'You know full [...]
to have an affai[r...]
boss!'

'You didn't mind my [...]' reminded Harriet wit[...] beside the point. I sa[...] and changed my mind about trying to "seduce" you, since you seem to like that word. Perhaps because it stops you from taking any responsibility over what just happened.'

'You kissed me, Alex. I didn't do a thing!'

'Nothing except look so deliciously sexy this morning that I haven't been able to think of anything else but making love to you all day.'

An already flustered Harriet honed in on his patently false wording. 'You don't want to *make love* to me at all,' she snapped. 'You want to have sex with me. That's a totally different scenario.'

'True,' he said, before walking slowly back towards her. 'But nothing changes the fact that we can't go back to the way it was between us, Harry. You want me as much as I want you—don't deny it,' he said, close enough now to reach out and place his large hands on her suddenly trembling shoulders.

Harriet somehow found her voice. 'That doesn't mean I have to do anything about it.'

'True again. But why deny yourself something which can give you pleasure? And I *can* give you pleasure, Harry,' he murmured, lifting his right hand off her shoulder to trace circles around her gasping lips. 'Lots of pleasure.'

Rich, Ruthless and Renowned

Billionaires secure their brides!

International tycoons Sergio, Alex and Jeremy were best friends at college. Bonded by their shared passion for business—and bedding beautiful women!—they formed The Bachelors' Club, which had only two goals:

1. Live life to the full.
2. Become billionaires in their own right!

But now, with the dotted line signed for the sale of their multibillion-dollar wine empire, there's one final thing left for each of the bachelors to accomplish: securing a bride!

The trilogy begins with Sergio's story in

The Italian's Ruthless Seduction

Continues with Alex's story in

The Billionaire's Ruthless Affair

And concludes with Jeremy's story—coming soon!

THE BILLIONAIRE'S RUTHLESS AFFAIR

BY
MIRANDA LEE

All rights reserved including the right of reproduction in whole
or in part in any form. This edition is published by arrangement with
Harlequin Books S.A.

This is a work of fiction. Names, characters, places, locations and
incidents are purely fictional and bear no relationship to any real
life individuals, living or dead, or to any actual places, business
establishments, locations, events or incidents. Any resemblance is
entirely coincidental.

This book is sold subject to the condition that it shall not, by way of
trade or otherwise, be lent, resold, hired out or otherwise circulated
without the prior consent of the publisher in any form of binding or
cover other than that in which it is published and without a similar
condition including this condition being imposed on the subsequent
purchaser.

® and TM are trademarks owned and used by the trademark owner
and/or its licensee. Trademarks marked with ® are registered with the
United Kingdom Patent Office and/or the Office for Harmonisation in
the Internal Market and in other countries.

First Published in Great Britain 2016
By Mills & Boon, an imprint of HarperCollins*Publishers*
1 London Bridge Street, London, SE1 9GF

© 2016 Miranda Lee

ISBN: 978-0-263-92120-5

Our policy is to use papers that are natural, renewable and recyclable
products and made from wood grown in sustainable forests. The logging
and manufacturing processes conform to the legal environmental
regulations of the country of origin.

Printed and bound in Spain
by CPI, Barcelona

Born and raised in the Australian bush, **Miranda Lee** was boarding-school-educated, and briefly pursued a career in classical music before moving to Sydney and embracing the world of computers. Happily married, with three daughters, she began writing when family commitments kept her at home. She likes to create stories that are believable, modern, fast-paced and sexy. Her interests include meaty sagas, doing word puzzles, gambling and going to the movies.

Books by Miranda Lee

Mills & Boon Modern Romance

Taken Over by the Billionaire
A Man Without Mercy
Master of Her Virtue
Contract with Consequences
The Man Every Woman Wants
Not a Marrying Man
A Night, A Secret...A Child

Rich, Ruthless and Renowned

The Italian's Ruthless Seduction

Three Rich Husbands

The Billionaire's Bride of Innocence

Visit the Author Profile page at
millsandboon.co.uk for more titles.

CHAPTER ONE

I SHOULD BE HAPPIER, Alex thought as he picked up his mug of coffee and carried it out onto the terrace of his penthouse apartment, shivering slightly when the crisp air hit his face. Not that it would be cold for long, the sun already peeping over the horizon. Winter in Sydney was a picnic compared to winter in London. He *was* glad to be back home. But not all that happy, for some reason.

Alex surveyed the panoramic view of the city skyline, telling himself that a man would have to be a fool not to be happy when he'd finally achieved everything he'd ever vowed to achieve.

At thirty-four, Alex was no fool. He was, in fact, a very successful businessman.

A Rhodes scholar, Alex had first become an entrepreneur back in England over a decade earlier, going into partnership with his two best friends from Oxford in a dilapidated old wine bar, which probably should have been demolished, but which they'd turned into a going concern. As it turned out, one wine bar had eventually become two, then three, then ten, till finally they'd formed a franchise.

Sergio's idea, that.

Alex smiled for the first time that morning. Thinking of Sergio always brought a smile to his face. Jeremy, too.

Yet those two were as different as chalk and cheese. Sergio was inclined to take life way too seriously at times, whereas Jeremy… Lord, where did one start with Jeremy? Though some people might describe him as a playboy, Alex knew Jeremy was a decent man at heart, generous and loyal, though with way too much charm and money for his own good. And he'd have even more money now, the recent sale of their wine bar franchise having made them all billionaires.

Alex's smile faded somewhat as he realised that the sale of their franchise had now severed the main connection between the three men. Whilst he didn't doubt they would always remain friends, it would not be the same as when they'd gathered together in London on a regular basis. Sergio had now returned to Milan to take up the reins of his family's ailing manufacturing business, whilst he himself would have no reason to return to England.

Still, that was life, Alex supposed. Nothing stayed the same. Time and tide waited for no man, he knew, a quick glance at his watch showing that it was almost eight.

He was going to be late for work, which was a rarity.

Harry would be wondering where he was. Alex hoped she wasn't upset over the way he'd spoken to her yesterday. Not that she'd seemed offended. Though relatively young, she was without doubt the best, most sensible PA he'd ever had.

Gulping down the rest of his coffee, he hurried back inside, stashed his mug in the dishwasher, snatched up his phone and keys, then headed for the lift. Just as the lift doors opened, his phone rang. A wry smile lit up Alex's face when he saw that it was Jeremy.

Speak of the devil!

'Jeremy…mate… I was just thinking about you.' Alex

strode into the lift and pressed the button for the basement car park.

'That's a worry,' Jeremy replied in that deeply masculine voice which always surprised people. 'Haven't you got anything better to do with your life? You should be out there making more millions. Though, perhaps not. You'd only give the lot away.'

Alex grinned. 'You've been drinking, haven't you?' It would be late evening in London.

'You could say that. I'm at a party. An engagement party.'

Alex suppressed a groan at the thought that another one of Jeremy's brothers—perhaps even his mother or father—were on their way to the altar again. You didn't have to look far to understand Jeremy's negative attitude towards love and marriage. Clearly, he didn't trust either to last.

Alex wasn't into love and marriage himself, either, but not for reasons of scepticism and cynicism. He knew full well that true love existed and lasted, if you found the right person. Alex just wasn't interested in finding his soul mate. He had personal reasons for staying a bachelor, the main one being the promise he'd made to his mother on her deathbed.

'God made you extra smart for a purpose, son,' she'd told him with her last breath. 'Promise me you won't waste your talents. Use them for good. Make a difference.'

Alex had done just that. But being a dedicated philanthropist took a lot of time and energy. He simply didn't have enough left over for a wife and family. Though, if he was strictly honest, Alex liked being a bachelor. Liked living by himself. Liked being free of emotional entanglements.

The lift doors opened at the basement and Alex headed for his nearby SUV at a clip.

'So who's getting hitched this time?' he asked Jeremy. 'Not your mother, I hope.' Jeremy's mother had divorced her third husband last year after she'd discovered he was sleeping with his personal trainer.

'No, thank God. No, this is someone far more surprising.'

'Really?' The mind boggled. 'Look, hold it a sec. Have to get in my car. I'm on my way to work.' Alex jumped in behind the wheel and swiftly connected his phone to Bluetooth. 'Right. All systems go,' he said as he backed out of his spot.

'Do you ever do anything except work?' Jeremy said drily.

'Sure I do. I eat out, work out and have lots of great sex. A bit like you, dear friend.'

'Are you still dating that Lisa chick, the girl you told me about with the grating giggle? Or did you break up with her as you said you were going to as soon as you got back to Sydney?'

'Yeah, she's gone,' Alex said with a scowl on his face. Lisa was still a sore point with him. He'd been going to tell her tactfully this last weekend that it was over between them when she'd actually had the hide to break up with him first, informing him that she'd taken a job on a cruise ship that was setting sail for Asia that very week.

He should have been relieved. Instead, he'd felt decidedly disgruntled. 'I don't want to talk about Lisa,' Alex ground out. 'I want to know which surprising person is getting married.'

'Trust me when I say that you're going to be more than surprised. It's Sergio. *He's* the one getting married.'

Though slightly taken aback, Alex was not exactly

shocked. 'What's so surprising about that? He said he was going to find himself a wife when he got back to Italy. It is a bit quick, though.'

Jeremy laughed. 'You don't know the half of it. The wedding's set for just over two weeks' time.'

'Good grief! Why all the hurry? The bride-to-be can't possibly be pregnant. He's only been back in Italy a little over a fortnight.'

'As far as I know, Bella's not pregnant.'

Alex's foot slammed on the brake, bringing an angry hoot of the horn from the car behind him. He was on the car park exit ramp at the time. Gathering himself, he drove on, trying to stay calm and not cause an accident.

'You shouldn't tell me something like that when I'm driving,' he said a lot more calmly than he was feeling. For Bella was *the* Bella, the darling of Broadway and Sergio's one-time stepsister. Sergio had confessed to his friends a couple of years back that he'd always had the hots for her. Naturally, they'd both urged him to move on and forget her.

Clearly, he hadn't taken their advice.

'Trust me, I'm just as shocked as you are,' Jeremy said in droll tones. 'Even worse, I've had to witness Sergio's crazed obsession first-hand.'

'What do you mean?'

'I knew Sergio was staying at his villa on Lake Como, so I decided to fly over yesterday and surprise him for his birthday.'

'Oh, God, his birthday. I forgot, as usual.'

'You always forget birthdays. Anyway, back to my story. Naturally, I thought Sergio would be alone. He'd said he wanted a holiday before tackling the family business. Apparently, I'd got that wrong. Because when I arrived, he was in Milan, with Bella installed at the villa.

She claimed she was suffering from burnout and had tried to rent the villa from Sergio, but he'd invited her to stay as his guest instead.'

Alex's teeth clenched down hard in his jaw. 'So the upshot is she wangled her way back into Sergio's life and then seduced him.'

'That's not how Sergio tells it. He says *he* seduced *her*.'

'That doesn't sound like Sergio.'

'I agree, but apparently he did. And then the poor bastard fell in love with her.'

'Yes, but did she fall in love with him back, or is this a case of like mother like daughter?' Bella's mother was a cold-blooded, ambitious woman who'd married Sergio's widowed father to finance her daughter's singing and dancing career, then divorced him once Bella's career had taken off. 'Does Bella know he's a billionaire now?'

'Don't know. It's been a madhouse here.'

Alex rolled his eyes. 'You must have got some impression of Bella's sincerity. Or lack of it.'

'Well, as unlikely as this will sound coming from an old cynic like me, I think she might be genuinely in love with Sergio.'

'Don't forget she's an actress,' Alex pointed out sharply.

'Now who's being a cynic? Anyway, the wedding's set for the thirty-first of July. I have no doubt that Sergio will be in contact with you shortly. He wants us both to be his best men. I told him we'd be honoured. So when he asks you, try to act thrilled, because there's no way he's going to change his mind about this. The man's crazy about her. All we can do is be there for him to pick up the pieces if and when everything goes belly-up.'

Alex wasn't sure how much help he could be from

Australia. But of course he would go to the wedding. He would be proud to stand at Sergio's side as his best man.

'Just book a flight that will get you to Lake Como the day before the wedding. No, make that two days before. I want to take you into Milan and have you fitted with a decent dinner suit. This might prove to be a disastrous marriage, but that's no excuse not to look our very best. We must do Sergio proud on the day. We are, after all, his best men.'

A lump formed in Alex's throat, rendering him speechless for a moment. Fortunately, Jeremy wasn't similarly afflicted.

'Have to go now, Alex. Claudia has just come out onto the terrace looking for me. Now, don't forget to book your flight, and for pity's sake sound thrilled when Sergio calls you. *Ciao*,' he said with a wry laugh. 'When in Rome, you know.' And he hung up.

Alex groaned at the thought of having to sound thrilled when Sergio contacted him. But he would do it for Sergio's sake. Fate wasn't being kind to him, letting him fall for a woman like Bella. Their getting married was a disaster waiting to happen.

Such thinking reinforced Alex's own decision never to get tangled up in the whole 'love and marriage' thing. Loving and losing someone—either through death or divorce—was never going to be on his agenda. No way would he risk ending up like his father, or becoming the victim of some clever gold-digger. That was why he always dated girls who never had a hope of ensnaring his heart. Girls who just wanted to have fun.

Alex quickly realised there would be no time for fun during the next two weeks. His nose would be pressed to the grindstone every single day. At least it would be when he finally got to the damned office. Poor Harry. She was probably close to sending out a search party!

Harriet didn't mind at all that her boss was running late that morning. When she'd arrived at the office shortly before eight, she'd been dreading having to tell him her news, news which she should have told him when he'd first come back from London. But at the time her emotions had been too raw. She would have wept in front of him. She knew she would. And she didn't want to do that. Alex would have been embarrassed. And so would she.

So she'd let the days tick away without confessing that her engagement to Dwayne was no more, her anxiety increasing as each day passed. She'd rather hoped her boss might notice that she wasn't wearing her engagement ring, but he hadn't. Alex didn't notice personal details like that. He was a man with tunnel vision most of the time. When at work, he worked.

It did irk Harriet slightly that no one else at Ark Properties had noticed, either. But that was her fault. Whilst she was friendly with everyone who worked there, she didn't socialise with the rest of the staff. She never went with them for drinks on a Friday night. Harriet had her own group of girlfriends she had drinks with, Emily of course being the main one. Then of course, up till recently, she'd had Dwayne.

Naturally, things would be different from now on, with no Dwayne to complain if she didn't hurry home after work. It worried Harriet, however, that her suddenly single status would change the wonderful working relationship she'd always had with Alex. He was a great boss. She liked him a lot and felt sure that he liked her back. Yet when she'd walked into his office to be interviewed for the job last year, Harriet had gained the immediate impression that she was a non-starter. Alex had looked her up and down with sceptical eyes. With hindsight, maybe he'd been worried that she might make a play for him. He was, after all, one of Sydney's most eligible bachelors.

Whatever; as soon as he'd discovered she was engaged, his attitude had changed. Though he'd still put her through the mill during the interview. She must have pleased him with her answers, because he'd hired her on the spot.

Of course, her résumé *had* been second to none—provided you overlooked her poor pass in her Higher School Certificate. Which Alex had, once she'd explained that her dad—who was a miner—had lost his job during her high school years and that the family finances had been so tight that she'd taken not one but *three* part-time positions to help make ends meet, her studies suffering as a result. A little white lie, that. But not one she felt guilty about. The boss of Ark Properties didn't need to know the ins and outs of her past life. Alex had seemed suitably impressed by her work ethic, plus her career in real estate. He didn't care that she'd never actually been a PA before. He wanted someone who could take over the office whenever he was away, which up till recently had been quite often. He had business ties in England which she wasn't privy to; Alex could be secretive at times.

But those business ties had apparently been wound up and he was back in Sydney permanently. Harriet might have felt pleased if she hadn't been in a state of apprehension at the time. That apprehension had now reached such a level that it was interfering with her sleep. So Harriet had resolved last night to bite the bullet and tell Alex the truth this morning. Which would have happened already if he'd been here when she'd arrived, she thought with a flash of irritation. All of a sudden, his being late didn't seem quite so desirable, the delay in confessing twisting her stomach into more knots.

Sighing at the sight of Alex's empty office, she headed straight for the staff room, where she filled the kettle in readiness for the mug of black coffee Alex always wanted first thing on arriving. He'd probably send her out for a bagel, too. That man was a bagel addict! Maybe she'd leave off telling him her news till he'd downed his coffee and bagel. Alex wasn't at his best till he'd eaten. The kettle on, she opened the overhead cupboard and took down one of the small tins of quite expensive cat food she kept there. The snapping sound of the ring pull had a rather large moggy dashing into the room, purring his welcome as he wound his way around Harriet's ankles.

'Hungry, Romany?' Harriet said, quickly scraping the food out onto a saucer and putting it down on the floor. The cat pounced, gobbling up the food like he was starving.

'You spoil that cat.'

Harriet whirled at the sound of Alex's voice, surprised that she hadn't heard him come in. He looked impossibly handsome as usual, dressed in a dark blue business suit which deepened the blue of his eyes and contrasted nicely with the fair hair. His shirt was a dazzling white, his tie a stylish blue-and-silver stripe.

'You ought to talk,' Harriet said, thinking of all her boss had done for Romany. 'Might I remind you that *you* were the one who insisted on buying all the top-of-the-line cat accessories.'

'Had to do something to stop my PA from crying her eyes out.'

'I wasn't doing any such thing.'

'You were close to,' he reminded her.

I suppose I was, she thought as she picked up the

plate, washed it thoroughly and put it away, not wanting any of the staff to start complaining about the smell of fishy cat food. Not that they would. They all loved Romany. Unlike Dwayne. He hadn't loved Romany at all; had complained like mad when Harriet had brought the poor starving animal home a couple of months ago after she'd found him cowering and crying under her car one Saturday night. He'd insisted she take it to the RSPCA the very next day, which she had, hopeful that they would find him a good home.

Impossible, they'd said. No one would want a seriously old cat like Romany. Unable to bear leaving him there to be put down, in desperation she'd taken him to work on the Monday, where she'd asked if anyone would give him a home. When no one had put their hand up, Alex had said he could be the office cat. Always a man of action, he'd immediately had a cat flap installed in the store room, then had taken Harriet out to buy whatever was necessary to keep the cat happy and clean. The cleaners had been informed of Romany's presence so that precautions could be taken for him not to escape.

Harriet recalled feeling overwhelmed by Alex's generosity and kindness at the time whilst seething with resentment over Dwayne's meanness. As she bent and scooped the cat up in her arms, she realised that the incident with Romany had been the beginning of the end of their relationship. Being an animal lover was, after all, one of her checklist points. After that, she'd begun to look at Dwayne with different eyes. The rose-coloured glasses that came with falling in love had definitely come off. His constant refusal to give any money to charity was a sore point. So was his not doing his share of housework around the flat. When she'd complained to Emily about this, she'd just laughed, saying Harry expected way too much from men.

'They expect their women to look after *them*,' her best friend had told her. 'It's in their DNA. They're the protectors and providers, whilst their women are the home-makers and nurturers.'

Harriet hadn't agreed with Emily, hoping the world had moved on from expecting women to be happy with such narrow roles in life. No way was she going to settle for less than what she wanted in life, which was an interesting career, as well as a husband who ticked all of the boxes on her Mister Right checklist. Dwayne had certainly ticked the first three, but had begun seriously falling down on the rest. His suggestion a month ago that she buy her wedding dress second-hand on the Internet had been the last straw!

'So has the kettle boiled?' Alex asked, interrupting Harriet's none-too-happy thoughts.

'Should have,' she said.

Dropping the cat gently on the tiled floor, she set about getting two mugs down from the overhead cupboard. 'It's not like you to be late,' she added, doing her best to ignore the instant churning in her stomach. Maybe she wouldn't tell him today after all...

'I slept in,' he replied. 'Then traffic was bad. I'm going to need a bagel with my coffee.'

'Fine. Oh, and, Alex...' she said before he had the opportunity to walk away and before she could procrastinate further. 'When you have a minute, I...um...I need to talk to you about something.'

He sighed a rather weary-sounding sigh. 'Look, Harry, if you're going to complain about the way I spoke to you yesterday, then don't bother. I'm sorry. All right? I was in a bad mood and I took it out on you, which I realise was unforgiveable, but I'm only human. If you must know, I broke up with Lisa at the weekend.'

'Oh,' she said, not really surprised. Of the three girls Alex had dated during the time she'd worked for him, Lisa had been the most annoying with that silly laugh of hers, not to mention the way she would drop into the office unannounced. Alex hadn't liked that, and neither had Harriet. 'I'm sorry,' she added a little belatedly.

'I'm not. Not really.' Alex stared at her hard for a long moment. 'You're not going to quit, are you?'

Her shocked expression must have soothed him, for his eyes immediately softened. But it underlined to Harriet that Alex was not a man who responded well to being crossed or thwarted. She'd always known he was a tough businessman, but she'd never seen him seriously angry. It wasn't in his nature to be mean, but she suspected he had a temper, like most men.

'No, nothing like that,' she said quickly.

'Then out with it, Harriet. I don't like to wait for bad news.'

'It's not bad news,' she said, startled by his calling her Harriet like that. She'd always liked the way he called her Harry. There was a subtle intimacy about it which made her feel like his friend as well as his assistant. Obviously, she'd been deluding herself in that regard.

'Well, not bad news for you,' she went on sharply, doing her best to control a whole range of emotions which began bombarding her. The sudden lump in her throat alarmed her.

'The thing is, Alex, I...I've broken off my engagement to Dwayne.'

His expression carried a measure of shock, quickly followed by one of genuine sympathy.

When tears pricked at her eyelids, panic was only a heartbeat away.

'I'm very sorry to hear that, Harry,' he said gently. 'Very sorry indeed.'

His calling her Harry like that completed her undoing, bringing a wave of emotion which shattered her pretend composure and sent a torrent of tears into her eyes.

CHAPTER TWO

ALEX'S SHOCK AT Harriet's news was eclipsed by her bursting into tears. For not once during the months she'd worked for him had she ever cried. Or come close to it, except perhaps over the cat. She was the epitome of common sense and composure, pragmatic and practical under pressure at all times. Even when he snapped at her—as he had yesterday—she just ignored him and went on with her job. Which he admired.

He didn't care for women who cried at the drop of a hat or used tears as a weapon. He'd been brought up by a woman who'd been very stalwart by nature, a legacy perhaps of being born poor in war-torn Hungary, she and Alex's father having migrated to Australia when they'd been just newlyweds. They'd hoped to make a better life down under. Unfortunately, that hadn't happened. But his mother had never complained, or cried.

'Crying doesn't get you anywhere,' his mother had told her three children often enough.

She had cried, however, when she'd found out she was dying of cervical cancer, a condition which could have been cured if she'd been diagnosed early enough.

Don't think about that, Alex. Attend to the here and now. Which is your usually calm PA sobbing her broken heart out.

After standing in the doorway for far too long, wondering how he'd forgotten that Harry was a woman with a woman's more sensitive emotions, Alex launched himself across the room and gathered her into his arms.

'There, there,' he said soothingly as he stroked her soft brown hair.

If anything she sobbed even harder, her shoulders shaking as her hands curled into fists and pressed against his chest. Romany meowed plaintively at his feet, obviously sensing distress in the air.

'Stop crying now,' he advised gently. 'You're upsetting the cat.'

She didn't stop crying and Romany ran off, the insensitive deserter. Alex wished he could do likewise. He didn't feel entirely comfortable holding Harry like this. He was never comfortable with excess emotion. Neither was he a touchy-feely kind of guy. He touched a woman only when he was about to make love to her.

'Oh! S-sorry.'

Alex's head swivelled round at the sound of Audrey's startled apology. Audrey was forty, divorced and a cynic and the expression on his receptionist's face suggested she'd instantly jumped to the conclusion that something of an intimate nature was going on between her boss and his PA. Alex knew he had to nip that idea in the bud before nasty rumours started flying around the office.

'Harriet is upset,' he said rather brusquely. 'She's broken off her engagement to Dwayne.'

Audrey's finely plucked eyebrows formed an even greater arch. 'Really? What did he do?'

Alex rolled his eyes at the woman's lack of compassion. All she seemed interested in were the grisly details. Though, now that he thought about it, Alex was curious about the circumstances as well. He could not imagine

Dwayne being unfaithful. He wasn't that kind of guy. Not that he knew him well. He'd met him only twice.

Alex had actually been surprised by Harriet's choice of fiancé. She was a very attractive girl—and smart as a whip—whereas Dwayne was just, well, ordinary, both in looks and intelligence. Alex had found him quite boring to talk to. He would have expected more interesting conversation from a high school history teacher, but Dwayne had come over as being interested in only his pay cheque and his holidays.

'More time to play golf,' he'd said rather avidly.

Perhaps that was what had gone wrong. Maybe he'd been spending too much time on the golf course and not enough time making love to his fiancée. Alex knew that if he was engaged to Harriet, he would spend quite a lot of time making love to her. Having her in his arms reminded him what a good figure she had.

When such thinking sparked a prickling in his groin, Alex decided to bring a swift end to his hugging Harriet so closely. Stepping back from the embrace, he leaned over to snatch a handful of tissues from the box that was kept on the counter and held them out towards her still-clenched hands.

'Dry your eyes,' he ordered.

She did as she was told, blowing her nose quite noisily.

'Now, I'm taking Harriet out for coffee. And we won't be back for a while,' he relayed to Audrey. 'Let the others know the situation when they come in, will you?'

'Will do,' Audrey replied.

'I…I'd like to fix my face before I go out anywhere,' Harriet requested.

'Fair enough,' Alex said. 'I'll meet you at the lifts in five minutes.'

* * *

Grabbing her handbag, Harriet dashed out of the office and along the corridor to the ladies' room, which thankfully was empty. She groaned when the vanity mirror showed flushed cheeks and red-rimmed eyes. Sighing, she splashed them with cold water, glad that she didn't wear eye make-up during the day. Otherwise she might have ended up looking like a raccoon.

Grabbing some paper towels, she dabbed her face dry, after which she swiftly replenished her red lipstick before running a brush through her shoulder-length brown hair. When it fell into its usual sleek curtain without a strand out of place, she conceded that her monthly appointment with one of Sydney's top stylists was worth every cent. It saved her heaps of time every morning and in moments like this. Because, when Alex said he'd meet her in five minutes, he meant five minutes. Patience was not one of her boss's virtues. Kindness was, however. And compassion. He'd shown both with Romany and now with her.

She should have known he'd be nice to her.

Not that she'd expected him to hug her like that. That had been a surprise. So had her bursting into tears in the first place. It wasn't like her to be so emotional. But she supposed it wasn't every day that your dreams for the future were shattered. Maybe if she'd cried buckets during the days after the split with Dwayne, she wouldn't have broken down just now. She hadn't even told Emily, knowing perhaps her friend's critical reaction. She'd just bottled up her feelings, then stupidly started worrying that telling Alex her news would jeopardise her job. As if he would be so cruel as to sack her because she was suddenly single. The very idea was ludicrous!

With a final swift glance at her reflection in the mirror, Harriet hurried from the ladies' room and strode quickly along the grey carpeted corridor which would bring her to the lift well. Alex was already there, his expression shuttered as he looked her up and down, probably searching for signs that she had herself under control. No way would he want her weeping by his side in public. She gave him a small, reassuring smile, but he didn't smile back, his gaze still probing.

'Better now?' he said.

'Much. You don't have to do this, you know,' she added, despite actually wanting to go and have coffee with him. 'We could just go back into the office and have coffee there.'

'Absolutely not. Audrey and the others can hold the fort.'

The lift doors opened and several office workers piled out, Ark Properties not being the only business with rooms on that particular floor, though theirs were the pick, with Alex's office having a wonderful view of the Harbour Bridge and the Opera House. 'Nothing like a good view of Sydney's spectacular icons to help sell property in Australia,' he'd told her on the day he'd hired her.

Harriet agreed wholeheartedly.

'So when did all this happen?' Alex asked her as he waved her into the now empty lift.

'The weekend you flew home from London,' she told him.

He threw a sharp glance over his shoulder as he pressed the ground-floor button.

'Why didn't you tell me straight away?' he went on before she could think of a suitable answer. 'Did you want to give yourself the opportunity to change your mind? Or for Dwayne to change it for you?'

'No. No, once I made up my mind, I knew I wouldn't

change it. Dwayne hasn't tried to change my mind, either. After our last argument, he knew it was over between us.'

'That must have been some argument.'

'It was.' A rueful smile teased the corners of her mouth. What would Alex say, she wondered, if he knew he'd been the subject of most of that last argument?

His eyes narrowed on her. 'Want to tell me about it?'

She looked up into his gorgeous blue eyes, then shook her head. 'I don't think that would be a good idea.'

'Well, I do,' he stated firmly just as the lift doors opened on the ground floor. Taking her arm, he steered her across the spacious lobby and through the revolving glass doors which led out onto the chilly city street.

'So which café do you prefer?' he asked, nodding towards each of the two casual eating establishments that flanked the entrance to their building. It occurred to Harriet that Alex had never actually taken her for coffee before. She'd lunched with him a few times—always with clients—but only at the kind of five-star restaurants which catered for businessmen of his status.

'That one has better bagels,' she said, pointing to the café on their left.

'That one it is, then.'

He found them an empty table at one of the windows which overlooked the street, seeing her settled before heading for the counter. Harriet found it odd watching him queue up to order food, thinking he wouldn't have done that too often. But then she recalled that he hadn't always been rich and successful.

When she'd secured a second and personal interview for this job, she'd looked him up on the Internet, unable to find out all that much information, the best being an article written about him for a men's magazine a couple of years back. Harriet had been surprised to discover that he'd come from a down-at-heel migrant family, living in government housing in the outer western suburbs of Sydney. His near-genius IQ had given him access to special schools for gifted children, followed by various financial grants to help him through university, culminating in his being awarded a Rhodes Scholarship.

The magazine article she'd read had outlined his rise to success in Sydney, first as a realtor based mainly in the western suburbs, then as a property developer with his head office in the heart of Sydney's CBD. The article made no mention of any business interests in England, or his personal life, except to say that he was one of Sydney's most eligible bachelors. There'd been no mention of his family or friends.

Harriet rolled her eyes at what happened when Alex reached the front of the queue. The very pretty young brunette behind the counter beamed at him as she took his order, her eyes and manner very flirtatious. Harriet found herself decidedly irritated, hating the thought that Alex might have already found a replacement for that silly Lisa. The sudden thought that she might be jealous seemed ludicrous. Jealous of whom? And of what? And, more to the point, *why*?

Harriet frowned, wondering and worrying that Alex's hugging her earlier might have unlocked feelings which she'd always had for him and which she'd successfully hidden, even from herself. Harriet couldn't deny that she'd liked the feel of his big, strong arms around her; she liked his bringing her here for coffee as well.

Whatever, when Alex turned away from the counter and started heading towards her, Harriet found herself looking at him with new eyes, the same new eyes which had examined Dwayne with brutal honesty and had found him sadly lacking.

The word 'lacking' would never apply to the boss of Ark Properties. He had everything that any woman would want. In a boyfriend, that was, but not in a prospective husband.

So lock this unwanted attraction of yours away again, Harriet, and look elsewhere for your life partner. Because it's never going to be Alex Kotana!

Perversely, however, as soon as he sat back down at their table, she opened her silly, jealous mouth and said waspishly, 'I suppose that happens to you all the time.'

'What?' he said, sounding perplexed.

Whilst kicking herself, Harriet quickly found a wry little smile and a more casual tone. 'The brunette behind the counter didn't half make it clear that you could have put her on your order, if you'd been so inclined.'

Alex smiled. 'She did, didn't she? Unfortunately, she's not my type.'

'You don't like brunettes?' Now that she thought about it, his last two girlfriends had been blondes. She'd never met the first one, who'd come and gone within a month of her becoming Alex's PA, so she didn't know if she was a blonde or not.

His eyes held hers for a rather long moment, making Harriet feel decidedly uncomfortable. She hoped her momentary jab of jealousy hadn't been obvious earlier. If it had, then she might not be lasting long in her job. It was a depressing thought. Her job meant the world to her. It was interesting and challenging and very well paid. Now that she didn't have Dwayne in her life, she needed her job more than ever.

'Sorry,' she said swiftly. 'I shouldn't be asking you personal questions like that. It's none of my business.'

Alex shrugged his powerful shoulders. 'No sweat. I'm about to ask you a personal question or two.'

'Oh?'

'Come now, Harry, you don't expect me not to be curious over why you broke up with Dwayne. That's why I brought you down here away from the prying eyes and ears in the office. To worm out all the grisly details. You must know that.'

Harriet sighed. 'There are no grisly details.' Just mundane ones.

'So you didn't discover he was a secret drunk, or a drug addict?'

'No!'

'You didn't come home and find him in bed with your best friend?'

'Lord no,' she said and laughed.

'Then what on earth did the man do?'

Harriet knew it was going to be difficult to explain without her seeming like some kind of nutcase. But she could see she would have to try. When Alex wanted to know something, he was like a dog with a bone.

'He just didn't measure up as husband material.'

'Ah,' Alex said, as though understanding perfectly what she was talking about. 'I rather suspected that his golf playing might have become a problem.'

Harriet just stared at him. 'I had no problem with Dwayne playing golf,' she replied, feeling somewhat confused. 'Though it didn't go down well when he bought a very expensive set of clubs the same day he suggested I buy my wedding dress on the Internet.'

Alex's brows lifted. 'He wanted you to buy a second-hand wedding dress?'

'Yes,' she admitted tartly.

'Ah,' he said in that knowing way again, Harriet gratified that her boss understood that Dwayne's penny-pinching suggestion might have been a deal breaker.

'My father was a mean man with money,' she found herself elaborating. 'I vowed when I was just a teenager that I would never marry a scrooge.'

'I fully agree with you. But didn't you know Dwayne was tight with money when you first started dating him?'

'He wasn't like that then. He used to spend money on me like water. Took me to the best restaurants, the best concerts, the best of everything.'

'Yes, well, a man like Dwayne would have had to pull out all stops to impress a girl like you. And he succeeded, didn't he? You fell for him and agreed to marry him. But once he had his ring on your finger, he dropped the ball. Am I right?'

'Very right,' Harriet agreed, then frowned. 'What do you mean by "a girl like me"?'

Alex smiled a crooked smile. 'It must have been very upsetting to find out that your Prince Charming was nothing but a frog. And a stingy frog at that. What I meant was that you were always a cut above Dwayne, not only in looks but in intelligence and personality. He must have known on first meeting you that he would have to lift his game in every department if he wanted to win the heart of the beautiful Harriet McKenna. But the fool couldn't keep it up, which is what happens when you play out of your league.'

Harriet flushed wildly at his compliments, not sure whether to believe him or not. Alex could be inclined to flattery on occasions. Not with her, but with clients. Though he had said she looked gorgeous the night they'd all attended that fundraising dinner back in March. She'd been wearing a new red cocktail dress which had looked well on her with her dark hair and eyes.

'So what was the final straw?' Alex went on. 'The wedding dress business? Or something else?'

'The wedding dress suggestion certainly brought things to a head. But I'd been unhappy for some time. And worried. It was obvious Dwayne wasn't the man I thought he was. He certainly wasn't acting like the man I fell in love with. He'd become lazy around the house. And with me.'

'You mean your sex life had suffered.'

Harriet laughed and blushed slightly. 'What sex life?'

'The man was a fool,' Alex said sharply. 'What did he honestly expect would happen if he started neglecting you in bed?'

'I have no idea,' Harriet said with a sigh, thinking to herself that she couldn't imagine Alex neglecting any of his girlfriends in bed. That man had testosterone oozing out of every pore of his gorgeous male body. 'He obviously didn't expect me to break off our engagement. He couldn't believe it at first. When I tried to explain the reasons why I'd fallen out of love with him, he went into a rage, accusing me of all sorts of crazy things.'

'Like what?'

Harriet could see Alex was determined to hear the truth behind the break-up.

'Like I no longer loved him because I'd fallen in love with you...

'As if I'd be stupid enough to do something like that,' she raced on before Alex had a chance to jump to any potentially dangerous conclusions.

CHAPTER THREE

THE ARRIVAL OF the brunette with his order of coffee and bagels could not have come at a better time, giving Alex the opportunity to hide his peeved reaction to Harriet's somewhat scoffing reply to Dwayne's accusation. A perverse reaction, in a way, considering he didn't want any woman falling in love with him. But it wasn't very flattering for Harry to tell him that her falling for him would be *stupid*!

His throwing the waitress one of his super-charming smiles was more the result of a bruised ego than his desire to capture the girl's interest. He'd been right when he'd said she wasn't his type. She'd been way too eager to please. As much as Alex liked to date pretty young things—and the brunette was just that—he preferred independent, spirited girls who didn't gush or grovel, and who didn't have a single gold-digging bone in their bodies. Alex had known immediately that the brunette was not of that ilk.

'Is there anything else you'd like, sir?' the brunette asked after carefully placing the coffee and bagel on the table, her attention all on him, not having cast a single glance in Harriet's direction.

'No, thanks,' he said and resisted the impulse to give her a tip. Harriet was already looking seriously irritated.

As the waitress departed, Harriet sent him a droll look.

'Yes, I know,' he said drily. 'It does happen to me all the time. But she's still not my type.'

'Then perhaps you shouldn't have flirted with her.'

Alex clenched his teeth hard in his jaw whilst he struggled to control his temper. 'And perhaps *you* should tell me why you find me so unlovable,' he retorted, still smarting over her earlier remark.

She blinked at his sharpness before dropping her eyes, taking a few seconds to pour the sugar into her coffee and looking up at him again. 'I never said you were unlovable, Alex. I said I would not be stupid enough to fall in love with you. That's an entirely different concept.'

Alex's bruised ego was not to be so easily mollified. 'Would you care to explain that last statement further? Why would it be so stupid for you to fall in love with me?'

'Aside from the fact that I'm your PA, you mean?' she threw at him.

He had to concede that that was an excellent reason. It was never a good idea to mix business and pleasure, something which he was in danger of forgetting.

'Point taken,' he said. 'Is that the only reason, then?'

She gave him a long, searching look that he found decidedly irritating. This was a Harriet he wasn't used to. Up till today she'd been the perfect PA, never complaining or criticising, calmly obeying his every wish and command. She'd never before looked at him in such an assessing and possibly judgmental fashion. He didn't like it. He didn't like it one bit.

Frankly, he preferred the Harriet who'd wept in his arms.

'You're not eating your bagel,' she said as she coolly stirred her flat white. 'And your coffee will get cold. You know how you hate lukewarm coffee.'

'I also hate not having my questions answered,' he ground out, sweeping up his mug of black coffee and glaring at her over the rim.

Harriet knew she had annoyed him; knew he'd taken her statement as a personal criticism. It had been seriously foolish of her to tell him about Dwayne's accusation. But it was too late now. Somehow she had to explain her remark without offending Alex further.

Make light of it, girl. Turn it round so that it's your failing and not his. And don't, for pity's sake, repeat the word 'stupid' in context with falling in love with him. No wonder he took umbrage!

'The thing is,' she said in a lighter, less emotional voice, 'I realised a few years back that if I wanted to get married and have children...which I did; which I still do, actually...that I had to stop dating a certain type of man. I—'

'And what type is that?' Alex interrupted before she could go on.

'Oh, you know. *Your* type.'

'*My* type?'

Oh, dear, she'd done it again. She'd opened her big mouth and put her foot in it. 'Well, not exactly your type, Alex,' she said with a 'butter wouldn't melt in her mouth' smile. 'You are rather unique. As you are aware, I've worked in real estate ever since I came to Sydney when I was twenty. Girls usually date men they meet at work. It was inevitable that I would end up dating real-estate salesmen. Invariably, they were tall and handsome, with the gift of the gab, but not exactly the most faithful kind of guy.'

'I see,' Alex said thoughtfully. 'Go on.'

Harriet was glad to see that Alex had lost his disgruntled expression, his blue eyes no longer cold and steely.

'By the time I turned twenty-seven, I decided I was wasting my time on men like that. So I sat down and made a checklist of what I wanted in a husband.'

'A checklist?' he repeated, looking both surprised and amused.

'Find it funny if you like. Emily certainly does.'

'Who's Emily? Your sister?'

'No. Emily's my best friend. She's an English teacher who flatted with me for a while. It was through her that I met Dwayne.'

'I did wonder how you two met. Frankly, I never thought you were all that well suited. Still, Dwayne must have met your checklist to begin with.'

Harriet sighed. 'I thought he did, till he moved in with me and eventually showed his true colours. I now appreciate that it's impossible to know a man's true character till you live with him. Dwayne certainly met the first three requirements. When I made up my checklist, I decided that I wouldn't even go out with a man till he ticked those three boxes. That way I hoped to avoid falling in love with any more Mr Wrongs.'

Alex's mind boggled over what those three requirements might be. Harriet was right about his finding the idea of a checklist funny. He did. Though he shouldn't have. Didn't he have a checklist of his own when it came to the girls he dated? They had to be in their early twenties, pretty and easy-going. He had a feeling, though, that Harriet's checklist would be a lot more fascinating. And, yes, very funny indeed.

'Do tell,' he said, trying to keep a straight face.

'Promise me you won't laugh.'

'I promise,' he said, but the corners of his mouth were already twitching.

'Okay, well, the first requirement is he can't be too tall or too short. Whilst I find tallness attractive, I've found that too-tall men are often arrogant, whilst too-short men can suffer from the "short man" syndrome.'

Alex realised that at six-foot-four he probably came into the 'too tall' category.

'Do you think I'm arrogant?' he asked.

'A little. But not in a nasty way.'

'Thank God for that. And requirement number two is?'

'He can't be too handsome or too ugly.'

Well, Dwayne had certainly been on the money there. As for himself… Harriet would probably label him in the 'too handsome' category.

'And number three?'

'He can't be too rich or too poor.'

'Right.' Well, that certainly ruled *him* out as a prospective date for Harriet. Not that he would ever ask her out. He'd have to be mad to date Harriet.

But, as he looked into her big brown eyes, Alex was struck by the startling realisation that that was exactly what he wanted to do. Take her out, then take her back to bed.

Bad idea, that, he thought and busied himself stuffing his mouth full of bagel whilst trying to work out where such a potentially self-destructive desire had come from. After all, Harriet didn't fit his own checklist for dating candidates any better than he fitted hers!

Still, it didn't take Alex all that long privately to admit that he'd secretly wanted to take Harriet to bed since the day he'd interviewed her ten months ago. The attraction had been there from the moment she'd walked into his office, looking deliciously nervous but beautifully turned out in a sleek black suit which had followed the curves of her very feminine figure. Her dark brown hair had been up in a professional and somewhat prissy style, but her lushly glossed mouth had betrayed her true nature. He'd immediately made the decision not to hire her, despite her excellent résumé—till he found out she was safely engaged, at which point he'd fooled himself into thinking he could ignore his hormones.

And he had, up till now.

They would have remained in control, too, if she hadn't broken up with Dwayne; if she hadn't cried and he hadn't hugged her. That had been the catalyst which had started the chemical reaction which saw him now being tempted to do something seriously stupid.

Thank God it was still just a temptation. He didn't have to act on it. Didn't have to suffer the humiliation of Harriet rejecting him, not just because he was her boss, but because he was too tall, too handsome *and* too rich.

His sudden laughter brought a reproving look into her velvety brown eyes.

'You promised you wouldn't laugh,' she chided him.

'Sorry. Couldn't help it.'

'In that case, I won't tell you the rest of my checklist. You'd probably crack up entirely.'

'You could be right, there. So I'll save up the rest of your checklist till a later date. Now, I think we should finish up here and get back to work.'

CHAPTER FOUR

HARRIET SIGHED AS she sat back down at her desk and turned on her computer. She hadn't wanted to go back to work; back to reality. She'd been enjoying having coffee with Alex, despite her many *faux pas*. She hadn't really minded his laughing at her checklist, which she now appreciated *was* rather funny. Whilst it did have some merit, such strategies simply didn't work out in real life, just like those silly matchmaking forms they made you filled in on online dating sites.

Most women ended up marrying men they met through work, Harriet accepted, thinking of her other married girlfriends. Actually, *all* her girlfriends were married, a thought which was rather depressing. Harriet was well aware that marriage and motherhood wasn't the only pathway to happiness and fulfilment in life, but it was her chosen pathway. That and a career. Yes, she wanted to have it all, which was possibly where she was going wrong. Having it all suddenly seemed beyond her grasp. This time next year, she'd be hitting thirty. After thirty, finding a husband became more difficult; all the good ones were already snapped up.

Even ordinary men like Dwayne weren't exactly thick on the ground. Maybe she shouldn't have been so quick to dump him. Maybe she should have ignored his fail-ings and accepted him for the imperfect specimen he was...

Harriet was pondering this conundrum when Alex strode out of his office and perched his far too perfect body on the corner of her thankfully large desk.

'A couple of things I forgot to tell you this morning,' he said as he hitched his right knee up into a more comfort-able position, indicating he was staying put for a while. 'First, I want you to book me a flight to Milan, arriving on the twenty-ninth of July.'

'Milan?' she echoed, forgetting that it wasn't a PA's job to question her boss, just to obey.

'Yes. Milan, Italy. One of my best friends from Ox-ford is getting married on the thirty-first. I've been or-dered to be there two days before the actual wedding so that I can be attired suitably for my job as best man. The other best man obviously fears I might show up in jeans and a T-shirt.'

Harriet blinked her astonishment at such a ludicrous idea. The night they'd attended that fundraising dinner back in March, Alex had walked into the hotel ballroom wearing a magnificent black tux. He'd quite literally taken her breath away.

'How ridiculous,' she scoffed. 'You are one of the best-dressed men I've ever met.'

'You haven't seen me when I'm slumming it. Jeremy has.'

'Jeremy?'

'The other best man and possibly the best-dressed rake in all of London.'

Harriet's eyes widened. 'Your best friend is a rake?'

'Birds of a feather flock together, you know.'

'You're not a rake,' she defended. 'You just pick the wrong girls to date. The reason they never last is that you get bored with them.'

Alex stared at Harriet and thought how right she was. He did get bored with the women he dated. But that was exactly what made them safe. They never touched him with any depth of feeling, never moved his soul. Leaving them behind was so damned easy.

The truth hit that he wasn't unhappy with his life so much, but he was bored. Bored with dating silly young girls. Bored with never having a decent conversation with a woman.

He hadn't been bored having coffee with Harriet this morning. He'd been alternately annoyed, then angry, then amused and, yes, aroused. A whole gamut of emotions. He hadn't been able to settle back down to work afterwards; he'd been looking for any reason to come out and talk to her again. Having Harriet book that flight for him had just been an excuse. He could quite easily have done it himself.

I'm not going to be able to resist this attraction, Alex finally conceded, *no matter what the danger*. He suspected she would not reject him; the sexual chemistry which had sprung up today was not all on his side. Alex had noticed her pique when the brunette in the café had flirted with him.

He still hesitated to ask her out on a regular date, sensing that it was too soon for such a move. Clearly, she was still hurting over the break-up with Dwayne. On top of that, she was his PA, one of the many reasons she'd given to explain why she would never fall in love with him. Not that he wanted her love, just her body. If truth be told, he didn't want Harry to be his next girlfriend. He just wanted to have an affair with her. A strictly sexual affair.

He should have been disgusted with himself. But Alex soothed his conscience by reassuring himself that he would never hurt Harry. He could give her pleasure and fun, something which he suspected had been in short supply in her life for some time.

The only problem was finding a way to achieve his aims without offending her.

An idea struck, one which would sound perfectly reasonable but which would give him the opportunity to act upon his feelings away from the office. Of course, there was always the risk that Harry would still reject his advances. And, yes, she might even be offended by them. Alex suspected she was a stickler for propriety in the workplace. But it was a risk he was prepared to take. It had been a long time since he'd lived on the edge, so to speak, and it excited him. *She* excited him.

His eyes met with hers, his gaze intense as he searched her face for a sign that he'd been right about her body language when they'd been having coffee together. Alex was gratified when a faint flush bloomed in her cheeks.

'My having to go to Italy for days on end couldn't have come at a worse time,' he said, schooling his own face into a concerned mask. 'I need to be continually hands-on with that golfing estate if it's going to be up and running by Christmas. Someone has to be up there every week to crack the whip. While I'm away, that person will have to be you, Harry.'

'*Me?*' she squawked.

'Yes, *you*,' he insisted. 'I've heard you over the phone to our contractors when they've been giving us grief. You are one tough cookie when you want to be.'

'But doesn't that job already have a foreman in charge?'

'Yes, but even the best foreman can get slack when he's working that far from the boss. If I hadn't been driving up there on a regular basis, we'd be even further behind than we are. I don't want any more delays.'

'Right,' she said, still looking a bit hesitant.

'I thought we could drive up there this Friday, stay overnight, then drive back on the Saturday. We'll stay overnight. And not in some dreary motel, either. Book us a two-bedroomed apartment at a five-star resort in Coffs Harbour. That's only a half-hour drive from the golf course. Somewhere near the ocean, with a balcony and a sea view. And make sure they have a decent restaurant. In fact, we might stay another night, then drive back on the Sunday. You deserve a break after what you've been through.'

CHAPTER FIVE

HARRIET DIDN'T KNOW what to say. She had travelled with Alex only once before. To the Gold Coast, to meet with some Japanese billionaires who'd been staying there at the Hotel Versace and who were potential clients for his new golf resort. But they'd travelled by plane and she'd taken a taxi to the airport by herself. She'd also stayed in a totally separate hotel room. The thought of staying with her way-too-sexy boss in an apartment—for possibly two nights—made her feel…what, exactly?

'Panic' came close to describing her reaction.

Before today, Harriet would have been supremely confident that Alex would never make a move on her. But things were different now. Lisa was past history and so was Dwayne. A new intimacy had sprung up between them, first when Alex had hugged her, and then when they'd had coffee together, an inevitable result once you started opening up about your private life to another person, even when that person was your boss. Harriet knew that men found her attractive. Why should Alex be any different?

And then there was her own silly self. She'd always been blindly attracted to men who were tall, handsome and, yes, super-successful, a failing which she'd worked hard to conquer. But she was in a highly vulnerable state at the moment and, when she faced it, when it came to tall, handsome and super-successful men, Alex was at the top of the heap. To stay with him in an apartment for two nights was asking for trouble.

She didn't need any more trouble in her life. She did, however, need her job; the mortgage on her Bondi apartment barely manageable now that she didn't have anyone to help with the payments. Having an affair with the boss was a sure way to lose her job. Harriet had been around long enough to know how such relationships ended.

'Thank you for your kind offer,' she said in her best businesslike voice. 'But I can't stay away for two nights. Emily is getting back from Bali on Saturday and we're having a catch-up lunch on Sunday.' This was a bald-faced lie. Emily was away for a further two months. Harriet knew, however, that she needed a decent excuse to get out of this. Alex didn't like being told no.

'Pity,' he muttered, then shrugged his shoulders, his indifference indicating he hadn't had any dastardly secret agenda when he'd suggested a two-night stay. He was just trying to be nice to her again. Truly, she was letting herself get carried away here, thinking he had seduction on his mind, a prospect which she had found perversely appealing and painfully flattering. Oh, dear... She seriously wished he'd get off the corner of her desk. Or alternatively stop swinging his foot like that. He was making her way too aware of his body, his very hunky, handsome male body.

Harriet picked up a biro so that she could pretend to take notes and not look at him.

'I'll get onto those bookings right away,' she said. 'I presume you'll be flying first class to Milan?' This with a quick glance his way.

'Of course,' he replied and smiled at her.

When Harriet's heart gave a lurch, she told herself quite fiercely just to stop it. But she might as well have tried to stop the tide from coming in. Why, oh why, did women find men like Alex so damned attractive? She supposed it was a primal thing, the female of the species blindly surrendering to the alpha male because that was the way of nature. But that didn't make it any easier to endure. The last thing she wanted was to start suffering from some silly crush.

'What about a date for the return flight?' she asked crisply.

'Mmm. Can't say I'm sure when that will be. I might spend a day or two with Jeremy in London after the wedding. It's summer over there at the moment. Look, just make it the one-way to Milan. I'll organise the return flight myself when I'm over there.'

'Fine. I'll scout around and see what's the best first-class deal. Might take me a while. First, I'll look up the various five-star resorts at Coffs Harbour,' she went on, putting the biro down and clicking on the computer to bring up resorts at Coffs Harbour. 'Get your tick of approval whilst you're here. Hmm… An ocean view, you said. With a balcony. It *is* winter, you know. I doubt we'll be spending too much time on an ocean-facing balcony.'

'Possibly not,' he agreed. 'But I like apartments with balconies. They're usually larger and have better light.'

'A balcony it is, then. Here's one which should suit— the Pacific View resort just south of Coffs Harbour. They have a two-bedroom spa suite available for Friday night which has a huge balcony with an ocean view.'

'And the other facilities?'

'Everything you could possibly want. There's a heated indoor pool as well as a gym and not one but two restaurants—one a bistro, the other *à la carte*.'

'Great.'

'Shall I book it, then?'

'Absolutely. Oh, and, Harry,' Alex added as he slid off the corner of her desk. *Finally.* 'Perhaps it might be best not to mention where we'll be staying to the rest of the staff, especially Audrey. She might jump to the wrong conclusion, the way she did this morning when she walked in on my hugging you. We don't want to start up any rumours, do we?'

'Absolutely not. Right you are, boss. Mum's the word.'

'Good girl,' he said, before heading back into his office.

Harriet almost laughed. Because all of a sudden she didn't want to be a good girl. She wanted to be a very bad girl. With Alex.

She was in the process of making the bookings when a courier walked in, holding a huge bouquet of assorted flowers.

'Someone's a lucky girl,' he said, smiling a goofy smile. 'The lady on reception said they were for you.'

Harriet's first hideous thought was that they were from Dwayne, in some vain attempt to get her back. But when she opened the card which accompanied the flowers, the words written there brought tears to her eyes for the second time that day.

Hope you're feeling better soon.
Love from Audrey.
PS The bum wasn't good enough for you, anyway.

The PS made her laugh, which came as a relief to the courier, who was looking worried.

'Everything's fine,' she said to him, waiting till he

left before going out to reception and thanking Audrey profusely.

'Flowers always make me feel better,' Audrey said. 'So does a glass of wine or two. Want to come have a drink with me after work?'

'Love to,' Harriet said. She'd missed her girls' nights out with Emily since she'd gone away.

'Great,' Audrey said. 'You should join the rest of us on Friday nights as well.'

'I will in future,' Harriet said. 'But I can't this Friday night. Have to go north with the boss to inspect his new golf resort. He has to go away overseas again soon and he wants me to keep a personal eye on things up there,' she added by way of explanation. 'So I need to see the lie of the land and meet the foreman.'

'That's a long drive. You'll have to stay somewhere overnight.'

'Probably. Still, there are plenty of motels up that way.'

'True.'

'I'd better get back to work or the slave driver might come looking for me.'

'He can be like that, can't he?'

'He's a workaholic, that's for sure.'

'I wouldn't like to do your job.'

'I don't mind. I like it.' An understatement. She *loved* her job.

'Don't you get fed up with being at his beck and call all the time? I mean, the things he asks you to do some-times.' Audrey rolled her eyes.

Harriet just laughed. Alex had been very up-front at her interview over the menial tasks he might ask her to do. She honestly didn't mind getting his bagels, buying presents for members of his family or even organising his dry-cleaning. Better than sitting at her desk all the time.

It wasn't till Harriet was sitting back down at that same desk that she realised she would enjoy the drive up to the golf estate this weekend very much if she wasn't starting to have these awkward feelings for Alex. Still, at least these days she was capable of resisting such self-destructive desires, having become wise to her own weaknesses where the opposite sex—and sex—was concerned. In time, these feelings would pass and she would meet someone else, someone who could satisfy her in bed and tick at least some of the boxes in her checklist, someone more in her league than the boss of Ark Properties.

The man himself suddenly materialised by her desk.

'So what's with the flowers?' he demanded, his face decidedly grim. 'I hope they're not from your idiot of an ex, trying to get back into your good books.'

'Hardly. They're from Audrey. Wasn't that sweet of her?'

'Very sweet. Look, I have to go out. Family emergency. Hold the fort till I get back.'

Harriet frowned at his swiftly departing back as well as his brusque manner. She wondered what kind of family emergency. He never talked about his family. Yet she knew he had a father still living, and a married older sister who had two children, a boy aged ten and a girl aged eight. She knew because she'd bought Christmas and birthday presents for them.

Maybe she would ask him about his family during the long drive north on Friday. And maybe not.

Friday now loomed in Harriet's mind as a day fraught with unspoken tension. Life, she decided, wasn't being very kind to her at the moment.

But then she looked at Audrey's flowers and smiled.

CHAPTER SIX

It took almost an hour for Alex to drive from the inner city out to Sarah's home in North Rocks. Sydney's traffic situation was getting worse with each passing year. No matter how many motorways they built, nothing seemed to ease the congestion, or the delays. But the level of his frustration when he finally pulled up outside the house he'd bought his sister some years back was not due to road rage but rage of a different kind.

Gritting his teeth, he jumped out from behind the wheel and stormed through the front gate, bypassing the front door and making his way hurriedly round to the back of the house to the entrance to the granny flat. The one-bedroomed very comfortable flat accommodated his father, his useless, drunken father, whom Sarah had kindly taken in but with whom Alex had totally run out of patience. He'd only come because Sarah had asked him to.

She was waiting for him in the doorway, startling Alex with how much she looked like his mother at around the same age. Both were petite and dark, though with blue eyes. Sarah was like her mother in nature, too, being strong and sensible. Alex loved her a lot and would do anything for her. He wasn't as fond of her husband, Vernon, who seemed to resent the things Alex bought for his family.

Though he'd taken the house, mortgage-free, hadn't he?

Still, Vernon did put up with his less than ideal father-in-law living with them, so he couldn't be all bad. Of course, he continued to benefit financially from the arrangement, Alex paying their rates and electricity.

'Where is he?' Alex asked, his tone sharp.

'On the floor in the bedroom,' Sarah answered, stepping back to let him enter.

The sight of his father sprawled on his back on the rug beside the bed was infinitely depressing. Not just because he was dead drunk but because of the deterioration of this once fine-looking man. Alex had inherited his looks from his father, who'd been a big blond hunk in his younger days. It was no wonder his mother had fallen for him. But there was nothing attractive about him now. Nothing at all.

'Good God,' he said, shaking his head as he stared down at the ruin at his feet. 'Whatever are we going to do with him?'

'It's not his fault, Alex,' Sarah said with her usual compassion. 'He started drinking to forget and now he can't stop. He's an alcoholic. It's a disease. A sickness.'

'Then he should agree to go into rehab.' Alex had lost count of the number of times he'd suggested rehab to his father, but it always fell on deaf ears. 'It's a pity we can't forcibly admit him.'

'I know. But you can't. He has to volunteer to go. Come on, help me lift him up onto the bed. I would have done it myself, but he's just too heavy and I can't afford to hurt my back again.'

Alex frowned. 'You've lifted him up off the floor before?'

'Only once. You were away and I didn't want to ask Vernon.'

'Don't try to lift him again, Sarah. Call an ambulance if you have to.'

Alex scooped his father up off the floor with ease and laid him down on top of the bed. He stirred slightly, making a disgusting snorting sound, before falling back into his drunken stupor, his mouth dropping wide open. His breath was foul. So was his whole body. He needed a bath, sooner rather than later. Then he needed a good talking-to. This situation simply couldn't go on. It wasn't fair to Sarah.

'I have to go to work soon, Alex,' Sarah said, anxiety in her strained face.

Sarah was an oncology nurse, an occupation which she'd decided on after their mother had died at home without too much in the way of nursing. It occurred to Alex that their mother's early and totally unnecessary death had resulted in two of her children choosing careers which they'd hoped would make a difference. Not so his pathetic father, who'd promptly fallen apart. His only decision about the future was to try to drink himself to death.

'You go,' Alex said. 'I'll stay with him.'

'That would be great. Thanks. Look, he honestly can't help it. He does try, you know. Sometimes he doesn't have a drink for weeks. I told him I wouldn't let him around the kids if he was drunk all the time. He even went to AA meetings. But last week was the anniversary of Mum's death. I found him at her graveside crying his eyes out. After that, he went on one of his benders.'

Alex sighed, finally finding some genuine compassion for the man who'd once been a decent enough father, if always a little weak. His mother had been the strength in the family and his father had adored her. He'd called her his soul mate, his rock. She'd always picked him up when he was down. Which was often, his work history not being the best. He'd constantly been made redundant, making money tight in the family. It had been inevitable that when she died he would fall apart.

Watching his father disintegrate over the years had reaffirmed Alex's own decision to steer clear of marriage, as well as avoiding any deeply emotional attachments. Loving a woman obsessively the way his father had loved his mother was not something Alex wanted in his life.

'I'll make sure he has a bath and eats some food,' Alex told his sister. 'And I'll wash those filthy clothes he's wearing. Then I'll do my best to talk to him, see if he'll try rehab. I have some contacts at the Salvation Army. They have some very good rehab places for alcoholics and addicts.'

'Oh, that would be wonderful!' Sarah exclaimed. 'Thank you, darling brother,' she added, coming forward to give him a hug, reminding him of that other hug he'd been involved in earlier that morning.

Sarah hurried off, leaving Alex alone with his father and his thoughts.

But he was no longer thinking about his father. He was thinking about Harriet and the danger of having an affair with a woman who was vastly different from his usual type of bed partner. Not only was she older and more intelligent, she was emotionally vulnerable at the moment. Frankly, Harriet was way more emotional that he would ever have imagined.

The risk he would be taking by sleeping with her was also far greater than he'd originally envisaged. What if she fell in love with him? Even worse, what if he fell in love with her? Hell! What in God's name had he been thinking? Clearly, he hadn't been thinking, not with his brain, anyway. He'd let his hormones take charge, let them cloud his usual good judgment when it came to matters concerning the opposite sex.

There was only one thing to do. He had to forget living on the edge and put Harriet firmly back into the strictly professional PA box which she'd occupied in his head for the past ten months. He actually would have called her and cancelled the trip up north if it wouldn't make him seem like a blithering idiot. He was thankful now that they would be staying in that apartment together for only one night. But, to be on the safe side, he'd put a dampener on his hormones by working out at length in the gym during the next two days. He'd also get out of the office as much as he could. There were several building projects he had underway around Sydney which he could visit. Out of sight was out of mind. By Friday morning, he'd have himself firmly under control again.

His father stirred again, this time opening his eyes, blinking blearily at Alex for several seconds before groaning.

'You're not going to lecture me again, son, are you?' he said wearily.

'No,' Alex replied in a firm, no-nonsense voice. 'This time, I'm going to tell you what you're going to do, and you're going to do it, whether you like it not.'

'Am I just?'

'Look, if you want to kill yourself, then do the decent thing and do it quickly. Just don't do it slowly in front of your daughter and your grandkids. They deserve better than that.'

'You don't understand,' he blubbered.

'Yeah, I do. Better than you think. You might not realise this, but Mum's death affected the whole family, not just you. You think Sarah and I didn't grieve? We did.

But eventually we all moved on, the way Mum would have wanted us to move on.'

His father looked away in shame.

'It's not too late, Dad,' Alex went on, his voice gentler. 'You can beat this thing if you want to. Sarah's going to need you when the kids get older. You could be here when she can't be. Keep an eye on them. Sarah's been good to you. Time for you to be good back to her. Time for you to step up to the plate and be a man.'

Tears sprung into his father's tired blue eyes. 'It's too late.'

'It's never too late,' Alex insisted. 'People can change, no matter how old they are. It won't be easy, but it will work, if you give it a chance. I'll help you, too, if you let me.'

'You're a good son.'

Alex experienced some guilt at this remark. He hadn't been such a good son. Sarah had been the one who'd shouldered most of the burden of looking after their father. He'd just opened his cheque book. But he vowed to do better in future.

'All right,' his father said with a resigned sigh. 'I'll give it a go.'

CHAPTER SEVEN

HARRIET SET HER alarm for five on Friday morning, having made arrangements with Alex to be at his place at six-thirty.

'Take a taxi on expenses,' he'd told her during the very brief appearance he'd made in the office last Wednesday morning, telling her at the same time that he wouldn't be in at all on the Thursday and that she was to use the extra time she would have to give their website a face-lift, something she'd been urging him to do for ages. He didn't explain any of his absences, as was often the case with Alex. She suspected it had something to do with his family emergency.

As the taxi sped towards Alex's Darling Harbour address, Harriet pondered again the nature of said emergency. She hoped none of his family was ill.

When the taxi pulled up to the kerb outside Alex's swish-looking apartment block, Harriet paid the fare, then climbed out, taking a few deep breaths as she waited for the driver to get her bag out of the boot. She no longer felt as nervous about this trip as she had the other day, but was not altogether calm. She'd spent an inordinate amount of time last night putting her wardrobe together for the two days, opting for smart casual, though at the last second she'd thrown in a dressy dress, in case Alex wanted to dine at the resort's *à la carte* restaurant.

Of course that had meant adding the right accessories to the growing pile of clothes.

'Going on holidays, love?' the taxi driver asked as he dropped the rather substantial bag by her feet.

'Something like that,' she replied.

'Hope it's somewhere a bit warmer than this,' he said jauntily as he climbed back in behind the wheel and sped off.

It was a bitterly cold morning, Sydney having been blasted by some air off the Antarctic overnight. Still, it would be warmer where they were going. Harriet had chosen to wear stretch black jeans for the drive, teaming them with black ankle boots and a cream cowl-necked jumper made of the softest mohair. She'd thrown on a fawn trench coat to keep out the early morning chill but which she would remove once they were underway. Alex's car was sure to be heated.

Pulling out her phone, she sent him a text to say she'd arrived.

Wait there, he texted back. I'll be right out.

Harriet was shivering by the time Alex pulled up next to her in his black Range Rover. She regretted not wearing a scarf; wearing her hair up was giving her no warmth around her neck.

'Get in,' he said as he jumped out. 'You look cold. I'll see to your bag.'

Harriet tried not to stare at him. But she'd never seen him in casual clothes before. He always wore a suit in the office. He looked great in a suit. In stone-washed grey jeans and a black leather jacket, however, he looked too hot for words. His fair hair was still wet from the shower, the top spiked up a bit, the sides and back clipped short.

She liked it that way. It was dead sexy, supplying an added edge to his already macho looks.

Harriet forcibly had to drag her eyes away, her heart alternatively flipping over, then sinking as she wrenched open the passenger door and climbed in.

And there I was, she thought irritably, *imagining I had this attraction under control.*

Hell on earth, thought Alex as he scooped up the bag and threw it in the back.

He'd taken one look at Harriet standing there, staring at him with those big brown eyes of hers, and he'd known for sure that this thing he felt for her wasn't a one-sided attraction. Alex was well versed in recognising the way women looked at him when they fancied him. And Harry fancied him. But possibly not as much as he fancied her. He was a man, after all, and she was seriously fanciable, especially in those sexy jeans and boots.

By the time Alex took his seat behind the wheel, his resolve not to act on the desire Harriet kept sparking in him was very definitely wavering, especially with her betraying her own feelings just now. Of course, his being her boss still created an ethical dilemma. Such relationships were definitely frowned upon, despite being quite common. Not always ideal, however. Inevitably, there came a time when the woman wanted more. Harriet would always want more. He wouldn't be doing her any favours by taking advantage of her, especially at this time in her life when she was on the rebound and emotionally vulnerable.

Hell, hadn't he been through this thought process before?

He'd already made up his mind to steer clear of her and that was what he should do. End of story. *So just be your normal, bossy self and for pity's sake keep your hands off! Then when you get back to Sydney tomorrow night, go out and find yourself a new girlfriend. With a bit of luck, by the time you go to work on Monday your head will be out of your trousers and back on business!*

Harriet forgot about taking off her coat, buckling up the seat belt over it and propping her large black handbag in her lap whilst doing her best to adopt a relaxed facade. But inside, that tension which she'd been fearing was gathering with force, making her jump slightly when Alex gunned the engine.

'You seem to have packed a lot for one night,' he said as he drove off.

Harriet managed a casual shrug of her shoulders. 'I'm never sure what clothes to take, so I always take more than I need.'

'It's a common female trait,' Alex said. 'When I took Hailey to Vanuatu for a long weekend, she had so much luggage I had to pay for extra baggage.'

Harriet had quite liked Hailey. Much better than Lisa. She didn't like any of Alex's girlfriends now, jealousy having raised its ugly head. Lord knew what she would do when the next one came along. And she would. There was nothing surer.

'I'll remember that when you take me to Vanuatu,' Harriet quipped.

Alex laughed. 'You mean you'd settle for Vanuatu? I would have thought Venice was more your style.'

Harriet winced as a memory hit her. 'You know, I wanted to go to Italy for my honeymoon. I'd always wanted to see Rome and Florence and, yes, Venice most of all. Imagine a city built on water! But Dwayne said

Italy was overrated and that Bali was just as good. And way cheaper.'

'He sounds like a gem,' Alex said drily.

Harriet snorted. 'Yes, a zircon. Everything about him was false.'

'You're well rid of him. But I have to confess I'm still curious over the other check-points on your list, the boxes Dwayne seemed to tick. At first, that is.'

'Oh, God,' Harriet groaned. 'Can't we just forget that stupid list?'

'Since *you* made that list, Harry, then I doubt it was stupid. Come on, tell your dear old boss all about it.'

She had to smile. The only thing right about that description of himself was the word 'boss'. 'Only if you give me your solemn word this time that you won't laugh.'

'If I do, I give you permission to hit me. Though not whilst I'm driving.'

They'd long passed through the harbour tunnel by then and were making their way towards Chatswood, the traffic growing with each passing minute. Like other big cities, Sydney never really slept.

'Well?' Alex prompted when she didn't say anything.

'Gosh, but you can be dogged at times,' she said, but smiling. It occurred to Harriet with a degree of surprise that their chatting away like this was making her relax. 'Okay, well, after Dwayne passed the first three boxes, the next one was that my husband-to-be was not to be boring or lazy.'

'Huh! I don't know about lazy, but I found him boring when I met him.'

'Yes, well, the rot was setting in by then. In the beginning, he showed me a good time. As for lazy... He went from sharing the housework and washing my car as well as his to being a couch potato.'

'I can understand how that would annoy someone as fastidious as you.'

Fastidious? Harriet wasn't sure if that was a compliment or a criticism.

'How am I fastidious?' she asked him enquiringly.

'Come now, Harry, you're a perfectionist! You always look great for starters, even at six-thirty in the morning. There's not a hair out of place, your make-up is on and your outfit is perfect for travelling. I'll also bet if I went into your place right now it would be spotless, with your bed made and the washing-up all done. Am I right?'

'Not at all. Yes, the bed is made and the washing-up done, but there's clothes all over my bed and the bulb in my bathroom isn't working. A perfectionist would have had it fixed by now instead of just moving a lamp in there so that I can see.'

'Really? I'm shocked.'

She had to smile. 'You're laughing at me again.'

'Never! Now, back to that fascinating checklist of yours. What comes after lazy and boring?'

'Look, I'm not going to go through every individual point with regard to Dwayne, except to say that he failed them all. I'll just recite the rest of the checklist the way it's written down.'

Alex smiled to himself; she clearly knew the list off by heart. 'My husband-to-be is to be easy-going and generous. He has to treat women as equals. He has to be a lover of animals and children. He has to have friends and interests other than work. He has to have empathy for others, especially those less fortunate than themselves. He has to be able to cook and doesn't think cleaning is beneath him. He has to respect me and trust me and love me and never, ever forget my birthday. And that's about it,' she finished, leaving off the last point which was about sex.

'Wow. That's some list. But what about sex? Don't you care what kind of lover he is?'

Harriet pursed her lips, a slight blush touching her cheeks. Trust Alex to notice that she'd bypassed that topic. She could never get anything past him at work, either.

'Well, naturally he has to satisfy me in bed,' she said, trying not to look as embarrassed as she felt.

'In that case, Dwayne must have satisfied you. At first, anyway?'

'I suppose so,' she said with a sigh. 'He could be quite good in bed when he wanted to be.'

'But not great.'

'No,' she admitted. 'Not great. Look, I don't feel comfortable talking about this,' she went on quite truthfully. The last thing she needed was to start thinking about sex when the object of her desire was sitting right next to her. 'Could we talk about something else? Work, perhaps, or the weather? And could you turn the heating down in this thing? It's very hot in here.'

Alex rarely felt shame, but he did at that moment. Asking Harriet personal questions like that was very definitely crossing the line, especially since he'd resolved not to act on the sexual feelings he'd been having about her. He couldn't help suspecting, however, that her flushed face was not entirely due to his putting the heater up too high.

Talking about sex could sometimes be very arousing, the brain being the most erotic area in the human body. The thought that she was sitting there in a turned-on state was not conducive to resisting temptation.

Gritting his teeth, Alex adjusted the temperature.

'I've turned the heating down,' he said. 'But perhaps you should take that coat off. I've only got a T-shirt on under my jacket, so I feel fine. You look like you've got a very warm jumper on.' And a very sexy-looking one, he'd noted earlier. All soft and furry, the kind you wanted to reach out and touch.

'I meant to take it off earlier,' she said. She was quick, the coat dispensed with in no time and her seat belt snapped back on.

'Throw it over onto the back seat,' he said when she went to lay the coat across her lap.

Alex glanced over at her as she twisted in her seat to do as he said, the movement bringing his attention to the swell of her breasts beneath her jumper. Her very nice breasts. It sent a message to his groin which made him wince.

Damn and blast! It wasn't Harriet who was sitting here in a turned-on state. It was his own stupid self. He should never have asked her about her sex life with Dwayne. He never should have organised this whole fiasco of a trip in the first place!

'I'll put the radio on,' he said brusquely. That way he wouldn't be tempted to ask her any more inappropriate questions. 'Do you want a news and chat channel? Or just music?'

CHAPTER EIGHT

'WHAT?' HARRIET COULDN'T think for a moment, her mind still on that look Alex had given her a moment ago. Had she imagined it or had he stared at her breasts?

Of course you were imagining it, you idiot, came the stern rebuke. *Why would he be ogling your very ordinary C-cups? They can't compare with Lisa's double Ds. Stop focusing on sex and just answer the man.*

'Just music, thanks,' she said, pressing her thighs together tightly in a vain attempt to bring her body under control, her silly, traitorous body which had become all hot and bothered. Talk about pathetic!

'Music,' Alex said to the computerised dashboard and a woman's voice came back with a request for more information. Whilst Harriet was technically savvy, her four-year-old car didn't have such advanced technology. She recalled Alex saying something about updating his SUV when he'd come back from London recently. So this had to be it.

'What kind of music do you like?' Alex asked her.

Harriet didn't really have a favourite style of music. But she supposed she had to say something. 'Country and Western.'

'Country and Western,' he commanded the computer and almost immediately a song came on that she liked.

'Amazing,' she said. 'You don't even have to insert a flash disc or a CD.'

'It's almost as brilliant as my PA.'

Harriet flushed with pleasure. This was another part of her job she liked—the way Alex would compliment her. Her previous bosses had never done that. Clearly, their fragile male egos had been threatened by her. Not so with Alex. Of course, there was nothing fragile about *his* ego. Or about him. He was a big man in every way.

'You did a brilliant job on our website, by the way,' he went on. 'I had a look at it last night and I was very impressed. It's better laid out and more user-friendly. And I like the way you included photos of the staff. Nothing like the personal touch.'

'That was Audrey's idea,' she admitted, not being one to take credit for something that someone else had suggested. 'We went out for drinks after work on Tuesday, and when I said I was going to revamp the website, she had quite a few excellent suggestions. She's an online shopping addict, so she knows what works and what doesn't.'

'She's a smart lady, Audrey. But inclined to gossip. Did you remember not to tell her we wouldn't be staying up here overnight?'

'Like you just said, Alex, she's smart. Audrey had already concluded we'd be staying somewhere overnight. But I let her think we'd be bunking down in separate rooms in an ordinary motel, not in an apartment at a five-star resort.'

'Good thinking. Did you organise someone to feed the cat while you're away?'

'Yes, Audrey's doing it.'

'That's good. Can't have the poor old thing passing

away from starvation while we're away. You'd blame me, and I don't think I could live with the guilt.'

'Don't be silly. You have nothing to feel guilty about where Romany is concerned. Did I ever thank you for letting him be the office cat?'

'Only about a hundred times.'

'Oh. Yes, well, it was still very good of you. Poor Romany,' she said with a sigh. 'I dare say he'll die soon. Still, at least we made the last part of his life a little happier.'

'You do spoil him rotten, Harry. Sometimes I almost feel jealous of that cat. Now, I don't want to stop again till we get to Port Macquarie, probably around eleven. I want to make the golf estate by two o'clock at the latest. Is that all right with you?'

'That's fine,' she agreed.

'If you need a break before then, just say so.'

'I'll be all right.'

'Good. Now, just settle back and relax and listen to the music. Eventually, though, I'll have to make some business calls. But not yet. It's still early.'

Harriet doubted that she would relax, but amazingly she did, the heated seats and the music melting away her earlier tension. She even drifted off to sleep, jolting awake when Alex started talking more loudly than the music. She listened, amazed at how much he could achieve on the phone in just a couple of hours, contacting all the foremen on his current building projects, demanding updates on their progress, giving them a hurry-up when needed.

Eleven saw them eating a disgustingly fattening lunch in the service centre near the turn-off to Port Macquarie, Alex scoffing at her comment that she'd end up with a backside the size of a bus if she ate that for lunch every day.

'No worries there, Harry. You would starve rather than eat this kind of food every day.'

'True,' she agreed.

'It doesn't hurt to bend your rules every once in a while, you know.'

She stared at him across the wooden bench, wondering what rules he was referring to. Probably that silly checklist of hers. Not that all of it was silly. In fact, a lot of those rules made perfect sense. The trouble was that men weren't perfect, so finding someone to fit all her far-too-many requirements was doomed to failure. All she could hope for was that the main ones might be fulfilled. The ones about love and respect and money and, yes, sex.

'You could be right, there,' she mused.

'I *am* right,' he pronounced. 'Now, drink up that cappuccino. Time to get going.'

He was back on the phone again as soon as they hit the road, chatting away with the sales team in the office, finding out how things were going and how many sales they'd had off their various plans. They had several blocks of units in a developmental stage, all of them in the far western suburbs and very reasonably priced. Most were likely to be sold before a single brick was laid. They also had a housing estate near where the new Sydney airport was to be built, which was proving popular with first-time buyers and builders. Harriet listened as Alex told each of the boys personally about his having to go away the week after next. When he finally finished talking, Harriet turned to glance his way.

'By the way, will *we* be handling the sales of the housing blocks on the golf estate, or are you going to give that job to local real-estate agents?'

'Both. And we'll advertise extensively online. That will be *your* job, Harry. Perhaps you can think about that while I'm away, since you won't be running around all the time getting your boss bagels and doing myriad other jobs which the lazy so-and-so could possibly do himself.'

Harriet laughed. 'I don't mind, really.'

'I know you don't. You are indispensable to me, Harry.'

'No one is indispensable, Alex.'

'You are to me. As selfish as it sounds, I'm almost glad that you've broken off your engagement. The thought of you getting married and leaving me to become a mother was filling me with dread.'

Harriet rolled her eyes. What a hopeless exaggerator he was! But, yes, it *was* selfish of him to say that. And rather insensitive.

'Sorry,' she said. 'But I still intend to get married and have at least one baby, so you'll just have to cope when that day comes. But don't worry. I have no intention of giving up my day job just because I'm pregnant. I'll waddle into the office right up to the last second. You might even have to drive me to the maternity ward if my husband is unavailable,' she added with a straight face.

CHAPTER NINE

ALEX WAS HORRIFIED at the thought, plus the image of Harry waddling into the office at some future date with a huge baby bump. He could see it now. Her desk would be littered with magazines that told you everything you needed to know about pregnancy and motherhood—plus everything you didn't need to know. She and Audrey would talk babies *ad infinitum*, spending every lunch hour buying baby clothes, not to mention oodles of those hideous stuffed toys. And, yes, there would be a bag packed and sitting in the corner, ready for the emergency of her suddenly going into labour.

'That won't be happening,' he ground out. 'Audrey can take you in a taxi.'

Harriet laughed. 'You should see your face. What's the problem, Alex? You're not afraid of babies, are you?'

'Immensely. They're noisy and messy and have no concept of doing what they're told.' He'd visited Sarah once or twice when she'd had newborns and had hardly slept a wink, what with the crying all night. It certainly wasn't something he craved for himself.

'No wonder you've stayed a bachelor if that's what you think.'

'It's what I think. Now, tell me what you think.'

'About what? Babies or bachelors?'

'No. About your surrounds. We're here.' And he pulled over to the side of the road and turned off the engine.

They were on the crest of a hill. Harriet's head swivelled round as she took in the land which would one day be an eighteen-hole golf course surrounded by privately owned homes and some holiday apartments. There would be a well-appointed club house, of course, as well as a small chapel with a lovely garden where weddings could be held. Big money in weddings, Alex had told her during the planning stage.

The land, she knew, had once been a banana plantation that had gone bust when the trees had developed some kind of fungus. A would-be entrepreneur had snapped it up for a bargain price, clearing the land before he himself had gone broke when his financing had fallen through and the stock market had crashed. Alex had stepped in, and here they were today.

She climbed out so that she could have a better look, standing on the grass verge with her hands on her hips whilst assembling her thoughts. The golf course itself looked nearly finished, but the buildings were still at the foundation stage, the rain obviously having held up that part of the project.

'Well?' Alex said as he came to stand beside her.

'It's going to be great. I love the artificial lakes. And the trees. But it's never going to be finished by Christmas,' she added.

Alex frowned. 'You're probably right. God, but I hate it when the weather works against me.'

'You can't control the weather, Alex.'

'I don't seem to be able to control anything much these days,' he muttered.

And then it happened. He turned towards her and she

saw it in his eyes—the very thing that she thought she'd imagined this morning. But she wasn't imagining this. The desire—no, the *hunger*—glittering in his sky-blue eyes was very real. Her hands slipped from her hips as she stared back at him, her heartbeat quickening.

Part of her didn't want him to want her like this. It would make Alex like all the other too-tall, too-handsome, too-successful men she'd slept with in the past. But there was no denying what he wanted, his hot gaze coveting her the way the big, bad wolf had coveted those three plump little pigs.

Unfortunately, Harriet knew she wouldn't prove to be the sensible pig who'd built his house out of bricks. She was the silly pig who'd built his house out of straw. One puff and it had fallen down.

Or one kiss, as it turned out.

He didn't say a word as he strode over and pulled her into his arms, all her defences dissolving well before his lips met hers. Her eyes closed as she lifted her mouth and her arms, sliding them up around his neck, pulling him close, her breasts flattening against his chest. Harriet could not recall a kiss affecting her as much as this kiss from Alex. Her head swirled as passion erupted within her like a volcano, her mouth gasping open. His arms tightened around her and his tongue delved deep.

Harriet had been kissed many times before—and by men who were good kissers. But Alex kissing her was something else entirely. His tongue moved back and forth in her mouth, then up, rubbing over the sensitive surface of her palate. She moaned with pleasure and excitement. She didn't want him ever to stop. She loved the way his hands started roaming over her back, sliding up and down her spine. One hand finally settled like a collar around the nape of her neck whilst the other splayed over her bottom, pressing her firmly against his erection. It blew her mind, just how hard he was.

The loud tooting of a horn plus some raucous catcalls had Alex wrenching away from her, his breathing ragged as he glowered at the passing car full of teenagers. Her eyes had flown open with the shock of his abandoning her so abruptly, leaving her still panting and flushed with heat.

'Damn,' he muttered, running his hands agitatedly through his short fair hair whilst scooping in several deep breaths. Shaking his head, he spun away from her, striding over to stand on the edge of the hill, his legs spread wide, his fists balled by his sides.

Harriet stayed where she was, staring over at him, dazed and more than a little shaken. It wasn't every day that she ached to have sex with a man within moments of their first kiss. Not that this was just any man, of course. This was Alex, her boss.

After staring down at the valley for several seconds, he whirled back to face her once more, though still keeping his distance.

'That shouldn't have happened,' he ground out. 'I never meant for that to happen.'

'No,' she said. Harriet didn't imagine for one moment that he had. 'Why did you do it, then?'

His laugh was very dry. 'Come now, Harry, don't play the ingénue with me. You've been around. You know how this works. If truth be told, I've been wanting to do that since the first day you walked into my office.'

Harriet blinked. 'What? You mean at my interview?'

'Yes, at your interview. Even then, I had some misgivings. But I fooled myself into thinking I could keep my hands off. I've never been partial to pursuing women who were in love with someone else, no matter how attractive I found them.' He dragged in a deep breath, then let it out slowly, his expression self-mocking. 'But fate conspired against me this week. I broke up with Lisa and you broke up with Dwayne. If I hadn't hugged you, then taken you out for coffee, none of this would ever have happened. I certainly wouldn't have organised for us to be alone like this.'

The meaning behind his last words took a few seconds to sink into Harriet's somewhat scattered brain, any flattery she'd been experiencing over his confessed attraction soon obliterated by shock.

'Are you saying that this so-called business trip was a deliberate ploy on your part to seduce me?' She'd imagined it might be for a brief moment earlier in the week, before dismissing the idea as ludicrous. 'You never really needed me to oversee this estate while you're away, did you?'

Alex shrugged his broad shoulders. 'No, I didn't need you to oversee this estate for me while I was away—and, yes, it was just an excuse to get you alone. Though I'm not keen on the word "seduce".'

'What else would you call it?' she threw at him angrily. 'You know full well I would never *want* to have an affair with you. You're my boss!'

'You didn't mind my kissing you just now,' he reminded her with brutal honesty. 'But all that is beside the point. I saw the folly of my ways in time and changed my mind about trying to *seduce* you, since you seem to like that word. Perhaps because it stops you from taking any responsibility over what just happened.'

'*You* kissed *me*, Alex. I didn't do a thing!'

'Nothing except look so deliciously sexy this morning that I haven't been able to think of anything else but making love to you all day.'

An already flustered Harriet homed in on his patently false words.

'You don't want to make love to me at all,' she snapped. 'You want to have sex with me. That's a totally different scenario.'

'True,' he said before walking slowly back towards her. 'But nothing changes the fact that we can't go back to the way it was between us, Harry. You want me as much as I want you. Don't deny it,' he said, close enough now to reach out and place his large hands on her suddenly trembling shoulders.

Harriet somehow found her tongue, despite it lying thick and dry in her parched mouth. 'That doesn't mean I have to do anything about it.'

'True again. But why deny yourself something which can give you pleasure? And I can give you pleasure, Harry,' he murmured, his right hand lifting off her shoulder to trace circles around her gasping lips. 'Lots of pleasure.'

'I didn't realise that you could be this wicked,' she choked out.

'There's nothing wicked about sexual pleasure, Harry,' he said, his bedroom-blue eyes going all smoky with desire. 'And there's nothing wrong with our having a sexual relationship, provided we keep it out of the office.'

He could say that, but she knew that if she did this—and her body was screaming at her to surrender—it might eventually cost her her job. Harriet knew of other women who'd had affairs with their bosses and they never came out on top. Never!

But her days of being weak where men were concerned was over. Harnessing every bit of backbone that she possessed, she stepped back, far enough to force his hand to drop away from her mouth and her still-burning lips. Her action surprised him, which made her smile a wry smile.

You don't know what you're dealing with where I'm concerned, Alex. But you'll learn.

'You're right,' she said crisply. 'About everything. But if we're going to have an affair, then I must set some rules.'

'Rules?' he echoed, his brows lifting skywards.

'Yes, rules.'

His rueful smile annoyed her, but she didn't let it show. She kept her cool and her resolve. Amazing, really, considering what she was about to do. Dwayne had been a big mistake, but Dwayne didn't have the power to hurt her as much as Alex could. Harriet had a history of falling madly in love with men like Alex. No matter how careful she was, it would probably still happen. But no way would he ever know that. The moment she felt even a smidgeon of love for him, her resignation would be on his desk.

'Shoot,' he said.

Harriet scooped in a calming breath before letting it out slowly. 'As you yourself said,' she began, her voice wonderfully cool and steady, 'there will be no sex in the office. That's a definite no-go. But also not during office hours. No sneaking out at lunchtime to some nearby hotel room.'

Alex scowled. 'Sounds like you've been down this road before.'

She hadn't, never having indulged in a secret affair before. All her relationships had been out in the open. But she wasn't about to tell Alex that. 'Like you said earlier, Alex, I've been here before.'

'Any other rules?' he asked, still sounding irritated.

'Only the obvious ones. You will use a condom at all

times.' She'd stopped taking the pill after breaking up with Dwayne. 'Also, whilst I'm sleeping with you, you don't sleep with anyone else. The day you take up with a new girlfriend, our relationship—such as it is—will be over.'

'Fair enough. Am I allowed any rules of my own?'

Harriet was taken aback. She hadn't anticipated this. 'But of course,' she said coolly.

'We will not have sex at all during the working week,' he surprised her by saying. 'When I work, I work hard. I can't afford to be wrecked the next day after being up half the night. But I expect you to spend every weekend with me. At my apartment,' he added. 'Starting from Friday night straight after work.'

A highly erotic thrill rippled through Harriet at the thought that he would want her that much. The prospect of spending every weekend at Alex's sexual beck and call was intoxicatingly exciting. She had no doubt he would be good in bed. No, he would be better than just good. He'd be fantastic. All of a sudden Harriet found it hard to concentrate on what she should be saying. But she had to. Her pride demanded it.

'Sorry,' she said crisply. 'No can do. I'll be going out for drinks on a Friday night with friends. I can't get to your apartment till much later in the evening.'

'No problem. I can wait. Waiting sometimes makes it better.'

Harriet suppressed a groan. She really was out of her league here. Yes, she'd had lovers before, but none quite like Alex. She could see that he was very experienced at playing erotic games. But there was no turning back. She wanted him too much.

'I also might have to go out with Emily on the odd

Saturday night,' she added, determined to make at least some show of independence.

'Can't you have your girls' night out during the week?'

'Sometimes, but not always. But back to the weekends. What do you mean by "at your apartment"? Aren't you ever going to take me out somewhere? For a drive, perhaps? Or to dinner, or to a show?'

'No. You're my PA, Harriet,' he added, showing her he meant business when he called her Harriet like that. 'You're also a marrying kind of girl. I don't want you to ever think that our affair has anything to do with love. It's about sex and sexual pleasure. It won't last. Maybe only a few weeks. But, let's face it, after what you've been through with Dwayne, you can afford a few weeks to indulge yourself in a purely selfish and strictly sexual relationship.'

Shock rippled through Harriet at the mention of Dwayne. Because she hadn't given him a second thought. The penny dropped that she hadn't been in love with Dwayne for a long time.

No, be honest, Harriet. You were never *in love with him. Yes, it was upsetting breaking up with him. But your heart wasn't broken, just your dreams.*

'When you're ready to move on,' Alex was saying, 'then just say so and we'll call it quits. Okay?'

Harriet just stared at him, stunned by the ruthlessness of his proposal and by her reaction to it. Sheer, unadulterated excitement. It was a struggle to stop the heat inside her body from reaching her face. Somehow, she managed.

'Okay?' he repeated, his eyes narrowing on hers.

'Okay,' she agreed, already afraid that calling it quits might prove impossible. Or it would whilst she was working for him. No matter what happened between them, it was perfectly clear that her days at Ark Properties were now numbered.

'Good,' he said, just a tad smugly. 'I'd kiss you to seal the deal, but I don't dare. After that last kiss, we'd probably end up having sex on the grass and, as much I occasionally fancy a quickie in the great outdoors, I prefer the comfort of a bed. Or a sofa. Or even a nice, warm spa bath.'

Harriet tried to banish the thought of having sex with Alex tonight in the spa bath, but it refused to go, evoking images which both aroused and tormented her. Dear God, but she could hardly wait!

'Now, we'd better get down there and pretend to do some work. I don't want Wally to think I made up some feeble excuse just so I could go away for a dirty weekend.'

But that's exactly what you did, Harriet thought dazedly as they both climbed back into the Range Rover. She didn't believe Alex's claim that he'd changed his mind about seducing her. He'd meant to have her all along. And now, he had her. Game, set and match!

CHAPTER TEN

ALEX STRUGGLED TO keep his focus on the job at hand in the two hours they spent with Wally, though he doubted the foreman noticed. He was too busy chatting away with Harriet and showing her everything. Wally seemed inordinately pleased that she would be visiting him in a couple of weeks' time, and not Alex. It seemed foolish to feel jealousy, but he did.

Alex might have worried about this uncharacteristic reaction more if his head hadn't been projecting forward to the evening ahead. He was impatient to have Harry in his arms again. Impatient to show her that he was the boss, even in the bedroom; that her ridiculous penchant for rules didn't apply to him. Yes, he would always use a condom. He wasn't a fool. But other than that he would not be dictated to, especially when she wanted him as much as he wanted her. He almost felt sorry for Dwayne. How could any man live up to that ridiculous checklist of hers? He'd have to be a saint.

Alex wasn't a saint. Not even remotely. But neither was he cruel or heartless. He was well aware that Harriet had just been through a tough time in her life. But he had no intention of hurting her. Hell, he would never hurt any woman, especially not Harry, whom he respected and admired enormously. Alex felt confident that having an affair with him would actually be good for her. It might encourage her to lighten up a bit. To live for the moment. To just have fun for a while.

By the time they left for the relatively short drive to the nearby resort, Alex had convinced himself that a strictly sexual affair with him was just what the doctor ordered for someone suffering over the break-up of a relationship.

Harriet didn't feel like chatting on the way to the resort, tension over the night ahead gathering in the pit of her stomach. Alex did his best to engage her in conversation, not very successfully. When he finally gave up asking her what she now saw as futile questions about the golf estate, she turned her head to gaze through the passenger window at her surrounds, noting idly that the countryside was very beautiful, with rolling hills and lush paddocks, the grass very green despite it being winter. Not many frosts this far north, she thought. Not to mention near the coast.

A sign came up saying that Coffs Harbour was only a few kilometres away.

By the time they turned into the resort, her nerves were jangling and her belly was as tight as a drum. Harriet still found it hard to believe that she was about to spend the night with Alex. *All* night, in his bed. Maybe even in his bath as well. It stunned her how quickly she had gone from engaged woman to suddenly single to her boss's secret mistress. Not that they'd actually done the deed yet. But it was a foregone conclusion. With the wild desires that were flooding her body at that moment, she couldn't have changed her mind even if she'd wanted to.

The resort was everything its website promised— several storeys high, the main building sat on a bluff overlooking the ocean. It faced north-east, with the back nestled into the rocky hillside. When they pulled into reception shortly after six, the sun had just set and dusk had arrived. Solar-powered lights were on everywhere, lining the circular driveway and winking in the tropical-style gardens. A parking valet descended on them as soon as Alex pulled up, taking care of their luggage while they went inside to book in.

Harriet was slightly taken aback when Alex told her to sit down whilst he handled everything. She was used to doing everything for him, but of course they were no longer just boss and employee; they were about to become lovers. She was glad to sit, her knees going to jelly at the thought.

The foyer was spacious and luxurious, with various seating arrangements dotted around. Over in a far corner was a bar and beyond that a large doorway with a sign over it, indicating the bistro-style restaurant she'd read about. She knew the *à la carte* restaurant was on the top floor, where the view of the ocean would be perfect during the daytime, as well as in the evening in summer, when daylight-saving time had it staying light till eight-thirty. She started thinking this would be the perfect place for future clients of their golf course to stay. She might contact the manager at a later date and see about their advertising on the Ark Properties website.

No sooner had Harriet thought that when she remembered she would probably not be working for Ark Properties for much longer. She sighed, then glanced over at where Alex was still at the desk, booking them in. Would it all be worth it? she wondered. Would the pleasure he'd promised live up to her expectations?

Harriet only had to recall the intoxicating expertise of his kiss to know the answer to that. Sex with Alex was going to be fantastic. Fantastic and unforgettable. It was the unforgettable part, however, which was the real worry. She couldn't imagine herself getting over him as quickly as she'd got over Dwayne. But when Alex turned from the desk and smiled over at her, all her concerns for the future fled. Her heart lurched as she watched him walk towards her. God, but he was gorgeous. Gorgeous and all hers. For now, anyway. Adrenaline shot through her veins, accompanied by the heat of a desire so strong that she wasn't sure she would be able to stand up.

'All done,' he said, still smiling. 'Our luggage has been sent up and they booked us a table for dinner at seven-thirty. Are you coming?' he said and held his hand out.

She put her much smaller hand in his large one, sucking in sharply when his fingers closed hot and strong around hers. He drew her up onto her feet, his mouth no longer smiling, his eyes darkening as they met hers.

'I'm not going to be able to wait till after dinner,' he said in a low, gravelly voice only she would hear. 'This is getting beyond bearing.'

'Yes,' she agreed, her face flushing wildly as everything she'd ever believed about herself was tipped on its head. She'd thought she knew how this kind of thing felt. She'd experienced sexual desire before. But this was different from *anything* she'd ever experienced.

'Don't say another word,' he growled and steered her hurriedly towards the bank of lifts against the back wall. 'When we get into the apartment, I want you to go to your bathroom and shower,' he told her on the way. 'I'll do the same in mine. Don't dress. Just put on one of their bathrobes. We'll meet in the living room. You have ten minutes. Not a second longer.'

There was another couple waiting to use the lifts and a fiercely aroused Harriet avoided their eyes. But she noticed when the woman started staring at Alex. It used to amuse Harriet when women ogled her boss, but this time she hated it with a passion, especially since this woman was young and attractive. Harriet knew she would have to get a grip on her jealousy if she was to survive her affair with Alex. He wasn't the type of man who'd appreciate a possessive lover.

She kept her eyes averted as they rode the lift upwards, the other couple alighting well before their own stop. Thank God. When the lift doors opened on their floor, Alex took her elbow and ushered her along the hallway.

The apartment was exactly as it had appeared on the website. Harriet already knew the floor plan by heart. The decor was no surprise, either, the website having detailed photos of all the rooms. The furniture was typical five-star-hotel furniture, comfy and classy. The colour palette was in blue, grey and white, the walls white, the carpet grey, the kitchen and bathrooms white.

Harriet didn't stop to look around, though she did notice that Alex actually had more luggage then she had, all their bags having been brought up and deposited in the entrance hall. She swept up her bag and walked swiftly through the living room and down the short hallway into the second bedroom, which she already knew had an *en suite* bathroom. Dropping her bag at the foot of the bed, Harriet raced into the bathroom, stripped off, then plunged into a hot, though far from relaxing, shower.

Harriet was way beyond relaxation. Alex had used the words 'beyond bearing' downstairs. She had already reached that point herself, her mind constantly filling with arousing images, her body balancing on a knife-edge of desire so sharp that the beating of the hot water against her erect nipples was actually painful. When she went to wash between her thighs, she had to stop for fear that she might come.

She was close. So very close. She had to stop thinking about Alex. Had to stop thinking about doing it with
him. Had to stop *thinking*. Oh, God...

Harriet snapped off the shower and almost fell out of
the cubicle, drying herself inadequately before drawing on the thick white bathrobe that was hanging on the
back of the door. A quick glance in the bathroom mirror showed pink cheeks and messed-up hair. Sighing,
she took her hair down, combing it with her fingers till
it fell around her face in its usual tidy curtain. There
seemed little point in bothering with make-up, though a
quick spray of deodorant might be a good idea. So would
cleaning her teeth. Dashing back into the bedroom, she
pulled out her toilet bag and returned to the bathroom to
attend to both matters.

More than ten minutes had definitely passed by the
time she forced her jelly-like legs to carry her towards the
bedroom door, her uncharacteristic tardiness not helped
by a new and rather undermining train of thought. As
much as she wanted Alex, she was suddenly terrified of
somehow disappointing him. Maybe he would find her
body too...well...ordinary. She didn't have spectacular
breasts, an overly curvy bottom or legs that went up to
her armpits. Her figure was very nice—she looked quite
good naked—but it was nothing out of the box.

And then there was the worry about her own performance in bed. She'd never had any complaints before,
but she suspected that Alex's standards were very high,
and very demanding. He'd already demonstrated dominant tendencies, his rules for their affair clearly trying
to turn her into some kind of submissive. And, whilst
Harriet found such a scenario exciting, she wasn't sure
how long she could sustain such a role. It went against
her basic nature. Harriet was very independent in spirit,

an organiser and a planner. Over the years she'd developed firm ideas over what she wanted in men and in life. Dwayne had gone as far as to call her bossy and controlling during their last argument, but Harriet didn't see herself that way.

Well, maybe a little…

It crossed her mind that her rather scandalous behaviour today could be her subconscious trying to break out of her usual sensible mould by doing something wild and rebellious.

Becoming the boss's secret mistress would certainly qualify as that!

CHAPTER ELEVEN

ALEX GLANCED UP when she entered the living room, his hands stilling on the bottle of champagne he was opening. It had been sitting in an ice bucket on the kitchen counter, along with two champagne glasses and a basket of fruit. Compliments of the management.

It had been over ten minutes since she'd fled his presence like the hounds of hell were after her. Her big brown eyes, he noted, looked just as they had that day he'd interviewed her. Deliciously nervous yet fiercely determined at the same time. He wondered how they would look when she was about to come. Would they grow wider, or scrunch up as she struggled not to let go?

He liked to prolong a woman's pleasure. Liked to prolong his own as well. Alex suspected, however, that there wouldn't be much prolonging this first time.

'Do you like champagne?' he asked.

She blinked, then stared at the bottle, as though she hadn't even seen it.

'Not really,' she replied. 'It gives me a headache.'

Alex laughed, then dumped the bottle back in the ice bucket. 'Well, we can't have that, can we? Should I make you some coffee, then? You must be thirsty.'

'I don't want anything,' she said before sucking in a deep breath. 'Just you.'

* * *

Harriet's bold admission shocked her. And him as well, judging by the startled look on his face.

But she simply hadn't been able to bear the thought of any more delay.

His surprised expression soon changed to one of hunger, his blue eyes clouding as they narrowed, then focused on her mouth.

She just wanted his hands on her naked body, and him inside her.

When he came out from where he'd been standing behind the breakfast bar, Harriet froze, needing all of her physical and mental strength to hold herself upright as he walked towards her. When he was close enough, he reached out and slowly undid the sash of the robe, Harriet's chest tightening as he parted it. When he slipped his hands inside and started playing with her tightly aching nipples, she gasped, then groaned. As much as she craved such attention, she craved him more.

'Please don't torture me, Alex,' she said shakily, her desperate eyes pleading with him.

'Don't torture *you*!' he exclaimed, then laughed. 'Sweetheart, you've been torturing me all day.' After shoving the ice bucket down to one end of the counter, he took a rough hold of her waist and hoisted her up onto the stone breakfast bar, pushing her back till her upper body was flat, parting her robe further, then parting her legs.

She could feel the cold of the stone counter through the robe, but she wasn't cold. Not at all. Harriet watched, eyes wide, as he moved to stand between her outspread legs, her head lifting a little when he unwound the sash on his own robe. She wanted to see him. Wanted to watch him.

Her mouth dried at the sight of his erection. He was

even bigger and harder than she'd imagined. And already sheathed with a condom.

'No, don't!' she cried out when he rubbed the tip against her clitoris, her nerve-endings already on the edge of release. 'Just do it.'

He swore, Harriet's head clunking back onto the bench top with relief when he pushed himself into her. Her relief was short-lived, however, as the dizzying pleasure of his possession was rapidly eclipsed by the speed and strength of the most intense orgasm she'd ever experienced. Spasm followed spasm, the sensations electrifying. Her mouth fell open as she dragged in a much-needed breath, her eyes closing when the room began to spin. They flew open again when Alex suddenly grabbed her hips, holding her captive with an iron grip as he came, his sex pulsating violently in tandem with her own contractions. Their mutual climax went on for ages, sating Harriet with the most overwhelming waves of pleasure.

Finally, their bodies grew still and calm, leaving Harriet lying there staring dazedly up at the ceiling whilst she struggled to gather her thoughts. For this was what she'd feared—a pleasure, a satisfaction, so out there that it would have her coming back for more, long after it wasn't wise. Hopefully, she wouldn't fall in love with Alex. Hopefully, she could keep it at just lust, or infatuation, or whatever this kind of sexual obsession was called. Already she was looking forward to those weekends where he wanted her to be at his sexual beck and call. There was nothing she wouldn't do for him. Nothing!

His lifting her up from the counter to hold her tenderly against him brought a moan of dismay to her lips. She didn't want tenderness from him. She just wanted sex. Alex might be able to indulge in tender post-coital embraces without letting his emotions get involved, but

Harriet wasn't of that ilk. She would have to put a stop to such hypocritical nonsense before disaster struck. After all, *he* was the one who said he just wanted a strictly sexual relationship. An affair, not a *love* affair. Which was exactly all *she* wanted from him. Clearly, he needed reminding of that fact.

Alex was taken aback when Harriet pulled back out of his arms.

'Wow,' she said as she lifted her hands to finger-comb her hair. 'I obviously needed that.'

Her remark sent Alex's teeth clenching down hard in his jaw. He hated to think that her urgent responses to him were the result of nothing but an intense sexual frustration. He preferred to believe she found him as attractive and desirable as he found her. He didn't like her implying that she was just scratching an itch with him. Surely she was just trying to find excuses for coming so quickly? Not that he cared. He'd come pretty quickly himself. And it had felt fantastic. Frankly, he hadn't had an orgasm that intense in living memory. Their coming together had helped, of course. God, the way she'd gripped his erection had been amazing. He could not wait to feel that again.

But he would have to wait, he supposed. They really should be getting dressed for dinner. But he was still inside her, damn it. And he wanted seconds.

Without asking, he slid his hands under her bottom and scooped her up off the counter. Thank God she was just a light little thing, but it still wasn't the most comfortable position with her legs dangling by her sides.

'What do you think you're doing?' she gasped, grabbing the lapels of his robe before thankfully wrapping her legs around him.

'That was a very nice entree, Harry,' he told her as he turned and carried her towards the main bedroom. 'But not nearly enough for me. My sexual appetite runs to five-course meals.'

He loved the wild glittering in her dilated eyes. She wanted seconds as much as he did.

'Don't worry,' he went on. 'We'll stop after the second course and save the rest till after we've eaten some real food. Nothing like a break to whet the appetite again.'

CHAPTER TWELVE

IT WAS AFTER seven-thirty by the time an elegantly dressed Alex steered a somewhat shell-shocked Harriet into the restaurant for dinner. Thankfully, she didn't look as shattered as she felt. The designer dress she was wearing, which had cost her a week's wages, fitted her figure like a glove, the emerald colour complementing her dark hair. Her make-up was perfect and her black patent leather bag matched her shoes, their four-inch heels giving her some much-needed height, especially when she was with Alex, who easily ticked her 'too tall' box.

Harriet did her best to exude an air of cool sophistication as their waiter showed them to their table. But it was a struggle to put aside the memories of what had just transpired. Less than twenty minutes earlier she had been stark naked in Alex's shower, her hands outstretched on the wet tiles, every muscle in her body tight as a drum as he teased her endlessly with a soapy sponge, then took her from behind, her moans muffled by the hot jets of water streaming over her back. She'd come quickly again, but Alex hadn't. He'd lasted and lasted and, astonishingly, when he'd finally come, so had she. Which was a first for her. She'd never come twice like that. Not in such a short space of time. Yet perversely, as soon as he'd withdrawn, she'd found herself wanting more. Before she'd been able to stop herself, she'd spun round and grabbed him, kissing him passionately.

It was Alex who'd put a stop to proceedings. Harriet flushed at the memory of his smacking her on the bottom and telling her not to be so greedy; that it was time to dress for dinner and she would just have to wait.

Harriet sucked in a deep breath as she sat down, the position reminding her that she was still on the sensitive side down there. Not sore, exactly. Just…sensitised. Feeling perversely embarrassed—really, what was there to be embarrassed about?—Harriet reached for the white linen serviette, flicking it open and placing it across her lap before the waiter did it for her.

'What would you like to drink?' Alex asked, forcing her to glance across the table at him.

Hopefully, her gaze was cooler than her cheeks. 'Something white and dry. But not too dry. I'll probably order seafood.'

'My thoughts exactly,' he replied, then handed the drinks menu to the hovering waiter, telling him to bring their best bottle of Verdelho.

'You trust him to pick for you?' she asked after the waiter hurried off.

'Why not? It's his job. I've never been a serious wine buff. I also don't drink much any more. I used to during my Oxford days—but I didn't have to pay for the wine at the time,' he added with a rather odd little smile.

'Why's that?'

'It's a long story. I might tell it to you one day, but not tonight. Tonight I want to find out a little more about you.'

'Me?'

'Yes, you, Harriet McKenna. So, tell me…what's your story? Before Dwayne, that is. I think I've heard enough about dear old Dwayne.'

Harriet pressed her lips tightly together. She really didn't want to open up any further to Alex. She'd already told him more than he needed to know.

'It's all in my résumé,' she said.

'Ah,' Alex said with a drily amused smile. 'You've decided to play the mysterious *femme fatale*, have you?'

Harriet shook her head at him. 'I'm not playing at anything, Alex. I'm simply keeping to the rules we set down when we started this strictly sexual affair. We don't need to know each other's life stories to have sex. In fact, telling each other all our past histories could be counter-productive. Exchanging confidences and secrets brings on emotional involvement. I don't want that. And neither do you.'

Absolutely not, Alex accepted. But, damn it all, he was curious about her. He suspected for the first time that there was a lot more to Harriet than he'd read in her résumé.

'We can't confine our conversations to sex, Harry. That could get a bit boring.'

'The sooner we get bored with each other, the better,' she replied. 'Then I can go back to just being your PA and you can find yourself another dolly-bird to sleep with.'

'I'm sick of sleeping with dolly-birds. I much prefer a woman I can talk to afterwards. Someone who's on the same wavelength as me. Someone like you, Harry.'

She rolled her eyes at him. 'In that case, we can talk about work as well as sex.'

Alex's exasperation was interrupted by the waiter arriving with the wine. Alex waved aside the tasting procedure and just asking him to pour, which he did, before placing the bottle in an ice bucket by the table.

'Would you like to order now, sir?' the waiter enquired.

'Come back in a few minutes,' Alex told him.

Harriet picked up her glass and took a sip. Alex did likewise, his mood turning dark as he glared over at her and thought how he much preferred her when she was naked and moaning with desire. No sooner had she put her clothes back on than the difficult woman was back, the one who liked rules and checklists, the one who was as intriguing as she was irritating.

Harriet picked up the menu and pretended to study the courses on offer, but her mind was still on things decidedly sexual. Various erotic images kept popping into her mind, all of them imaginative and wickedly exciting. In the end, she gave up, putting her menu down and picking up her wine glass.

'You order for me, will you?' she asked after a deep swallow of the wine. 'I'm not fussy, especially where seafood is concerned.'

'Right. How about we skip the entree and share a seafood platter? I'm not in the mood for waiting ages between courses.'

Harriet shivered as their eyes met across the table. When he looked at her like that, she wouldn't have minded skipping the whole meal.

'Fine,' she said and took another gulp of wine.

He frowned at her. 'I'd go easy on the alcohol till the food arrives, if I were you. Drinking too much on an empty stomach is never a good idea.'

Harriet's sigh carried exasperation. In truth, the alcohol *was* going straight to her head, but so what? It stopped her worrying about what she was doing and what she was suddenly craving. She was glad when the waiter came back and took their order; glad even when Alex's phone rang, leaving her to sit there and sip her wine in silence while he answered it, her ears pricking up when she heard Alex use the word 'dad'. She'd never heard him talking to family before. Not at work, anyway.

'That's good, Dad,' he was saying. 'No, it's not going to be easy, but it's the only way.'

A short silence, then he added, 'I'm proud of you. Look, I'll talk to you some more tomorrow. I'm out at dinner at the moment. With a very pretty lady.' This with a smile over at her. 'Yes, Dad, I will. Hang in there. Bye for now.'

He hung up, his smile disappearing as he put the phone away.

'My father,' he said unnecessarily, then added, 'He was the family emergency the other day.'

'Oh?' Harriet questioned, not wanting to pry, but naturally curious.

There was instant regret in Alex's eyes. Clearly, he wished he could snatch back those words. But then he shrugged and said bluntly, 'My father's a drunk. He's been living with my sister, Sarah, and giving her grief. Without going into unnecessary detail, I was finally able to get him to go into rehab this week. Hopefully, it will work, but I won't be holding my breath. Still, it gives poor Sarah a decent break.'

Harriet could see that talking about the situation was difficult for him. At the same time, she felt that perhaps he needed to talk about it. Men were their own worst enemy sometimes. They were poor communicators when it came to emotional issues. She wondered if Alex was secretly worried that he might become a drunk, too; that he might have inherited his father's weakness. It would explain why he was careful with alcohol.

'That's sad, Alex. Has your dad always been a heavy drinker?' she asked gently, forcing him to talk about it.

'No. Not at all. It didn't start till after my mother died. She was the love of his life. And the rock in the family. When he lost her from cancer way too early, he couldn't cope. None of us coped all that well. We all adored her, you see. Sarah was devastated. I can't begin to describe how I felt. I found it hard to come to terms with the fact that if she'd been diagnosed earlier, she would probably still be alive.

'Still, none of us kids handled our grief by turning to the bottle. My brother, Roy, eventually took off to the minefields in Western Australia, where he worked seven days a week and made a small fortune for himself. I gather he's married with children now, but we hardly ever hear from him. Sarah became an oncology nurse before getting married and having a family of her own.'

He stopped talking then and lifted his wine glass to his lips, leaving Harriet up in the air as to how *he* had coped with his mother's death. Whilst Harriet could see the danger in continuing with this conversation—her heart had already turned over in sympathy for Alex—she simply could not bear the suspense of not knowing.

'And you, Alex?' she prodded quietly. 'How did *you* cope?'

He shrugged, feeling uncomfortable. He put his glass down and smiled, though the smile didn't reach his eyes. 'I went to Oxford, found two great mates and joined the Bachelor's Club.'

Harriet's eyebrows arched in genuine surprise. 'What on earth is the Bachelor's Club?'

'I thought you didn't want to exchange personal details,' he reminded her.

'That was before.'

'Before what?'

'Before you whetted my curiosity.'

He laughed and the sparkle was back in his eyes. 'Women!' he exclaimed, but on a teasing note.

'Yes, yes, I know. Can't live with them, can't live without them.'

'True. I, for one, could not survive without a woman in my life. And in my bed,' he added, bringing Harriet back to cold, hard realty with a jolt. 'But I have found that the pleasure of a woman's company does come at a price. They invariably want to know way too much about your life, both past and present.'

Harriet stiffened at the injustice of this remark. 'I didn't ask you to tell me about your father's drinking problem, or your mother's death. You volunteered the information.'

He sighed and that bleakness was back in his eyes. 'So I did. Foolish of me. Could you forget I ever mentioned it? It's a rather depressing topic.'

Harriet wondered which one. His father's drinking problem or his mother's death? She suspected the latter. He must have loved his mother very much. Clearly, his way of coping initially with her death had been to run away from his life here in Australia by studying in England, making friends there and joining this Bachelor's Club.

'I only asked you about the Bachelor's Club, Alex,' she pointed out. 'If you don't want to tell me about it, then fine.'

Their meal arrived at that opportune moment, a simply huge platter full of the most delicious seafood. The tantalising smells wafted up to Harriet's nose, making her mouth water.

'Gosh, that looks good,' she said and the waiter smiled at her. So did Alex.

'Tuck in, then,' he said once the waiter had departed. 'I don't know about you, but I'm suddenly starving.'

They both tucked in, Harriet sampling a little bit of everything. Oysters, lobster, crab, scallops and fish pieces, along with side dishes of French fries and salad. They didn't talk much, and when they did, it was about the food. Alex ordered a second bottle of wine at one stage, though in the end they drank only half of it. He didn't mention the Bachelor's Club again and Harriet decided to let the matter drop. She could read between the lines, anyway. Unlike his sister and brother, Alex had decided that love and marriage were not for him. Maybe he was afraid of the responsibility that marriage entailed. And the emotion. Maybe he was afraid of falling in love. Or maybe he simply wasn't capable of falling in love, his mother's tragic death having killed off that particular part of him. Whatever, Alex obviously liked his life as a bachelor and had no intention of changing. Only a very foolish woman would start thinking—or hoping—that she would be the one to change him.

Harriet liked to think that she wasn't a very foolish woman.

Enjoy what you're doing whilst it lasts, she told herself as she wiped her fingers with her serviette. *Then do what Alex always does—move on!*

CHAPTER THIRTEEN

ALEX GLANCED ACROSS the table and wondered what was going on in Harry's mind. A somewhat defiant light had come into her eyes all of a sudden. Or was it determined? Whatever, he knew that his affair with her was not going to be like any affair he'd ever had before. How could it be? She was different from his usual choice of bed partner. Older, more intelligent and more difficult to control.

Not in bed, though. In a matter of minutes he'd torn down her defences and had her blindly surrendering to his wishes. Clearly, she was a passionate creature whose desire for sex easily matched his. That episode in the shower had been seriously hot. *She* was seriously hot. One night with her would definitely not be enough. One *month* seemed too inadequate as well. Which was a worry. He didn't want to want *any* woman too much. Harriet might start thinking he wanted more from her than just sex. Which he definitely didn't. He liked his life the way it was. He liked being a bachelor with no emotional ties.

It had been a mistake to confide in her the way he had. Big mistake. Like she'd said, confiding in people led to emotional involvement. Alex resolved not to do that again. Right. Time to finish up this meal and take her up to bed, where there would be very little talking.

Not on his part, anyway. His tongue would be otherwise occupied. By the time he finished with her tonight, asking him questions about his past life would be the last thing on her mind.

'Do you want dessert?' he asked, only out of sheer politeness.

'Heavens, no,' she replied. 'I've had more calories today than I usually eat in a week.'

'Rubbish. What about coffee?'

'No. I'd rather not sit here any longer, if you don't mind. I can always make us some coffee up in the apartment.'

Alex smiled. 'I do like a girl who knows what she wants.'

'I suppose you think I want you,' she said, her remark surprising him, then annoying him. Damn, but she was a difficult woman. A great PA, but a pain in the neck as a lover.

'That thought did cross my mind when you kissed me in the shower earlier,' he said in droll tones.

At least he had the satisfaction of seeing a guilty colour enter her cheeks.

'It's been some time since I've had any decent sex,' she said, defiance quickly back in her eyes. 'If I wasn't on the rebound from my relationship with Dwayne, you would never have made it to first base with me.'

The corners of his mouth tilted up into a sardonic smile. 'You honestly believe that?'

Harriet stifled a groan of dismay. What on earth had possessed her to start this type of tit-for-tat conversation? Not only was it dishonest of her, it was potentially humiliating. But, oh…how she'd hated seeing that smug look on his far-too-handsome face, as though it was a foregone conclusion that she would do whatever he wanted.

Her pathetic effort to pull his male ego down a peg or two was already in danger of backfiring on her; Alex's bedroom-blue eyes were glittering at her in a wickedly sexy fashion. Clearly, he meant to show her that she was talking rubbish. Which she was. That was the problem.

But she'd be darned if she was going to admit anything. Squaring her shoulders, she found a cool smile from somewhere.

'You do think you're irresistible, don't you?'

'Not at all, but I know what I know. You want me as much as I want you. I'm not afraid to admit it, but you are, for some reason. Silly, really. There's nothing to be gained from your pretending this has something to do with your breaking up with Dwayne. That was just the catalyst which threw us together. You've fallen in lust with me, Harry, and I with you. That's the cold, hard truth of it. Now, do stop putting obstacles in the way of our pleasure. And do stop wasting time. We should be in bed by now, doing what I do very well, and which you have already told me you like a lot. Come...'

When he stood up and reached out his hand towards her, Harriet gave up and gave in.

'You really are an arrogant bastard,' she muttered as she placed her hand in his and let him pull her up onto slightly unsteady feet. Possibly her light-headedness was due to the wine she had drunk, but Harriet doubted it. More likely it was due to the waves of desire that were currently washing through her body. Sweeping up her bag with her free hand, she let Alex steer her from the restaurant, leaving a forlorn-looking waiter in their wake. When she dared to say something, Alex just shrugged and said the charge for the meal would be added to his room account.

Alex didn't say a word to her during their lift ride

upwards, or during the short walk along the hallway, the silence only adding to the sexual tension which was gripping Harriet with cruelly frustrating tentacles. Every muscle in her body was tight with need. When she glanced over at Alex, she was taken aback at the tension she glimpsed in *his* face. He hadn't lied to her. He wanted her as much as she wanted him. It was a sinfully seductive thought.

Once they were alone, with the door locked behind them, he turned and yanked her into his arms.

'No more nonsense now,' he ground out after his ravaging kiss reduced them both to heavy breathing. 'You have five minutes to be naked in my bed.'

Alex's lack of sexual inhibition was overwhelming. Yet exciting at the same time.

'Well, what are you waiting for?' he asked, a dry amusement in his voice and eyes.

'You're not just an arrogant bastard,' she threw at him. 'You're a wicked devil as well!' And with that she whirled and flounced off, his laughter following her.

As Alex hurriedly stripped off in the bedroom, he smiled at the memory of the shock that had zoomed into her eyes. Harriet claimed to have been around, but he suspected that her idea of 'been around' was totally different from his. She wasn't even close to being the sophisticated woman of the world she liked to think she was. Not a *femme fatale*, either. But he liked that about her; liked that she could still be shocked.

He couldn't wait to shock her some more.

After a quick trip to the bathroom, Alex collected a new box of condoms from his gym bag, placed it on the bedside table, then climbed, naked, into the bed, his heart thudding with anticipation, his erection bordering on painful. He regretted now not jumping into a cold shower for a couple of minutes, scowling as he conceded he was not going to be able to last all that long the first time. Still, they had all night. He was not a once-a-night man; his sexual stamina was something he'd worked on over the years.

Where *was* that infernal woman? he thought, frustrated as he glared at the still-empty doorway. Five minutes had well and truly gone by now.

Harriet knew she'd passed her five-minute deadline, but she simply could not summon up the courage to walk stark naked into Alex's bedroom. She would have put on the white towelling bathrobe she'd worn earlier, except that it wasn't in her bathroom any more. It was out there somewhere. She hadn't packed a dressing gown, well aware that a five-star resort would provide one. In the end, she grabbed the PJs she'd brought with her and pulled them on. They were hardly the sexiest of outfits, the long pants and long sleeves covering almost every inch of her. And then there were the unfortunate little-girl colours. The bottom was pink-and-white stripes, the top plain white with little pink love hearts all over it. Emily had bought them for her for her birthday last year.

Thinking of Emily made Harriet groan. Her best friend would have a fit if she knew what she was doing at this moment. Which meant she would never tell her. By the time Emily got back from her holiday, her affair with Alex would probably be over. Taking a couple of deep breaths, Harriet turned and walked from the room with her chin held high. She was shaking inside when she thought of Alex's reaction. He liked to have his orders obeyed...

He was waiting for her on the bed, sitting up with just

a sheet over him, a mountain of pillows stuffed behind his head, his magnificent chest bare, his handsome face scowling. But not for long; major amusement rocketed into his eyes as they raked her up and down. He didn't laugh out loud, but he was close.

'I like your idea of naked,' he said, shooting her a heart-stopping smile.

Her stomach flipped right over. 'Sorry. I just couldn't do it.'

'You have no reason to be shy, Harry. You have a very beautiful body.'

Now her *heart* flipped over. *Oh, Harriet, Harriet. Be careful. You don't want to fall in love with this devil. He'll eat you alive.*

She gave him a long, considering look as she walked over to the side of the bed closest to where he was lying. 'I do *not* have a very beautiful body, Alex,' she denied quietly. 'It's nice enough, but not anything special. Please do not feel you have to flatter me. Trust me when I say it's not necessary—I'm a sure thing here.'

Now he laughed. 'That's good to know. When you came in wearing that, I thought you might have changed your mind.'

'Not at all.'

'Then perhaps you could take them off now,' he suggested.

'Is that an order?'

'Not at all,' he replied, cleverly echoing her own words. 'Would you like me to do it for you?'

Yes, she thought with a dizzying rush of desire. But it was imperative she keep some control in all this. Harriet already feared that once she was naked in his bed she might be lost for ever. It was one thing to have a couple of raunchy encounters out of bed, another thing entirely to spend the whole night in his arms.

Scooping in a steadying breath, she slipped off the bottom half of the PJs first, tossing it onto the armchair in the corner, before turning her attention to the top half. Crossing her arms, she lifted it up over her head, hotly aware of the way his eyes were glued to her. When at last she stood naked before him, it took all of her mental and physical strength not to tremble, or to flee. The raw hunger in his gaze was both seductive and terrifying. Had any man ever wanted her like this, and vice versa? Alex had said they'd fallen in lust with each other. Harriet hoped that was all it was.

'And you think you're not anything special,' he growled, shaking his head at her. Throwing back the sheet to reveal his own stunning nakedness, Alex stretched out his hand towards her. 'Now come here, you gorgeous thing, you. I can't wait another second.'

CHAPTER FOURTEEN

HARRIET WOKE IN the same position she'd fallen asleep, lying on her side with Alex's body wrapped around hers like two spoons. His arms were wrapped tightly around her waist, her bottom pressed up against his stomach. She didn't dare move, but whilst her body remained still, her brain was active, reliving their long night of lovemaking.

No, not lovemaking, she amended. *Your long night of sex, dummy. Don't start thinking of it as lovemaking.*

But it had *felt* like lovemaking at the time, she conceded, Alex proving to be a surprisingly tender lover. Imaginative, yes, and totally uninhibited—the things he did with his tongue!—but never had Harriet felt one second of disgust, or even embarrassment. He had a beguiling way about him which bypassed such feelings, caressing her at length between acts of actual intercourse, playing with her body with sometimes shocking intimacy. Yet she had never felt shock, only excitement and pleasure, along with the most amazing orgasms. So many that she had lost count.

Alex had been so right when he'd said she'd fallen in lust with him. She had. Totally.

Her sigh was the sigh of a thoroughly sated woman.

She should have been appalled with herself. But she wasn't. She wasn't even appalled with him. Yet she definitely should have been. If truth be told, Alex was nothing but an arrogant devil with the morals of an alley cat, who thought he could indulge in a strictly sexual affair with his PA, then just shrug her off when he grew bored with her in bed. Which he would. That was the nature of the beast. His admission that he'd always fancied her went some way to excusing his behaviour. But if that was the case, then he should never have hired her, damn him. His lust had become a time bomb waiting to happen.

I never stood a chance, she realised.

Her sigh this time had nothing to do with satisfaction.

'Will you stop all that sighing?' Alex muttered into her hair.

Harriet automatically stiffened, her buttocks tensing when her legs straightened.

He groaned, his hands lifting to cup her breasts as he rolled over onto his back, taking her with him. Panic filled Harriet as the evidence of his erection sent jabs of desire rocketing through her own infatuated flesh. She tried to wriggle away from him, but he held her tight.

'Hand me a condom, beautiful,' he purred into her ear. 'My hands are otherwise occupied.'

Which they were, his palms rubbing over her still-erect nipples, sending unnecessary messages to that part of her which seemed always to be ready for him. Her legs fell apart of their own volition, her belly tightening.

'Haven't you had enough?' Harriet protested, but weakly, her hand already reaching for the condom.

'Not even remotely,' he replied.

Alex had plenty of opportunity to think about that telling reply during the drive back to Sydney. Harry had refused to put off her Sunday lunch with her friend, despite his doing his best to persuade her over breakfast to stay another night. Whilst she was extremely compliant in bed—*and* in the spa bath this morning—she became a different woman once she was up and dressed, reverting to the difficult one who was not amenable to persuasion.

Alex's decision when he woke this morning to change the rules of their affair looked in danger of failing. When he'd suggested that they meet up at least one night during the week, she had been quick to say no, reminding him that that wasn't what they'd agreed on. She would come to his apartment next Friday night and not before.

Alex couldn't contemplate waiting that long before he made love to her again.

It came to Alex after he'd been driving in a somewhat frustrated silence for over two hours that his PA's hot-as-hell behaviour last night might be worrying her. In his experience, women weren't as pragmatic about sex as men. They read into things. They sometimes invented complications where there weren't any.

Slanting a quick glance her way, he saw that the set of her mouth was tight, her hands gripping her handbag in her lap with unnecessary force. Silly girl. Didn't she know that there was nothing wrong with what they'd done last night? They were consenting adults. Grown-ups. Yet she was sitting there, acting like some guilty schoolgirl or an adulterous wife. Okay, so the suddenness of their affair—and the fieriness of their passion for each other—was on the startling side. But why fight it? Why not just go with the flow and enjoy what they could share till the fire had burned out, after which they could call it quits and she could go back to the life she'd mapped out for herself?

Another reason for her grim mood suddenly crossed Alex's mind. Maybe she was worried that their affair might cost her her job.

He had to say something to reassure her.

'I would never fire you, Harry,' he said. 'If that's what's bothering you.'

Her head turned his way, but she was wearing sunglasses and he couldn't see what was going on in her eyes.

'I know that,' came her rather cool reply.

'Then what *is* bothering you? Are you regretting last night?'

He was taken aback when she laughed. 'Of course,' she said. 'Sleeping with the boss is never a good idea, even if he promises not to fire you when he grows bored with you in bed.'

'I can't see that happening in a hurry,' he muttered. And he meant it. Which was a first for him. Alex had a low boredom threshold at the best of times. He was always looking for new challenges, new goals and, yes, new girlfriends.

Of course, Harry would never be a proper girlfriend. She was going to be his secret mistress, one who would be at his sexual beck and call only at weekends. Stupid rule, that. He had been an idiot ever to suggest such a masochistic arrangement.

'I have no illusions,' came her firm pronouncement, 'about how this affair of ours will end.'

Maybe it will never end, Harry, came the unexpected thought. *Maybe I will keep you as my secret mistress for ever.*

It was a truly wicked thought. But a hell of an appealing one. People said you could never have your cake and eat it, too. But maybe he could. At least for a while. There was no hurry for her to get married, surely? She was only twenty-nine. Women got married later these days. And had children later. He would have to let her go eventually, he supposed. But till then he aimed to make her his. *Without* all these silly rules.

For the first time during this exasperating drive, Alex's black mood lifted. Knowing what you wanted in life was always a good thing, he accepted. And he wanted Harriet. Not just for a few weeks. For much, *much* longer than that.

'It's never a wise thing to think about endings, Harry,' he said, adopting his best salesman voice. 'Far better to live in the moment. The only assurance we have in life is the here and now. You like having sex with me, don't you?'

She sighed. 'You know I do.'

'Then stop stressing and just enjoy. We could be dead tomorrow.'

When he glanced over at her, he saw that she was frowning.

'I can't think like that,' she said. 'I have to plan. *You* plan. You plan all the time. So stop giving me this "live in the moment" nonsense, Alex. If you think you can persuade me to change my mind where the rules of our affair are concerned, then you can think again.'

Alex gritted his teeth. Lord, but she would try the patience of a saint. And he was no saint. He was, however, a man who rose to a challenge.

Relaxing the clenched muscles in his jaw took an effort, but he managed before shooting her a warmly amused smile. 'Can't blame a man for trying, Harry. Last night was so fabulous that I find it unbearable to wait another week to sample some more of your bewitching charms.'

'*You* were the one who claimed sex was better if you wait.'

He smiled with amusement at the cleverness of her

mind. And the sharpness of her wit. 'Yes, well, there's waiting and waiting. I was talking about a few hours on that occasion, not a whole week. I would imagine that by Friday night I'll be ready to explode.'

'Too much information,' she threw at him.

He laughed, then she laughed, breaking the tension that had been building since they'd set off.

'That's better,' he said.

'Better?' she echoed.

'I wasn't looking forward to sitting next to Miss Grumpy all the way back to Sydney.'

'I wasn't grumpy. I was just…thinking.'

'Thinking is almost as bad as planning. Or so Jeremy tells me. He doesn't believe in either.'

'Your best friend, Jeremy? The rake from London?'

'The one and the same.'

'He sounds very shallow.'

'Oh, he is. He admits it. But he's also intelligent and charming and the most wonderful friend I've ever had. Outside of Sergio, that is.'

'I presume it's Sergio, then, who's getting married.'

'Yes, the poor devil.'

'Why do you say it like that? What have you got against marriage?'

'Don't misunderstand me. I have nothing against marriage. It's the woman he's marrying that worries me.'

'What's wrong with her?'

For a split second, Alex hesitated. But then he told her. All about Sergio and Bella, detailing their past history and their current romance. She was taken aback at the identity of the bride-to-be, of course. Bella was very well known in Australia. But so was her reputation with men.

'I can understand why you're worried,' she said.

'Thank God someone agrees with me. Jeremy has

some doubts, but he believes that they're genuinely in love.'

'It does happen, you know. People do fall in love.'

'Not that quickly. It's nothing but lust. Which is not a recipe for marital happiness. You need to be best friends as well as lovers. Soul mates, for want of a better word.'

'In an idealistic world, perhaps. Life is not always quite so accommodating.'

'I suppose so. I have an awful feeling that Sergio loves Bella, but that she's only in it for the money. Being a billionaire is not always an advantage when it comes to finding true love.'

'Well, you don't have to worry about that, Alex. You're not interested in finding true love.'

'You are absolutely correct. That kind of love is not for me.'

Harriet wondered just *why* Alex was so against falling in love. He must have been badly hurt at one stage to feel so strongly about it. Before she could come to any conclusion, he turned and smiled at her.

'The turn-off for Taree is coming up. What say we get off the freeway and go have some lunch?'

CHAPTER FIFTEEN

IT WAS AFTER five before Alex pulled up outside her flat. Harriet was annoyed with herself when she asked him if he'd like to come up for a cup of coffee. What had happened to her resolve to keep some control over their affair and her own silly self? To invite him into her home was a foolish move. But it was done now.

Of course, he said yes, that big, bad wolf smile on his face.

At least he carried her bag up the stairs for her, her flat being on the second floor of the rather ancient red-brick building. There were eight units in all, hers at the front of the building facing east, though not with an ocean view, being a couple of streets back from the beach.

'Nice place you've got here, Harry,' Alex said even before she'd shown him inside. He knew she owned it. She'd said so when he'd interviewed her.

'I like it,' she replied, fishing out her key and opening the front door.

'*Very* nice,' he said once he went inside and glanced around.

His compliment pleased her, Harriet being on the house-proud side, something she'd learned from her mother, who had instilled in her daughter good habits when it came to keeping her home clean and tidy. Harriet's good taste in furniture and furnishings, however, was something she'd learned for herself after coming to Sydney. Selling expensive real estate did give one a yearning for having nice things around.

Her two-bedroomed flat wasn't overly large, but by painting all the walls and ceilings white, and not overfurnishing the rooms, she'd achieved the effect of making it look larger than it was. Both the kitchen and bathrooms were white, but that was not her doing. They'd been renovated shortly before she'd bought the place.

'Could you point me to the bathroom, Harry?' Alex asked.

She did, reminding him that the light in there wasn't working due to her poor DIY skills.

'Give me a bulb, then,' Alex said. 'I'll fix it while I'm here. You go make the coffee.'

He joined her in the kitchen a couple of minutes later. 'All fixed,' he said.

'Thank you,' she said. 'I didn't realise you would be such a good handyman.'

He laughed. Not a happy laugh. More a dry one. 'When you grow up living in government housing, you learn to do all minor repairs yourself. If there was one thing Dad did teach me growing up, it was how to change light bulbs and tap washers. I can also fix leaking toilets and blocked drains. So, if your kitchen sink ever gets blocked up...' he added, smiling wryly.

'I will call a plumber,' Harriet finished for him, at the same time wondering if Alex had called his dad today like he promised last night. She hadn't heard him do so. Still, it really wasn't her business to remind him. It wasn't like they were at work, when she often reminded him to do things. He could be forgetful at times. Oh, Lord, maybe she *should* say something...

'You're frowning,' he said. 'On top of that, you've stopped making the coffee. What gives?'

Harriet turned to look at him. 'I'm worried that you might have forgotten to ring your dad. You promised him last night that you would call him today.'

Alex shook his head at her. 'I should never have told you about him.'

'Well, you *did*,' she replied, feeling quite angry with his attitude. 'And I'm glad you did. Now at least I know that you're human, with personal problems like the rest of us.'

His eyebrows lifted. 'Wow, Harry, you have quite a temper on you, don't you? Something you've managed to keep hidden from me all these months.'

'A PA doesn't lose her temper with her boss. But a secret mistress is another thing entirely. Tamper with a woman's emotions and you have to pay the price.'

'I don't want to tamper with your emotions. Just your body.'

'Same thing, Alex. I'm a woman. Our bodies and our emotions are linked. Unlike men. It always amazes me how some men can compartmentalise their lives. Work over here and women over there. In the past, you've cleverly chosen to sleep with empty-headed young things who haven't given you any trouble. Let me warn you in advance, Alex, that I might give you trouble.'

His eyes narrowed on her. 'Are you warning me that you might fall in love with me?'

'I certainly hope not,' she said quite truthfully. 'But don't expect me to be entirely happy with this…relationship. Yes, I love having sex with you, and yes, I love working for you. But I'm going to find it increasingly hard to separate the two. Please appreciate that I might have to quit in the end.'

'Quit work or quit me?'

'Both.'

'I won't let you.'

A shiver of alarm ran down her spine at the sheer arrogance of him.

'You won't have any choice in the matter.'

'We'll see about that,' he ground out. 'Forget the coffee. I'm going home. But first a little taste of what you can expect next Friday night.'

Five minutes later, he was gone, leaving Harriet reeling with shock. She sagged back against the kitchen counter, her legs weak with desire. What a cruel devil he was, kissing her like that, then touching her like that, bringing her to the brink of release, then just abandoning her, his eyes glittering with a chilling resolve when his head finally lifted.

The week that stretched ahead of her would be unbearable. But of course Alex wanted it to be. That was why he'd just done what he'd done.

I should never have challenged him like that, Harriet conceded as she levered herself away from the kitchen counter, pulled her bra back into place, then did up her jeans. She'd known from the start that she was way out of her league, tangling with someone like Alex.

Try as she might, however, Harriet could not regret going to bed with him. How could she regret something which had brought her so much pleasure? Alex excited her as no man had ever excited her. He was a fabulous lover, with a way about him that was both seductive and oddly romantic. The compliments he'd made about her body last night were so sweet. Harriet knew she wouldn't be the one to call it quits. But *he* would one day, and this inevitability would happen sooner rather than later if she didn't lighten up a bit. She really had to stop acting the way she had earlier today. And just now. She had to start doing what Alex suggested. Live for the moment. Concentrate on just having fun!

It came to Harriet that she'd never been a 'just have fun' girl. She'd always been so serious. But it wasn't too late, surely? She could do fun, couldn't she? Not every relationship had to be about finding Mr Right. After the fiasco with Dwayne, that could definitely wait for a while. As for that stupid checklist of hers, that was definitely going to be thrown out the window.

Satisfied with her new resolve, Harriet made her way back into the living room, where Alex had left her bag. She had just picked it up when her phone rang. Dropping the bag, she walked over to where she'd placed her handbag on the dining table, retrieved her phone, then groaned. It was Emily. Oh, Lord. She had a sinking feeling that Emily might have found out about Dwayne.

'Hi, Em,' she said with false brightness. 'How's it going with the holiday?'

'Don't you say hi to me like that, Harriet McKenna. Why didn't you ring and tell me that you've broken up with Dwayne? All those text messages about work and not a single word about what's really important.'

Harriet scooped in a deep breath, then let it out slowly before answering.

'Why do you think?' she finally asked. 'I knew you wouldn't be on my side and I wasn't in the mood for a lecture.'

'Don't be silly. Of course I'm on your side. You're my best friend. Dwayne doesn't mean a thing to me. Okay, so I thought you and he were a good match, but it's what *you* think that really counts. Obviously, you decided he wasn't the right man for you.'

A huge lump had filled Harriet's throat at this unexpected show of support from Emily. She'd been so sure that she would be critical.

'No, he wasn't,' she choked out. 'I…I…' Her voice cut out as her whole chest filled with emotion, tears threatening. Silly, really, given she'd already realised she hadn't loved Dwayne.

'Oh, Harriet. Hon,' Emily said gently. 'I didn't mean to upset you.'

Harriet gulped, then cleared her throat. 'I thought you'd be mad at me.'

'Never. I just worry about you, that's all. I want you to be happy.'

'I want to be happy, too.'

'Then perhaps you should stop looking for Mr Perfect to marry and just have fun for a while,' Emily suggested. 'You're still young, Harriet. Plenty of time for you to get married yet.'

'You're so right, Em. I've been thinking exactly the same thing.'

CHAPTER SIXTEEN

'GOT ANYTHING SPECIAL planned for this weekend?' Audrey asked Harriet.

Friday night had finally arrived and the two women were sharing a bottle of white wine at the nearby hotel where the staff of Ark Properties gathered for drinks every Friday night after work. Audrey and Harriet were sitting at a quiet table in a dark corner, whilst the boys were gathered at the bar drinking beer and watching the Friday night football game. Alex was noticeably absent, as he'd been from the office most of the week, finding any and every excuse to go out—minus his PA—from business lunches to doing site-checks of all their current building projects. He'd claimed he had to have everything on track before leaving for Milan the following week, though Harriet suspected he just didn't want to be around her lest he be tempted to go back on his word.

When she'd arrived at work last Monday morning, a bagel already in hand, she'd made Alex coffee and taken both into his office, where she'd apologised for being so uptight the other night. She'd promised to lighten up in future, adding that she didn't want to live her life according to rules, and it would be all right with her if he wanted to see her before Friday night. He'd stared at her for a long moment, then told her that he would prefer to wait till Friday as they'd originally agreed upon. Although surprised and a little hurt, the new live-for-the-moment, just-have-fun Harriet simply smiled and said fine. Whatever.

But it had been a long, long week.

'No, nothing special,' Harriet told Audrey, hoping the lie didn't show in her eyes. 'I might try to catch up on housework. I usually give the flat a thorough clean on a Saturday, but I was away last Saturday.'

'That's right. You were up north with Alex. How did that go, by the way?'

Harriet shrugged. 'Okay. I think Alex was annoyed that the rain had delayed things so much. No way is that golf course going to be open by Christmas.'

'It's supposed to rain all next week, too,' Audrey said. 'Not just here in Sydney, but all the way up the coast.'

Harriet groaned. 'He's not going to be too thrilled with that.'

'Nothing you can do about the weather,' Audrey said. 'Where did you stay?'

'Oh, some place near Coffs Harbour. Quite nice, really. You know Alex. He wouldn't stay at a dump.'

'Why should he? I mean, he's seriously rich. And seriously sexy. I would watch yourself with him, if I were you.'

'What do you mean?'

'You know what I mean. Now that Dwayne's out of the picture...' Audrey shrugged, then took another sip of her wine.

No way did Harriet want any of the staff ever to know about her affair with Alex. Though they might twig after she resigned. But it wouldn't matter then.

'He's not really my type,' Harriet said. 'But I know

what you mean. He *is* handsome, but personally I don't like arrogant men.'

Audrey frowned at her over the rim of her glass. 'I thought you liked Alex.'

'Well, yes, I do. And to be fair, he's not all that arrogant. But he can be annoying at times.'

'Yes, I can see that. Rich bachelors like him are not used to considering other people's feelings. They don't mean to be selfish or self-centred, but they are.'

'You've got it in one,' Harriet stated, thinking that was Alex's biggest flaw. His selfishness. At the same time, however, he could be kind, generous and even rather sweet. She would never forget what he'd done for Romany.

But he should never have pursued *her*. That had not been kind, or sweet. It had been seriously selfish. He could have slept with just about any other woman in Sydney, but he had to pick her.

Such thinking suddenly annoyed Harriet, who'd determined to put aside the critical habits of her old, serious self and embrace a more easy-going attitude to life and men. So, instead of criticising Alex in her head, she focused on his good points. He gave oodles of money to charity, was a caring son and a fabulous lover. This last fact reminded her that in less than two hours she'd be in his arms again, being made love to in ways she'd only ever dreamt about. The anticipation of what was in store for her tonight had her shifting restlessly in her seat. Her phone suddenly ringing startled her, the identity of the caller startling her as well.

'Hi there,' she answered, careful not to say Alex's name.

'I presume you're still at the pub,' he ground out.

'Yes, I am.'

'Don't say my name,' he warned her sharply.

'I won't. What's up?' If he was calling to tell her not to come, she would just die.

'Is there any chance you can make it before nine?' he asked.

Nine was the time he'd designated before he'd left the office that morning, giving her a key-card at the same time so that she could access the building and the private lift to the penthouse.

'I'm going insane here,' he added thickly.

The passion and the urgency in his voice was both flattering and arousing. Not that Harriet needed arousing. She was already burning for him.

'Me, too,' she said quietly.

'Have you eaten?'

'Not yet.'

'Then don't. I've organised something for later. Can you come straight away?'

'I should be able to. I'll catch a taxi and meet you there ASAP. Bye.'

Putting her phone away, she rose and threw Audrey an apologetic smile. 'Sorry to abandon you so early, but I'm needed.'

'Oh?'

'A married girlfriend of mine has the chance of a rare night out while her husband minds the baby, so we're off to a movie together.'

'What are you going to see?'

'Have no idea. Have to go. See you on Monday.' And she bolted before Audrey could ask her any more awkward questions.

The hotel was within walking distance of the taxi rank down at the quay. Harriet didn't have to wait too long before she was climbing into the back seat and giving the driver Alex's address. But it was Friday night, of course, with Friday night traffic. Her level of frustration rose when it took ten minutes to go three blocks. She sent Alex a text message explaining she was on her way but the traffic was heavy.

No sweat, came his reply. I'll meet you downstairs.

He was standing on the pavement by the time she climbed out of the taxi, dressed in a black tracksuit with a white T-shirt underneath and white trainers. Harriet still had on the tailored black suit and white silk blouse that she'd worn to work, actually having planned to go home before coming here tonight to shower and change into something more feminine. She'd also planned to put on the new sexy black underwear that she'd bought this week.

During the ride in the taxi, she'd regretted not having the opportunity to dolly herself up for Alex, but at the sight of him she no longer cared. The way he was looking at her made her not care about anything but being here with him.

He didn't say a word, just took her arm and urged her through the revolving glass doors inside the foyer, which was modern and spacious with a large reception desk, behind which sat two burly security guards studying computer screens. They didn't even look up as Alex steered her across the vast expanse of marble tiled floor to an alcove which housed the lifts. There were four in all, Alex choosing the one marked for private use only. The doors opened immediately, Alex ushering her into the lavishly appointed lift that had lots of brass and glass, along with far too much lighting. Harriet could see her reflection everywhere, forcing her to note her flushed face and her over-bright eyes.

'How long have you lived here?' she asked him in an

effort to break the tension which was almost killing her. If her heart beat any faster, she was sure it would explode.

Alex pressed the button which had the lift doors closing with barely a sound before he turned and answered her.

'About three years. I bought it off-plan five years ago before it was even built and before the market went crazy. God, but it's been a long week. I have to kiss you, Harry. I simply can't wait.' He pulled her into his arms and kissed her right there in the lift. Even when it reached its destination, and the doors slid quietly open, the kissing didn't stop. By then he'd rammed her up against the mirrored back wall, the coldness of the glass seeping through her jacket. Not that she cared. She was way too hot to care about such a small discomfort. By then her handbag had fallen from numb fingers and her arms were wrapped tightly around his neck. His hands were much busier, hitching up her skirt, pushing aside her panties.

She moaned when his fingers found their target. God, she was close to coming. And she didn't care. She *needed* to come. *Yes, yes, just keep doing that*; all her muscles tensed in anticipation of release from the madness which was possessing her.

His taking his hand away brought a groan of despair, her eyes flying open when his head lifted. His expression was wry and knowing.

'Sorry, but I had to stop,' he said.

She just stared at him, her heartbeat still haywire. 'You're cruel,' she said shakily.

'Sometimes you have to be cruel to be kind. I didn't have a condom with me and I was close to losing control. For some reason kissing you does that to me,' he said and reached out to run a single fingertip over her still-burning mouth. 'I suspect you have some secret aphrodisiac in this red lipstick you always wear.'

She couldn't speak, all her attention on that tantalising fingertip.

His eyes darkened on her, aware no doubt of the extent of her desire.

'Come,' he said, this time taking her arm more gently.

Alex guided her across a wide entrance hall and into a huge living room which was beautifully appointed, filled with glass and white leather furniture which shouted money. The floors were all grey marble tiles, but the rugs were thick, soft and more colourful. The artwork on the walls were probably originals, not the framed prints which graced her own flat.

'This way,' he said, leading her past a semi-circular shaped alcove in which sat a circular glass dining table beautifully set for two, with elegant silver placemats and tall candles just waiting to be lit.

'That's for dinner later,' he told her, perhaps noting the direction of her eyes.

'It looks lovely.' She hadn't expected anything so romantic.

'I've ordered a meal to be delivered at ten from a local restaurant. And there's two bottles of chilled white wine waiting for you in the fridge.'

'You've thought of everything,' she said, taken aback by his thoughtful attention to detail.

'I try to please. I would have been showered and properly attired if my passion for you hadn't got the better of me. But while I was waiting for you to arrive, I realised I could kill two birds with one stone.'

'Sorry. I'm not following you.'

'You will. This way…'

He took her down a tiled hallway and into the master bedroom, which was large, spacious and thankfully nothing like a playboy's bedroom, other than the fact that the bed was king-sized. The floor was covered in a lush cream carpet, the furniture made in a dark wood, the furnishings in various shades of cream and brown. She loved the brass-based bedside lamps with their stylish cream shades and the gorgeous tapestry which hung above the bedhead. It was a park scene—Parisian, since it had the Eiffel Tower in the background. The colours were glorious.

'I love that tapestry,' she said as he led her past it.

'It's a recent purchase. An investment, really. I don't put my money in stock and shares. I prefer property. And art.'

Harriet couldn't afford to invest in art. But at least she did have her flat, which had already doubled in value since she'd bought it.

'In here,' he directed and guided her into an *en suite* bathroom which had to be seen to be believed. It was larger than her bedroom with a modern toilet and bidet, a sunken spa bath, a double vanity and a shower stall built for two. Or possibly three. But it wasn't any of those things which made her gasp. It was the candles which were dotted around the bath, all lit and giving out the most incredible vanilla fragrance.

'Did you do this for me?' she asked, amazed and touched.

His smile was warm, soft and faintly apologetic. 'I wanted to make it up to you for being a bit of a bastard last Monday. All I can say in my defence is that I knew I wouldn't be able to get all the work done that I needed to do before I went away if I started meeting up with you. And making love to you. And not getting any sleep. As it was, I didn't sleep all that well anyway, despite working my butt off in the gym every evening. All I could think about was you, Harry.'

'Oh…' she said, in danger of melting into a puddle. 'I…I didn't sleep very well, either.'

His smile was slow, sexy and incredibly arousing. 'That's nice to know,' he said as he turned on the bath taps, adjusted the temperature, then tipped in what looked like bubble bath. 'Can you wait a bit longer?' he asked her as he turned back to face her.

'What? Yes. No. Yes, I… I suppose so.'

'Good. Now I'm going to take off all your clothes.'

'What?'

'Don't think about it. Just let me do it.'

She didn't think about it, and she let him do it, dazed by the feeling of blissful helplessness which took possession of her as he slowly removed each item of clothing. First came her jacket, which he folded and placed on the vanity counter top. Her blouse followed, then her bra.

How weird it felt to be standing before Alex, naked to her waist. Weird, yet wickedly exciting. Her skirt came next, then her shoes, leaving her with nothing on but a black satin thong and a pair of lace-topped stay-up stockings.

Once she was naked, he took a step back and just looked at her.

'That's how I've been picturing you all week,' he said thickly, his eyes raking over her.

She'd done a lot of picturing of her own, her many erotic fantasies underlining just how much in lust with Alex she was. Lord, if he didn't make love to her soon, she was going to faint with desire. Her head was spinning, whilst the rest of her was on fire.

'Aren't you going to get undressed?' she asked him shakily.

'Of course. Do you want to watch?'

Oh, Lord, she was seriously out of her depth here.

He didn't strip slowly, but he didn't hurry, either. Once naked, he turned off the taps, then extracted a condom from a nearby drawer, ripping it open with his teeth before drawing it on with practised swiftness. She tried not to stare, but he was just so big and hard and ready. She wanted him inside her right now.

'I...I don't think I can wait much longer,' she told him shakily.

He smiled a wry smile. 'Me neither, beautiful.'

Taking her shoulders, he turned her to face the vanity mirror. Without his saying a word, she knew what he wanted her to do. She reached out to grip the edges of the marble bench top, moved her legs apart, then bent forward, dropping her head so that she couldn't see the wantonness in her eyes. She gasped when he stroked down the curve of her spine, caressing her bottom before taking a firm hold of her hips and doing what she was desperate for him to do.

Oh, God, she thought as her head spun and her body rocketed to a release that saw her crying out like some wild, wounded animal. He came soon after her, pulling her upright as his flesh shuddered within hers. When their eyes finally met in the mirror, his smile stunned her. For it was soft and sweet, making her heart lurch in a way that might have worried her at any other time. But her mind was on other things at that moment.

'I like the new you, Harry,' he said, a wicked twinkle in his eye. 'Now, let's go get in that bath.'

CHAPTER SEVENTEEN

I DON'T WANT her to go, Alex thought as he reluctantly followed Harry to the lift doors.

He'd never enjoyed a weekend so much in years. Never enjoyed a woman so much in years. It wasn't just the sex part—though that was fabulous—it was her company, her conversation, her intelligence. Alex hadn't realised till that weekend how much he craved being with a woman as smart as she was. And Harriet was smart. Perhaps not academically. She didn't have degrees to her name. But she had smarts of a different kind. She was quite well-read, too, he'd found out. Plus she was never at a loss for words. Or opinions. They hadn't spent the whole weekend having sex, though Friday night had been full on. Understandable, given they'd both been somewhat frustrated at the time.

After a long sleep-in on the Saturday, he'd driven her back to her place so that she could get a change of clothes. When he then suggested they drive out somewhere for lunch, she hadn't objected, so he'd headed west toward the Blue Mountains, showing her the parcels of land he'd bought near the proposed new airport at Badgery's Creek on the way. Her praise over his plan to build affordable housing for the people who would one day work at the airport had pleased him no end. He rarely told anyone about his charitable efforts, most people not being interested. But Harry had seemed genuinely impressed.

After lunch at a trendy café in Katoomba, they'd visited the Three Sisters, where Harry had taken heaps of photos of the iconic mountaintops, insisting he be in most of the shots. It had been a fun day. By the time they'd arrived back at his apartment, however, he'd been more than ready to take her to bed. He'd ordered Chinese that night and they'd eaten it whilst they watched a movie, their naked bodies wrapped in a mohair rug he kept on the sofa. Then it had been back to bed, where they'd stayed on and off for the whole of Sunday, only rising to shower and eat.

When Harry had said around five that she really had to go home, he'd tried to change her mind with some more lovemaking. But it had worked only temporarily. By five-thirty she was adamant that it was time for her to go. Sighing, he said he would drive her home. But he still hated the thought of her going. When the temptation arose to ask her to move in with him, he was totally taken aback. That was not what he wanted in life. Besides, he was pretty sure that Harry would say no. She just wanted to have fun with him, not live with him. Though he didn't abandon the idea altogether...

'Come with me,' he said when they stopped at a set of lights during the drive to her place. 'To Italy.'

Harriet's head whipped round, his offer clearly having thrown her. 'I can't do that,' she said at last. 'People at work will talk.'

'They don't have to know. I'll go into the office on Monday and say you've come down with a bad case of flu. I'll say I've given you the week off.'

He could see that she was tempted. Seriously tempted.

'I don't know, Alex,' she said slowly. 'I don't think it's a good idea.'

'Well, I do. You can come to the wedding with me, then afterwards I'll take you to Venice for a couple of days.'

'Venice,' she repeated, her eyes going all misty. 'I've always wanted to go to Venice.'

The lights went green and he drove on. 'Then let me take you there,' he said.

She shook her head at him. 'You are a wicked man, do you know that?'

'It has been said of me before. But I don't think it's wicked to offer to take you to Italy with me. You'll love Lake Como.'

'I dare say I will. I've heard it's very beautiful. But I won't go to the wedding with you. I wouldn't be comfortable doing that. They are *your* friends, Alex, not mine.'

Alex knew when he'd pushed things as far as he could.

'Very well. I'll book you into a nearby hotel on the lake whilst I'm doing my best man act. You can do a few touristy things by yourself that day. Then, after the wedding, I'll join you and we'll go to Venice together.'

'Won't that take longer than a week?'

He shrugged. 'Not much longer. Look, as things stand I won't be back by next weekend. I don't know about you, but I've enjoyed this weekend more than even I envisaged. I love your company, Harry, in bed *and* out. Come with me. Please…'

Harriet didn't speak again for a full minute. 'I should say no,' she said. But there was a smile in her voice.

He grinned. 'Possibly. But you're not going to. You're going to fly first class with me to Italy.'

'No,' she replied with a firmness which shocked him. 'I'm not.'

Before he could give vent to his frustration, she added, '*You* can fly first class, but *I'll* be in economy. I wouldn't feel comfortable having you pay that much money for my flight.'

'But I can afford it,' he told her.

'I don't care what you can afford. I will not be bought, Alex. I'm not that kind of girl.'

'Would you compromise by going business class?'

She heaved a resigned sigh. 'I suppose that would be all right. But I will be paying for my own ticket. I also want to pay half of all our hotel expenses. And before you object, I assure you, *I* can afford it. I'll just use the money I saved up for my wedding. I only lost the deposit on the reception venue when I broke up with Dwayne, so I have plenty left.'

Alex frowned. 'But surely your parents were going to pay for your wedding?'

Her laugh sounded bitter. 'My parents and I are estranged,' she told him. 'They wouldn't have come to my wedding even if I'd invited them. Which I had no intention of doing.'

Shock at this statement was quickly followed by curiosity.

'What on earth happened between you?'

'My father happened, that's what,' she stated with a bitterness which stunned him.

Alex recalled her telling him something at her interview about her father losing his job when she'd been a teenager, which was why she'd had to go out to work instead of studying. He'd been a miner up in the Singleton area. But that was all he knew about her family.

'He was a pig,' Harriet bit out. 'A male chauvinist pig.'

Whoa, Alex thought. They were pretty heavy words.

'What did he do?' Alex asked.

'What didn't he do?' she threw at him. 'First, he thought women were only put on this earth to wait on him hand and foot. Mum and I were treated like servants. Never with love or caring. My brothers were spoiled rotten, whilst I got nothing. He bought them everything they wanted, whereas I was given only the barest essentials. I lived in second-hand uniforms and clothes. If it hadn't been for gifts from relatives, I would never have had anything new.'

Alex could hardly believe what he was hearing. He'd been critical of his father at times, but he was still a loving parent. What little money he'd earned, he'd given to his children.

'I lied when I told you that Dad had lost his job,' Harriet went on. 'He never did. He always earned a good salary. But Mum and I never saw any of it. So, once I was old enough to get a job or three, I did so.' A small, very bitter smile curved her mouth. 'Naturally, Dad was furious when I refused to hand over any of my salaries.'

'He didn't hit you, did he?' Alex despised men who hit women.

'No. He wasn't a physically violent man, just verbally and emotionally abusive. I hated him.'

'Understandable. So I'm presuming you didn't have your parents' approval when you came to Sydney to pursue a career in real estate?'

'They had absolutely no idea of my plans. But I always knew what I was going to do. First, I saved up for a car. Not a new car, of course. But not bad, either. I also secretly went to college at night, doing an advanced computer course as well as getting my real-estate licence. Then, as soon as I turned twenty, I left home and drove the two hundred kilometres to Sydney.'

'That was brave of you,' he said, admiring her enormously.

'I didn't see it that way. I just knew I had to leave home and make a life for myself. I had enough money saved to survive for a few weeks till I got a job. And I booked into a backpackers' lodge till then as it was relatively cheap.'

'Did you tell your parents you were going or did you just up and leave?'

'Mum knew I was going, but Dad was at work when I left. I did ring home to tell Mum I'd arrived safely, but Dad answered and promptly disowned me, saying I was ungrateful and that he didn't want to set eyes on me ever again.'

'You're right. He is a pig. I hope you told him where to go.'

'I did indeed. In no uncertain terms. Then when I asked to speak to my mother, he hung up. I did ring again the next day when I knew he'd be at work, but Mum also hung up on me.'

Her sad sigh was very telling. 'Clearly, she'd been ordered not to talk to me, and she was too scared to defy him. I'd hoped I might be able to persuade her to leave him, but I soon saw that was never going to happen. I knew from that moment on that I was on my own. My life would be what *I* made it. No one was going to help me.'

Alex was beginning to understand exactly where that checklist had come from. It went a long way back.

'Well, you've done a very good job,' he complimented her. 'I was seriously impressed when I read your résumé, working your way up from being a receptionist to getting a job in sales. Not for any old company, either. For one of Sydney's top realtors. Frankly, I was a bit surprised when you applied for the job as my PA. You probably could have made more money staying in sales.'

'Life isn't all about money, Alex.'

'It's still nice to have it,' he replied.

'True. Right, we're nearly there. I suggest you just let me off outside my place, Alex. There'll be no parking in my street on a Sunday afternoon.'

She was right. There wasn't. 'Are you absolutely sure you have to go home?' he tried one last time. 'I could always turn around and take you back to my place for the night.'

'Alex, just stop it,' she said firmly. 'If I'm going to Italy with you on Tuesday, I have lots of things to do.'

'Give me a kiss before you go.'

She laughed. 'Good try, Alex.' And she was out of the car like a shot, leaning in to grab her overnight bag before waving and running inside.

Alex just sat there for a long moment, then drove slowly back to his place, feeling more alone than he ever had in his life before. Once there, he wandered around like a lost sheep for a while till in desperation he rang Sergio and talked for a good twenty minutes, unlike his previous congratulatory call, which had been rather brief. By the time he hung up, Alex saw what Jeremy meant about their friend being genuinely in love with Bella. He was utterly obsessed with the woman, unable to form a sentence without her name being in it. Alex hoped like hell that Sergio's love was returned. Falling that deeply in love could be dangerous enough. Even worse if it was one-sided.

Seeking more reassurance on the matter, he rang Jeremy, who clearly didn't appreciate being woken on a Sunday morning before noon.

'Alex,' he growled. 'Do you know what time it is?'

'I guess that depends on where you are. London or Lake Como?'

'Neither. I'm in Paris.'

'What are you doing in Paris?'

'What do you think I'm doing in Paris? Go back to sleep, *mon amie*,' he murmured to whoever was in bed beside him. 'So what drama is unfolding in your life that you feel you have to call me at this ungodly hour? It had better be life threatening, or you're a dead man.'

'No drama on my front,' he said, though his mind flew to a certain brunette who was definitely giving him grief. 'I've just been talking to Sergio. Hell, Jeremy, the poor man is seriously infatuated, isn't he?'

'Seriously in love, more like it. And Bella is, too, so you can stop worrying about their marriage. I'm beginning to think that it just might work.'

'How can you be sure? About *her* feelings, that is?'

'I can just tell. The way they look at each other and speak about each other. It's positively sickening. If I ever act like that around a woman, I want you to shoot me.'

Alex laughed. 'I don't have a gun.'

'I'll give you one. We have several in the gun room at the family's country estate.'

'Remind me not to go there with you any more.'

'Don't be ridiculous, you love it there. What say we pop down together for a few days after the wedding? It's lovely in Cornwall in the summer.'

At any other time, he would have said yes. But as much as he loved Jeremy's excellent company, it could not compare with being in Venice with Harriet. Not that he could say that.

'Sorry. No can do. I have to get back here ASAP. I'm up to my ears in work.'

Jeremy sighed. 'Truly, Alex, someone is going to have to take you in hand one day and teach you how to relax.'

Alex smiled as he thought about where Harry's hand had been earlier today. Not that he'd felt in any way relaxed at the time.

'Well, if anyone could teach me how to relax, it would be you,' he said. 'If R and R was a sport, you'd win the gold medal every four years.'

Jeremy chuckled. 'I'll take that as a compliment. But honestly, dear friend, all work and no play makes Alex a dull boy.'

'In that case, you'll be pleased to know I've been playing all weekend.' As soon as the bragging words were out of his mouth, he regretted them.

'*Really?* Do tell.'

'Sorry, mate, I'm not a kiss-and-tell kind of guy.'

'So, how old is this latest bimbo of yours?'

'I'll have you know she's in her late twenties. And no bimbo.'

'I'm impressed. What does she do for a crust?'

Alex had to think quickly. He could hardly say she was his PA. 'She's in real estate,' he said.

'Even better. Nothing worse than dating someone with very little between her ears.'

Alex had noticed over the years that Jeremy preferred intelligent girls, provided they were beautiful as well as brainy.

'So, who did you bring to Paris?' Alex asked.

'No one. Marlee lives in Paris. She's an editor. I'm going to put her in charge of my French office.'

'Combining business and pleasure is never a good idea,' Alex said with considerable irony.

'What rubbish. I've had some of my best sex by doing just that. Look, something's just come up. So I should go. Text me the details of your flight and I'll meet you at Milan airport. *Au revoir.*'

Alex had no time to open his mouth before Jeremy hung up. Smiling wryly over what it was that had come up, Alex put down his phone, then made his way out to the kitchen, where he poured himself a large glass of Scotch, added a few ice cubes, then returned to the living room, sipping slowly. Calling his two best friends hadn't helped all that much. He still missed Harriet and she'd been gone only an hour or so. The thought that he might be falling in love with her started worrying him. He didn't want to fall for her any more than she wanted to fall for him. They had different goals in life. Vastly different.

It was still just lust, he reassured himself. On both their parts. Still, to take her to Italy with him and romance her in Venice was playing with fire, especially when it came to *her* feelings. Women loved that kind of thing.

But it was no use. He wanted to do it. Wanted to see the pleasure in her eyes.

So he ignored the risk and sent her a text telling her to cancel his original first-class booking ASAP and to book two business-class seats for them on the same flight, or an equivalent one.

Will do, she texted back.

Ten minutes later, she texted him the details of their flight, at which point he gave in and rang her.

They talked for close to an hour.

CHAPTER EIGHTEEN

'OH, THIS IS HEAVENLY!' Harriet exclaimed once they settled into their business-class seats, Alex insisting Harriet have the window seat, with him right beside her.

It was early evening on the Monday, take-off in ten minutes. Only one brief stopover, in Dubai, then straight on to Malpensa airport, where they would arrive on Tuesday midmorning, Milan time.

'Thank you, Alex,' she said, turning her head to look over at him.

'For what? You paid for your own ticket.' He was still slightly exasperated with her over that. He'd wanted to spoil her. Make her feel special. Make up to her for what her mean and disgustingly unfair father had done. She'd told him a few more details about her father's appalling treatment last night. It had made him so angry, he'd felt like driving up to Singleton and teaching the man a lesson. When questioned about her mother, Harriet had also confessed that she sent her mother birthday and Mother's Day cards every year, with money enclosed, but never received a reply. How heartbreaking was that?

'Thank you for persuading me to come with you,' she said with the loveliest smile.

He reached over and took her hand in his. 'My pleasure,' he said softly.

* * *

Once again, Harriet's heart turned over and this time she noticed. For a split second she started worrying that she was falling in love with Alex, but just as quickly she decided to ignore any such worry. What would be, would be. She wasn't going to spoil this trip by stressing over future complications. She was going to have fun. And live in the moment.

A flight attendant materialised by their seats, with a tray holding glasses of champagne.

'Champagne, sir? Madam?' he asked.

'The lady doesn't drink champagne,' Alex replied.

'Can I get you anything else, sir? Some white wine, perhaps?'

'When will you be serving dinner?'

'About half an hour after take-off.'

'We'll have a bottle of wine with our meals. Perhaps some juice for now. What kind, Harriet?'

'I prefer orange,' she replied.

'Orange juice for two,' Alex relayed.

'Very good, sir. I'll be back shortly.'

Harriet loved the way Alex took command of situations. It had been sweet of him to remember about the champagne, and very sweet of him to insist on coming to pick her up today when it had been really out of his way. She could just have easily caught a taxi. She was glad she hadn't; his authoritative presence defused her tension over the trip, replacing anxiety with excitement, especially after he'd reassured her that everything was under control at the office. She had momentarily contemplated telling Emily about her affair with Alex. But only momentarily. She didn't want Emily to say anything negative or critical.

Of course, it was probably silly of her to have let Alex

persuade her to accompany him to Italy. Nothing could come of it. Nothing except…

Harriet brought herself up short before she could start thinking of the future again. Instead, she concentrated on the plusses of her affair with Alex. After all, how could she possibly regret having him as her lover? He was incredibly good in bed; last weekend had been the most amazing experience of her life. He was good out of bed, too, proving to be a fun companion, nothing at all like his often serious persona at work. As for this trip… Harriet vowed to enjoy every single moment. The prospect of spending more time alone with Alex was exciting enough, but to spend that time with him in stunning places like Lake Como and Venice was almost too good to be true. She had to keep glancing over at him to remind herself that it *was* true.

'Yes?' he queried after she'd probably looked at him one time too many.

'Nothing. Just checking that you're real.'

The steward arrived with the orange juice, relieving Harriet of having to explain her rather cryptic remark. It was freshly squeezed juice, and deliciously chilled, just the way she liked it. Harriet sipped it and sighed.

'I don't think I'll ever be able to fly anything but business class from now on,' she said.

'That can be arranged,' Alex said. 'I was thinking of taking you to Rio during our Christmas break.'

Harriet's heart skipped a beat at the thought that he was planning so far ahead. Christmas was five months away. As much as she was tempted just to say yes to anything he suggested, she could not afford to let him think she would settle for being his secret mistress for the rest of her life.

Her smile was light. 'What happened to the Alex who said I should just live for the here and now?'

'He was a fraud. And an opportunist. I've always been a planner, Harry. Just like you.'

'Well, that's a shame. Because I think that that particular Alex might have had the right idea. I've always worried too much about the future. Always planned too much. And where did it get me in the end? Nowhere.'

'I don't know about that, Harry. You have a nice flat near Bondi Beach, money in the bank, the best boss in the world and an even better lover.'

She had to laugh. 'You *are* an arrogant devil.' Not to mention so handsome that every woman on this plane had craned to look at him as they boarded. Harriet had felt so proud to be the woman by his side, resolving to wallow in the experience whilst it lasted.

It was the lasting part, however, that kept coming back to haunt her. Harriet knew in her heart that by Christmas this would all be over. Oh, dear, she was doing it again. Worrying about the future.

The thought sent a sad sigh escaping her lungs.

'You do that a lot, you know,' Alex said.

'Do what?'

'Sigh.'

'Sorry.'

'No need to apologise. It's just that I sometimes wonder what's behind the sigh.'

'Nothing serious. It's just a habit of mine, a way of relieving tension.'

'You're afraid of flying?'

Afraid of flying and dying and falling in love with the wrong man. Again.

'A little,' she admitted.

'Then here…take my hand. We're about to take off.'

* * *

Alex took her hand and squeezed it tight, feeling the tension in her as the jumbo airbus zoomed along the wet runway—it had started to rain—before lifting into the air slowly but safely. When the jet levelled off at God knew what height, she sighed again, then took her hand out of his. Alex wished she hadn't. He'd liked holding her hand.

When Alex sighed, Harriet leant over and poked him. '*You're* doing it now.'

He sent her a droll look. 'Maybe it's catching.'

'Maybe you're not the big, brave boy you pretend to be.'

'I never pretend, Harry. I don't like flying, but I'm not scared of it. What's the worst that can happen? The plane crashes and you die. There are worse ways to go.'

Harriet nodded, her big brown eyes turning soft. 'You're thinking of your mother, aren't you?'

Despite the sympathetic note in her voice, Alex could not stop his heart from hardening at the memory of what that wonderful woman had suffered. And so unnecessarily. It had blighted him, knowing he could do nothing to ease her pain. He'd been holding her hand when she'd taken her last breath. He could still see the look on his father's face when he realised she had gone. Poor bastard. Hopefully, this time he'd stick with the rehab and get his life back on track. When he'd rung him earlier today, he'd sounded good.

'Or is it your dad you're worrying about?' Harriet asked.

Her intuition touched him. 'Not really. You were right the first time. I was thinking of my mother.'

He glanced over at Harriet and smiled. 'But let's not

talk about sad things. We're off to Italy, to beautiful Lake Como and then on to amazing Venice, which, I might add, I have never seen.'

Harriet's eyes lit up with surprise. 'You haven't?'

'Nope. It will be the first time for both of us. I've been to Lake Como, of course. Jeremy and I holidayed with Sergio at his family villa quite a lot over the years.'

'You three are very close, aren't you?'

'Yep. Have been since our Oxford days.'

'Which is where you all joined that Bachelor's Club.'

'We didn't join it. We *formed* it. There were just the three of us. But that's ancient history now. In reality, the Bachelor's Club is no more. Once Sergio turned thirty-five, he decided to get married, so that was virtually the end of it.'

'What did his turning thirty-five have to do with it?'

'That was the age we vowed to stay bachelors till. And the age we aimed to become billionaires by.'

'Heavens. And did you? Become billionaires, I mean?'

Alex hesitated to tell her, out of habit. He'd always kept the extent of his wealth a secret, well aware that having heaps of money sometimes brought out the worst in people. Men envied and women grovelled. He quickly realised, however, that Harriet was not that type of woman. He'd never met a more independent, less grovelling female in his life.

'Yes, we did,' he admitted.

'*All* of you?'

Clearly, she was taken aback. Alex smiled, both at her and the memory of how their financial goals had finally been reached. Though just in time.

'It took many years, of course,' he explained. 'You don't become a billionaire overnight.'

'I would imagine not. So how *did* it happen?'

'Shortly after we started the Bachelor's Club, the three of us went into partnership in a wine bar. It was basically a dump, but the location was good. Very close to the university and between two restaurants. We worked hard to turn it into a hip and happening place. At least, Sergio and I worked hard. Jeremy provided the money. He was the wealthy one in our group. Anyway, to cut a long story short, we didn't stop at one wine bar. We eventually had several, all done out the same way. In the end, they were so successful that we formed a franchise. That was how we became billionaires. A little while ago, we sold the WOW franchise to an American company.'

'Oh, my goodness!' Harriet exclaimed. 'You owned the WOW wine bars? That's amazing! Emily and I go to the one in town all the time. They're so cool.'

'They are indeed. But we didn't own any of them in the end. We sold the ones we originally owned years ago. We just owned the franchise.'

'So, that's what you were doing in London recently? Selling the franchise?'

'Yes.'

'I did wonder what business interests you had over there.'

'Well, now you know.'

Harriet fell silent for a long moment before turning to look at him. 'Do you mind if I ask why you three boys decided to stay bachelors in the first place? I mean, I know most men these days don't rush to the altar, but they usually want to settle down eventually. It seems strange that all three of you wanted to stay single so much that you actually formed a club.'

'Look, it was just a bit of fun to begin with. We were all pretty sloshed at the time. Though underneath the fun we all had some serious reasons for embracing bachelor-hood. Sergio was still bitter over his father marrying a gold-digger. Jeremy was anti-marriage due to the number of divorces in his family. As for myself...I'd vowed on my mother's deathbed to spend my life making enough money to make sure no one had to suffer what my family did. Making that sort of money—and making a difference—is hard. I didn't see myself ever having the time or the energy to marry and have children of my own. Remaining a bachelor suited my goals.'

Or, it *had*...

Alex could not ignore the fact that he'd reached his goals now. So maybe it was time to change his mind about staying a bachelor. Maybe it was time to face his inner demons and admit to himself that all he'd just said to Harriet was just rubbish. The truth was, he was afraid of falling in love. Afraid of ending up like his pathetic father.

It was a crazy fear. Irrational, really. Other than in looks, he was nothing like his father. But fear was not always logical.

He gazed into Harriet's lovely face and wished he could be more like Sergio. Fearless and brave when it came to matters of the heart. But he was more like Jeremy, tainted by life's negative experiences, wary of feeling anything too deeply.

'What are you thinking?' she asked.

'Just how lovely you are,' he returned.

Her smile was wry. 'You shouldn't lie to me, Alex. You weren't thinking that at all.'

'You're right. I was thinking that it's rather sad that the Bachelor's Club is no longer relevant. It was a seriously fun club to belong to.'

'No doubt. But I think your Bachelor's Club is past its use-by date, Alex.'

'Only for one of us, Harry. Jeremy and I will soldier on.'

Her lips pursed. 'I have a feeling I won't like this Jeremy.'

Alex had to smile. 'Yes, you will. *Everyone* likes Jeremy.'

CHAPTER NINETEEN

THE CAPTAIN HAD just announced their descent into Milan when Alex turned to her.

'I didn't want to say anything earlier,' he said. 'I wanted you to enjoy the flight and not stress over anything, but Jeremy is going to meet me at the airport. Whilst I'm in Milan, I'm to be whisked off to some tailoring establishment to have a fitting for my suit for the wedding, after which we have to pick up Sergio at his factory, then drive down to Lake Como together.'

Harriet's heart sank. She didn't want to meet any of his rich friends, especially this Jeremy character.

'But won't that be awkward? How are you going to explain me?'

'I'm not,' he replied. 'We won't leave the plane together. You can go first. I know I said we were going to take the train down to Lake Como together, and I was going to see you safely booked into the hotel before I left you, but that was before Jeremy insisted on meeting me.'

Harriet could feel panic setting in. She was a confident girl travelling by train around Sydney, but to travel alone in a strange country was daunting.

'Stop worrying,' he said, seeing alarm in her face. 'I've booked you a hire car which will take you from the airport to the hotel door. The driver will be waiting for you in arrivals, holding up a card with your name on it. He'll help you with your luggage and so forth. I asked for a driver who spoke good English so that you wouldn't feel uncomfortable. Now, stop looking at me like that.'

'Like what?'

'Like I'm abandoning you in a strange land.'

'Sorry. I know it's not your fault.'

'I'll ring you when I can. Or text you if I can't.'

'All right,' she said and sighed.

'And stop that damn sighing,' he snapped. 'You could have come to the wedding with me, but you refused.'

'I wouldn't have fitted in.'

'Rubbish. It's not too late to change your mind, you know. Come with me. Be with me.'

'But what about the hire car? And the booking at the hotel?'

'Nothing that can't be sorted out.'

'I don't know, Alex. Are you sure?'

Not even remotely, he thought. But he couldn't bear to see her go off alone, looking unhappy and worried. He'd brought her here. It was his job to look after her.

'Positive,' he said. 'Now, I don't want to hear another word about it. You're coming with me and that's that.'

Her smile did things to him that shouldn't be allowed. Dear God, if he didn't watch himself, he would fall in love with her. And that would never do.

'I'll just go along to the ladies' and freshen up,' she said.

'Better be quick. We'll be landing soon.'

'I'm always quick,' she told him with a wry smile. 'I have a boss who gives me five-minute deadlines all the time.'

'What a bastard.'

'He can be.'

'I'll have to have a word with him.'

'He won't listen. He never listens.'

'Stupid as well.'

She laughed, then left him. He watched her make her way down the aisle, her neat little backside encased in stylish black slacks. She wore black a lot, usually teaming it with white tops. Harriet's top today was a simple but expensive-looking white T-shirt. He watched her walk back towards him five minutes later, her dark hair swinging in a sleek curtain around her shoulders, her glossy red lipstick a perfect foil for her black-and-white outfit. Though not classically beautiful, Harriet's face was strikingly attractive, her big dark eyes her best feature.

'That's better,' she said as she sat down and clicked her seat belt into place. 'Can't have your best friends looking down their noses at me.'

'They'll love you,' he said, confident that neither Sergio nor Jeremy would make any girlfriend of his feel bad. Which was exactly how he would introduce Harriet. Not as his PA. As his new girlfriend. Jeremy wouldn't care that he was sleeping with one of his staff, but Sergio might.

Alex tried to remember if he'd ever told his friends his relatively new PA's name. He vaguely recalled saying something about her the last night they'd had dinner together a few weeks ago. Yes, he'd called her Harry, Jeremy having picked up that that was probably a nickname. Sergio, however, had been very distracted that night, his mind clearly on Bella. He was unlikely to remember what his PA was called.

Alex decided to clue Jeremy in on who Harriet really was, but he would keep Sergio in the dark. He wasn't in the mood for any lectures where his private life was concerned, especially from Sergio, who was stupidly about to marry a possible gold-digger!

The plane's landing was as smooth as silk, their disembarking just as trouble-free. They were whisked through Customs without a hitch, Alex collecting and loading their luggage on a trolley before proceeding to the arrivals area, an anxious-looking Harriet by his side.

Jeremy, as luck would have it, was standing not that far from a uniformed chauffeur who was holding up a card with Harriet's name on it. It wasn't till that moment that Alex thought of a way to soothe some of Harriet's nervousness over having to spend too much time with his friends.

'Jeremy! Mate!' he called out and steered Harriet in his direction.

CHAPTER TWENTY

JEREMY WASN'T ANYTHING like Harriet had been imagining. Since Alex virtually had described him as the best-dressed rake in London, she'd pictured a handsome but dissolute-looking man with slicked-back hair and heavy-lidded eyes, wearing a designer suit and sporting a lot of expensive jewellery.

The man who waved back at Alex *was* handsome, but he looked disgustingly healthy with a nice tan and sparkling blue eyes. His hair wasn't oily or slicked back. It was clearly freshly washed, brown and collar-length, with a boyish wave which fell across his high forehead. As for his clothes...they looked expensive but were very casual. Not a bit of jewellery, either, Harriet noted as they drew closer. No earrings or rings or even a watch.

When he threw his arms around Alex in a huge bear hug, Harriet was astounded, then oddly touched. It wasn't often that you saw grown men hug each other with such genuine warmth and affection.

'God, it's great to see you,' Jeremy said at the same time, astounding Harriet even more with the richness and depth of his voice, which seemed at odds with his size. Though far from short—he was only a couple of inches shorter than Alex—his frame was much leaner. His shoulders were broad enough, but the rest of his body was very slender. He could easily have made money as a model, or as a narrator, with that gorgeous voice of his.

Harriet couldn't remember what he did for a living. She didn't think Alex had actually told her. Just that he was a rich friend from Oxford and was a fellow member of their Bachelor's Club, which meant he, too, had recently become a billionaire. He *looked* rich; money had a way of clinging to a man like an invisible cloak.

When he cheekily winked at Harriet over Alex's shoulder, she got a glimpse of his much-vaunted charm.

'So, who's this gorgeous creature, Alex?' he asked as he stepped back to look her up and down, his blue eyes twinkling. 'You never mentioned you were bringing someone with you.'

'It was a last-minute decision. This is Harriet,' Alex introduced. 'My PA. And my new girlfriend,' he added before Harriet could be offended. 'I usually call her Harry, but in present company I think Harriet is called for.'

She saw the drily amused look Jeremy gave Alex. 'You sneaky devil,' he said, then grinned. 'And you had the hide to tell me that business and pleasure don't mix!'

'There are exceptions to every rule,' Alex said and smiled a wry smile at a slightly startled Harriet. 'I didn't say anything because I agreed to keep our affair a secret. But there's no need for secrets over here, though I think I might not tell Sergio she's my PA. Sergio isn't as much of a free spirit as you are, Jeremy. Without going into too many details, I have to speak to that chauffeur over there. He was going to drive Harriet down to a hotel at Lake Como, but I've persuaded her to change her plans and come to the wedding with me.'

'And rightly so,' Jeremy pronounced warmly as Alex walked off, leaving Harriet to fend alone in his friend's perversely bewitching company. It was simply impossible not to like him. She wasn't sexually attracted to him, but she could understand why lots of women had fallen under his spell over the years. He possessed a personal charisma which she imagined could be overpowering if he was also your physical type.

'It's wonderful to see Alex dating a real woman for a change,' he said. 'Though slightly disconcerting.'

'Disconcerting?'

'I don't want to be the only one left a bachelor in our Bachelor's Club. Oops. Maybe I shouldn't have said that. Has Alex told you about the Bachelor's Club?'

'Yes. I know all about it.'

'That's a relief. Thought I'd put my big foot in it just then. Sergio's broken ranks, but Alex and I are still committed bachelors. We both believe it's best for a girl to know the lie of the land before she gets in too deep. Or is it too late for that?' he added with a sudden searching look.

Oh, God. Why did she have to blush?

'I see,' he said, his brows drawing together.

'No, you don't,' she said quickly. 'Look, I know Alex isn't into love or marriage. I'm not a fool. I recently broke up with my fiancé and I'm not looking for love or commitment of any kind. I'm just having a much-needed fling. It won't last. When it's over, I'll move on and so will Alex.'

'Are you quite sure about that?'

'Quite sure,' she said coolly and glanced over at Alex, who was still talking to the chauffeur. Just then, he glanced back at her, smiled, then hurried over, the chauffeur in his wake.

'Right. All settled. Jeremy, am I right in guessing you didn't drive yourself to the airport? Knowing you, you either had Sergio drop you off or you took a taxi.'

'I hate it when people know me that well,' he said, but without looking offended at all. 'Yes, Sergio dropped me off, then went on to his office. He's getting everything organised there before he and Bella fly off to New York.'

'Thought that might be the case,' Alex said. 'Anyway, I've organised for Lucca here to take us all to the tailor. After we're finished there, we'll drop you off back at Sergio's office, Jeremy, then I'll accompany Harriet down to the hotel I booked her into on Lake Como. Everyone, this is Lucca,' he finally introduced. 'Lucca, this is Harriet and Jeremy.'

Relief swamped Harriet at Alex not insisting that she stay at Sergio's villa on Lake Como. Now that she'd met Jeremy, she wasn't quite so nervous about meeting Sergio—whom she was sure would be nice to her as well—but she didn't want to spend every minute of the next two days in their company. Besides, it was only natural that the three friends would like to spend some time together. Clearly, that didn't happen too often these days.

'I'll tell you what,' Harriet butted in before he could put his plans into motion. 'Why don't you and Jeremy take a taxi to wherever it is you have to go and I'll have Lucca take me straight down to the hotel? To be honest,' she added, 'I feel seriously jet-lagged. You're an experienced traveller, Alex, but I'm not. I hardly slept a wink on that flight. Now, please, don't worry about me. I'll be fine. I'm going to go straight to bed once I check in, and sleep for hours, so don't go calling me for ages. Tonight'll be soon enough.'

'Are you sure?' Alex asked.

'Absolutely. I'm quite capable of looking after myself, like we originally planned. Go have some fun with your friends.'

He leant forward and gave her a peck on the cheek. 'You're a darling.'

His sweet words sent tears pricking at her eyes.

'Off you go,' she said hurriedly before she could embarrass herself totally. 'Lucca will look after me, won't you, Lucca?'

Lucca, who was a good-looking lad of no more than twenty, nodded enthusiastically. '*Si*. You will be safe with me.'

'Safe' was not quite the word Harriet would have used to describe Lucca's driving. Thankfully, the road from Milan to Lake Como was first class, but good God, didn't they have speed limits in Italy? If they did, Lucca was oblivious to them. Once off the freeway, fortunately he did slow down enough for Harriet to take in the sights. And what sights they were! Never had she seen such a beautiful spot as Lake Como, with its surrounding snow-capped mountains and magnificent villa-dotted shores.

The boutique hotel they were heading for was once a private villa, according to its website. The pictures of it looked beautiful, and the setting peaceful, which was why she'd booked it. But flat, one-dimensional photographs did not replicate the experience of seeing the place in real life, Harriet was soon to appreciate, especially on a warm summer's day with a clear blue sky.

When the hotel came into view, she was overwhelmed by the sheer grandeur of the ancient stone building gleaming a soft white in the sunshine. The magnificence of the grounds and the view of the lake were just as spellbinding. Harriet's eyes were everywhere as she followed Lucca into the grand foyer with its vaulted ceiling and spectacular marble staircase. She'd been in some nice hotels in Sydney over the years, but there was nothing at home like this. It was like stepping back in time to a world of splendour, elegance and opulent luxury, a feeling enhanced when she finally lay down on her antique four-poster bed in her exquisitely furnished room.

She didn't really want to go to sleep just yet. She wanted to wander in the garden and sit on the terrace which overlooked the lake. Instead, the excitement of the trip and the length of the flight finally caught up with her and she couldn't stop herself from drifting off, her last thought being that she hoped Alex was enjoying himself.

Alex finally became aware of the fact that Jeremy had been uncharacteristically quiet during their trip to the tailor. After the fitting was finished, Alex suggested they go have a spot of lunch somewhere. He was curious about what was bothering Jeremy. He suspected it was something to do with Harriet; Alex wondered what she'd said to him that had rendered him unusually taciturn.

They found a café nearby which wasn't too crowded. Summer in Milan was high tourist season, with all the cafés and restaurants doing excellent business. Alex had by then removed his suit jacket and rolled up his sleeves, but he was still on the warm side. Fortunately, the café was air-conditioned.

'Okay, so what's bugging you?' Alex asked after the waitress had departed with their order of wraps and coffee.

Jeremy widened ingenuous blue eyes. 'Why would you think something's bugging me?'

'Don't try to con me, Jeremy. I know you, remember?'

Jeremy shrugged. 'Okay, but you might not like what I have to say.'

'Let me be the judge of that.'

'Are you in love with this girl, Alex?'

His question stunned Alex. It was certainly not what he'd been expecting.

'No,' he said. 'I'm not.' Not yet, anyway.

'I see.' Jeremy began making circles on the table with his index finger, an old habit of his when he was thinking. Finally, he stopped and looked up at Alex. 'Harriet told me she's not interested in love or commitment from you. She says she's having a fling on the rebound.'

Alex only just contained his exasperation. 'I leave you with her for five minutes and she tells you her innermost thoughts and feelings. How on earth did you manage that?'

'It's a talent I inherited,' Jeremy said with a perfect poker face. 'All the Barker-Whittle males are born charmers. But that's beside the point.'

'And the point is?'

'I know you very well, Alex, the same way you know me. It's not like you to become involved with an employee, especially your PA. You're nothing like me. You have hidden depths. And a capacity for caring which I simply don't possess.'

'Don't undersell yourself, dear friend. You have a great capacity for caring. Look how you always remember everyone's birthdays.'

'Stop trying to be funny, Alex. This is serious.'

'What is?'

Jeremy's blue eyes turned a steely grey. 'I have this awful feeling that you're heading for an even worse disaster than Sergio's marriage.'

'In what way?'

'I'm worried you're going to fall in love with this girl and she's going to break your heart.'

Alex was taken aback. 'I can't see that happening.'

Jeremy shook his head. 'This is not going to end well, Alex.'

'Everything will work out fine, Jeremy. Harry and I are just having a bit of fun together. Lighten up, for pity's sake. It's not like you to worry so much.'

Jeremy heaved a frustrated sigh. 'You're right. I'm in danger of becoming a worrywart. And a workaholic. Ever since I bought my book business, I've changed.'

'I didn't notice much of a change when I rang you the other night,' Alex pointed out drily. 'You were happily bedding your French editor with your usual *laissez-faire* attitude. Ah…our wraps are here.'

Both men tucked into the food and didn't speak for a couple of minutes.

'I do know what you mean about changing, though,' Alex went on finally. 'I've changed, too, this past year. Possibly it's because we're getting older. Just think, both you and I will be thirty-five before the year is out. I hope we'll always stay friends, despite the tyranny of distance, but our lives are now taking different paths.'

'God, that sounds wretched. I already miss you and Sergio both. Terribly.'

Alex was touched by his words, but not surprised. Of the three friends, Jeremy had always been the softest, and the most sentimental. He *never* forgot birthdays. It came to Alex that Jeremy's *laissez-faire* attitude to life might hide a deep-seated loneliness. His upbringing, though privileged, had not been easy. He'd been sent to boarding school when he was eight, where his slight frame and pretty-boy looks had resulted in lots of bullying. It wasn't till puberty had hit that he'd found his feet, his voice breaking and his height shooting up to over six feet, putting paid to the bullying. But his less than positive experiences at school, plus his parents' constant divorcing and remarrying, had left lots of emotional scars.

'Who knows?' Alex said casually. 'Maybe *you'll* fall in love one day.'

'*What?*'

Alex laughed. 'You should see the look on your face.'

'Well, it isn't every day that one of my best friends says something to me so outrageous. I would possibly tolerate it from Sergio, now that he's about to embrace wedded bliss. But I expected better from a fellow dedicated bachelor.'

'I was only joking. Come on, finish up that coffee. Then we'll go pick up Sergio.'

Dragging Sergio away from work was not an easy task, but Jeremy managed it when he promised to tell Sergio some fascinating news, but only once they were on their way to Lake Como. Alex knew exactly what he had in mind, but went along with it. After all, if he was going to bring Harriet to the wedding, Sergio had to know about her.

'Okay, out with it!' an impatient Sergio demanded within thirty seconds of leaving the factory. Jeremy leant forward from where he was sitting in the back seat, kindly having given Alex the passenger seat.

'Alex brought a girl with him. No, no, strike that. He brought a *woman*.'

Sergio shot Alex a surprised look. 'A woman, eh? What happened?'

'I finally grew bored with dating dolly-birds whose IQs were smaller than their bra size.'

Jeremy chuckled. 'That's a good one, Alex.'

'So how did you meet this woman?' Sergio asked.

'Through work. She's in real estate.' He'd instructed Jeremy not to mention she was his PA.

'What's her name?' Sergio asked.

'Harriet.'

'Classy name.'

'She's a classy girl.'

'I thought she was a woman.'

'She is. But she's not that old. Late twenties.'

'Around Bella's age, then. I presume she's attractive.'

'*Very* attractive,' Jeremy jumped in. 'Brunette. Slim. She's also nicely independent. I met her at the airport.'

'So where the hell *is* she?' Sergio asked.

'By now she's settled in at the Villa Accorsi. You know it?'

'Of course. But why is she staying at a hotel when we have plenty of room at my place?'

'She didn't want to stay there. To be honest, she didn't even want to come to the wedding, but I talked her into it.'

'Are you serious about this Harriet?'

'Silly question, Sergio,' Jeremy intoned drily. 'Alex is never serious about *any* girl.'

'But it's clear this one is different. He wouldn't have brought her all this way if he didn't at least like her a hell of a lot.'

'I do like her a hell of a lot,' Alex confessed. 'But we've only been dating a short while. She's also just getting over a broken engagement. When Harry told me she'd always wanted to go to Italy, I impulsively asked her along—something I'll start to regret if my friends start harassing me over my intentions.'

When Sergio fell broodingly silent, Alex worried that he might have come down a bit heavy.

'Look, I'm sorry, I—'

'It's your PA you should apologise to,' Sergio broke in sharply. 'Did you honestly think I wouldn't remember? You called her Harry that night at dinner a few weeks back. The odds of both your new girlfriend and your PA being called Harry are at lotto-winning level, so let's cut the crap and tell the truth. You're having sex with your personal assistant—most likely on the sly—and you're using this trip as an excuse to have some more.'

Alex sighed heavily, whilst Jeremy remained conspicuously silent, both of them having been on the end of Sergio's disapproval more than once over the years.

'It's not like that,' Alex said defensively.

'Then what's it like?'

'We're just having some fun together. It's nothing serious.'

Jeremy's snort didn't help.

'Harry needs some fun right now,' Alex went on firmly. 'I would never hurt her.'

Now Sergio snorted.

Alex decided he'd heard enough. 'Hey, just cut it with the "high and mighty" stuff, buddy. From what I've heard, your intentions weren't exactly pure as the driven snow when you invited Bella to stay at your villa.'

Sergio had the grace to apologise.

'I was just thinking,' Jeremy piped up. 'We should have your stag party tonight. That way we won't be hung over for the wedding. What do you say, Sergio?'

'I say good thinking. I still have half a case of that gorgeous red you sent me last Christmas.'

'Great. And we'll order in some of those fantastic pizzas we ate last time. You like pizza, don't you, Alex?'

'I like good pizza.'

'These are the best. So that's settled. Another bonus is it leaves Alex free to spend tomorrow to do some sightseeing with Harriet. He could even stay the night with her. Then they can come to the wedding together the next morning.'

'You'd better watch it, Jeremy,' Alex said. 'You're turning into a planner.'

'You could be right,' he agreed. 'Like I told you, since I bought my book business I seem to have developed a strange compulsion for being organised. When I was working for the family bank, I didn't give a damn about nine-to-five, or even turning up at my desk at all. I did most of my business via my phone. Now I'm getting obsessed with marketing meetings and publishing deadlines and all sorts of weird things.'

Both Sergio and Alex laughed.

'We'll make a businessman out of him yet,' Alex said.

'Stranger things have happened, I suppose,' Jeremy remarked.

'About tomorrow night,' Sergio piped up. 'With the wedding at eleven, I'd be more comfortable if you spent that night with us at my place, Alex. I don't want anything going wrong.'

'Fair enough,' Alex said. 'How will Harriet get to the wedding, then?'

'I'll book her a water taxi to pick her up at the hotel around ten. They have their own jetty.'

'Okay.' Alex didn't mind. He would have all day with her, more than enough time to show her some sights *and* have late-afternoon delight in her hotel room. He wondered what Harriet was doing right at this moment. Hopefully, she was having a good rest and not feeling lonely or abandoned. He would call her later. Or perhaps he would just text her; tell her they were having their stag party tonight and that he would join her tomorrow morning. Yes, perhaps that would be better. He didn't want her thinking he simply *had* to hear the sound of her voice.

CHAPTER TWENTY-ONE

WHEN HARRIET WOKE, she wasn't sure where she was for a split second. But then she remembered. She was in Italy, in a gorgeous hotel on the shores of Lake Como.

Unfortunately, she was also alone. Harriet pulled a face. What she would not give to have Alex by her side at this moment.

Thinking of Alex had her rolling over, picking up her phone and turning it back on. Good Lord! It was almost seven o'clock. She'd slept for hours. She hoped he hadn't tried to ring her. She quickly checked. No. No missed calls, but one message, informing her that they were having Sergio's stag party that night so that they wouldn't be hung over for the wedding. This would also leave tomorrow free for him to spend with her.

Harriet's spirits immediately lifted.

'Ring me when you wake up,' he'd added before signing off.

She did so straight away, just the sound of his voice filling her with joy.

'Did you have a good sleep?' he asked.

'Very good.'

They talked for ages, Alex telling her of all the places he planned to take her the next day. Sergio had offered the use of his speedboat. It sounded wonderful. Still, she would enjoy going anywhere with Alex.

'Hey!' She heard a deep male voice call out. Jeremy, no doubt. He did have a distinctive voice.

'Girlfriends aren't allowed at stag parties,' he said. 'Not even via the phone.'

Harriet's heart turned over at the word 'girlfriend'. It sounded wonderful as well, though she'd better not get used to it. That would only be her title here, in this fantasy world, on this fantasy getaway. Once they got back to the real world at home, she would revert to being Alex's PA, plus his secret bit on the side.

It was a depressing thought.

Then don't think about that, Harriet, she lectured herself. *Live in the moment.* That was the order of the day.

'I'd better go,' Alex said. 'See you tomorrow morning around nine-thirty.'

'That early?'

'Don't worry. I won't be drinking too much. I'll leave that up to Sergio and Jeremy. I'll give you a call when I'm on my way. Bye, sweetheart.'

That evening seemed endless, despite the excellence of the meal she had in a local restaurant. She kept thinking about Alex, then about tomorrow. She could hardly wait.

She woke very early the next day, already excited. Unfortunately, it was still over three hours before Alex was due to join her. Showering, dressing and titivating took up a good hour and a half, and Harriet used up another hour having a leisurely breakfast out on the huge back terrace that overlooked the lake. The day promised to be warm again, but not too warm, with a smattering of cloud in the sky. She was lingering over a third cup of coffee when her phone pinged. Snatching it up, she read the message from Alex with a pounding heart.

I'm on my way, it said. Be on the lookout for the boat. It's red, so it should be easy to spot.

Harriet stood up and made her way over to stand at the stone railing that enclosed the terrace. Her eyes scanned the lake, looking for a red speedboat. There were myriad assorted craft on the water. Ferries, water taxis, sailing boats, jet skis and, yes, several speedboats, none of them red.

And then she saw it, cutting across the wake of a ferry, jumping the waves, Alex at the wheel, his fair hair glinting golden in the sunshine. He arrived like a hero from an action movie, Harriet only then noticing the hotel jetty at the bottom of some stone steps. Spotting her watching him from the terrace, he waved, jumped out of the boat, tied a rope around a post, then dashed up the steps towards her, dashingly handsome in white shorts and a navy polo. He gathered her to him and kissed her thoroughly, uncaring of the other guests sitting at tables nearby. When he finally let her come up for air, Harriet didn't care, either.

'You're looking good for a man who should have a hangover,' she said, cupping his face and pretending to inspect his eyes. Lord, but he had beautiful eyes, blue as the sky overhead, and with lashes that any woman would kill for.

'I told you I wouldn't drink much.'

'Have you had breakfast?'

'Would you believe that I have? Maria insisted on cooking an omelette.'

'Who's Maria?'

'Sergio's housekeeper. She wanted to pack me a picnic lunch, but I said no to that. So, are you ready to go? First, we're going over to Bellagio. You can't visit Lake Como without visiting the town of Bellagio. It's called "the pearl of Lake Como".'

'Sounds lovely.'

'It is. Very old, of course, but fascinating. Seeing all the main places of interest there will take us all morning. We'll have lunch there, too. Their restaurants are second to none. Then after lunch we'll motor down to Como. That's a beautiful town. After that I'll take you for a leisurely drive around the whole lake. You can see a lot from the water. I'll show you Sergio's villa, plus the one next door, the countess's. It's very grand. That's where they're having the wedding and the reception afterwards.'

'It's not going to be a big wedding, is it?'

Alex laughed. 'Hardly. Counting the celebrant and the photographer, there'll be just eleven of us. So don't start stressing that it's some huge celebrity shindig, because it isn't.'

Harriet had to admit she was relieved. She hadn't packed a dress suitable for a seriously formal do. But she *had* brought along her red cocktail dress, the one Alex had admired. That would do.

'Now, are you ready to go? You look ready. And you look very lovely, might I add. If I hadn't had our itinerary all worked out, I'd whisk you off upstairs for a quickie.'

'I don't much like quickies,' Harriet said, doing her best to ignore the wild jab of desire coursing through her veins.

He chuckled. 'You are such a little liar. I'm almost tempted to show you just how much. But I think I'll make you wait.'

'I can wait,' she told him. 'Provided you give me a little taster occasionally.'

'And what would that involve?'

'Nothing much. Just hold my hand and kiss me at regular intervals so that I don't go cold on you.'

'Done!'

* * *

Alex hadn't enjoyed himself so much in years. He'd been to Lake Como a few times as Sergio's guest, and he'd seen the various sights on offer, but there was something about seeing them through Harriet's delighted eyes which made the experience even more pleasurable, and infinitely more satisfying. Of course, it didn't hurt holding her hand or kissing her more times than he could count. By the time they docked at the hotel jetty in the late afternoon, he was more than ready to steer her up the amazing staircase to her room without further ado.

She made no objection to sharing a shower with him, or having what turned out to be a quickie under the jets of hot water, Alex coming with a speed that bothered him a bit, knowing that Harriet had been left panting and unsatisfied. Still, he made it up to her afterwards with an hour of leisurely love-play in bed, during which she came three times before he reached for a condom once more.

'Hate to love you and leave you,' he said afterwards, 'but I don't want to drive that boat across the lake at night. Sergio is a nervous enough bridegroom without my adding to his worries, so I promised I'd be back before dark.'

Harriet propped herself up on one elbow and watched him dress.

'How am I getting to the wedding?' she asked.

'Sergio's booked you a water taxi for ten. It'll bring you to his villa. I'll meet you down at his jetty and we'll all go over to the countess's place together.'

'I still can't believe how amazing her place is. I mean, Sergio's villa was grand enough, but hers is like a palace.'

'It *is* magnificent, but it's not as big as it looks. The setting up against the hillside makes it look larger.'

When Harriet reached for her phone and took a photo of him, he groaned. 'Will you stop doing that? You've already taken heaps of photos of me today.'

'Yes, but none with your shirt off.'

'I hope none of them shows up on social media,' he warned her.

Harriet shrugged. 'I'm not into social media on a personal basis. It has its uses, but I don't particularly want to give other people—even friends—a blow-by-blow description of my life.'

'Sensible girl. But, to be on the safe side, perhaps you'd better not take any snaps at the wedding tomorrow. Sergio has a passion for privacy.'

'In that case, he shouldn't be marrying Bella, should he?'

Alex laughed. 'You could be right there. Okay, I'll reassure Sergio that any photos you take are for your personal use only. They won't be gracing the glossies, or anywhere else.'

Harriet smiled. 'Good. Because I really want to take some photos. Not just of the bride. I especially want one of you and your two friends together.'

Alex bent down and gave her a kiss on the cheek. 'I'd like that. Have to go now, Harry. Sorry I wasn't able to take you out to dinner tonight.'

'No worries. I'll have room service, then read one of the books I downloaded onto my tablet back home before I left.'

'What kind of books?'

'Mostly thrillers, with a few romances thrown in. What do you suggest I try?'

'Not a romance. Romancing you is *my* job.'

'And you're very good at it, too. Lord knows what I'm going to do when you grow bored and don't want to have

sex with me any more. I'm already seriously addicted to
your unique brand of lovemaking.'

'I wouldn't worry about that, if I were you,' he said
ruefully. 'There's no danger of my growing bored with
you for a long time yet.' And wasn't that the truth!

It was actually a relief to hear that Harriet didn't envisage ending their affair any time soon. Alex couldn't bear
the thought of her telling him one day that it was over between them. It would happen, of course. She didn't love
him. Basically, she was just in it for the sex. Same as him.

Are you sure that's still true, Alex? questioned that
inner voice that had been plaguing him ever since Jeremy had brought up the subject of love. *Are you sure that
your feelings for her haven't already changed to something far deeper than a combination of liking and lust?*

Alex clenched his jaw down hard, refusing to listen to
such rubbish. It was all Jeremy's fault, which was ironic,
considering *his* attitude to love and marriage. Alex decided that it was the romantic setting that was making
him feel things he didn't normally feel. Paris might be
called the city of love, but Italy was the country of love.
He would have to watch himself tomorrow at the wedding, and then in Venice. If he wasn't careful, before he
knew it he'd be asking Harriet to marry him. Which was
pretty stupid, considering he was the last man on earth
she would marry. *So just put all these thoughts of love
back into Pandora's box, Alex, and get yourself out of
here. Pronto!*

'Must fly,' he told her, and with one last peck on the
cheek he was gone.

CHAPTER TWENTY-TWO

HARRIET COULD NOT imagine a more perfect wedding. The lack of a church filled to the brim with guests didn't seem to matter, despite her own dream to have that kind of traditional wedding. Or it had been, till she witnessed this one. Admittedly, the setting for the ceremony was idyllic, on the wide stone terrace of a magnificent villa overlooking Lake Como. Plus the weather was beautiful, the skies blue overhead and the summer sun not too hot.

But it was the unique bridal party that dazzled Harriet the most. It wasn't often that there were no bridesmaids, just the bride, groom and two best men. She didn't know whose photograph to take first, they were all so good-looking. The bride, of course, was more than dazzling. Harriet had already known Bella was beautiful. She'd seen her on television and in the gossip magazines. Dressed as a bride, however, she was breathtaking. Yet her gown was simple, a sleek floor-length sheath in pearl satin which skimmed her figure rather than clung. She wore no veil. With that gorgeous mane of white-blonde hair, she didn't need a veil. Her jewellery was just as simple. A fine gold chain with a single pearl pendant, along with pearl-drop earrings.

She and Sergio looked brilliant standing together, his darkly handsome looks the perfect foil for Bella's exquisite blonde beauty. Harriet took heaps of photos, including several of the three friends together. She didn't have an opportunity to meet Bella before the actual ceremony, but Sergio had spoken to her at length as she'd walked with the men from Sergio's villa to the countess's. Such a nice man; a real gentleman. He'd made her feel so welcome, which was good of him, considering she was a wedding crasher.

The countess had been very sweet as well. Her name was Claudia and she was a widow. But a very merry one, Harriet deduced by her flashy clothes and flirtatious manner, especially towards Jeremy. Not that he seemed to mind. Alex had eventually confirmed her suspicions that the two of them might have been lovers at some stage, despite their age difference.

Which didn't surprise Harriet. Nothing would surprise Harriet about Jeremy's behaviour where women were concerned. She even caught him winking at the mother of the bride, who was still attractive and possibly younger than Claudia. The only other guests were Sergio's housekeeper, Maria, and her husband, Carlo, who obviously thought the marriage a marvellous idea, judging by the wide smiles on their faces.

By the time the celebrant—a portly and loquacious Italian named Giovanni—pronounced Sergio and Bella husband and wife, Claudia and the mother of the bride were dabbing at their eyes, though not enough to spoil their make-up.

Harriet felt teary herself, partly because she always cried at weddings, but mostly because she knew she would never marry the man *she* loved. Oh, dear God. She *did* love Alex, didn't she? There was no longer any doubt in her mind. She'd suspected as much yesterday but had pushed the dreaded thought away. When her eyes automatically went to him, more tears threatened. Fortunately, he didn't notice; the official photographer—a tall, thin woman in her forties—had pounced on the bridal party for more photos, leaving Harriet to battle her emotions in private.

Time to get a grip, girl, she lectured herself after slipping her phone back into her black clutch bag. *Go talk to the countess. Or Bella's mother. Whatever, just do something, and for pity's sake, no more silly crying!*

Alex felt impatient for the reception luncheon to be over, despite the happiness of the occasion and the quality of the food. They were sitting at the sumptuous table in Claudia's opulent dining room, being given course after mouth-watering course. Harriet was on his right side and Jeremy on his left, both of them obviously enjoying the lavish meal a lot more than he was. His mind was definitely elsewhere, his gaze drifting over the table to Sergio and Bella, who didn't seem to be eating much. They were too busy gazing adoringly into each other's eyes. Alex finally agreed with Jeremy that Bella did love Sergio; the way she looked at him was rather persuasive. But he would reserve judgment till their marriage had passed the hurdle of Sergio abandoning the family business in order to move to New York with her.

They were actually flying there later this evening, which was the reason for the morning wedding. Knowing this, Alex had booked a hire car to pick both himself and Harriet up at her hotel later that afternoon and take them straight to Venice, where he'd booked them into one of the city's most luxurious hotels. The suite he'd picked had cost a bomb, but he didn't care. He worked hard. Why shouldn't he spoil himself? Alex suspected, however, that it was Harriet whom he wanted to spoil.

He watched her out of the corner of his eye, thinking how lovely she looked today. She was wearing the same red cocktail dress she'd worn to the charity dinner earlier this year, the one which had given him wicked thoughts all that night. Or had they been jealous thoughts? He certainly hadn't liked the thought of her going home with that dullard Dwayne. She'd always deserved someone better.

But you're not better, that annoying voice piped up once again. *Except perhaps in bed. You're selfish and ruthless, and a total waste of time. She'd be better off without you in her life. Really, your behaviour has been quite shameless. So do the right thing, Alex, and once you get home let her go.*

But he didn't want to let her go. He couldn't. Not yet.

Harriet tried to pretend she was having a wonderful time, but she wasn't. The food was marvellous, yes, but there was way too much of it. The only reason she kept eating was that she didn't want to offend the countess, who'd obviously gone to a lot of trouble to make the wedding a success. She couldn't wait to get out of there and be alone with Alex once more; couldn't wait to go to Venice. Lake Como was lovely, but somehow seeing Sergio and Bella getting married here today had temporarily spoiled the place for her. Venice would be much better. Out of sight was out of mind, or so they said. She didn't want to think about love and marriage. She had to get her mind back to reality, which was that she was having a strictly sexual affair with Alex. Nothing more.

Before she'd left Sydney to come to Italy, Harriet had vowed to enjoy the trip for what it was. But somehow the enjoyment she'd experienced yesterday was in danger of disintegrating. Which was a shame. When she sighed, Alex gave her a nudge.

'None of that infernal sighing,' he muttered under his breath.

Harriet gave him a rueful smile. 'It's just that I'm full,' she whispered. 'I can't eat another bite.'

'Then don't.'

'I won't,' she said and put down her cutlery.

Jeremy leaned forward and shot a questioning glance down the table. 'You don't want your dessert?'

'I'm full,' Harriet answered.

'Pass it along to me. I need added fortification for the night ahead.'

'Don't even ask,' Alex informed her drily as he passed along her dessert.

'He really is very naughty,' Harriet said after Jeremy had dropped them back at the hotel in Sergio's speed-boat. The happy couple had by then departed, and Alex wasted no time in getting Jeremy to drive them across the lake. The hire car he'd booked was due to pick them up in less than an hour.

'But you can't help liking him,' she added as they hurried up the steps towards the hotel entrance.

'You don't fancy him, do you?' Alex said, his voice sharp.

'Don't be silly. He's not my type at all.'

'Why not?'

'He just isn't. You're my type, Alex, as you very well know. There's no need to be jealous.'

'I'm not jealous,' he denied. But he was. Fiercely jealous. The thought of Harriet even fancying another man brought a sour taste to his mouth. The thought of her having sex with another man didn't bear thinking about. The only man allowed to have sex with her was *him*!

'How long will it take you to pack?' he asked her.

'Not long. Why?'

He gave her a look which spoke a thousand words. Less than a minute later, Harriet was up against the bedroom door, her panties in tatters on the floor, her legs wrapped around Alex's waist while he pumped up into her with primal passion. As they both came, Alex thanked his lucky stars that he'd had enough foresight to put a condom in his jacket pocket that morning, perhaps anticipating a moment such as this. He shuddered at the thought of what he might have done if he hadn't.

Alex held her close, not wanting to let her go. But he really had to. Time was moving on.

Slowly, gently, he eased out of her, then headed for the bathroom. What he saw there brought a groan of dismay to his lips. Talk about life being cruel. After flushing the toilet, he adjusted his clothes, washed his hands and walked slowly back into the bedroom. Harriet was sitting on the side of the bed, looking slightly dishevelled.

'What is it?' she asked straight away on seeing worry stamped on his face.

'I hate having to tell you this,' he said, his heart sinking, 'but the condom broke.'

'Oh,' she said, then just sat there, silent and thoughtful.

'Is it a dangerous time of the month for you?'

CHAPTER TWENTY-THREE

HARRIET DIDN'T HAVE to think too long to know that it was. Extremely dangerous.

Her first reaction to the possibility of falling pregnant by Alex was despair. If it had been anyone else, she might have had a chance of being happy about having a baby. She'd always wanted to be a mother by the time she was thirty. But she knew having a child would be the last thing *he* wanted.

It took a while for Harriet to see the situation with a calmer mind, but she eventually came to a decision. If she had been unlucky enough to fall pregnant—or lucky enough, depending on how you looked at it—then the problem would be hers.

Finally, she looked up. 'I won't lie to you,' she said. 'There is a chance that I might fall pregnant. It's close to the middle of my cycle. But I also might not. Pregnancies don't always happen, even when people are trying to have a baby. We'll just have to wait and see.' She'd already decided not to tell him if she did. Still, whether she did or not, she was going to resign. She simply could not go on having wildly passionate sex with Alex and pretending it was just lust. She loved the man. But if she told him so, he would dump her cold. Even if it turned out that she wasn't pregnant, how could she continue to work for him under such circumstances? It had all become impossible. Going to Venice with him was impossible, too.

She smothered a sigh and made the hardest decision of her life.

'I'm sorry, Alex, but I can't go to Venice with you. Not now. I just want to go home.'

'But there's no need to do that. We could go buy you one of those morning-after pills. Then you won't have to worry.'

You mean you *won't have to worry*, Harriet thought unhappily. Still, she supposed it was a sensible suggestion and one which she hadn't thought of. Silly, really. It would solve the problem. Though not *all* of her problems.

'I still want to go home, Alex,' she said, the stark reality of their affair having finally sunk in. She simply could not go on pretending that she didn't love him; that all she cared about was fun and games. 'Look, I'll buy a morning-after pill at the airport. They always have pharmacies at airports. Then neither of us will have to worry. Now, please...just take me home.'

He stared at her for a long moment. 'All right,' he finally said, and Harriet let out a huge sigh of relief.

When they arrived at the airport, Harriet found a pharmacy and asked for the morning-after pill. But, as it turned out, the rules in Italy were different from some other parts of the world. You couldn't just buy one over the counter; you had to have a doctor's prescription to get the pill. She was told that the public health clinic in Milan would give her a prescription, but it wouldn't be open till the following morning, and there was often a several-hours wait to be seen.

Harriet decided fate was telling her something and they boarded their flight without said pill.

'But what if you *are* pregnant?' Alex asked, face grim.

'I'll cross that bridge when I come to it. But you don't have to worry, Alex. If I am pregnant, then I'll take care of it.'

'What do you mean by that?'

'I mean I'll take care of it,' she snapped. 'Now, if you don't mind, I don't want to talk about it any more.'

CHAPTER TWENTY-FOUR

ALEX WENT TO work extra early that Monday morning, mostly because he'd been awake for hours. Sleep had been elusive during the two and a half weeks since his return from Italy, something he wasn't used to. It had been especially elusive last night, knowing that Harriet had made a doctor's appointment for first thing this morning to find out if she was pregnant. She'd refused to use one of the home testing kits you can buy over the counter—despite being a few days late—claiming they weren't always accurate and she needed to be sure. She'd also refused to do other things, like talk to him more than strictly necessary. She wouldn't even have coffee with him.

The past two weeks at work had been sheer hell.

The moment Alex let himself into the office, the cat sauntered over to him, purring as he wound himself around his ankles.

'At least you still love me,' Alex muttered.

Not that Harriet had ever loved him. But she had liked him. And desired him. Now she couldn't seem to stand the sight of him, which really wasn't fair, in Alex's humble opinion. It wasn't *his* fault that the damned condom broke.

'Come on, Romany,' he said with a weary sigh. 'Let's go get you some food.'

That done, he made himself a mug of black coffee before taking it into his office and slumping down behind his desk. As he sat there, sipping slowly, he tried to work out exactly why Harriet was so angry with him. And she was. She tried to hide her antagonism towards him, but it had been there, in her body language, right from the time they'd had the disastrous news about the morning-after pill. Harriet had even looked perversely pleased when he'd informed her that the only seats left on the first available flight home were first class. Alex had soon twigged that this was because she would have her own space and not have to sit next to him. Or talk to him. From the moment they'd arrived back, she'd cut him dead, saying it was over between them and taking a taxi home.

Every day since, Alex had tried to work out what he would do and how he would feel if she *was* pregnant.

Clearly, Harriet had no intention of keeping the baby if she was. Her savage 'I'll take care of it' had indicated exactly what she would do. Alex knew that if he'd accidentally impregnated any other girl he'd been involved with over the years, he would not have objected to this course of action.

But you didn't love any of those girls. You love Harriet, he accepted at long last. *If she is going to have your baby, you will want her to keep it.*

Shock at this astonishing realisation propelled Alex forward in his chair, some coffee sloshing onto his tie and shirt front. Swearing, he banged the mug down on his desk and stood up, reefing his clothes off before the coffee burned his skin. Fortunately, there was a brand-new shirt and tie in the bottom drawer of his desk, courtesy of his brilliant PA, who thought of every eventuality before it had even happened.

What in God's name would he do without her? Alex's heart lurched at the very real possibility that Harriet would soon exit from his life altogether. She hadn't said anything yet, but he could *feel* it. She meant to move on, and there was absolutely nothing he could do to stop her. As time ticked away, he began to hope that she *wasn't* pregnant. Maybe then things might settle back to normal.

Not a very logical thought.

The next two and a half hours were agony. He couldn't think about work. Instead, he tried filling in the time till Harriet arrived by ringing his father and then Sarah. His father didn't want to talk. He was off to his morning exercise class, his perky voice actually irritating Alex, which was perverse. Sarah couldn't talk, either. She had to drive the kids to school, then go on to work, saying she would talk to him later. He contemplated calling Jeremy and confiding the situation to him. But it would be the middle of the night in London and no doubt Jeremy would not be alone.

In the end, Alex wandered downstairs into the café where he'd taken Harriet that fateful day not all that long ago. After ordering a bagel and another coffee, he sat down at the same table and stared through the window at the passing parade whilst his inner tension escalated to a level he'd never experienced before. By the time a pale-faced Harriet showed up for work shortly before eleven, Alex's temples were pounding and his shoulder blades ached.

At least she didn't keep him waiting. She came straight into his office, stood in front of his desk and said bluntly, 'I'm not pregnant. So you can breathe easier now.'

He actually did let out a huge breath, having found that his heartbeat had been temporarily suspended. He could not help but notice that she noticed, a small, rueful smile on her lips.

'The doctor said I'm late because I'm stressed,' she went on before he could say a single word. 'Which leads me to my next announcement. I'm resigning. Right now. I can't work for you any more, Alex. I'm sorry to leave you in the lurch like this, but you can get a temp till you can fill my position permanently. There are plenty of good agencies who specialise in excellent temps. I seem to recall you were working with a temp before you found me, so you'll know what to do. I'd take Romany with me, but animals still aren't allowed in my building. Besides, he'd miss this place now. It's his home. I'll ask Audrey to keep an extra eye on him on my way out.

'It's been a pleasure working for you, Alex,' she finished up while he just sat there, pole-axed. 'Up till recently, that is. Still, what happened was as much my fault as yours. You didn't force me to sleep with you, or do any of the other things we did together. As for a reference, I'm sure that when asked you will give me a good one. You might be a selfish man, but you're not a vindictive one. Goodbye, Alex. No, please don't say anything. I've made up my mind and you won't change it.'

So saying, she whirled and was gone, Alex staring at the empty doorway without moving a muscle till Audrey stormed in a couple of minutes later, looking outraged.

'Harriet's just left,' she informed him unnecessarily. 'She told me she'd quit, but she wouldn't tell me why. As if I can't guess!'

Alex suppressed a sigh as he snapped forward on his chair and adopted his firm 'boss face'. 'Why Harriet resigned is none of your business, Audrey. Please go back to Reception.'

'I always thought you were heartless where women

were concerned,' she spat at him. 'I just didn't realise how heartless. That girl's fallen in love with you. That's why she's quit. Blind Freddie could see how unhappy she's been these last couple of weeks. It's you! You seduced her that Friday you took her away with you, didn't you?'

'I did not seduce Harriet and she's not in love with me,' he stated, trying not to sound as shaken as he felt. 'So please don't go saying any of that to the others.'

'I wouldn't be bothered. But, just so you know in advance, I'll be looking around for another job. Even if you didn't do anything wrong with her, I don't want to work for a man who'd let a fantastic girl like Harriet just walk out without fighting to keep her. Don't you care how upset she is?'

'Of course I care. But she can be very stubborn.'

'But if she's not in love with you, then why did she leave?'

'I don't know, Audrey. Maybe it has something to do with her break-up with Dwayne. Maybe she just needs a change.'

'But she *loved* working for you.'

Alex was as close to weeping as he'd been in decades. 'Look, I'll give her a call later and see if I can change her mind.' Even as he said the placating words, he knew he wouldn't do any such thing. It was over.

'Go back to work, Audrey,' he said.

After she left, Alex sat there for ages, thinking about everything Audrey had said.

You seduced her. She's in love with you. If she's not in love with you, then why did she leave?

Could he be wrong in assuming she *didn't* love him? If she did love him, it would explain a lot, especially if she thought he didn't love her.

And why *wouldn't* she think that, when he'd gone to

such great lengths to make her understand that he didn't do love and marriage; that any relationship they had was strictly sexual?

God, but he was an idiot!

Jumping up, he pulled on his jacket, grabbed his keys and headed out, telling Audrey as he passed Reception that he was off to get Harriet back.

'Just as well,' she threw after him.

Ten minutes later, Alex was only a block from the office, stuck in traffic.

'Damn!' he swore. He thought about ringing Harriet but decided that wouldn't be good enough. He had to do this face-to-face. There was no option but to wait.

CHAPTER TWENTY-FIVE

HARRIET WAS CURLED up on her sofa, no longer crying but feeling terrible, when there was a knock on her flat door. It was a rather timid knock, so she knew it wasn't Alex come to demand she return to work. Not that he would. Alex wouldn't run after any woman.

Probably a neighbour, needing something.

It was Betty from next door, wanting to borrow an onion. She was a dear old love who found it hard enough to get up and down the stairs, let alone walk to the corner shop just to buy an onion. Harriet was happy to give her one.

'Thanks, pet,' she said. 'I saw you come home earlier. Not feeling well? You do look a little peaky.'

'I had a bad headache,' Harriet invented. 'But it's gone now. In fact, I was just about to go out for a walk along the beach.'

'Wish I could come with you, pet, but these old legs of mine won't cooperate. Thanks for the onion.'

After Betty left, Harriet forced herself to put on leggings, trainers and a light sweater, then set off for a power walk to the beach. Exercise always did her good, as did the sight of the sea. There was something calming about watching the waves roll into shore. Something…spiritual.

The first sight of the blue ocean lifted her spirits.

You will survive this, Harriet, she told herself. *And, just think, soon you'll have a baby to love.* How wonderful was that?

By the time Alex reached Harriet's address he was not a happy man, his frustration increasing when he couldn't find a parking spot in her street for love nor money. In the end, he parked in someone's driveway, knocked on their door and gave the startled woman a hundred dollars to let his SUV stay there for a couple of hours. Alex figured he might need a couple of hours to convince Harriet that he really, truly loved her. Lord knew what he was going to do if she didn't love him back and didn't give a damn.

It wasn't like Alex to entertain negative thinking, but it wasn't every day that he fell in love. He understood now why he'd been afraid of it. Because he had known, subconsciously, that when and if he fell in love it would be very deeply. Not to have his love returned would shatter him.

His tension increased as he hurried up the stairs of Harriet's block of flats, his heart pounding along with his feet. When he knocked loudly on her door, the sound echoed through the whole building. When she didn't answer, he knocked again. And again. And again.

A door opened along the way and an elderly lady peeped out. 'If you're looking for Harriet, she's gone for a walk along the beach.'

'Right. Thanks.'

Alex took off in the direction of nearby Bondi Beach, his long legs bringing him there in less than a minute. Thankfully, the beach wasn't all that crowded. He searched along the wide stretch of sand but didn't see her. And then she came into view, walking briskly along the promenade towards where he was standing in front of the Pavilion. She stopped as soon as she saw him, her body language not good. Her chin came up, her hands curling into fists by her sides. He couldn't see the expression in her eyes, as she was wearing sunglasses. But he got the impression of barely controlled anger and heaps of exasperation.

In the end, she covered the few metres which separated them, her hands finding her hips as she planted herself right in front of him.

'What are you doing here?' she bit out.

'I went to your flat, but you weren't there. Your neighbour told me where to find you.'

'That's not what I asked you. Look, you're wasting your time, Alex. I'm not coming back to work for you and that's that!'

'I haven't come to talk to you about work,' he returned in what he hoped was a calm voice. *Someone* had to be calm. Still, he took the level of her ongoing anger as a positive sign. She really didn't have that much reason to be angry with him. Not unless her emotions were involved.

'Neither am I going to keep sleeping with you!' she said in a voice loud enough to have passers-by stare over at them.

'Could we possibly have this discussion in private, Harry? I don't appreciate your telling the world about our personal business.'

At least she had the good grace to blush.

'Come on,' he said, taking her elbow and leading her away from several curious onlookers. 'We'll go back to your place and have things out there.'

'There are no things to have out,' she muttered.

'I beg to differ. We have lots of things to have out,

mostly concerning your misconception about my feelings for you.'

Her laugh was wry and bitter. 'I was *never* in any doubt over your feelings for me, Alex.'

'You could be wrong, you know.'

Harriet knew she wasn't wrong. The only reason Alex had come after her was because he didn't like being left in the lurch, either in his office or in his bed.

'If you think you can seduce me again, then you have another think coming.'

'I never seduced you in the first place, Harry. You came to my bed willingly.'

'You know what I mean. You engineered our being alone together so it would be harder for me to resist you.'

'I plead guilty to that one.'

Wrenching her arm out of his hold, she hurried ahead of him, not saying another word till she was standing by her front door fumbling with her keys.

'You can come in,' she threw over her shoulder at him. 'But not for long. It won't take long anyway, because there's nothing you can possibly say to make me change my mind on this. We're over, Alex. As hard as it might be for a man of your ego, I suggest you learn to take no for an answer.'

'Hell, but you don't make things easy on a man, do you?' he ground out as he strode after her into her living room. 'I almost pity poor old Dwayne.'

'I suggest you leave Dwayne out of this,' she snapped, banging the door after him and tossing her sunglasses onto the hall table. 'Now, just get on with what you have to say.'

'Okay, I will. The thing is, Harriet, that I love you.

Sorry if that's not the most romantic of declarations, but it's hard to be romantic when you're this angry.'

Harriet would wonder afterwards if she looked as shocked as she felt. All she could remember in hindsight was that her heart stopped beating and her body seemed to freeze on the spot. Nothing worked. Not her brain, her tongue or anything.

He started pacing, throwing snatches of words at her as he circumnavigated the room with long, angry strides.

'I know I said I didn't do love... And I don't...or I didn't... Till you came along. You changed everything... Loving you changed everything...'

He finally ground to a halt in front of her again, his handsome face all flushed and frustrated.

'I love you, Harriet. And I want to marry you. I even want to have babies with you, which believe me is such an astonishing concept that it took me a while to get my head around it. But once I did, I saw that it could be wonderful. You'd make a marvellous mother. When you told me this morning that you weren't pregnant, I actually felt disappointed. But I could hardly tell you that because at the time I thought you didn't love me back. But then Audrey stormed in and told me that you probably did. So then I got to thinking that maybe you did love me, that that was the reason for your anger. But now that I'm here, I'm not so sure.'

He took abrupt hold of her shoulders and dragged her close. 'Tell me that I'm not wrong, Harry,' he demanded in a passionate voice which fairly vibrated through the air. 'Tell me that you love me, because if you don't, I don't know what I'll do.'

Harriet's eyes swam with the impact of his declaration. He loved her. Alex loved her. He even wanted to marry her and have babies with her. Oh, God...

'Please don't cry,' he said, then gathered her to him. 'Just tell me that you love me.'

'I love you,' she choked out against his throat. 'Oh, Alex...'

His heart almost burst with happiness and relief. She loved him. She really loved him.

'And you'll marry me, even if I don't tick your check-boxes for a husband?'

'You tick the most important ones. But, Alex...'

His heart tightened at the sudden wariness in her voice. Holding her at arm's length, he looked deep into her still-teary eyes. 'What is it? What's wrong?'

'Nothing. I hope... It's just that I...I never imagined that you loved me. You were always so adamant that our relationship was about nothing but fun and sex. I honestly believed that if I was pregnant you'd try to talk me into having a termination. So I lied to you this morning. I lied and I...I'm sorry...'

His shock was evident. But it was quickly followed by delight. 'So you *are* pregnant?'

She nodded, still looking slightly guilty. 'I thought I was doing the right thing at the time.'

'I can understand that. So you were planning on raising our child all alone, were you?'

'I...I might have told you about it when it was too late for a termination.'

'I sincerely hope so. Still, you're going to *have* to marry me now,' he said, smiling.

'If you insist.'

'I insist.'

He kissed her then, the kissing leading to more than kissing. Lots more. Finally, they moved into her bedroom.

Afterwards, Harriet snuggled into Alex's arms, happier than she'd ever been in her life.

'I can't believe that you love me,' she murmured.

'Fishing for compliments, Harry?' he said softly and kissed the top of her head.

'Not really. But feel free to give them, if you like.'

He laughed. 'In that case, be assured that I love everything about you, including your obsessive sense of independence.'

'I'm not that bad. Surely?'

'You don't think it obsessively independent to not tell the father of your child that you're pregnant?'

'I would have told you. In the end.'

'I hope so. So when are we getting married?'

'Not too soon. I don't want a rushed wedding, Alex. How about we have the wedding in that little chapel you're building up at the golf resort?' she suggested, thinking it would be romantic to marry near where they'd first got together.

'But that won't be finished for months!' he protested.

'Does it matter?'

'Would you live with me in the meantime?'

'Of course. But I won't be selling this flat. It can be the beginning of my property portfolio.'

'Done!' he said. 'What about work? Will you come back to work for me?'

'I don't see why not.'

'Thank God for that. If you don't, I would never be able to show my face around there ever again. Audrey called me heartless. She even threatened to get another job. The only one who loves me there is Romany.'

'Don't be silly. Everyone there loves you. You're a great boss.'

'I don't care about everyone else. Just about you.'

'Oh, Alex…' The tears came hard and fast then, tears of happiness and relief, all the emotion and tension Harriet had been bottling up over the past month finally set free.

Alex drew her close, his heart squeezing tight at the thought that he might have lost her today. Lost her *and* his child. It had been a close call. Too close for comfort. Never again, he vowed, would he let her doubt his love for her. Never, ever again. And, as he held her even closer, he felt sure that his mother would be pleased that he'd finally found true love with a wonderful girl like Harriet. Being a philanthropist was all very well, but being a good husband and father was just as important.

'By the way,' he whispered into her hair. 'After the wedding, I'm taking you to Venice for our honeymoon.'

* * * * *

In case you missed it, book one in the
RICH, RUTHLESS AND RENOWNED *trilogy,*
THE ITALIAN'S RUTHLESS SEDUCTION,
is available now!
And look out for book three, Jeremy's story,
coming soon!

Uncover the wealthy Di Sione family's sensational
secrets in the brand-new eight-book series
THE BILLIONAIRE'S LEGACY,
beginning with
DI SIONE'S INNOCENT CONQUEST
by Carol Marinelli
Also available this month

'I don't care what you think!'

How could Javier be so cool and composed when she was all over the place? Except, of course, she knew how. Sophie was just so much more affected by him than he was by her, and she could see all her pride and self-respect disappearing down the plughole if she didn't get a grip on the situation *right now*.

She cleared her throat and stared at him and through him. 'I...we have to work alongside one another for a while and...and this was just an unfortunate blip. I would appreciate it if you never mention it again. We can both pretend that it never happened—because it will never happen again.'

Javier lowered his eyes and tilted his head to one side, as if seriously considering what she had just said.

So many challenges in that single sentence. Did she really and truly believe that she could close the book now that page one had been turned?

He'd tasted her, and one small taste wasn't going to do. Not for him and not for her. Whatever her back story, they both needed to sate themselves in one another. And sooner or later it *would* happen...

Cathy Williams can remember reading Mills & Boon books as a teenager, and now that she is writing them she remains an avid fan. For her, there is nothing like creating romantic stories and engaging plots, and each and every book is a new adventure. Cathy lives in London, and her three daughters—Charlotte, Olivia and Emma—have always been, and continue to be, the greatest inspirations in her life.

Books by Cathy Williams

Mills & Boon Modern Romance

Seduced into Her Boss's Service
The Wedding Night Debt
A Pawn in the Playboy's Game
At Her Boss's Pleasure
The Real Romero
The Uncompromising Italian
The Argentinian's Demand
Secrets of a Ruthless Tycoon
Enthralled by Moretti
His Temporary Mistress
A Deal with Di Capua
The Secret Casella Baby
The Notorious Gabriel Diaz

The Italian Titans

Wearing the De Angelis Ring
The Surprise De Angelis Baby

One Night With Consequences

Bound by the Billionaire's Baby

Visit the Author Profile page at
millsandboon.co.uk for more titles.

A VIRGIN
FOR VASQUEZ

BY
CATHY WILLIAMS

All rights reserved including the right of reproduction in whole
or in part in any form. This edition is published by arrangement with
Harlequin Books S.A.

This is a work of fiction. Names, characters, places, locations and
incidents are purely fictional and bear no relationship to any real
life individuals, living or dead, or to any actual places, business
establishments, locations, events or incidents. Any resemblance is
entirely coincidental.

This book is sold subject to the condition that it shall not, by way of
trade or otherwise, be lent, resold, hired out or otherwise circulated
without the prior consent of the publisher in any form of binding or
cover other than that in which it is published and without a similar
condition including this condition being imposed on the subsequent
purchaser.

® and TM are trademarks owned and used by the trademark owner
and/or its licensee. Trademarks marked with ® are registered with the
United Kingdom Patent Office and/or the Office for Harmonisation in
the Internal Market and in other countries.

First Published in Great Britain 2016
By Mills & Boon, an imprint of HarperCollins*Publishers*
1 London Bridge Street, London, SE1 9GF

© 2016 Cathy Williams

ISBN: 978-0-263-92120-5

Our policy is to use papers that are natural, renewable and recyclable
products and made from wood grown in sustainable forests. The logging
and manufacturing processes conform to the legal environmental
regulations of the country of origin.

Printed and bound in Spain
by CPI, Barcelona

A VIRGIN
FOR VASQUEZ

CHAPTER ONE

JAVIER VASQUEZ LOOKED around his office with unconcealed satisfaction.

Back in London after seven years spent in New York and didn't fate move in mysterious ways…?

From his enviable vantage point behind the floor-to-ceiling panes of reinforced rock-solid glass, he gazed down to the busy city streets in miniature. Little taxis and little cars ferrying toy-sized people to whatever important or irrelevant destinations were calling them.

And for him…?

A slow, curling smile, utterly devoid of humour, curved his beautiful mouth.

For him, the past had come calling and that, he knew, accounted for the soaring sense of satisfaction now filling him because, as far as offices went, this one, spectacular though it was, was no more or less spectacular than the offices he had left behind in Manhattan. There, too, he had looked down on busy streets, barely noticing the tide of people that daily flowed through those streets like a pulsing, breathing river.

Increasingly, he had become cocooned in an ivory tower, the undisputed master of all he surveyed. He was thirty-three years old. You didn't get to rule the concrete jungle by taking your eye off the ball. No; you kept focused, you eliminated obstacles and in that steady, onward and upward march, time passed by until now...

He glanced at his watch.

Twelve storeys down, in the vast, plush reception area, Oliver Griffin-Watt would already have been waiting for half an hour.

Did Javier feel a twinge of guilt about that?

Not a bit of it.

He wanted to savour this moment because he felt as though it had been a long time coming.

And yet, had he thought about events that had happened all those years ago? He'd left England for America and his life had become consumed in the business of making money, of putting to good use the education his parents had scrimped and saved to put him through, and in the process burying a fleeting past with a woman he needed to consign to the history books.

The only child of devoted parents who had lived in a poor *barrio* in the outskirts of Madrid, Javier had spent his childhood with the driving motto drummed into him that to get out, he had to succeed and to succeed, he had to have an education. And he'd had to get out.

His parents had worked hard, his father as a taxi driver, his mother as a cleaner, and the glass ceiling had always been low for them. They'd managed, but only just. No fancy holidays, no flat-screen tellies for the house, no chichi restaurants with fawning waiters. They'd made do with cheap and cheerful and every single penny had been put into savings for the time when they would send their precociously bright son to university in England. They had known all too well the temptations waiting for anyone stupid enough to go off the rails. They had friends whose sons had taken up with gangs, who had died from drug overdoses, who had lost the plot and ended up as dropouts kicked around on street corners.

That was not going to be the fate of their son.

If, as a teenager, Javier had ever resented the tight controls placed on him, he had said nothing.

He had been able to see for himself, from a very young age, just what financial hardship entailed and how limiting it could be. He had seen how some of his wilder friends, who had made a career out of playing truant, had ended up in the gutter. By the time he had hit eighteen, he had made his plans and nothing was going to derail them: a year or two out, working to add to the money his parents had saved, then university, where he would succeed because he was bright—brighter than anyone he knew. Then a high-paying job. No starting at the ground level and making his way up slowly, but a job with a knockout financial package. Why not? He knew his assets and he had had no intention of selling himself short.

He wasn't just clever.

Lots of people were clever. He was also sharp. Sharp in a streetwise sort of way. He possessed the astuteness of someone who knew how to make deals and how to spot where they could be made. He knew how to play rough and how to intimidate. Those were skills that were ingrained rather than learnt and, whilst they had no place in a civilised world, the world of big business wasn't always civilised; it was handy having those priceless skills tucked up his sleeve.

He'd been destined to make it big and, from the age of ten, he had had no doubt that he would get there.

He'd worked hard, had honed his ferocious intelligence to the point where no one could outsmart him and had sailed through university, resisting the temptation to leave without his Master's. A Master's in engineering opened a lot more doors than an ordinary degree and he wanted to have the full range of open doors to choose from.

And that was when he had met Sophie Griffin-Watt.

The only unexpected flaw in his carefully conceived life plan.

She had been an undergraduate, in her first excitable year, and he had been on the last leg of his Master's, already considering his options, wondering which one to take, which one would work best for him when he left university in a little under four months' time.

He hadn't meant to go out at all but his two housemates, usually as focused as he was, had wanted to celebrate a birthday and he'd agreed to hit the local pub with them.

He'd seen her the second he'd walked in. Young, impossibly pretty, laughing, head flung back with a drink in one hand. She'd been wearing a pair of faded jeans, a tiny cropped vest and a denim jacket that was as faded as the jeans.

And he'd stared.

He never stared. From the age of thirteen, he'd never had to chase any girl. His looks were something he'd always taken for granted. Girls stared. They chased. They flung themselves in his path and waited for him to notice them.

The guys he'd shared his flat with had ribbed him about the ease with which he could snap his fingers and have any girl he wanted but, in actual fact, getting girls was not Javier's driving ambition. They had their part to play. He was a red-blooded male with an extremely healthy libido—and, as such, he was more than happy to take what was always on offer—but his focus, the thing that drove him, had always been his remorseless ambition.

Girls had always been secondary conquests.

Everything seemed to change on the night he had walked into that bar.

Yes, he'd stared, and he'd kept on staring, and she hadn't glanced once at him, even though the gaggle of girls she was with had been giggling pointing at him and whispering.

For the first time in his life, he had become the pursuer. He had made the first move.

She was much younger than the women he usually dated. He was a man on the move, a man looking ahead to bigger things—he'd had no use for young, vulnerable girls with romantic dreams and fantasies about settling down. He'd gone out with a couple of girls in his years at university but, generally speaking, he had dated and slept with slightly older women—women who weren't going to become clingy and start asking for the sort of commitment he wasn't about to give them. Women who were experienced enough to understand his rules and abide by them.

Sophie Griffin-Watt had been all the things he'd had no interest in and he'd fallen for her hook, line and sinker.

Had part of that driving obsession for her been the fact that he'd actually had to try? That he'd had to play the old-fashioned courting game?

That she'd made him wait and, in the end, had not slept with him?

She'd kept him hanging on and he'd allowed it. He'd been happy to wait. The man who played by his own rules and waited for no one had been happy to wait because he'd seen a future for them together.

He'd been a fool and he'd paid the price.

But that was seven years ago and now...

He strolled back to his chair, leant forward and buzzed his secretary to have Oliver Griffin-Watt shown up to his office.

The wheel, he mused, relaxing back, had turned full circle. He'd never considered himself the sort of guy who would ever be interested in extracting revenge but the opportunity to even the scales had come knocking on his door and who was he to refuse it entry...?

* * *

'You did what?'

Sophie looked at her twin brother with a mixture of clammy panic and absolute horror.

She had to sit down. If she didn't sit down, her wobbly legs would collapse under her. She could feel a headache coming on and she rubbed her temples in little circular movements with shaky fingers.

Once upon a time, she'd been able to see all the signs of neglect in the huge family house, but over the past few years she'd become accustomed to the semi-decrepit sadness of the home in which she and her brother had spent their entire lives. She barely noticed the wear and tear now.

'What else would you have suggested I do?' There was complaint in his voice as he looked at his sister.

'Anything but that, Ollie,' Sophie whispered, stricken.

'So you went out with the guy for ten minutes years ago! I admit it was a long shot, going to see him, but I figured we had nothing to lose. It felt like fate that he's only been back in the country for a couple of months, I just happen to pick up someone's newspaper on the tube and, lo and behold, who's staring out at me from the financial pages…? It's not even as though I'm in London all that much! Pure chance. And, hell, we need all the help we can get!'

He gestured broadly to the four walls of the kitchen which, on a cold winter's night, with the stove burning and the lights dimmed, could be mistaken for a cosy and functioning space but which, as was the case now, was shorn of any homely warmth in the glaring, bright light of a summer's day.

'I mean…' His voice rose, morphing from complaint to indignation. 'Look at this place, Soph! It needs so much work that there's no way we can begin to cover the cost.

It's eating every penny we have and you heard what the estate agents have all said. It needs too much work and it's in the wrong price bracket to be an easy sell. It's been on the market for two and a half years! We're never going to get rid of it, unless we can do a patch-up job, and we're never going to do a patch-up job unless the company starts paying its way!'

'And you thought that running to…to…' She could barely let his name pass her lips.

Javier Vasquez.

Even after all these years the memory of him still clung to her, as pernicious as ivy, curling round and round in her head, refusing to go away.

He had come into her life with the savage, mesmerising intensity of a force-nine gale and had blown all her neat, tidy assumptions about her future to smithereens.

When she pictured him in her head, she saw him as he was then, more man than boy, a towering, lean, commanding figure who could render a room silent the minute he walked in.

He had had presence.

Even before she'd fallen under his spell, before she'd even spoken one word to him, she'd known that he was going to be dangerous. Her little clutch of well-bred, upper-middle-class friends had kept sneaking glances at him when he'd entered that pub all those years ago, giggling, tittering and trying hard to get his attention. After the first glance, she, on the other hand, had kept her eyes firmly averted. But she hadn't been able to miss the banging of her heart against her ribcage or the way her skin had broken out in clammy, nervous perspiration.

When he'd sauntered across to her, ignoring her friends, and had begun talking to her, she'd almost fainted.

He'd been doing his Master's in engineering and he

was the cleverest guy she'd ever met in her life. He was so good-looking that he'd taken her breath away.

He'd been also just the sort of boy her parents would have disapproved of. Exotic, foreign and most of all… unashamedly broke.

His fantastic self-assurance—the hint of unleashed power that sat on his shoulders like an invisible cloak— had attracted and scared her at the same time. At eighteen, she had had limited experience of the opposite sex and, in his company, that limited experience had felt like no experience at all. Roger, whom she had left behind and who had been still clinging to her, even though she had broken off their very tepid relationship, had scarcely counted even though he had been only a couple of years younger than Javier.

She'd felt like a gauche little girl next to him. A gauche little girl with one foot poised over an unknown abyss, ready to step out of the comfort zone that had been her privileged, sheltered life.

Private school, skiing holidays, piano lessons and horse riding on Saturday mornings had not prepared her for anyone remotely like Javier Vasquez.

He wasn't going to be good for her but she had been as helpless as a kitten in the face of his lazy but targeted pursuit.

'We could do something,' he had murmured early on when he had cornered her in that pub, in the sort of seductive voice that had literally made her go weak at the knees. 'I don't have much money but trust me when I tell you that I can show you the best time of your life without a penny to my name…'

She'd always mixed with people just like her: pampered girls and spoilt boys who had never had to think hard about how much having a good night out might cost.

She'd drifted into seeing Roger, who'd been part of that set and whom she'd known for ever.

Why? It was something she'd never questioned. Oliver had taken it all for granted but, looking back, she had always felt guilty at the ease with which she had always been encouraged to take what she wanted, whatever the cost.

Her father had enjoyed showing off his beautiful twins and had showered them with presents from the very second they had been born.

She was his princess, and if occasionally she'd felt uneasy at the way he'd dismissed people who were socially inferior to him, she had pushed aside the uneasy feeling because, whatever his faults, her father had adored her. She'd been a daddy's girl.

And she'd known, from the second Javier Vasquez had turned his sexy eyes to her, that she was playing with fire, that her father would have had a coronary had he only known...

But play with fire she had.

Falling deeper and deeper for him, resisting the driving desire to sleep with him because...

Because she'd been a shameless romantic and because there had been a part of her that had wondered whether a man like Javier Vasquez would have ditched her as soon as he'd got her between the sheets.

But he hadn't forced her hand and that, in itself, had fuelled her feelings towards him, honed and fine-tuned them to the point where she had felt truly alive only when she'd been in his company.

It was always going to end in tears, except had she known just how horribly it would all turn out...

'I didn't think the guy would actually agree to see me,' Oliver confessed, sliding his eyes over to her flushed, distressed face before hurriedly looking away. 'Like I said, it was a long shot. I actually didn't even think he'd remember who I was... It wasn't as though I'd met him more than a couple of times...'

Because, although they were twins, Oliver had gone to a completely different university. Whilst she had been at Cambridge, studying Classics with the hope of becoming a lecturer in due course, he had been on the other side of the Atlantic, going to parties and only intermittently hearing about what was happening in her life. He'd left at sixteen, fortunate enough to get a sports scholarship to study at a high school, and had dropped out of her life aside from when he'd returned full of beans during the holidays.

Even when the whole thing had crashed and burned a mere few months after it had started, he had only really heard the edited version of events. Anyway, he had been uninterested, because life in California had been far too absorbing and Oliver, as Sophie had always known, had a very limited capacity when it came to empathising with other people's problems.

Now she wondered whether she should have sat him down when he'd eventually returned to the UK and given him all the miserable details of what had happened.

But by then it had been far too late.

She'd had an engagement ring on her finger and Javier had no longer been on the scene. Roger Scott had been the one walking up the aisle.

It didn't bear thinking about.

'So you saw him...' *What did he look like? What did he sound like? Did he still have that sexy, sexy smile that could make a person's toes curl?* So much had happened over the years, so much had killed her youthful dreams about love and happiness, but she could still remember, couldn't she?

She didn't want to think any of those things, but she did.

'Didn't even hesitate,' Oliver said proudly, as though

he'd accomplished something remarkable. 'I thought I'd have to concoct all sorts of stories to get to see the great man but, in fact, he agreed to see me as soon as he found out who I was...'

I'll bet, Sophie thought.

'Soph, you should see his office. It's incredible. The guy's worth millions. More—billions. Can't believe he was broke when you met him at university. You should have stuck with him, sis, instead of marrying that creep.'

'Let's not go there, Ollie.' As always, Sophie's brain shut down at the mention of her late husband's name. He had his place in a box in her head, firmly locked away. Talking about him was not only pointless but it tore open scabs to reveal wounds still fresh enough to bleed.

Roger, she told herself, had been a learning curve and one should always be grateful for learning curves, however horrible they might have been. She'd been young, innocent and optimistic once upon a time, and if she was battle-hardened now, immune to girlish daydreams of love, then that was all to the good because it meant that she could never again be hurt by anyone or anything.

She stood up and gazed out of the patio doors to the unkempt back garden which rolled into untidy fields, before spinning round, arms folded, to gaze at her brother. 'I'd ask you what he said...' her voice was brisk and unemotional '...but there wouldn't be any point because I don't want to have anything to do with him. He's...my past and you shouldn't have gone there without my permission.'

'It's all well and good for you to get sanctimonious, Soph, but we need money, he has lots of it and he has a connection with you.'

'He has no connection with me!' Her voice was high and fierce.

Of course he had no connection with her. Not unless

you called *hatred* a connection, because he would hate her. After what had happened, after what she had done to him.

Suddenly exhausted, she sank into one of the kitchen chairs and dropped her head in her hands for a few moments, just wanting to block everything out. The past, her memories, the present, their problems. *Everything.*

'He says he'll think about helping.'

'What?' Appalled, she stared at him.

'He seemed very sympathetic when I explained the situation.'

'Sympathetic.' Sophie laughed shortly. The last thing Javier Vasquez would be was sympathetic. As though it had happened yesterday, she remembered how he had looked when she had told him that she was breaking up with him, that it was over between them, that he wasn't the man for her after all. She remembered the coldness in his eyes as the shutters had dropped down. She remembered the way he had sounded when he had told her, his voice flat and hard, that if he ever clapped eyes on her again it would be too soon... That if their paths were ever to cross again she should remember that he would never forget and he would never forgive...

She shivered and licked her lips, resisting the urge to sneak a glance over her shoulder just to make sure that he wasn't looming behind her like an avenging angel.

'What exactly did you tell him, Ollie?'

'The truth.' He looked at his twin defensively. 'I told him that the company hit the buffers and we're struggling to make ends meet, what with all the money that ex of yours blew on stupid ventures that crashed and burned. He bankrupted the company and took us all down with him.'

'Dad allowed him to make those investments, Oliver.'

'Dad...' His voice softened. 'Dad wasn't in the right place to stop him, sis. We both know that. Roger got away with everything because Dad was sick and getting sicker, even if we didn't know it at the time, even if we were all thinking that Mum was the one we had to worry about.'

Tears instantly sprang to Sophie's eyes. Whatever had happened, she still found it hard to blame either of her parents for the course her life had eventually taken.

Predictably, when her parents had found out about Javier, they had been horrified. They had point-blank refused to meet him at all. As far as they were concerned, he could have stepped straight out of a leper colony.

Their appalled disapproval would have been bad enough but, in the wake of their discovery, far more than Sophie had ever expected had come to the surface, rising to the top like scum to smother the comfortable, predictable lifestyle she had always taken for granted.

Financial troubles. The company had failed to move with the times. The procedures employed by the company were cumbersome and time-consuming but the financial investment required to bring everything up to date was too costly. The bank had been sympathetic over the years as things had deteriorated but their patience was wearing thin. They wanted their money returned to them.

Her father, whom she had adored, had actually buried his head in his hands and cried.

At the back of her mind, Sophie had stifled a spurt of anger at the unfairness of being the one lumbered with these confidences while her brother had continued to enjoy himself on the other side of the world in cheerful, ignorant bliss. But then Oliver had never been as serious as her, had never really been quite as responsible.

She had always been her father's 'right-hand man'.

Both her parents had told her that some foreigner blown in from foreign shores, without a penny to his name, wasn't going to do. They were dealing with enough stress, enough financial problems, without her *taking up with someone who will end up being a sponge, because you*

know what these foreigners can be like... The man prob-
ably figures he's onto a good thing...

Roger was eager to join the company and he had inherited a great deal of money when his dear parents had
passed away. And hadn't they been dating? Wasn't he already like a member of the family?

Sophie had been dumbstruck as her life had been
sorted out for her.

Yes, she had known Roger for ever. Yes, he was a perfectly okay guy and, sure, they had gone out for five minutes. But *he wasn't the one for her* and she'd broken it off
even before Javier had appeared on the scene!

But her father had cried and she'd never seen her dad
in tears before.

She had been so confused, torn between the surging
power of young love and a debt of duty towards her parents.

Surely they wouldn't expect her to quit university when
she was only in her first year and loving it?

But no. She'd been able to stay on, although they hoped
that she would take over the company alongside Roger,
who would be brought on board should they cement a
union he had already intimated he was keen on.

He was three years older than her and had experience
of working for a company. He would sink money into
the company, take his place on the board of directors...

And she, Sophie had read between the lines, would
have to fulfil her obligations and walk up the aisle with
him.

She hadn't been able to credit what she had been hearing, but seeing her distraught parents, seeing their shame
at having to let her down and destroy her illusions, had
spoken so much more loudly and had said so much more
than mere words could convey.

Had Roger even known about any of these plans? Was

that why he'd been refusing to call it quits between them even though they'd been seeing one another for only less than eight months before she had left for university? Had he already been looking to a future that involved her parents' company?

She had called him, arranged to see him, and had been aghast when he had told her that he knew all about her parents' situation and was keen to do the right thing. He was in love with her, always had been...

With no one in whom to confide, Sophie had returned to university in a state of utter confusion—and Javier had been there. She had mentioned nothing but she had allowed herself to be absorbed by him. With him, she could forget everything.

Swept along on a heady tide of falling in love, the panic she had felt at what was happening on the home front had been dulled. Her parents had not mentioned the situation again and she had uneasily shoved it to the back of her mind.

No news was good news. Wasn't that what everyone said?

She surfaced from the past to find a drink in front of her and she pushed it aside.

'I've got another appointment to see the bank tomorrow,' she said. 'And we can change estate agents.'

'For the fourth time?' Oliver gave a bark of laughter and downed his drink in one gulp. 'Face it, Soph. The way things are going, we'll be in debt for the rest of our lives if we're not careful. The company is losing money. The house will never sell. The bank will take it off our hands to repay our overdraft and we'll both be left homeless. It's not even as though we have alternative accommodation to return to. We don't. You bailed university to get married and moved into the family pile with Roger. I may have stayed on to get my diploma, but by the time I got back here everything had changed and we were both in it together. Both here, both trying to make the company work...' His voice had acquired the bitter, plaintive edge Sophie had come to recognise.

She knew how this would go. He would drink away his sorrows and wake up the following morning in a blurry, sedated haze where all the problems were dulled just enough for him to get through the day.

He was, she had been forced to accept, a weak man not made for facing the sort of situation they were now facing.

And she hated that she couldn't do more for him.

He was drinking too much and she could see the train coming off the tracks if things didn't change.

Did she want that? Wasn't there too much already on her conscience?

She shut down that train of thought, shut down the deluge of unhappy memories and tried hard to focus on the few bright things in her life.

She had her health.

They might be struggling like mad trying not to drown but at least Mum was okay, nicely sorted in a cottage in Cornwall, far from the woes now afflicting herself and her brother.

It might have been a rash expenditure given the dire financial circumstances, but when Gordon Griffin-Watt had tragically died, after a brief but intense period of absolute misery and suffering, it had seemed imperative to try to help Evelyn, their mother, who was herself frail and barely able to cope. Sophie had taken every spare penny she could from the scant profits of the company and sunk it all into a cottage in Cornwall, where Evelyn's sister lived.

It had been worth it. Her mother's contentment was the brightest thing on the horizon, and if she was ignorant about the extent of the troubles afflicting her twins, then that was for her own good. Her health would never be able to stand the stress of knowing the truth: that they stood to lose everything. One of the sweetest things Gordon Griffin-Watt had done had been to allay her fears about their financial situation while dealing with his own disastrous health problems, which he had refused to tell his wife about. She had had two strokes already and he wasn't going to send her to her grave with a third one.

'Vasquez is willing to listen to what we have to say.'

'Javier won't do a thing to help us. Trust me, Ollie.' *But he would have a merry time gloating at how the mighty had fallen, that was for sure.*

'How do you know?' her brother fired back, pouring himself another drink and glaring, challenging her to give him her little lecture about staying off the booze.

'Because I just do.'

'That's where you're wrong, sis.'

'What do you mean? What are you talking about? And should you…be having a second drink when it's not yet four in the afternoon?'

'I'll stop drinking when I'm not worrying 24/7 about whether I'll have a roof over my head next week or whether I'll be begging in the streets for loose change.' He drank, refilled his glass defiantly, and Sophie stifled a sigh of despair.

'So just tell me what Javier had to say,' she said flatly. 'Because I need to go and prepare information to take with me to the bank tomorrow.'

'He wants to see you.'

'He…*what*?'

'He says he will consider helping us but he wants to discuss it with you. I thought it was pretty decent of him, actually…'

A wave of nausea rushed through her. For the first time

ever, she felt that at the unseemly hour of four in the afternoon she could do with a stiff drink.

'That won't be happening.'

'You'd rather see us both living under a bridge in London with newspapers as blankets,' Oliver said sharply, 'rather than have a twenty-minute conversation with some old flame?'

'Don't be stupid. We won't end up *living under a bridge with newspapers as blankets*...'

'It's a bloody short drop from the top to the bottom, Soph. Can take about ten minutes. We're more than halfway there.'

'I'm seeing the bank tomorrow about a loan to broaden our computer systems...'

'Good luck with that! They'll say no and we both know that. And what do you think is going to happen to that allowance we give Mum every month? Who do you think is going to support her in her old age if we go under?'

'Stop!' Never one to dodge reality, Sophie just wanted to blank it all out now. But she couldn't. The weight of their future rested on her shoulders, but Oliver...

How could he?

Because he didn't know, she thought with numb defeat. What he saw was an ex who now had money and might be willing to lend them some at a reasonable rate for old times' sake. To give them a loan because they had nowhere else to turn.

She could hardly blame him, could she?

'I told him that you'd be at his office tomorrow at six.' He extracted a crumpled piece of paper from his pocket and pushed it across the table to her.

When Sophie flattened it out, she saw that on it was a scribbled address and a mobile number. Just looking at those two links with the past she had fought to leave behind made her heart hammer inside her.

'I can't make you go and see the man, Sophie.' Oliver stood up, the bottle of whisky in one hand and his empty glass in the other. There was defeat in his eyes and it pierced her heart because he wasn't strong enough to take any of this. He needed looking after as much as their mother did. 'But if you decide to go with the bank, when they've already knocked us back in the past and when they're making noises about taking the house from us, then on your head be it. If you decide to go, he'll be waiting for you at his office.'

Alone in the kitchen, Sophie sighed and rested back in the chair, eyes closed, mind in turmoil.

She had been left without a choice. Her brother would never forgive her if she walked away from Javier and the bank ended up chucking her out. And her brother was right; the small profits the company was making were all being eaten up and it wouldn't be long before the house was devouring far more than the company could provide. It was falling down. Who in their right mind wanted to buy a country mansion that was falling down, in the middle of nowhere, when the property market was so desperate? And they couldn't afford to sell it for a song because it had been remortgaged…

Maybe he'd forgotten how things had ended, she thought uneasily.

Maybe he'd changed, mellowed. Maybe, just maybe, he really would offer them a loan at a competitive rate because of the brief past they'd shared.

Maybe he'd overlook how disastrous that brief past had ended…

At any rate, she had no choice, none at all. She would simply have to find out…

CHAPTER TWO

SOPHIE STARED UP at the statement building across the frenzied, busy street, a soaring tower of glass and chrome.

She'd never had any driving desire to live in London and the crowds of people frantically weaving past her was a timely reminder of how ill-suited she was to the fierce thrust of city life.

But neither had she ever foreseen that she would be condemned to life in the tiny village where she had grown up, out in rugged Yorkshire territory. Her parents had adored living there; they'd had friends in the village and scattered in the big country piles sitting in their individual acres of land.

She had nothing of the sort.

Having gone to boarding school from the age of thirteen, her friends were largely based in the south of England.

She lived in a collapsing mansion, with no friends at hand with whom she could share her daily woes, and that in itself reminded her why she was here.

To see Javier.

To try to pursue a loan so that she could get out of her situation.

So that she and her brother could begin to have something of a life free from daily worry.

She had to try to free herself from the terror nibbling away at the edges of her resolute intentions and look at the bigger picture.

This wasn't just some silly social visit. This was...*a business meeting.*

She licked her lips now, frozen to the spot while the crowds of people continued to swerve around her, most of them glaring impatiently. There was no time in London to dawdle, not when everyone was living life in the fast lane.

Business meeting. She rather liked that analysis because it allowed her to blank out the horrifying personal aspect to this visit.

She tried to wipe out the alarming total recall she had of his face and superimpose it with the far more manageable features of their bank manager: bland, plump, semi-balding...

Maybe he had become bland, plump and semi-balding, she thought hopefully as she reluctantly propelled herself forward, joining the throng of people clustered on the pavement, waiting for the little man in the box to turn green.

She had dressed carefully.

In fact, she wore what she had planned to wear to visit the bank manager: black knee-length skirt, crisp white blouse—which was fine in cool Yorkshire, but horribly uncomfortable now in sticky London—and flat black pumps.

She had tied her hair back and twisted it into a sensible chignon at the nape of her neck.

Her make-up was discreet and background: a touch of mascara, some pale lip gloss and the very sheerest application of blusher.

She wasn't here to try to make an impression. She was here because she'd been pushed and hounded into a corner and now had to deal with the unfortunate situation in a brisk and businesslike manner.

There was no point travelling down memory lane because that would shatter the fragile veneer of self-confidence she knew she would need for this...*meeting*.

Another word she decided she rather liked.

And, at the end of the day, Oliver was happy. For the first time in ages, his eyes had lit up and she'd felt something of that twin bond they had shared when they'd been young but which seemed to have gone into hiding as their worries had begun piling up.

She took a deep breath and was carried by the crowd to the other side of the road as the lights changed. And then she was there, right in front of the building. Entering when most of the people were heading in the opposite direction because, of course, it was home time and the stampede to enjoy what remained of the warm weather that day was in full swing.

She pushed her way through the opaque glass doors and was disgorged into the most amazing foyer she had ever seen in her entire life.

Javier, naturally, didn't *own* the building, but his company occupied four floors at the very top and it was dawning on her that when Oliver had labelled him a 'billionaire' he hadn't been exaggerating.

You would have to have some serious money at your disposal to afford to rent a place like this, and being able to afford to rent four floors would require *very* serious money.

When had all that happened?

She'd reflected on that the evening before and now, walking woodenly towards the marble counter, which at six in the evening was only partially staffed, she reflected on it again.

When she'd known him, he hadn't had a bean. Lots of

ambition, but at that point in time the ambition had not begun to be translated into money.

He had worked most evenings at the local gym in the town centre for extra cash, training people on the punching bags. If you hadn't known him to be a first-class student with a brain most people would have given their right arm for, you might have mistaken him for a fighter.

He hadn't talked much about his background but she had known that his parents were not well off, and when she had watched him in the gym, muscled, sweaty and focused, she had wondered whether he hadn't done his fair share of fighting on the streets of Madrid.

From that place, he had gone to...*this*: the most expensive office block in the country, probably in Europe... A man shielded from the public by a bank of employees paid to protect the rich from nuisance visits...

Who would have thought?

Maybe if she had followed his progress over the years, she might have been braced for all of this, but, for her, the years had disappeared in a whirlpool of stress and unhappiness.

She tilted her jaw at a combative angle and squashed the wave of maudlin self-pity threatening to wash away her resolve.

Yes, she was told, after one of the women behind the marble counter had scrolled down a list on the computer in front of her, Mr Vasquez was expecting her.

He would buzz when he was ready for her to go up.

In the meantime...she was pointed to a clutch of dove-grey sofas at the side.

Sophie wondered how long she would have to wait. Oliver had admitted that he had had to wait for absolutely ages before Javier had deigned to see him and she settled in for the long haul. So she was surprised when, five minutes later, she was beckoned over and told that she could take the private lift to the eighteenth floor.

'Usually someone would escort you up,' the blonde woman told her with a trace of curiosity and malicious envy in her voice. 'I suppose you must know Mr Vasquez…?'

'Sort of,' Sophie mumbled as the elevator doors pinged open and she stepped into a wonder of glass that reflected her neat, pristine, sensible image back at her in a mosaic of tiny, refracted detail.

And then, thankfully, the doors smoothly and quietly shut and she was whizzing upwards, heart in her mouth, feeling as though she was about to step into the lion's den…

She was on her way up.

Javier had never been prone to nerves, but he would now confess to a certain tightening in his chest at the prospect of seeing her in a matter of minutes.

Of course he had known, from the second her brother had entered his offices with a begging bowl in his hand, that he would see Sophie once again.

As surely as night followed day, when it came to money, pride was the first thing to be sacrificed.

And they needed money. Badly. In fact, far more badly than Oliver had intimated. As soon as he had left, Javier had called up the company records for the family firm and discovered that it was in the process of free fall. Give it six months and it would crash-land and splinter into a thousand fragments.

He smiled slowly and pushed his chair back. He linked his fingers loosely together and toyed with the pleasurable thought of how he would play this meeting.

He knew what he wanted, naturally.

That had come as a bit of a surprise because he had

truly thought that he had put that unfortunate slice of his past behind him, but apparently he hadn't.

Because the very second Oliver had opened his mouth to launch into his plaintive, begging speech, Javier had known what he wanted and how he would get it.

He wanted *her*.

She was the only unfinished business in his life and he hadn't realised how much that had preyed on his mind until now, until the opportunity to finish that business had been presented to him on a silver platter.

He'd never slept with her.

She'd strung him along for a bit of fun, maybe because she'd liked having those tittering, upper-class friends of hers oohing and aahing with envy because she'd managed to attract the attention of the good-looking bad boy.

Didn't they say that about rich, spoilt girls—that they were always drawn to a bit of rough because it gave them an illicit thrill?

Naturally, they would never *marry* the bit of rough. That would be unthinkable!

Javier's lips thinned as he recalled the narrative of their brief relationship.

He remembered the way she had played with him, teasing him with a beguiling mixture of innocence and guileless, sensual temptation. She had let him touch but he hadn't been able to relish the full meal. He'd been confined to starters when he had wanted to devour all courses, including dessert.

He'd reached the point of wanting to ask her to marry him. He'd been offered the New York posting and he'd wanted her by his side. He'd hinted, saying a bit, dancing around the subject, but strangely for him had been too awkward to put all his cards on the table. Yet she must have suspected that a marriage proposal was on the cards.

Just thinking about it now, his insane stupidity, made

him clench his teeth together with barely suppressed anger.

She was the only woman who had got to him and the only one who had escaped him.

He forced himself to relax, to breathe slowly, to release the cold bitterness that had very quickly risen to the surface now that he knew that he would be seeing her in a matter of minutes.

The woman who had…yes…*hurt him*.

The woman who had used him as a bit of fun, making sure that she didn't get involved, saving herself for one of those posh, upper-class idiots who formed part of her tight little circle.

He was immune to being hurt now because he was older and more experienced. His life was rigidly controlled. He knew what he wanted and he got what he wanted, and what he wanted was the sort of financial security that would be immune to the winds of change. It was all that mattered and the only thing that mattered.

Women were a necessary outlet and he enjoyed them but they didn't interrupt the focus of his unwavering ambition. They were like satellites bobbing around the main planet.

Had he only had this level of control within his grasp when he'd met Sophie all those years ago, he might not have fallen for her, but there was no point in crying over spilt milk. The past could not be altered.

Which wasn't to say that there couldn't be retribution…

He *sensed* her even before he was aware of the hesitant knock on the door.

He had given his secretary the afternoon off. He'd been in meetings all afternoon, had returned to his offices only an hour previously, and something in him wanted to see Sophie without the presence of his secretary around.

He had brought Eva back with him from New York.

A widow in her sixties, originally from the UK anyway with all her family living here, she had been only too glad to accompany him back to London. She could be trusted not to gossip, but even so...

Seeing Sophie after all this time felt curiously *intimate*.

Which was something of a joke because *intimacy* implied some level of romance, of two people actually wanting to be in one another's company...

Hardly the case here.

Although, if truth be told, he was almost *looking forward* to seeing the woman again, whilst she...

He settled back in his leather chair and mused that *he* was probably the last person in the world *she* wanted to see.

But needs must...

'Enter.'

The deep, controlled tenor of that familiar voice chilled Sophie to the bone. She took a deep breath and nervously turned the handle before pushing open the door to the splendid office which, in her peripheral vision, was as dauntingly sophisticated as she had mentally predicted.

She had hoped that the years might have wrought changes in him, maybe even that her memory might have played tricks on her. She had prayed that he was no longer the hard-edged, proud, *dangerous* guy she had once known but, instead, a mellow man with room in his heart for forgiveness.

She'd been an idiot.

He was as *dangerous* as she remembered. More so. She stared and kept on staring at the familiar yet unfamiliar angles of his sinfully beautiful face. He'd always been incredibly good-looking, staggeringly exotic with finely chiselled features and lazy dark eyes with the longest eyelashes she had ever seen on a guy.

He was as sinfully good-looking as he had been then,

but now there was a cool self-possession about him that spoke of the tough road he had walked to get to the very top. His dark, dark eyes were watchful and inscrutable as she finally dragged her mesmerised gaze away from him and made her way forward with the grace and suppleness of a broken puppet.

And then, when she reached the chair in front of his desk, it dawned on her that she hadn't been invited to sit down, so she remained hovering with one hand on the back of the chair, waiting in tense, electric silence...

'Why don't you sit down, Sophie?'

He looked at her, enjoying the hectic colour in her cheeks, enjoying the fact that she was standing on shaky legs in front of him, in the role of supplicant.

And he was enjoying a hell of a lot more than that, he freely admitted to himself...

She was even more beautiful than the image he had stored in his mind carefully, as he had discovered, wrapped in tissue paper, waiting for the day when the tissue paper would be removed.

He couldn't see how long or short her hair was but it was still the vibrant tangle of colour it had been when he had first met her. Chestnut interweaved with copper with strands of strawberry blonde threaded through in a colourful display of natural highlights.

And she hadn't put on an ounce over the years. Indeed, she looked slimmer than ever. Gaunt, even, with smudges of strain showing under her violet eyes.

Financial stress would do that to a person, he thought, especially a person who had been brought up to expect the finest things in life.

But for all that she was as beautiful as he remembered, with that elusive quality of hesitancy that had first attracted him to her. She looked like a model, leggy, rangy and startlingly pretty, but she lacked the hard edges of someone with model looks and that was a powerful source of attraction. She had always seemed to be ever so slightly puzzled when guys spun round to stare at her.

Complete act, he now realised. Just one of the many things about her that had roped him in, one of the many things that had been fake.

'So...' he drawled, relaxing back in his chair. 'Where to begin? Such a long time since we last saw one another...'

Sophie was fast realising that there was going to be no loan. He had requested an audience with her *because he could*, because he had *known* that she would be unable to refuse. He had asked to see her so that he could send her away with a flea in her ear over how he thought he had been treated by her the last time they had been together.

She was sitting here in front of him simply because revenge was a dish best served cold.

She cleared her throat, back ramrod-straight, hands clutching the bag on her lap, a leftover designer relic back from the good old days when money, apparently, had been no object.

'My brother informs me that you might be amenable to providing us with a loan.' She didn't want to go down memory lane and, since this was a business meeting, why not cut to the chase? He wasn't going to lend them the money anyway, so what was the point of prolonging the agony?

Though there was some rebellious part of her that was compelled to steal glances at the man who had once held her heart captive in his hand.

He was still so beautiful. A wave of memories washed over her and she seemed to see, in front of her, the guy who could make her laugh, who could make her tingle all over whenever he rested his eyes on her; the guy who had lusted after her and had pursued her with the sort of intent and passion she had never experienced in her life before.

She blinked; the image was gone and she was back in the present, cringing as he continued to assess her with utterly cool detachment.

'Tut-tut-tut, Sophie. Don't tell me that you seriously expected to walk into my office and find yourself presented with a loan arrangement all ready and waiting for you to sign, before disappearing back to…remind where it is… the wilds of Yorkshire?' He shook his head with rueful incredulity, as though chastising her for being a complete moron. 'I think we should at least relax and chat a bit before we begin discussing…*money*…'

Sophie wondered whether this meant that he would actually agree to lend them the money they so desperately needed.

'I would offer you coffee or tea, but my secretary has gone for the day. I can, of course…' He levered himself out of the chair and Sophie noted the length and muscularity of his body.

He had been lean and menacing years ago, with the sort of physical strength that can only be thinly hidden behind clothes. He was just as menacing now, more so because he now wielded power, and a great deal of it.

She watched as he made his way over to a bar, which she now noticed at the far side of his office, in a separate, airy room which overlooked the streets below on two sides.

It was an obscenely luxurious office suite. All that was missing was a bed.

Heat stung her cheeks and she licked her lips nervously. For all she knew, he was married with a couple of kids, even though he didn't look it. He certainly would have a woman tucked away somewhere.

'Have a drink with me, Sophie…'

'I'd rather not.'

'Why not?'

'Because…' Her voice trailed off and she noted that he had ignored her completely and was now strolling towards her with a glass of wine in his hand.

'Because…what?' Instead of returning to his chair, he perched on the edge of his desk and looked down at her with his head tilted to one side.

'Why don't you just lay into me and get it over and done with?' she muttered, taking the drink from him and nursing the glass. She stared up at him defiantly, her violet eyes clashing with his unreadable, dark-as-night ones. 'I knew I shouldn't have come here.'

'Lay into you?' Javier queried smoothly. He shrugged. 'Things happen and relationships bite the dust. We were young. It's no big deal.'

'Yes,' Sophie agreed uneasily.

'So your brother tells me that you are now a widow…'

'Roger died in an accident three years ago.'

'Tragic. You must have been heartbroken.'

'It's always tragic when someone is snatched away in the prime of their life.' She ignored the sarcasm in his voice; she certainly wasn't going to pretend to play the part of heartbroken widow when her marriage had been a sham from beginning to end. 'And perhaps you don't know but my father is also no longer with us. I'm not sure if Ollie told you, but he suffered a brain tumour towards the end. So life, you see, has been very challenging, for me and my brother, but I'm sure you must have guessed that the minute he showed up here.' She lowered her eyes and then nervously sipped some of the wine before resting the glass on the desk.

She wanted to ask whether it was okay to do that or whether he should get a coaster or something.

But then, really rich people never worried about silly little things like wine glass ring-marks on their expensive wooden desks, did they?

'You have my sympathies.' Less sincere condolences had seldom been spoken. 'And your mother?'

'She lives in Cornwall now. We...we bought her a little cottage there so that she could be far from... Well, her health has been poor and the sea air does her good... And you?'

'What about me?' Javier frowned, eased himself off the desk and returned to where he had been sitting.

'Have you married? Got children?' The artificiality of the situation threatened to bring on a bout of manic laughter. It was surreal, sitting here making small talk with a guy who probably hated her guts, even though, thankfully, she had not been subjected to the sort of blistering attack she had been fearing.

At least, not yet.

At any rate, she could always walk out...although he had dangled that carrot in front of her, intimated that he would indeed be willing to discuss the terms and conditions of helping them. Could she seriously afford to let her pride come in the way of some sort of solution to their problems?

If she had been the only one affected, then yes, but there was her brother, her mother, those faithful employees left working, through loyalty, for poor salaries in the ever-shrinking family business.

'This isn't about me,' Javier fielded silkily. 'Although, in answer to your question, I have reached the conclusion that women, as a long-term proposition, have no place in my life at this point in time. So, times have changed for you,' he murmured, moving on with the conversation. He reached into his drawer and extracted a sheet of paper, which he swivelled so that it was facing her.

'Your company accounts. From riches to rags in the space of a few years, although, if you look carefully, you'll see that the company has been mismanaged for somewhat longer than a handful of years. Your dearly departed husband seems to have failed to live up to whatever promise there was that an injection of cash would rescue your family's business. I take it you were too busy playing the good little wife to notice that he had been blowing vast sums of money on pointless ventures that all crashed and burned?'

Sophie stared at the paper, feeling as though she had been stripped naked and made to stand in front of him for inspection.

'I knew,' she said abruptly. *Playing the good little wife?* How wrong could he have been?

'You ditched your degree course to rush into marriage with a man who blew the money on…oh, let's have a look…transport options for sustainable farmers…a wind farm that came to nothing…several aborted ventures into the property market…a sports centre which was built and then left to rot because the appropriate planning permission hadn't been provided… All the time your father's once profitable transport business was haemorrhaging money by the bucketload. And you knew…'

'There was nothing I could do,' Sophie said tightly, loathing him even though she knew that, if he were to lend them any money, he would obviously have to know exactly what he was getting into.

'Did you know where else your husband was blowing his money, to the tune of several hundred thousand?'

Perspiration broke out in a fine, prickly film and she stared at him mutinously.

'Why are you doing this?'

'Doing what?'

'Hanging me out to dry? If you don't want to help, then please just say so and I'll leave and you'll never see me again.'

'Fine.' Javier sat back and watched her.

She had never lain spread across his bed. He had never seen that hair in all its glory across his pillows. He had felt those ripe, firm breasts, but through prudish layers of clothes. He had never tasted them. Had never even *seen* them. Before he'd been able to do any of that, before he'd been able to realise the powerful thrust of his passion and his *yearning*, she had walked away from him. Walked straight up to the altar and into the arms of some little twerp whose very existence she had failed to mention in the months that they had been supposedly going out.

He had a sudden vision of her lying on his bed in the penthouse apartment, just one of several he owned in the capital. It was a blindingly clear vision and his erection was as fast as it was shocking. He had to breathe deeply and evenly in an attempt to dispel the unsettling and un-welcome image that had taken up residence in his head.

'Not going to walk out?' Javier barely recognised the raw lack of self-control that seemed to be guiding his re-sponses.

He'd wanted to see her squirm but the force of his an-tipathy took him by surprise because he was realising just how fast and tight she had stuck to him over the years.

Unfinished business. That was why. Well, he would make sure he finished it if it was the last thing he did and then he would be free of the woman and whatever useless part of his make-up she still appeared to occupy.

'He gambled.' Sophie raised her eyes to his and held his stare in silence before looking away, offering him her averted profile.

'And you knew about that as well,' Javier had a fleet-ing twinge of regret that he had mentioned any of this. It had been unnecessary. Then he remembered the way she had summarily dumped him and all fleeting regret van-ished in a puff of smoke.

She nodded mutely.

'And there was nothing you could have done about that either?'

'I don't suppose you've ever lived with someone who has a destructive addiction?' she said tightly. 'You can't just sit them down for a pep talk and then expect them to change overnight.'

'But you *can* send them firmly in the direction of professional help.' Javier was curious. The picture he had built of her had been one of the happily married young wife, in love with Prince Charming, so in love that she had not been able to abide being away from him whilst at university—perhaps hoping that the distraction of an unsuitable foreigner might put things into perspective, only for that gambit to hit the rocks.

Then, when he had inspected the accounts closely, he had assumed that, blindly in love, she had been ignorant of her loser husband's uncontrolled behaviour.

Now...

He didn't want curiosity to mar the purity of what he wanted from her and he was taken aback that it was.

'Roger was an adult. He didn't want help. I wasn't capable of manhandling him into a car and driving him to the local association for gambling addicts. And I don't want to talk about...about my marriage. I... It's in the past.'

'So it is,' Javier murmured. When he thought about the other man, he saw red, pure jealousy at being deprived of what he thought should have been his.

Crazy.

Since when had he considered any woman *his possession*?

'And yet,' he mused softly, 'when is the past ever *really* behind us? Don't you find that it dogs us like a guilty conscience, even when we would like to put it to bed for good?'

'What do you mean?'

'You ran out on me.'

'Javier, you don't *understand...*'

'Nor do I wish to. This isn't about understanding what motivated you.' And at this point in time—this very special point in time when the tables had been reversed, when she was now the one without money and he the one with the bank notes piled up in the coffers—well, she was hardly going to tell the whole truth and nothing but the truth when it came to motivations, was she? Oh, no, she would concoct some pretty little tale to try to elicit as much sympathy from him as she could...

'I'm not asking you to give me money, Javier. I...I'm just asking for a loan. I would pay it all back, every penny of it.'

Javier flung back his head and laughed, a rich, full-bodied laugh that managed to lack genuine warmth. 'Really? I'm tickled pink at the thought of a Classics scholar, almost there but never graduated, and her sports scholarship brother running any company successfully enough to make it pay dividends, never mind a company that's on its last legs.'

'There *are* directors in the company...'

'Looked at them. I would ditch most of them if I were you.'

'You *looked at them*?'

Javier shrugged. His dark eyes never left her face. 'I probably know more about your company than you do. Why not? If I'm to sink money into it, then I need to know exactly what I will be sinking money into.'

'So...are you saying that you'll help?'

'I'll help.' He smiled slowly. 'But there's no such thing as a free lunch. There will be terms and conditions...'

'That's fine.' For the first time in a very long time, a cloud seemed to be lifting. She had underestimated him. He was going to help and she wanted to sob with relief. 'Whatever your terms and conditions, well, they won't be a problem. I promise.'

CHAPTER THREE

'PERHAPS WE SHOULD take this conversation somewhere else.'

'Why?' The suggestion of leaving with him for *somewhere else* sent little shivers of alarm skittering through her.She could scarcely credit that she was sitting here, in this office, facing this man who had haunted her for years. All the things that had happened ever since that first tentative step as a young girl falling hopelessly in love with an unsuitable boy lay between them like a great, big, murky chasm.

There was just so much he didn't know.

But none of that was relevant. What was relevant was that he was going to help them and that was enough.

'Because,' Javier drawled, rising to his feet and strolling to fetch his jacket from where it lay slung over the back of one of the expensive, compact sofas in the little sitting area of the office, 'I feel that two old friends should not be discussing something as crass as a business bailout within the confines of an office.'

Two old friends?

Sophie scrutinised the harsh angles of his face for any inherent sarcasm and he returned her stare with bland politeness.

But his bland politeness made her feel unaccountably uneasy.

He'd never been polite.

At least, not in the way that English people were polite. Not in the middle-class way of clinking teacups and saying the right things, which was the way she had been brought up.

He had always spoken his mind and damned the consequences. She had occasionally seen him in action at university, once in the company of two of his lecturers, when they had been discussing economics.

He had listened to them, which had been the accepted polite way, but had then taken their arguments and ripped them to shreds. The breadth and depth of his knowledge had been so staggering that there had been no comeback.

He had never been scared of rocking the boat. Sometimes, she wondered whether he had privately relished it, although when she'd once asked him that directly, he had burst out laughing before kissing her senseless—at which point she had forgotten what she had been saying to him. Kissing him had always had that effect on her.

A surge of memories brought a hectic flush to her cheeks.

'Is this your new way of dressing?' he asked and Sophie blinked, dispelling disturbing images of when they had been an item.

'What do you mean?'

'You look like an office worker.'

'That's exactly what I am,' she returned lightly, following him to the door, because what else could she do? At this point, he held all the trump cards, and if he wanted to go and have their business chat sitting on bar stools in the middle of Threadneedle Street, then so be it. There was too much at stake for her to start digging her heels in and telling him that she felt more comfortable discussing business in an office.

She had come this far and there was no turning back now.

This floor was a sanctum of quiet. It was occupied by CEOs and directors, most of whom were concealed behind opaque glass and thick doors. In the middle there was a huge, open-plan space in which desks were cleverly positioned to allow for maximum space utilisation and minimum scope for chatting aimlessly.

The open space was largely empty, except for a couple of diligent employees who were too absorbed in whatever they were doing to look up at them as they headed for the directors' lift.

'But it's not exactly where you wanted to end up, is it?' he asked as the lift doors quietly closed, sealing them in together.

It didn't matter where she looked, reflections of him bounced back at her.

She shrugged and reluctantly met his dark eyes.

'You don't always end up where you think you're going to,' she said tersely.

'You had big plans to be a university lecturer.'

'Life got in the way of that.'

'I'm sure your dearly departed husband wouldn't like to be seen as someone who got in the way of your big plans.'

'I don't want to talk about Roger.'

Because the thought of him no longer being around was still too painful for her to bear. That thought struck Javier with dagger-like precision. The man might have been a waste of space when it came to business, and an inveterate gambler who had blown vast sums of money that should have been pumped into saving the company, yet she had loved him and now would have nothing said against him.

Javier's lips thinned.

He noted the way she scurried out of the lift, desperate to put some physical distance between them.

'When did you find out that the company was on the brink of going bust?'

Sophie cringed. She wanted to ask whether it was really necessary to go down that road and she knew that she had to divorce the past from the present. He wasn't the guy she had loved to death, the guy she had been forced to give up when life as she knew it had suddenly stopped. That was in the past and right now she was in the company of someone thinking about extending credit to the company. He would want details even if she didn't want to give them.

But there was a lot she didn't want to tell him. She didn't want his contempt or his pity and she knew she would have both if she presented him with the unadorned truth. That was if he believed her at all, which was doubtful.

'I knew things weren't too good a while back,' she said evasively. 'But I had no idea really of just how bad they were until...well, until I got married. '

Javier felt the dull, steady beat of jealousy working its poisonous way through his body.

He was painfully reminded of the folly of his youth, the naivety of imagining that they would have a future together. The poor foreigner working his way up and the beautiful, well-spoken, impeccably bred English girl who just so happened to be the apple of her father's adoring and protective eye.

At the time, he had thought himself to be as hard as nails and immune to distraction.

He'd set his course and he had been cocky enough to imagine that no ill winds would come along to blow him off target.

Of all the girls on the planet, he had found himself blown off target by one who had set her course on some- one else and had been playing with him for a bit of fun, stringing him along while her heart belonged to some- one else.

'And then...what?'

'What do you mean?' She nervously played with her finger, where once upon an unhappy time there had been a wedding ring.

She hadn't paid much attention to where they were going, but when he stood back to push open a door for her, she saw that they were at an old pub, the sort of pub that populated the heart of the City.

She shimmied past him, ducking under his outstretched arm as he held the door open for her. She was tall at five foot ten, but he was several inches taller and she had a memory of how protected he had always made her feel. The clean, masculine scent of him lingered in her nostrils, making her feel shaky as she sat down at a table in the corner, waiting tensely while he went to get them some- thing to drink. She knew she should keep a clear head and drink water but her nerves were all over the place. They needed something a little stronger than water.

Outside it was hot and she could glimpse a packed garden but in here it was cool, dark and relatively empty.

The sun worshippers were all drinking in the evening sun.

Trying to elicit details about her past was not relevant. Javier knew that and he was furious with himself for suc- cumbing to the desire to know more.

Just like that, in a matter of minutes, she had managed to stoke his curiosity. Just like that, she was back under his skin and he couldn't wait to have her, to bed her, so that he could rid himself of the uncomfortable suspicion that she had been there all along, a spectre biding its time until it could resurface to catch him on the back foot.

For a man to whom absolute control was vital, this slither of susceptibility was unwelcome.

He realised that when he tried to think of the last woman he had slept with, a top-notch career woman in New York with legs to her armpits, he came up blank. He couldn't focus on anyone but the woman sitting in front of him, looking at him as though she expected him to pounce unexpectedly at any minute.

She had the clearest violet eyes he had ever seen, fringed with long, dark lashes, and the tilt of them gave her a slightly dreamy look, as though a part of her was on another plane. He itched to unpin her neat little bun so that he could see whether that glorious hair of hers was still as long, still as unruly.

'Well?' Javier demanded impatiently, hooking a chair with his foot and angling it so that he could sit with his long legs extended. He had brought a wine cooler with a bottle of wine and one of the bartenders placed two glasses in front of them, then simpered for a few seconds, doe-eyed, before reluctantly walking back to the bar.

'Well...what?'

'What was the order of events? Heady marriage, fairy-tale honeymoon and then, lo and behold, no more money? Life can be cruel. And where was your brother when all this was happening?'

'In America.' She sighed.

'By choice, even though he knew?' With the family company haemorrhaging money, surely it would have been an indulgence for Oliver to have stayed in California, enjoying himself...

'He didn't know,' Sophie said abruptly. 'And I don't know why...how all this is relevant.'

'I'm fleshing out the picture,' Javier said softly. 'You've

come to me with a begging bowl. What did you think I was going to do? Give you a big, comforting hug and write out a cheque?'

'No, but…'

'Let's get one thing straight here, Sophie.' He leant forward and held her gaze. She couldn't have said a word even if she had wanted to. She could hardly breathe. 'You're here to ask a favour of me and, that being the case, whether you like it or not, you don't get to choose what questions to answer and what questions to ignore. Your private life is your business. Frankly, I don't give a damn. But I need to know your levels of capability when it comes to doing business. I need to know whether your brother is committed to working for the company, because if he was left to enjoy four years of playing sport in California, then I'm guessing he wouldn't have returned to the sick fold with a cheerful whistle. Most of the directors of the company aren't worth the money they're being paid.'

'You know how much they're being paid!'

'I know everything worth knowing about your crippled family company.'

'When did you get so…so…*hard*?'

Roughly around the same time I discovered what sort of woman I'd been going out with, Javier thought with the sour taste of cynicism in his mouth.

He leant back and crossed his legs, lightly cradling the stem of the wine glass between his long fingers.

'You don't make money by being a sap for sob stories,' he informed her coolly, keen eyes taking in the delicate bloom of colour in her cheeks. 'You've come to me with a sob story.' He shrugged. 'And the bottom line is this—if you don't like the direction this conversation is going, then, like I said before, you're free to go. But of course, we both know you won't, because you need me.'

He was enjoying this little game of going round the houses before he laid all his cards on the table, before she knew exactly what the terms and conditions of her repayment would be.

It wouldn't hurt her to realise just how dangerously close the company was to imploding.

It wouldn't hurt her to realise just how much she needed him...

'If you knew about your husband's hare-brained schemes and addiction to gambling, and you allowed it to go under the radar, then are you a trustworthy person to stand at the helm of your company?'

'I told you that there was nothing I could do,' she said with a dull flush.

'And if your brother was so clueless as to what was happening on the home front, then is *he* competent enough to do what would need to be done should I decide to help you out?'

'Ollie...doesn't have a huge amount of input in the actual running of things...'

'Why?'

'Because he's never been interested in the company and, yes, you're right—he's always resented the fact that he had to finally return to help out. He's found it difficult to deal with not having money.'

'And you've found it easy?'

'I've dealt with it.'

Javier looked at her narrowly and with a certain amount of reluctant admiration for the streak of strength he glimpsed.

Not only had she had to face a tremendous fall from the top of the mountain, but the loss of her husband and the father she had adored.

Yet there was no self-pity in the stubborn tilt of her chin.

'You've had a lot to deal with, haven't you?' he murmured softly and she looked away.

'I'm no different from loads of people the world over who have found their lives changed in one way or another. And, now that you've got the measure of the company, will you lend us some money or not? I don't know if my brother told you, but the family house has been on the market for over two years and we just can't seem to sell it. There's no appetite for big houses. If we could sell it, then we might be able to cover some of the expenses...'

'Although a second mortgage was taken out on it...'

'Yes, but the proceeds would go a little way to at least fixing certain things that need urgent attention.'

'The dated computer systems, for example?'

'You really did your homework, didn't you? How did you manage that in such a small amount of time? Or have you been following my father's company over the years? Watching while it went downhill?'

'Why would I have done that?'

Sophie shrugged uncomfortably. 'I know you probably feel... Well, you don't understand what happened all those years ago.'

'Don't presume to think that you know what goes on in my head, Sophie. You don't. And, in answer to your preposterous question, I haven't had the slightest clue what was going on in your father's company over the years, nor have I cared one way or the other.' He saw that the bottle was empty and debated whether or not to get another, deciding against it, because he wanted them both to have clear heads for this conversation.

When he knew that he would be seeing her, he had predicted how he would react and it hadn't been like this.

He'd thought that he would see her and would feel nothing but the acid, bilious taste of bitterness for having been played in the past and taken for a chump.

He'd accepted that she'd been in his head more than he'd ever imagined possible. A Pandora's box had been opened with her brother's unexpected appearance at his office. Javier had recognised the opportunity he had been given to put an end to her nagging presence, which, he now realised, had been embedded in him like a virus he'd never managed to shake off.

He would have her and he had the means to do so at his disposal.

She needed money. He had vast sums of it. She would take what was offered because she would have no choice. His *terms and conditions* would be met with acquiescence because, as he had learned over the years, money talked.

He had slept with some of the world's most desirable women. It had followed that whatever she had that had held him captive all those years ago, she would lose it when he saw her in the flesh once again. How could she compete with some of the women who had clamoured to sleep with him?

He'd been wrong.

And that was unbelievably frustrating because he was beginning to realise that he wanted a lot more from her than her body for a night or two.

No, he *needed* a lot more from her than her body for a night or two.

He wanted and needed *answers* and his curiosity to pry beneath the surface enraged him because he had thought himself above that particular sentiment when it came to her.

Nor, he was discovering, did he want to take what he knew she would have no choice but to give him in the manner of a marauding plunderer.

He didn't want her reluctance.

He wanted her to come to him and in the end, he reasoned now, if revenge was what he was after, then wouldn't that be the ultimate revenge? To have her want him, to take her and then to walk away?

The logical part of his brain knew that to want revenge was to succumb to a certain type of weakness, and yet the pull was so immensely strong that he could no more fight it than he could have climbed Mount Everest in bare feet.

And he was enjoying this.

His palate had become jaded and that was something he had recognised a while back, when he had made his first few million and the world had begun to spread itself out at his feet.

He had reached a place in life where he could have whatever he wanted and sometimes having everything at your fingertips removed the glory of the chase. Not just women, but deals, mergers, money…the lot.

She wasn't at his fingertips.

In fact, she was simmering with resentment that she had been put in the unfortunate position of having to come to him, cap in hand, to ask for his help.

He was a part of her past that she would rather have swept under the carpet and left there. He was even forced to swallow the unsavoury truth that he was probably a part of her past she bitterly regretted ever having gone anywhere near in the first place.

But she'd wanted him.

That much he felt he knew. She might have played with him as a distraction from the main event happening in her life somewhere else, or maybe just to show off in front of her friends that she had netted the biggest fish in the sea—which Javier had known, without a trace of vanity, he was.

But perhaps she hadn't actually banked on the flare of physical attraction that had erupted between them. She had held out against him and he had seen that as shyness, youthful nerves at taking the plunge… He'd been charmed by it. He'd also been wrong about it, as it turned out. She'd held out against him because there had been someone else in her life.

But she'd still fancied him like hell.

She'd trembled when he'd traced his finger across her collarbone and her eyes had darkened when their lips had touched. He hadn't imagined those reactions. She might have successfully fought that attraction in the end and scurried back to her comfort zone, but, for a brief window, he'd taken her out of that comfort zone...

Did she imagine that she was now immune to that physical attraction because time had passed?

He played with the thought of her opening up to him like a flower and this time giving him what he had wanted all those years ago. What he wanted now.

He wondered what she would feel when she found herself discarded.

He wondered whether he would really care or whether the mere fact that he had had her would be sufficient.

He hadn't felt this *alive* in a long time and it was bloody great.

'I was surprised when your brother showed up on my doorstep, so to speak, in search of help.'

'I hope you know that I never asked him to come to see you.'

'I can well imagine, Sophie. It must cut to the quick having to beg favours from a man who wasn't good enough for you seven years ago.'

'That's not how it was.'

Javier held up one hand. 'But, as it happens, to see you evicted and in the poorhouse would not play well on my conscience.'

'That's a bit of an exaggeration, don't you think?'

'You'd be surprised how thin the dividing line is between the poor and the rich and how fast places can be swapped. One minute you're on top of the world, the ruler of everything around you, and the next minute you're lying on the scrap heap, wondering what went wrong. Or I could put it another way—one minute you're flying upwards, knocking back all those less fortunate cluttering your path, and the next minute you're spiralling downwards and the people you've knocked back are on their way up, having the last laugh.'

'I bet your parents are really sad at the person you've become, Javier.'

Javier flushed darkly, outraged at her remark, and even more outraged by the disappointed expression on her lovely face.

Of course, in those heady days of thinking she was his, he had let her into his world, haltingly confided in her in a way he had never done with any woman either before or since. He had told her about his background, about his parents' determination to make sure he left that life behind. He had painted an unadorned picture of life as he had known it, had been amused at the vast differences between them, had seen those differences as a good thing, rather than an unsurmountable barrier, as she had. If she'd even thought about it at all.

'I know you've become richer than your wildest dreams.' She smiled ruefully at him. 'And you always had very, very wild dreams...'

The conversation seemed to have broken its leash and was racing away in a direction Javier didn't like. He frowned heavily at her.

'And now here we are.'

'You once told me that all your parents wanted was for you to be happy, to make something of your life, to settle down and have a big family.'

Javier decided that he needed another drink after all.

He stood up abruptly, which seemed to do the trick, because she started, blinked and looked up at him as if suddenly remembering that she wasn't here for a trip down memory lane. Indeed, that a trip down memory lane was the very last thing she had wanted.

He'd forgotten that habit of hers.

He was barely aware of placing his order for another bottle of wine at the bar and ordering some bar snacks because they were now both drinking on fairly empty stomachs. He hadn't a clue what bar snacks he ordered, leaving it to the guy serving him to provide whatever was on the menu.

She was filling up his head. He could feel her eyes on him even as he stood here at the bar with his back to her.

Whatever memories he'd had of her, whatever memories he'd kidded himself he'd got rid of and had buried, he was now finding in a very shallow grave.

She'd always had that habit of branching out on a tangent. It was as if a stray word could spark some improbable connection in her head and carry her away down unforeseen paths.

There were no unforeseen paths in this scenario, he thought grimly as he made his way back to the table, where she was sitting with the guarded expression back on her face.

The only unforeseen thing—and it was something he could deal with—was how much he still wanted her after all this time.

'I should be getting back,' she said as he poured her a glass of wine and nodded to her to drink.

'I've ordered food.'

'My ticket...'

'Forget about your ticket.'

'I can't do that.'

'Why not?'

'Because I'm not made of money. In fact, I'm broke. There. Are you satisfied that I've said that? I can't afford to kiss sweet goodbye to the cost of the ticket to get me down here to London. You've probably forgotten how much train tickets cost, but if you'd like a reminder, I can show you mine. They cost a lot. And if you want to do a bit more gloating, then go right ahead.' She fluttered her hand wearily. 'I can't stop you.'

'You'll need to pare down the staff.'

'I beg your pardon?'

'The company is top-heavy. Too many chiefs and very few Indians.'

Sophie nodded. It was what she had privately thought but the thought of sitting down old friends of her parents and handing them their marching orders had been just too much to contemplate. Oliver couldn't have done that in a million years and, although she was a heck of a lot more switched on than he was, the prospect of sacking old retainers, even fairly ineffective old retainers, still stuck in her throat.

Few enough people had stuck by them through thin times.

'And you need to drag the business into this century. The old-fashioned transport business needs to be updated. You need to take risks, to branch out, to try to capture smaller, more profitable markets instead of sticking to having lumbering dinosaurs doing cross-Channel deliveries. That's all well and good but you need a lot more than that if your company is to be rescued from the quicksand.'

'I…' She quailed at the thought of herself and Oliver, along with a handful of maybe or maybe not efficient directors, undertaking a job of those proportions.

'You and your brother are incapable of taking on this challenge,' Javier told her bluntly and she glared at him even though he had merely spoken aloud what she had been thinking.

'I'm sure if you agree to extend a loan,' she muttered, 'we can recruit good people who are capable of—'

'Not going to happen. If I sink money into that business of yours, I want to be certain that I won't be throwing my money into a black hole.'

'That's a bit unfair.' She fiddled with the bun which, instead of making her feel blessedly cool in the scorching temperatures, was making her sweaty and uncomfortable. As were the formal, scratchy clothes, so unlike her normal dress code of jeans, tee shirts and sneakers.

She didn't feel like the brisk, efficient potential client of someone who might want to extend a loan. She felt awkward, gauche and way too aware of the man looking at her narrowly, sizing her up in a way that made her want to squirm.

This wasn't the guy she had known and loved. He hadn't chucked her out of his office but, as far as feelings went, there was nothing there. There wasn't a trace of that simmering attraction that had held them both mesmerised captives all those years ago. He wasn't married but she wondered whether there was a woman in his life, someone rich and beautiful like him.

Even when he'd had no money, he could have had any woman he wanted.

Her mind boggled at the thought of how many women would now fall at his feet because he was the guy who had the full package.

A treacherous thought snaked into her head...

What if she'd defied her parents? What if she'd carried on seeing Javier? Had seen where that love might have taken them both?

It wouldn't have worked.

Despite the fact that she had grown up with money,

had had a rich and pampered life, money per se was not what motivated her. For Javier, it was the only thing that motivated him.

She looked at him from under her lashes, taking in the cut of his clothes, the hand-tailored shoes, the mega-expensive watch around which dark hair curled. He *breathed* wealth. It was what made him happy and made sense of his life.

She might be stressed out because of all the financial worries happening in her life, but if those worries were removed and she was given a clean slate, then she knew that she wouldn't really care if that slate was a rich slate or not.

So, if she'd stayed with him, she certainly wouldn't have been the sort of woman he'd have wanted. She might talk the talk but her jeans, tee shirts and sneakers would not have been found acceptable attire.

They'd had their moment in time when they'd both been jeans and tee shirts people but he'd moved on, and he would always have moved on.

The attraction, for him, would have dimmed and finally been snuffed out.

The road she'd taken had been tough and miserable and, as things had turned out, the wrong one. But it would be silly to think that she would have been any happier if she'd followed Javier and held the hand he'd extended.

'We can go round the houses discussing what's fair and what's unfair,' he said in a hard voice. 'But that won't get us anywhere. I'm prepared to sink money in, but I get a cut of the cake and you abide by my rules.'

'Your rules?' She looked at him in bewilderment.

'Did you really think I'd write a cheque and then keep my fingers crossed that you might know what to do with the money?' He'd had one plan when this situation had first arisen—it had been clean and simple—but now he didn't want clean and simple. He needed to get more immersed in the water...and he was looking forward to that.

'I will, to spell it out, want a percentage of your business. There's no point my waiting for the time when you can repay me. I already have more money than I can shake a stick at, but I could put your business to some good use, branch out in ways that might dovetail with some of my other business concerns.'

Sophie shifted, not liking the sound of this. If he wanted a part of their business, wouldn't that involve him *being around*? Or was he talking about being a silent partner?

'Does your company have a London presence at all?' Javier was thoroughly enjoying himself. Who said the only route to satisfaction was getting what you wanted on demand? He'd always been excellent when it came to thinking outside the box. He was doing just that right now. Whatever he sank into her business would be peanuts for him but he could already see ways of turning a healthy profit.

And as for having her? Of course he would, but where was the rush after all? He could take a little time out to relish this project...

'Barely,' she admitted. 'We closed three of the four branches over the years to save costs.'

'And left one open and running?'

'We couldn't afford to shut them all...even though the overheads are frightening.'

'Splendid. As soon as the details are formalised and all the signatures are in place, I will ensure that the office is modernised and ready for occupation.'

'It's already occupied,' Sophie said, dazed. 'Mandy works on reception and twice a week one of the accountants goes down to see to the various bits of post. Fortunately nearly everything is done by email these days...'

'Pack your bags, Sophie. I'm taking up residence in your London office, just as soon as it's fit for habitation, and you're going to be sitting right there alongside me.'

Not quite the original terms and conditions he had intended to apply, but in so many ways so much better...

CHAPTER FOUR

'I DON'T KNOW what you're so worried about. His terms and conditions seem pretty fair to me. In fact, better than fair. He's going to have a percentage interest in the company but at least it'll be a company that's making money.'

That had been Oliver's reaction when she had presented him, a fortnight ago, with the offer Javier had laid out on the table for her to take or reject.

He had been downright incredulous that she might even be hesitating to eat from the hand that had been extended to feed her. In a manner that was uncharacteristically pro-active for him, he had called an extraordinary meeting of the directors and presented them with Javier's plan, and Sophie had had to swallow the unpalatable reality that her past had caught up with her and was now about to join hands with her present.

Since then, with papers signed and agreements reached at the speed of light, the little office they had kept open in Notting Hill had been awash with frantic activity.

Sophie had refused to go. She had delegated that task to her brother, who had been delighted to get out of York-shire for a couple of weeks. He had reported back with gusto at the renovations being made and, inside, Sophie had quailed at the way she felt, as though suddenly her life was being taken over.

She knew she was being ridiculous.

Javier had agreed to see them because of their old connection but there had been nothing there beyond that historic connection. He had made no attempts to pursue any conversations about what had happened between them. He had been as cool as might have been expected given the circumstances of their break-up and she was in no doubt that the only reason he had agreed to help them was because he could see a profit in what was being offered.

Money was what he cared about and she suspected that he would be getting a good deal out of them. They were, after all, in the position of the beggars who couldn't be choosers.

Hadn't he greeted her with all the information he had accumulated about the company?

He had done his homework and he wouldn't be offering them a rescue package if he wasn't going to get a great deal out of it.

She brushed her skirt, neatened her blouse and inspected herself in the mirror in the hallway, but she wasn't really seeing her reflection. She was thinking, persuading herself that his attitude towards her made everything much easier. For him, the past was history. What he had with her now was a business deal and one that had fallen into his lap like a piece of ripe fruit that hadn't even needed plucking from the tree.

Maybe in some distant corner of his mind there was an element of satisfaction that he was now in a position to be the one calling the shots, but if that was the case, he would have to have cared one way or another about her and he didn't.

The effect he still had on her was not mutual. And even her responses to him were an illusion, no more than a reminder of the power of nostalgia, because truthfully her heart was safely locked away, never again to be taken out to see the light of day.

She blinked and focused on the tidy image staring back at her. Everything in place. In a few minutes the taxi would come to take her to the station. A month ago, she would have hit the bus stop, which was almost a mile away, but he had deposited a large advance of cash in the company account to cover expenses and to ensure that everyone on the payroll was compensated for the overtime which they had contributed over the months and which had not been paid.

She would take the taxi to the station and then the train down to London so that she could see the final, finished product, the newly refurbished offices in which she would be stationed for as long as it took to get things up and running.

'How long do you think that's going to take?' she had asked Javier on day one, heart thumping at the prospect of being in an office where, on a whim, he could descend without warning.

He had shrugged, his dark-as-night eyes never leaving her face. 'How long is a piece of string? There's a lot of work to do with the company before it begins to pull its weight. There's been mass wastage of money and resources, expenditures that border on criminal and incompetent staff by the bucketload.'

'And you're going to…er…be around, supervising…?'

His eyes had narrowed on her flushed face. 'Does the prospect of that frighten you, Sophie?'

'Not in the slightest,' she had returned quickly. 'I would just be surprised if you managed to take time off from being the ruler of all you surveyed to help out an ailing firm. I mean, don't you have minions who move in when you take over sick companies?'

'I think I might give the minions a rest on this particular occasion,' he had murmured softly.

'Why?' Sophie had heard the thread of desperation in her voice. She couldn't be within five feet of him without her body reliving the way he had once made it feel, playing stupid games with her mind.

'This is a slightly more personal venture for me, Sophie,' he had told her, leaning across the boardroom table where both of them had remained after the legal team had exited. 'Maybe I want to see that the job is done to the highest possible standard given our…past acquaintanceship.'

Sophie hadn't known whether to thank him or quiz him, so she had remained silent, her eyes helplessly drifting down to his sensual mouth before sliding away as heat had consumed her.

With a little sigh, she grabbed her handbag as she heard the taxi circle the gravelled forecourt, and then she was on her way, half hoping that Javier wouldn't be there waiting at the office when she finally arrived, half hoping that he might be, and hating herself for that weakness.

She had no idea what to expect to find. The last time she had visited this particular office had been two years previously, when she and Oliver had been trying to decide which of the offices to shut. She remembered it as spacious enough but, without any money having been spent on it at all, it had already been showing telltale signs of wear and tear. That said, it had been the biggest and the least run-down, so they'd been able to amalgamate the diminishing files and folders there from the other offices.

Not for the first time, as she was ferried from north to south, she thought about how clueless she had been about the groundbreaking changes that had been happening right under her nose.

Ollie, at least, had had the excuse of being abroad, be-

cause he had left on his sports scholarship two years before she had gone to Cambridge. He'd been a fresh-faced
teenager wrapped up in his own life, with no vision of
anything happening outside it.

But she had still been living at home, in her final years
at school. Why hadn't she asked more probing questions
when her mother's health had begun to fail? The doctor
had talked about stress, and now Sophie marvelled that
she hadn't dug deeper to find out what the stress had been
all about, because on the surface her mother could not
have been living a less stressed-out life.

And neither had she questioned the frequency with
which Roger's name had cropped up in conversations or
the number of times he'd been invited along to the house
for various parties. She had been amused at his enthusi-
asm and had eventually drifted into going out with him;
she had never suspected the amount of encouragement he
had got from her parents.

All told, she had allowed herself to be wrapped up in
cotton wool. So when that cotton wool had been cruelly
yanked off, she had been far more shell-shocked than she
might otherwise have been.

Everything had hit her at once. She had been bom-
barded from all sides and, in the middle of this, had had
to wise up quickly to the trauma of discovering just how
ill her father was and the lengths he had gone to to protect them all from knowing.

She should have been there helping out long before
the bomb had detonated, splintering shrapnel through
their lives.

If she had been, then perhaps the company could have
taken a different direction. And, if it had taken a different
direction, then she wouldn't be here now, at the mercy of
a guy who could still send her senses reeling, whatever
her head was telling her.

Once in London, Sophie took a black cab to the premises of the office in Notting Hill.

Oliver had told her that things were coming along brilliantly but he had undersold just how much had been done in the space of a few days. It wasn't just about the paint job on the outside or the impressive potted plants or the newly painted black door with its gold lettering announcing the name of the company.

Standing back, Sophie's mouth fell open as she took in the smart exterior. Then the door opened and she was staring at a casually dressed Javier, who, in return, stared back at her as he continued to lounge indolently against the door frame. Arms folded, he was already projecting the signs of ownership so that, as she took a few tentative steps towards him, she felt herself to be the visitor.

'Wow.' She hovered, waiting for him to step back, which he did after a couple of seconds, taking his time to unfold his gloriously elegant body and then stand aside so that she had to brush past him, immediately turning around and establishing a safe physical distance between them. 'It's completely changed on the outside.'

'There's no point having an office that repels potential clients,' Javier said drily.

Yet again, she was in work attire. The sort of clothes that drained her natural beauty.

'Why have you shown up wearing a suit?' he asked, strolling past her and expecting her to follow, which she duly did. 'And where is your bag? You do realise that you will be relocating to London for the foreseeable future?'

'I've been giving that some thought…'

Javier stopped and turned to look at her. 'Forget it.'

'I beg your pardon?'

'Remember the terms and conditions? One of them is that you relocate down here so that you can oversee the running of the London arm of the business.'

'Yes, but—'

'No *buts*, Sophie.' His voice was cool and unyielding. He hooked his fingers on the waistband of his black jeans, which sat low on his lean hips, and held her stare. 'You don't get to dip in and out of this. You're on the letterhead, along with your brother, and of course myself. Don't think that you're going to reap the rewards without doing any of the hard graft. I intend to oversee proceedings initially but I need to be assured that you and your brother won't run the company back into the ground the second my back's turned. Don't forget, this isn't a charity gesture of goodwill on my part. I'm not parting with cash if I don't think that there will be a decent return on my investment.'

Sophie thought that she'd been right. It was all about the money for him. Yes, there was a personal connection, but the animosity of their break-up wasn't paramount in his decision to help them. What mattered was that he was being handed a potentially very profitable business with an age-old reputation at a very cheap price because she and Oliver were desperate.

She imagined that, once the company was sorted, its reputation would not only be repaired but would ensure gold-plated business and a return of all the customers they had sadly lost over the years.

Right now, Oliver had an interest in a third of the company, but he would quickly lose interest and, she foresaw, would cash in his shares, take the money and head back to California, where he could continue his sporting career in a teaching capacity.

In due course, Javier would have invested in a very worthwhile project at a very good price.

And their past history did not figure in the calculations. In fact, she wondered whether he felt anything at all about what had happened between them.

'I thought I might commute down.'

Javier burst out laughing before sobering up to look at her with a gimlet-eyed warning. 'I wouldn't even entertain that notion if I were you,' he informed her in the sort of voice that did not expect contradiction. 'In the first few weeks there will probably be a great deal of overtime, and hopping on and off a train to try to get the work done just isn't going to cut it.'

'I have nowhere to stay here.' Once upon a time, there had been a snazzy apartment in Kensington but, she had discovered, that had been mortgaged up to the hilt when the company had started shedding customers and losing profit. It had been sold ages ago.

'Your brother has stayed in a hotel when he's been down.' Javier's eyes roved over her flushed face. 'But,' he mused with soft speculation, 'as you're going to be here for considerably longer, I have already made arrangements for you to have use of one of my apartments in Notting Hill. You'll be within convenient walking distance of the company. No excuse for slacking off.'

'No!' She broke out in clammy perspiration.

'Reason being…?'

'I…I can't just decamp down here to London, Javier!'

'This isn't something that's open to debate.'

'You don't understand.'

'Then enlighten me.' They hadn't even stepped foot into the renovated office and already they were arguing.

He couldn't credit that he had originally played with the thought of helping her in return for having her. He couldn't think of anything less satisfying than having her blackmailed into coming to him as a reluctant and resentful partner when he wanted her hot, wet and willing…

He also couldn't credit that he had simplistically imagined that one scratch would ease this itch that had surfaced with such surprising speed the second her brother had opened that door back into the past. The more he saw of her, the more he *thought* of her, the more dangerously deep his unfinished business with her felt. One or two nights wasn't going to be enough.

'I have to keep an eye on the house,' she said with obvious reluctance.

'What house?'

'The family home.'

'Why? Is it in imminent danger of falling down if you're not at hand with some sticking plaster and masking tape?'

Bitter tears sprang to her eyes and she fought them down as a red mist of anger swirled through her in a tidal rush.

'Since when did you get so arrogant?' she flung at him. They stared at one another in electric silence before she broke eye contact to storm off, out of the beautiful reception area, which she had barely noticed at all, and into the first set of offices.

It took a couple of seconds before Javier was galvanised into following her.

Being accused of *arrogance* was not something he was accustomed to. Indeed, being spoken to in that accusatory, critical tone of voice was unheard of. He caught her arm, tugging her to face him and then immediately releasing her because just the feel of her softness under his fingers was like putting his hand against an open flame. It enraged him that she could still have this effect on him. It enraged him that, for the first time in living memory, and certainly for the first time in many, many years, his body was refusing to obey his mind.

'Are you sure it's the house you need to be close to?' he growled.

'What are you talking about?'

'Maybe there's a man lurking in the background...'

Javier was disgusted to realise that he was fishing. Did
he care whether there was some lame boyfriend in the
background? She wasn't married and that was the main
thing. He would never have gone near any woman with
a wedding ring on her finger, but if she had a boyfriend
somewhere, another one of those limp ex–public school
idiots who thought that a polished accent was all that it
took to get you through life, well…

All was fair in love and war…

Sophie reddened. The dull prickle of unpleasant memories tried to surface and she resolutely shoved them back
where they belonged, in the deepest corners of her mind.

'Because, if you have, then he'll just have to take a back
seat for…however long it takes. And word of warning—
my apartment is for sole occupation only…'

'You mean if there was a guy in my life, and I happened to be living in one of your apartments, I wouldn't
be allowed to entertain him?'

Javier looked at her appalled expression and swatted
away the uncomfortable feeling that he was being pigeon-
holed as some kind of dinosaur when that couldn't have
been further from the truth. Having reached the soaring
heights the hard way, he made a conscious effort to ensure
that the employees of his company were hand-picked for
all the right reasons: talent, merit and ability. He made
sure that there were no glass ceilings for women, or for
those who had had to struggle to find their way, as he had.

He was not the sort of guy who would ever have dreamt
of laying down pathetic rules about men being kept apart
from women, like teenagers in boarding schools overseen
by strict house masters.

So what was he doing right now? And how was it that
he had no intention of doing otherwise?

'I mean you're probably going to be working long
hours. The distraction of some man who wants you back

home to cook his meal by five-thirty isn't going to work'
was the most he would offer.

Sophie laughed shortly. If only he knew...

'There's no man around to distract me,' she said in a
low voice. 'And, yes, as a matter of fact the house *is* falling down, and Oliver won't be there because he's been
dispatched to France to see what's happening to the company over there...'

'Your house is falling down?'

'Not literally,' Sophie admitted. 'But there's a lot
wrong with it and I'm always conscious of the fact that
if it springs a leak and I'm not there to sort it out, well...'

'Since when has your house been falling down?'

'It doesn't matter.' She sighed and began to run her fingers through her hair, only to realise that she had pinned
it up, and let her hand drop to her side. She looked around
her but was very much aware of his eyes still on her, and
even more aware that somehow they were now standing
way too close for comfort.

'You've done marvellous things with the space.' She
just wanted to get away from the threat of personal quiz-
zing. She took a few steps away from him and now took
time really to notice just how much *had* been done. It was
not just a paint job; everything seemed very different from
what she remembered.

It seemed much, much larger and that, she realised,
was because the space within the first-floor office block
had been maximised. Partitions had been cleverly put in
where before there had been none. The dank carpeting
had been replaced with wooden floors. The desks and
furniture were all spanking new. She listened and nodded
as he explained the dynamics of the place being manned
and who should be working the London office. The client list would have to be updated. The sales team would

need to be far more assertive. He had identified useful gaps in the market that could be exploited.

Everything was perfect. There were two private offices and she would be occupying one. Again she nodded because, like it or not, she was going to be here, in London.

'But,' she said when the tour had been concluded and they were in the pristine, updated kitchen, sitting at the high-tech beaten metallic table with cups of steaming coffee in front of them, 'I still don't feel comfortable leaving the house and I don't want to live in one of your apartments.' *He would have a key... He would be able to walk in unannounced at any given time... She could be in the shower and he could just stroll in...*

Her nipples tightened, pushing against her lacy bra and sending tingles up and down, in and out and through her from her toes to her scalp. She licked her lips and reminded herself that if he felt anything towards her at all it would be loathing because of what had happened between them in the past. Although, in reality, he couldn't even be bothered to feel such a strong emotion. What he felt was...indifference.

So if he were to let himself in, which he most certainly wouldn't, the shower would be the last place he would seek her out. Her responses were all over the place and it wouldn't be long before he started to realise that she wasn't as immune to him as she was desperately trying to be.

'I'll bring your brother back over.'

'No! Don't...'

'Why not?' Javier raised his eyebrows expressively, although he knew the reason well enough. Oliver didn't want to be stuck in Yorkshire and he didn't see his future with the family business. He resented the penury into which they had been thrust and, although he recognised the importance of rebuilding what had fallen into disrepair, he really thought no further than what that personally meant for him. Given half a chance, he would have cashed in his shares and headed for the hills. In due course he would, which would be interesting should Javier decide he wanted more than he had. That was unlikely, because once he was done with getting what he wanted, he would be more than happy to disappear and leave the running of the business to an underling of his choice.

'He's enjoying being in Paris.'

'And that's how it's always been, isn't it?' Javier asked softly and Sophie raised translucent violet eyes to look at him with a frown.

'What do you mean?'

'I remember how you used to talk about your twin.' He had resolved not to go down any maudlin, reminiscing roads but now found that he couldn't help himself. 'The party animal. Off to California while you stayed behind to do your A levels. Praised for being sporty and indulged at a time when most kids that age would have had their head in textbooks to make sure they passed exams. When he came down to see you, he barely stayed put. He managed to make friends in five seconds and then off he went to see what nightclubs there were. He had his fun, enjoyed Mummy and Daddy's money and never had to face up to any grim realities because by then he was in California on his sports scholarship...

'I bet no one ever filled him in about the reality of the company losses, not even you...not even when they were glaringly obvious. I'll bet he only found out the extent of the trouble when you couldn't hide it from him any longer. Did your beloved ex-husband likewise conspire to keep your immature brother in the dark?'

'I told you.' Sophie stiffened at the mention of her ex-husband. 'I don't want to talk about Roger.'

Javier's lips tightened. The more she shied away from

all mention of her ex, the more his curiosity was piqued. He was bitterly reminded of his pointless *wondering* when she had dumped him, when she had told him that she was destined to marry someone else... When she had married a guy whom he had found himself researching on the Internet even though it had been an exercise in masochism.

He had learned strength from a very young age. It had taken a great deal of willpower to avoid the pitfalls of so many of his friends when he had been growing up in poverty in Spain. The easy way out had always been littered with drugs and violence, and that easy way had been the popular route for many of the kids he had known. He had had to become an island to turn his back on all of that, just as he had had to develop a great deal of inner strength when he had finally made it to England to begin his university career. He had had to set his sights on distant goals and allow himself to be guided only by them.

Sophie had taken his eye off the ball, and here she was, doing it again.

The sooner he got her out of his system, the better.

'So your brother stays in Paris,' he said, with the sort of insistence that made her think of steamrollers slowly and inexorably flattening vast swathes of land. 'I could get someone to house-sit and daily look for walls falling down...'

'You might think it's funny, Javier, but it's not. You might live in your mansion now, and you might be able to get whatever you want at the snap of a finger, but it's just not funny when you have to watch every step you take because there might just be a minefield waiting to explode if you put your foot somewhere wrong. And I'm surprised you have no sympathy at all, considering you... you were...'

'I was broke? Penniless? A poor immigrant still trying to get a grip on the first rung of that all-important ladder? I feel it's fair to say that our circumstances were slightly different.'

'And, in a way, you probably have no idea how much worse it makes it for me.' She swung her head away. Her prissy, formal clothes felt like a straitjacket and her tidy bun nestled at the nape of her neck was sticky and restricting.

Without thinking, she released it and sifted restless fingers through the length of her tumbling hair.

And Javier watched. His mouth went dry. Her hair cascaded over her shoulders and down her back, a vibrant wash of colour that took his breath away. He had to look away but he knew that he was breathing fast, imagining her naked, projecting how her body would feel were he to run his hands along its shapely contours.

'You're right. Oliver has always been protected,' she told him bluntly. He might very well be the first person she was telling this to. It was a truth she had always kept to herself because to have voiced it would have felt like a little betrayal. 'He only found out about…everything when Dad's illness was finally revealed, and even then we didn't tell him that the company was on its last legs. In fact, he returned to California and only came back after the…the accident when… Well, he came back for Dad's funeral, and of course Roger's, and by then he had to be told.

'But his heart isn't in getting the company up and running. His heart isn't in the house either. Mum's now living in Cornwall and, as far as Ollie is concerned, he would sell the family home to the highest bidder if there was anyone around who was in the slightest bit interested. He doesn't give a hoot if it all falls down in a pile of rubble just so long as we got some money for the rubble. So, no, he wouldn't be at all happy to leave Paris to house-sit.'

She took a deep, shaky breath. 'The house hasn't been maintained for years. It always looked good on the outside, not that I ever really *looked*, but it turned out that there were problems with the roof and subsidence that had never been sorted. There's no money left in the pot to sort that stuff out, so I keep my eyes peeled for anything that might need urgent attention. The worse the house is, the less money we'll get, if we ever manage to sell at all. I can't afford for a leak to spring in the cellar and start mounting the stairs to the hallway.' She sighed and rubbed her eyes.

'Why did you let him get away with it?' It was more of a flat, semi-incredulous statement than a question and Sophie knew exactly who he was talking about even though no name had been mentioned.

'I don't want to talk about that. It's in the past and there's no point stressing about the stuff you can't change. I just have to deal with the here and now...'

'Oliver,' Javier ploughed on, 'might be indifferent and clueless when it comes to business, but you clearly have the capacity to get involved, so why didn't you? You knew what was happening.'

'Mum wasn't in good health. Hadn't been for ages. And then Dad's behaviour started getting weird...erratic... Suddenly everything seemed to be happening at the same time. We found out just how ill he was and then, hard on the heels of that, the full repercussions of...of Roger's gambling and all the bad investments began coming to light. There was no one at the helm. All the good people were leaving. Lots had already left, although I didn't know that at the time, because I'd never been involved in the family business. It was...chaos.'

Even in the midst of this tale of abject woe, Javier couldn't help but notice that there was no condemnation of her scoundrel husband. Loyalties, he thought with a sour taste, were not divided.

'So I'll get a house-sitter,' he repeated and she shook

her head. He had already infiltrated her life enough. She wasn't sure she could cope with more.

'I'll come here,' she conceded, 'and go home at the weekends.' She breathed in deeply. 'And thank you for the use of an apartment. You have to let me know...I don't have a great deal of disposable income, as you can imagine, but please let me know how much rent I will owe you.'

Javier sat back and looked at her from under sinfully long lashes, a lazy, speculative look that felt like a caress.

'Don't even think of paying me rent,' he told her silkily. 'It's on the house...for old times' sake. Trust me, Sophie, I want you...' he paused fractionally '...there at the helm while changes are taking place, and what I want, I usually get...whatever the cost.'

CHAPTER FIVE

SOPHIE LOOKED AROUND her and realised guiltily that, after two weeks' living in the apartment Javier had kindly loaned her, refusing to countenance a penny in payment, she was strangely *happy*.

The apartment was to die for. She still found herself admiring the décor, as she was doing right now, having just returned from the office and kicked off her stupid pumps so that she could walk barefoot on the cool, wooden floor.

She had expected minimalist with lots of off-putting glossy white surfaces, like the inside of a high-tech lab. Images of aggressive black leather and chrome everywhere had sprung to mind when she had been handed the key to the apartment by his personal assistant, who had accompanied her so that the workings of the various gadgets could be explained.

She had assumed that she would be overwhelmed by an ostentatious show of wealth, would be obliged to gasp appropriately at furnishings she didn't really like and would feel like an intruder in a foreign land.

The Javier of today was not the teasing, warm, sexy, funny guy she had once known. The today Javier was tough, rich beyond most people's wildest dreams, ruthless and cutting edge in his hand-tailored suits and Italian shoes. And that would be reflected in any apartment he owned.

She'd been surprised—shocked, even—when she was shown the apartment.

'It's had a makeover,' the personal assistant had said in a vaguely puzzled voice, but obviously far too well-trained to comment further. 'So this is the first time I'm seeing the new version...'

Sophie hadn't quizzed her on what it had been like previously. Tired and in need of updating, she had assumed. He'd probably bought a bunch of apartments without even seeing them, the way you do when you have tons of money, and then paid someone handsomely to turn them into the sort of triple-A, gold-plated investments that would rent for a small fortune and double in value if he ever decided to sell.

Whoever had done the interior design had done a great job.

She padded towards the kitchen, which was cool, in shades of pale grey with vintage off-white tiles on the floor and granite counters that matched the floor.

Everything was open-plan. She strolled into the living room with a cup of tea and sank into the cosy sofa, idly flicking on the television to watch the early-evening news.

It was Friday and the work clothes had been dumped in the clothes hamper. Javier had told her that it was fine to dress casually but she had ignored him.

Keep it professional; keep it businesslike... she had decided.

Jeans and tee shirts would blur the lines between them...at least for her...

Not, in all events, that it made a scrap of difference how she dressed, because, after the first day, he had done a disappearing act, only occasionally emailing her or phoning her for updates. A couple of times he had visited the branch when she had been out seeing customers, trying to drum up business, and she could only think that he had timed his arrivals cleverly to avoid bumping into her.

He didn't give a passing thought to her, whilst she, on the other hand, couldn't stop thinking about him.

She didn't think that she had ever really stopped thinking about him. He'd been in her head, like the ghost of a refrain from a song that wouldn't go away.

And now she couldn't stop thinking about him. Worse than that, she spent every day at the office anticipating his unexpected arrival and was disproportionately disappointed when five-thirty rolled round and he'd failed to make an appearance.

Her heart skipped a beat when she opened up her emails and found a message from him waiting for her.

Her throat went dry when she heard the deep, sexy timbre of his voice on the end of the line.

She was in danger of obsessing over a guy who belonged to her past. At least, emotionally.

He'd suddenly reappeared on the scene, opening all sorts of doors in her head, making her think about choices she had made and bringing back memories of the horror story that had followed those choices.

He made her think about Roger. He was curious about her ex. She sensed that. Perhaps not curious in a personal way, but mildly curious, especially because so many things didn't quite add up. Why, he had asked her, hadn't she intervened when she'd known that he was blowing vast sums of money gambling? When she'd discovered the scale of the financial problems with the company? Why hadn't she acted more decisively?

But, of course, that was the kind of person he was. Someone who was born and bred to act decisively. He could never begin to understand how easy it was just to get lost and find yourself in a fog, with no guiding lights to lead you out.

She had grown up a lot since then. She had had to. And, in the process of taking charge, she had realised just how feeble her brother was when it came to making decisions and taking difficult paths.

When she looked back at herself as she had been seven years ago, it was like staring at a stranger. The carefree girl with a life full of options was gone for ever. She was a woman now with limited options and too many bad memories to deal with.

Was that why she was now obsessing over Javier, someone she had known for such a short space of time? Was it because he reminded her of the girl she used to be? Was it obsession by association, so to speak?

He made her think things she would rather have forgotten but he also made her heart skip a beat the way it once used to when she'd been with him.

And more than that, he made her body feel alive the way it hadn't for years. Not since him, in fact. He made her feel young again and that had a very seductive appeal.

With an impatient click of her tongue, she raised the volume of the television, determined not to waste the evening thinking about Javier and remembering what life had been like when they had been going out.

She almost didn't hear the buzz of the doorbell, and when she did, she almost thought that she might have made a mistake because no one could possibly be calling on her.

Since she had moved to London, she had kept herself to herself. She knew a couple of people who had relocated from the northern branch but the London crew, all very able and super-efficient, were new and she had shied away from making friends with any of them.

For starters, although it wasn't advertised and in all

probability none of them knew, she was more or less their boss. And also…did she really want anyone knowing her backstory? It was just easier to maintain a healthy distance, so there was no way whoever had buzzed her from downstairs was a colleague on the hunt for a Friday night companion.

She picked up the intercom which allowed her to see her unexpected visitor and the breath left her in a whoosh.

'You're in.' Javier had come to the apartment on the spur of the moment. Since she'd started at the London office, he had seen her once, had spoken to her six times and had emailed her every other day. He had purposefully kept his distance because the strength of his response to her had come as a shock. Accustomed to having absolute control over every aspect of his life, he had assumed that her sudden appearance in his highly ordered existence would prove interesting—certainly rewarding, bearing in mind he intended to finish what had been started seven years previously—and definitely nothing that he wouldn't be able to handle.

Except that, from the very minute he had laid eyes on her, all that absolute certainty had flown through the window. The easy route he had planned to take had almost immediately bitten the dust. He'd had every intention of coolly trading his financial help for the body he had been denied, the body he discovered he still longed to touch and explore.

She'd used him and now he'd been given a golden opportunity to get his own back.

Except, he'd seen her, and that approach had seemed worse than simplistic. It had seemed crass.

There was no way he was going to pursue her and showing up at the workplace every day would have smelled a lot like pursuit, even though he had every right to be there, considering the amount of money he was sinking into the failing company.

He wanted her to come to him but staying away had been a lot more difficult than he'd dreamed possible.

Like someone dying of thirst suddenly denied the glass of ice-cold water just within his reach, he had found himself thinking about her to the point of distraction, and that had got on his nerves.

So here he was.

Sophie frantically wondered whether she could say that she was just on her way out. His unexpected appearance had brought her out in a nervous cold sweat. She had been thinking about him, and here he was, conjured up from her imagination.

'I...I...'

'Let me in.'

'I was just about to...have something to eat, actually...'

'Perfect. I'll join you.'

That wasn't what she'd had in mind. What she'd had in mind was a lead-up to a polite excuse and an arrangement to meet when she had some sort of defence system in place. Instead, here she was, hair all over the place, wearing jogging bottoms and an old, tight tee shirt bought at a music festival a dozen years ago and shrunk in the wash over time.

'Come on, Sophie! I'm growing older by the minute!'

'Fine!' She buzzed him in, belatedly remembering that it was actually *his* apartment, so he had every right to be here. And not only was it *his* apartment, but she wasn't paying a penny towards the rent, at his insistence.

She scrambled to the mirror by the front door, accepted that it was too late to start pinning her hair back into something sensible, and even though she was expecting him, she still started when he rapped on the door.

He'd obviously come straight from work, although, *en*

route, he had divested himself of his tie, undone the top couple of buttons of his shirt and rolled his sleeves to his elbows. Her eyes dipped to his sinewy forearms and just as quickly back to his face.

'You look flustered,' Javier drawled, leaning against the door frame and somehow managing to crowd her. 'I haven't interrupted you in the middle of something pressing, have I?' This was how he remembered her. Tousled and sexy and so unbelievably, breathtakingly *fresh*.

And *innocent*.

Which was a bit of a joke, all things considered.

Dark eyes drifted downwards, taking in the outline of her firm, round breasts pushing against a tee shirt that was a few sizes too small, taking in the slither of flat belly where the tee shirt ended and the shapeless jogging bottoms began. Even in an outfit that should have done her no favours, she still looked hot, and his body responded with suitable vigour.

He straightened, frowning at the sudden discomfort of an erection.

'I haven't managed to catch much of you over the past couple of weeks.' He dragged his mind away from thoughts of her, a bed and a heap of hurriedly discarded clothes on the ground. 'So I thought I'd try you at home before you disappeared up north for the weekend.'

'Of course.'

There was a brief pause, during which he tilted his head to one side, before pointedly looking at the door handle.

'So...' He looked around him at his apartment with satisfaction. He'd had it redone. 'How are you finding the apartment?'

Some might say that he'd been a little underhand in the renovating of the apartment, which had been in perfectly good order a month previously. He'd walked round it, looking at the soulless, sterile furnishings, and had been able to picture her reaction to her new surroundings: disdain. He had always been amused at her old-fashioned tastes, despite the fact that she had grown up with money.

'I imagine your family home to be a wonder of the most up-to-the-minute furnishings money can buy,' he had once teased, when she'd stood staring in rapt fixation at a four-poster bed strewn with a million cushions in the window of a department store. She'd waxed lyrical then about the romance of four-poster beds and had told him, sheepishly, that the family home was anything but modern.

'My mum's like me,' she had confessed with a grin. 'She likes antiques and everything that's old and worn and full of character.'

Javier had personally made sure to insert some pieces of character in the apartment. He, himself, liked modern and minimalist. His impoverished family home had been clean but nearly everything had been bought second-hand. He'd grown up with so many items of furniture that had been just a little too full of character that he was now a fully paid-up member of all things modern and lacking in so-called character.

But he'd enjoyed hand-picking pieces for the apartment, had enjoyed picturing her reaction to the four-poster bed he had bought, the beautifully crafted floral sofa, the thick Persian rug that broke up the expanse of pale flooring.

'The apartment's fine.' Sophie stepped away from him and folded her arms. 'Better than fine,' she admitted, eyes darting to him and then staying there because he was just so arresting. 'I love the way it's been done. You should congratulate your interior designer.'

'Who said I used one?' He looked at her with raised eyebrows and she blushed in sudden confusion, because to picture him hand-picking anything was somehow... *intimate*. And of course he would never have done any such thing. What über-rich single guy would ever waste time hunting down rugs and curtains? Definitely not a guy like Javier, who was macho to the very last bone in his body.

'I'm afraid there's not a great deal of food.' She turned away because her heart was beating so fast she could barely breathe properly. His presence seemed to infiltrate every part of the apartment, filling it with suffocating, masculine intensity. This was how it had always been with him. In his presence, she'd felt weak and pleasurably helpless. Even as a young guy, struggling to make ends meet, he'd still managed to project an air of absolute assurance. He'd made all the other students around him seem like little boys in comparison.

The big difference was that, back then, she'd had a remit to bask and luxuriate in that powerful masculinity. She could touch, she could run her fingers through his springy, black hair and she'd had permission to melt at the feel of it.

She'd been allowed to want him and to show him how much she wanted him.

Not so now.

Furthermore, she didn't *want* to want him. She didn't *want* to feel herself dragged back into a past that was gone for good. Of course, foolish love was gone for good, and no longer a threat to the ivory tower she had constructed around herself that had been so vital in withstanding the years spent with her husband, but she didn't want to feel that pressing, urgent *want* either…

She didn't *want* to feel her heart fluttering like an adolescent's because he happened to be sharing the same space as her. She'd grown up, gone through some hellish stuff. Her outlook on life had been changed for ever because of what she'd had to deal with. She had no illusions now and no longer believed that happiness was her right. It wasn't and never would be. Javier Vasquez belonged to a time when unfettered optimism had been her constant companion. Now, not only was the murky past an unbreachable wall between them, but so were all the changes that had happened to her.

'I wasn't expecting company.' She half turned to find him right behind her, having followed her into the kitchen.

The kitchen was big, a clever mix of old and new, and she felt utterly at home in it.

'Smells good. What is it?'

'Just some tomato sauce. I was going to have it with pasta.'

'You never used to enjoy cooking.' Yet again, he found himself referring to the past, dredging it up and bringing it into the present, where it most certainly did not belong.

'I know.' She shot him a fleeting smile as he sat down at the table, angling his chair so that he could extend his long legs to one side. 'I never had to do it,' she explained. 'Mum loved cooking and I was always happy to let her get on with it. When she got ill, she said it used to occupy her and take her mind off her health problems, so I never interfered. I mean, I'd wash the dishes and tidy behind her, but she liked being the main chef. And then…'

She sighed and began finishing the food preparation, but horribly aware of those lazy, speculative eyes on her, following her every movement.

Javier resisted the urge to try to prise answers out of her. 'So you learned to cook,' he said, moving the conversation along, past the point of his curiosity.

'And discovered that I rather enjoyed it.' She didn't fail to notice how swiftly he had diverted the conversation from the controversial topic of her past, the years she had spent after they had gone their separate ways. His initial curiosity was gone, and she told herself that she was very thankful that it had, because there was far too much she could never, would never, tell him.

But alongside that relief was a certain amount of disappointment, because his lack of curiosity was all wrapped up with the indifference he felt for her.

She suddenly had the strangest temptation to reach out and touch him, to stroke his wrist, feel the familiar strength of his forearm under her fingers. What would he do? How would he react? *Would he recoil with horror or would he touch her back?*

Appalled, she thrust a plate of food in front of him and sat down opposite him. She wanted to sit on her treacherous hands just in case they did something wildly inappropriate of their own accord and she had to remind herself shakily that she was a grown woman, fully in control of her wayward emotions. Emotions that had been stirred up, as they *naturally* would be, by having him invade her life out of the blue.

She heard herself babbling on like the village idiot about her culinary exploits while he ate and listened in silence, with every show of interest in what she was saying.

Which was remarkable, given she had just finished a lengthy anecdote about some slow-cooked beef she had tried to cook weeks previously, which had been disastrous.

'So you like the apartment,' Javier drawled, eyes not leaving her face as he sipped some wine. 'And the job? Now that the work of trying to repair the damage done over the years has begun?'

'It's…awkward,' Sophie told him truthfully.

'Explain.'

'You were right,' she said bluntly, rising to begin clearing the table, her colour high. 'Some of the people my father trusted have let the company down badly over the years. I can only think that employing friends was a luxury my father had when he started the company, and he either continued to trust that they were doing a good job or he knew that they weren't but found it difficult to let them go. And then...'

'And then?' Javier queried silkily and Sophie shrugged.

'Getting rid of them never happened. Thankfully the majority have now left, but with generous pension payments or golden handshakes...' Yet more ways money had drained away from the company until the river had run dry.

'The company is in far worse shape than even I imagined...'

Sophie blanched. She watched as he began helping to clear the table, bringing plates to the sink.

'What do you mean?'

'Your father didn't just take his eye off the ball when he became ill. I doubt his eye had ever really been fully on it in the first place.'

'You can't say that!'

'I've gone through all the books with a fine-tooth comb, Sophie.' He relieved her of the plate she was holding and dried it before placing it on the kitchen counter, then he slung the tea towel he had fetched over his shoulder and propped himself against the counter, arms folded.

Javier had always suspected that her father had been instrumental in her decision to quit university and return to the guy she had always been destined to marry. Even though she had never come right out and said so; even though she had barely had the courage to look him in the face when she had announced that she'd be leaving university because of a family situation that had arisen.

He had never told her that he had subsequently gone to see her parents, that he had confronted her father, who had left him in no doubt that there was no way his precious daughter would contemplate a permanent relationship with someone like him.

He wondered whether the old man's extreme reaction

had been somehow linked to his decline into terminal ill health, and scowled as he remembered the heated argument that had resulted in him walking away, never looking back.

This was the perfect moment to disabuse her of whatever illusions she had harboured about a father who had clearly had little clue about running a business, but the dismay on her face made him hesitate.

He raked his fingers uncomfortably through his hair and continued to stare down at her upturned face.

'He was a terrific dad,' she said defensively, thinking back to the many times he had taken the family out on excursions, often leaving the running of the company to the guys working for him. 'Life was to be enjoyed' had always been his motto. He had played golf and taken them on fantastic holidays; she recognised now that ineffective, relatively unsupervised management had not helped the company coffers. He had inherited a thriving business but, especially when everything had gone electronic, he had failed to move with the times and so had his pals who had joined the company when he had taken it over.

In retrospect, she saw that so much had been piling up like dark clouds on the horizon, waiting for their moment to converge and create the thunderstorm of events that would land her where she was right now.

Javier opened his mouth to disabuse her of her girlish illusions and then thought of his own father. There was no way he would ever have had a word said against him, and yet, hadn't Pedro Vasquez once confessed that he had blown an opportunity to advance himself by storming out of his first company, too young and hot-headed to take orders he didn't agree with? The golden opportunity he had walked away from had never again returned and he had had to devote years of saving and scrimping to get by on the low wages he had earned until his retirement.

But Javier had never held that weak moment against him.

'Your father wouldn't be the first man who failed to spot areas for expansion,' he said gruffly. 'It happens.'

Sophie knew that he had softened and something deep inside her shifted and changed as she continued to stare up at him, their eyes locked.

She could scarcely breathe.

'Thank you,' she whispered and he shook his head, wanting to break a connection that was sucking him in, but finding it impossible to do so.

'What are you thanking me for?'

'He was old-fashioned, and unfortunately the people he delegated to were as old-fashioned as he was. Dad should have called a troubleshooter in the minute the profits started taking a nosedive, but he turned a blind eye to what was going on in the company.'

And he turned a blind eye to your ex as well...

That thought made Javier stiffen. Her father had been old-fashioned enough to hold pompous, arrogant views about *foreign upstarts*, to have assumed that some loser with the right accent was the sort of man his daughter should marry.

But that wasn't a road he was willing to go down because it would have absolved Sophie of guilt and the bottom line was that no one had pointed a gun to her head and forced her up the aisle.

She had *wanted* to take that step.

She had *chosen* to stick with the guy even though she knew that he was blowing up the company with his crazy investments.

She had *watched* and *remained silent* as vast sums of vitally needed money had been gambled away.

She had *enabled*. And the only reason she had done that was because she had loved the man.

He turned away abruptly, breaking eye contact, feeling the sour taste of bile rise to his mouth.

'The company will have to be streamlined further,' he told her curtly. 'Dead wood can no longer be tolerated.' He remained where he was, hip against the counter, and watched as she tidied, washed dishes, dried them and stayed silent.

'All the old retainers will end up being sacked. Is that it?'

'Needs must.'

'Some of the old guys have families… They're nearing retirement—and, okay, they may not have been the most efficient on the planet, but they've been loyal…'

'And you place a lot of value on loyalty, do you?' he murmured.

'Don't you?'

'There are times when common sense has to win the battle.'

'You're in charge now. I don't suppose I have any choice, have I?'

Instead of soothing him, her passive, resentful compliance stoked a surge of anger inside him.

'If you'd taken a step back,' he said with ruthless precision, 'and swapped blind loyalty for some common sense, you might have been able to curb some of your dear husband's outrageous excesses…'

'You truly believe that?' She stepped back, swamped by his powerful, aggressive presence, and glared at him.

The last thing Javier felt he needed was to have her try to make feeble excuses for the man who had contributed to almost destroying her family business. What he really felt he needed right now was something stiff to drink. He couldn't look at her without his body going into instant and immediate overdrive and he couldn't talk to her without relinquishing some of his formidable and prized self-control. She affected him in a way no other woman ever had and it annoyed the hell out of him.

'What else is anyone supposed to believe?' he asked with rampant sarcasm. 'Join the dots and you usually get an accurate picture at the end of the exercise.'

'There was no way I could ever have stopped Roger!' Sophie heard herself all but shout at him, appalled by her outburst even as she realised that it was too late to take it back. 'There were always consequences for trying to talk common sense into him!'

The silence that greeted this outburst was electric, sizzling around them, so that the hairs on the back of her neck stood on end.

'Consequences? What consequences?' Javier pressed in a dangerously soft voice.

'Nothing,' Sophie muttered, turning away, but he reached out, circling her forearm to tug her back towards him.

'You don't get to walk away from this conversation after you've opened up a can of worms, Sophie.'

There were so many reasons this was a can of worms that she didn't want to explore. On a deeply emotional level, she didn't want to confront, yet again, the mistakes she had made in the past. She'd done enough of that to last a lifetime and she especially didn't want to confront those mistakes aloud, with Javier as her witness. She didn't want his pity. She didn't want him to sense her vulnerability. He might no longer care about her, but she didn't want to think that he would be quietly satisfied that, having walked out on him, she had got her comeuppance, so to speak.

'It's not relevant!' she snapped, trying and failing to tug her arm out of his grasp.

'Was he…? I don't know what to think here, Soph…'

That abbreviation of her name brought back a flood of memories and they went straight to the core of her, burning a hole through her defence mechanisms. Her soft mouth trembled and she knew that her eyes were glaz-

ing over, which, in turn, made her blink rapidly, fighting
back the urge to burst into tears.

'He could be unpredictable.' Her jaw tightened and
she looked away but he wouldn't allow her to avoid his
searching gaze, tilting her to face him by placing a finger
gently under her chin.

'That's a big word. Try breaking it down into smaller
components...'

'He could be verbally abusive,' she told him jerkily.
'On one occasion he was physically abusive. So there you
have it, Javier. If I'd tried to interfere in his gambling,
there's no accounting for what the outcome might have
been for me.'

Javier was horrified. He dropped his hand and his fingers clenched and unclenched. She might have fancied
herself in love with the guy but that would have been dis-
illusionment on a grand scale.

'Why didn't you divorce him?'

'It was a brief marriage, Javier. And there is more to
this than you know...'

'Did you know that the man had anger issues?' Javier
sifted his fingers through his hair. Suddenly the kitchen
felt the size of a matchbox. He wanted to walk, unfettered;
he wanted to punch something.

'Of course I didn't, and that certainly wasn't the case
when... You don't get it,' she said uneasily. 'And I'd really rather not talk about this any more.'

Javier had been mildly incredulous at her declaration
that her descent into penury had been tougher to handle
than his own lifetime of struggle and straitened circumstances. She, at least, had had the head start of the silver
spoon in the mouth and a failing company was, after all,
still a company with hope of salvation. The crumbling
family pile was still a very big roof over her head.

Now there were muddy, swirling currents underlying

those glib assumptions, and yet again, he lost sight of the clarity of his intentions.

He reminded himself that fundamentally nothing had changed. She had begun something seven years ago and had failed to finish it because she had chosen to run off with her long-time, socially acceptable boyfriend.

That the boyfriend had failed to live up to expectation, that events in her life had taken a fairly disastrous turn, did not change the basic fact that she had strung him along.

But he couldn't recapture the simple black-and-white equation that had originally propelled him. He wondered, in passing, whether he should just have stuck to his quid pro quo solution: 'you give me what I want and I'll give you what you want'.

But no.

He wanted so much more and he could feel it running hot through his veins as she continued to stare at him, unable to break eye contact.

Subtly, the atmosphere shifted. He sensed the change in her breathing, saw the way her pupils dilated, the way her lips parted as if she might be on the brink of saying something.

He cupped her face with his hand and *felt* rather than heard the long sigh that made her shudder.

Sophie's eyelids felt heavy. She wanted to close her eyes because if she closed her eyes she would be able to breathe him in more deeply, and she wanted to do that, wanted to *breathe him in*, wanted to touch him and scratch the itch that had been bothering her ever since he had been catapulted back into her life.

She wanted to kiss him and taste his mouth.

She only realised that she was reaching up to him when she felt the hardness of muscled chest under the palms of her flattened hands.

She heard a whimper of sheer longing which seemed to come from her and then she was kissing him…tongues entwining…exploring…easing some of the aching pain of her body…

She inched closer, pressed herself against him and wanted to rub against his length, wanted to feel his nakedness against hers.

She couldn't get enough of him.

It was as if no time had gone by between them, as if they were back where they had been, a time when he had been able to set fire to her body with the merest of touches. Nothing had changed and everything had changed.

'No!' She came to her senses with horrified, jerky panic. 'This is…I am *not* that girl I once was. I… *No!*'

She'd flung herself at him! She'd practically assaulted the man like a sex-starved woman desperate to be touched! He didn't even care about her! She'd opened up and on the back of that had leapt on him and had managed to surface only after damage had been done!

Humiliation tore through her. She went beetroot-red and stumbled backwards.

'I apologise for that.' She immediately went on the attack. 'It should never have happened and I don't know what came over me!' She ran her fingers through her hair and tried to remain calm but she was shaking like a leaf. 'This isn't what we're about! Not at all.'

Javier raised his eyebrows and her colour deepened.

'There's only business between us,' she insisted through clenched teeth. 'I must have had…I don't normally drink…'

'Now, isn't that the lamest excuse in the world?' Javier murmured. 'Let's blame it on the wine…'

'I don't care what you think!' How could he be so *cool and composed* when she was all over the place? Except, of course, she knew how. Because she was just so much more affected by him than he was by her and she could see all her pride and self-respect disappearing down the plug hole if she didn't get a grip on the situation *right now*.

She cleared her throat and stared, at him and through him. 'I... We have to work alongside one another for a while and...this was just an unfortunate blip. I would appreciate it if you never mention it again. We can both pretend that it never happened, because it will never happen again.'

Javier lowered his eyes and tilted his head to one side as if seriously considering what she had just said.

So many challenges in that single sentence. Did she really and truly believe that she could close the book now that page one had been turned?

He'd tasted her and one small taste wasn't going to do. Not for him and not for her. Whatever her backstory, they both needed to sate themselves with one another and that was what they would do before that place was inevitably reached where walking away was an option.

'If that's how you want to play it.' He shrugged and looked at her. 'And from Monday,' he said with lazy assurance, 'bank on me being around most of the time. We both want the same thing, don't we...?'

'What?' Confused, the only thought that came to her was *each other*—that, at any rate, was the thing that *she* wanted, and she could *smell* that it was what he wanted as well.

'For us to sort out the problems in this company as quickly as possible,' he said in a voice implying surprise that she hadn't spotted the right answer immediately. 'Of course...'

CHAPTER SIX

'No.'

'Give me three good reasons and maybe I'll let you get away with that response.'

Sophie stared at Javier, body language saying it all as she supported herself on her desk, palms flattened on the highly polished surface, torso tilted towards him in angry refusal.

True to his word, he had more or less taken up residence in the premises in Notting Hill.

He wasn't there *all* the time. That would actually have been far easier for her to deal with. No, he breezed in and out. Sometimes she would arrive at eight-thirty to find him installed at the desk which he had claimed as his own, hard at it, there since the break of dawn and with a list of demands that had her on her feet running at full tilt for the remainder of the day.

Other times he might show up mid-afternoon and content himself with checking a couple of things with members of staff before vanishing, barely giving her a second glance.

And there had been days when he hadn't shown up at all and there had been no communication from him.

After six weeks, Sophie felt as though she had been tossed in a tumble dryer with the speed turned to high. She had been miserable, uncertain and fearful when she had had to deal with the horrendous financial mess into which she had been plunged. After her marriage, that had just felt like a continuation of a state of mind that had become more or less natural to her.

Now, though...

She was none of those things. She was a high-wire walker, with excitement and trepidation fighting for dominance. She leapt out of bed every morning with a treacherous sense of anticipation. Her pulses raced every time she took a deep breath and entered the office. Her blood pressure soared when she glanced to the door and saw him stride in. Her heart sang when she saw him stationed at his desk first thing, with his cup of already tepid black coffee on the desk in front of him.

Life was suddenly in technicolor and it scared the living daylights out of her. It had become obvious that she'd never got him out of her system and she seemed to have no immunity against the staggering force of his impact on all her senses. Her heart might be locked away behind walls of ice but her body clearly wasn't.

'I don't have to give you any reasons, Javier.' She was the last man standing and had been about to leave the office at a little after six when Javier had swanned in and stopped her in the act of putting on her jacket.

'Quick word,' he had said, in that way he had of presuming that there would be no argument. He'd then proceeded to lounge back in his chair, gesturing for her to drop what she was doing and take the seat facing him across his desk.

That had been half an hour ago.

'You do, really.' He looked at her lazily. Despite the fact that the largely young staff all dressed informally, Sophie had stuck it out with her prissy work outfits, which ranged from drab grey skirts and neat white blouses to drab black skirts and neat white blouses, all worn with the same flat

black pumps. The ravishing hair which he had glimpsed
on the one occasion when he had surprised her weeks ago
at the apartment had gone back into hiding. Woe betide
she actually released it from captivity between the hours
of eight-thirty and five-thirty!

'Why?'

'Because I think it would work.'

'And of course, because *you* think it would work,
means *I* have to agree and go along with it!'

'How many of the programmes that I've set in motion
over the past couple of months have failed?'

'That's not the point.'

'Any? No. Is the company seeing the start of a turn-
around? Yes. Have the sales team been reporting gains?
Yes.' He folded his hands behind his head and looked at
her evenly. 'Ergo, this idea makes sense and will gener-
ate valuable sales.'

'But I'm not a model, Javier!'

'That's the point, Sophie. You're the face of your company. Putting your image on billboards and in advertising campaigns will personalise the company—half the
battle in wooing potential customers is making them feel
as though they're relating to something more than just a
name and a brand.'

She stared at him mutinously and he gazed calmly
back at her.

The waiting game was taking longer than he had anticipated and he was finding that he was in no rush to
speed things up. He was enjoying her. He was enjoying
the way she made him feel and it wasn't just the reaction
of his body to her. No, he realised that the years of having whatever he wanted and whoever he chose had jaded
him. This blast from the past was...*rejuvenating*. And who
didn't like a spot of rejuvenation in their lives? Of course,
he would have to hurry things along eventually, because

bed was the conclusion to the exercise before normal service was resumed and he returned to the life from which he had been taking a little holiday.

But for the moment...

He really liked the way she blushed. He could almost forget that she was the scheming young girl who had played him for an idiot.

'So we just need to talk about the details. And stop glaring. I thought all women liked to show off their bodies.'

Sophie glared. 'Really, Javier? You really think that?'

'Who wouldn't like to be asked to model?'

'Is that the message you've got from...from the women you've been out with?'

Javier looked at her narrowly because this was the first time she had ventured near the question of his love life. 'Most of the women I've been out with,' he murmured, 'were already catwalk models, accustomed to dealing with the full glare of the public spotlight.'

She'd wondered. Of course she had. Now she knew. Models. Naturally. He certainly wouldn't have dated normal, average women holding down normal, average jobs. He was the man who could have it all and men who could have it all always, but always, seemed to want to have models glued to their arm. It was just so...*predictable*.

'You've stopped glaring,' Javier said. 'Which is a good thing. But now there's disapproval stamped all over your face. What are you disapproving of? My choice of woman?'

'I don't care what your choice of girlfriends has been!'

'Don't you?' He raised his eyebrows. 'Because you look a little agitated. What's wrong with models? Some of them can be relatively clever, as it happens.'

'Relatively clever...' Sophie snorted. Her colour was high and the look in his sinfully dark eyes was doing

weird things to her, making her feel jumpy and thrillingly excited.

Making her nipples tighten…stoking a dampness between her thighs that had nothing to do with her scorn for his choice of dates, whoever those nameless dates had been.

Instant recall of that kiss they had shared made her breath hitch temporarily in her throat.

Just as she had stridently demanded, no mention had been made of it again. It was as though it had never happened. Yes, that was exactly what she had wanted, but it hadn't stopped her constantly harking back to it in her head, reliving the moment and burning up just at the thought of it. How could a bruised and battered heart take second billing to a body that seemed to do whatever it felt like doing?

'You used to tell me that you liked the fact that I had opinions!'

'Many models have opinions—admittedly not of the intellectual variety. They have very strong opinions on, oh, shoes…bags…other models…'

Sophie felt her mouth twitch. She'd missed his sense of humour. In fact, thinking about it, he'd been the benchmark against which Roger had never stood a chance. Not that he had ever been in the running…

In fact, thinking about it, wasn't he the benchmark against which every other man had always been set and always would be? When would that end? How could she resign herself to a half-life because she was still wrapped up in the man in front of her? Because that intense physical reaction just hadn't died and could still make itself felt through all the layers of sadness and despair that had shaped the woman she was now.

She hadn't looked twice at any guy since she'd been on her own. Hadn't even been tempted!

Yet here she was, not only wanting to look but wanting to touch...

Why kid herself? Telling herself to pretend that that kiss had never happened didn't actually mean that it had disappeared from her head.

And telling herself that she should feel nothing for a guy who belonged to her past, a guy who wasn't even interested in her, didn't actually mean that she felt nothing for him.

Lust—that was what it was—and the harder she tried to deny its existence, the more powerful a grip it seemed to have over her.

And part of the reason was because...he *wasn't* indifferent, was he?

Heart racing, she looked down and gave proper house room in her head to all those barely discernible signals she had felt emanating from him over the past few weeks.

For starters, there had been *that kiss*.

She'd felt the way his mouth had explored hers, hungry and greedy and wanting more.

And then, working in the same space, she'd lodged somewhere in the back of her head those accidental brushes when he had leant over her, caging her in in front of her computer so that he could explain some detail on the screen.

She'd committed to memory the way she had occasionally surprised his lazy dark eyes resting on her just a fraction longer than necessary.

And sometimes...didn't he stand just a little too close? Close enough for her to feel the heat from his body? To smell his clean, masculine scent?

Didn't all of that add up to something?

She didn't know whether he was even aware of the dangerous current running between them just beneath the surface. If he was, then it was obvious that he had no intention of doing anything about it.

And then, one day, he would no longer be around.

Right now, he was making sure that his investment paid off. He had sunk money into a bailout, and he wasn't going to see that money flushed down the drain, so he was taking an active part in progressing the company.

But soon enough the company would be on firmer ground and he would be able to retreat and hand over the running of it to other people, herself included.

He would resume his hectic life running his own empire.

And she, likewise, would return to Yorkshire to take up full-time residence in the family home, which she would be able to renovate at least enough to make it a viable selling proposition.

They would part company.

And she would be left with this strange, empty feeling for the rest of her life.

She felt guilty enough about the way they had broken up. On top of that, he would remain the benchmark against which no other man would ever stand a chance of competing for ever.

She should have slept with him.

She knew that now. She should have slept with him instead of holding on to all those girlish fantasies about saving herself for when that time came and she knew that they would be a permanent item, for when she was convinced that their relationship was made to stand the test of time.

If she'd slept with him, he would never have achieved the impossible status of being the only guy capable of turning her on. If she'd slept with him, she might not feel so guilty about the way everything had crashed and burned.

Was it selfish now to think that, if she righted that oversight, she might be free to get on with her life? Things were being sorted financially but what was the good of that if, emotionally, she remained in some kind of dreadful, self-inflicted limbo?

She wasn't the selfish sort. She had never thought of herself as the kind of pushy, independent type who took what she wanted from a man to satisfy her own needs.

The opposite!

But she knew, with a certain amount of desperation, that if she didn't take what she wanted now she would create all sorts of problems for herself down the line.

She wondered whether she could talk to her mother about it and immediately dismissed that thought because, as far as Evelyn Griffin-Watt was concerned, Javier was a youthful blip who had been cut out of her life a long time ago, leaving no nasty scars behind.

Besides, her mother was leading an uncomplicated and contented life in Cornwall; was it really fair to bring back unpleasant memories by resurrecting a long, involved conversation about the past?

'Okay.'

'Come again?'

'I'll do it.'

Javier smiled slowly. In truth, the whole modelling idea had sprung to mind only the day before, and he had anticipated defeat, but here she was...agreeing after a pretty half-hearted battle. At least, half-hearted for her.

'Brilliant decision!'

'I was railroaded into it.'

'Strong word. I prefer *persuaded*. Now, I have a few ideas...'

Sophie peeped through a crack in the curtains and looked down into the courtyard which had been tarted up for the day into a vision of genteel respectability.

The shoot had been arranged in the space of a week, during which time Sophie had spoken to various media types and also to various stylists. She imagined that they were being paid a phenomenal amount for the day because they had all bent over backwards to pay attention to what she had said.

Which hadn't been very much because she had no idea what questions to ask other than the obvious one: *How long is it all going to take?*

Javier hadn't been at any of those meetings, choosing instead to delegate to one of the people in his PR department, but that hadn't bothered Sophie.

In a way, she'd been glad, because she had a plan and the element of surprise was a big part of the plan.

Except, the day had now arrived and the courtyard was buzzing with cameramen, the make-up crew, the director, producer and all the other people whose roles were, quite frankly, bewildering. And where was Javier? Nowhere to be seen.

It was today or it was not at all.

She dropped the curtain and turned to the full-length mirror which the stylist had installed in the bedroom because the small one on the dressing table *'just won't do, darling!'*

The brief which she had agreed on with Javier would have her standing next to a gleaming articulated lorry bearing the company logo, in dungarees, a checked shirt and a jaunty cowboy hat on her head.

Sophie had decided to take it up a notch and the reflection staring back at her had dumped the dungarees in favour of a pair of shorts with a frayed hem. The checked shirt remained the same, but it was tied under her breasts so that her flat stomach was exposed, and there was no jaunty cowboy hat on her head. Instead, she had slung it on her back so that her hair was wild and loose.

Javier had vaguely aimed for something wholesome and appealing, a throwback to the good old days of home-baked bread and jam, which was some of the cargo transported in the lorries. He'd suggested that it would be a nice contrast to the new face of the business, which was streamlined and fully up to spec on the technological front, which it hadn't been before. Something along the lines of the home-baked bread getting from A to B before it had time to cool from the oven and Sophie's image was going to sell the absolute truth of that.

She had taken it up a notch from wholesome to wholesome *and sexy*.

It had been her brainwave when she had sat there, numbly recognising that she would never, ever get over him if she didn't sleep with him, if she didn't seduce him into bed. He'd been in her head for years and she couldn't think of another way to make sure that he was knocked off the position he occupied there.

She'd never seduced anyone in her life before. Just thinking about doing something like that was terrifying, but when it came to her emotions, she had to be proactive. As proactive as she had been dealing with the mess she'd been left to clear up in the company.

She wasn't a simpering teenager any more, seeing the future through rose-tinted specs and believing in happy-ever-after endings.

She was an adult, jaded by experience, who would be left nursing regret for the rest of her life if she didn't give this a shot. And so what if she failed? What if he looked at her get-up and burst out laughing? So, she might have a moment's humiliation, but that would be worth the life-time she would have had thinking about an opportunity that had passed her by, an opportunity to claim what she knew could have been hers all those years ago.

The time had come to take a chance.

Except, it didn't look as though the wretched man was going to show up!

Her nerves were shot, her pulses were racing and she hadn't eaten since lunchtime the previous day because of the shot nerves and the racing pulses...

She was a mess and it was all going to be for nothing because Javier had obviously had his brainwave and then allowed his minions to realise it while he stepped back from the scene of the action.

She slunk down to the courtyard with a white bath-robe over her screamingly uncomfortable outfit and was immediately appropriated by a host of people whose only function seemed to be to get her ready for *the shoot*.

She allowed herself to be manoeuvred while disappointment cascaded through her in waves.

No Javier. No big seduction. It had taken absolutely everything out of her. And there was no way she was going to do this again. She wasn't going to set herself the task of staging seductive scenes in the hope of igniting something that probably wasn't there for him anyway, whatever stupid signals she thought she'd read!

A mirror was brought for her to inspect herself. Sophie barely glanced at the fully made-up face staring back at her. After the tension of the past couple of days, and the nervous excitement of earlier this morning as she had got dressed, she now felt like a balloon that had been deflated before it had made it to the party.

She was aware of orders being shouted and poses she was being instructed to adopt.

No one had questioned the slight change in outfit. She was Javier's personal pet project and no one dared question her for fear that she would report unfavourably back to their boss.

She was supposed to turn up in denim and a checked top with a cowboy hat and they knew what the direction of the shoot should be. The outfit was daring, though, and the poses were therefore slightly more daring than perhaps originally choreographed.

She had her back to the camera team, one hand resting lightly on the shining lorry, looking over her shoulder with a smile, when she heard his roar from behind her.

She'd given up on Javier coming.

But before she'd clocked his absence, she had somehow imagined him standing amongst the crew, goggle-eyed as he looked at her, wanting her as much as she wanted him and knowing that he had to have her. She'd pictured him waiting impatiently until the crew had packed up and gone and then...

Her wanton thoughts had not formulated much beyond that point. There would be a lot of ground to cover before the scene shifted from impatient seduction to the satisfied aftermath.

'What the hell is going on here?'

Sophie stumbled back against the lorry and the entire assembled crew stared at Javier in growing confusion, aware that they had done something wrong but not quite sure what.

Javier strode forward through them like a charging bull, face as black as thunder.

'You!' He pointed to the director of the shoot, who jumped to attention and began stammering out his consternation, puzzled as to what the problem was. The shoot was going very well. Indeed, if Javier wanted, he could see what was already in the bag. It was going to do the job and sell the business like hot cakes straight from the oven. Sophie was a brilliant model. No temper tantrums and no diva pouting. She was perfect for the job and the fact that she was part-owner of the company was going to be a nice touch. They'd make sure they got that in in the backdrop...

Javier held up one cold, imperious hand. 'This was not what I wanted!' he snapped. He looked across to Sophie with a scowl and she folded her arms defensively.

'They have no idea what you're going on about, Javier,' she said sweetly, strolling towards him although she was quaking inside, unable to tear her eyes away from his strident masculinity. He dominated the space around him, a towering, forbidding figure who clearly inspired awe, fear and respect in equal measure.

It was an incredible turn-on to think that this was the guy who had once teased her, told her that she made him weak, the guy whose eyes had flared with desire whenever they had rested on her.

The guy she wanted so much that it hurt.

The guy she was prepared to risk humiliation for.

'Consider this shoot over for the day.' He directed the command at the director but his eyes were focused on Sophie as she moved to stand right in front of him.

He cursed the overseas phone call that had held him up and then the traffic on the motorways and B-roads that wound their way to her family home. If he'd arrived when he had originally planned, he would have…

Made sure that she didn't step one delicate foot out of the house dressed in next to nothing.

He was shocked by his sudden regression to a Neanderthal, which was the very opposite of the cool composure he prided himself on having.

Hands thrust deep into his pockets, he continued to stare at her with ferocious intent while the entire assembled crew hurriedly began packing their equipment and disappearing fast.

Sophie heard the gravelly chaos of reversing cars and SUVs but she was locked into a little bubble in which the only two people who existed were herself and Javier.

'That wasn't the outfit we agreed on.' His voice was

a low, driven snarl and she tilted her chin at a mutinous angle.

'Checked shirt...*tick*. Denim...*tick*. Stupid cowboy hat...*tick*. Trainers...*tick*...'

'You know what I mean,' Javier gritted, unable to take his eyes off her.

'Do I?' She hadn't realised how chilly it was and she hugged herself.

'You're cold,' he said gruffly, removing his jacket and settling it around her shoulders. For a second, she just wanted to close her eyes and breathe in the scent from it.

And this was what it was all about. This *hunger* that had never gone away, but which *had* to go away, because if it didn't it would eat away at her for ever. And there was only one way of it just *going away and leaving her alone*.

'Tell me,' she pressed huskily. 'Why are you so furious? It wasn't fair of you to send all those poor people packing. They were only doing their job.'

'That's not the way I see it,' Javier growled. The jacket, way too big, drowned her and it was really weird the way that just made her look even sexier. He shifted in an attempt to ease the discomfort of his erection. Was she wearing a bra? He didn't think so and that made him angry all over again.

'How do you see it?'

'The brief was for you to look wholesome!' He raked his fingers through his hair and shook his head. This was the first time he had ventured to her family home but he hadn't noticed a single brick. His entire focus was on her. She consumed him. 'The attractive girl next door! Not a sex siren out to snag a man! How the hell is *that* supposed to sell the company?'

'I thought that sex sold everything?'

'Is that why you did it? Was that your concept of positive input? Dressing up in next to nothing and draping yourself over that lorry like a hooker posing in a motor-bike shot?'

'How *dare you*?' But she flushed and cringed and knew that there was some justification for that horrible slur. She barely stopped to think that in summer there were many, many girls her age who went out dressed like this and thought nothing of it. She just knew that it wasn't *her*.

'The entire crew,' he delineated coldly, 'must have had a field day ogling you. Or maybe that was what you had in mind. Is that it? Has living in London kick-started an urge to push the limits? Have you realised how much tamer your life up here was?'

'I didn't do this so that any of the crew could *ogle me*.' She fought to maintain his cool, disapproving stare and took a deep breath. 'I did this so that...' Her voice faltered. Her hands were clammy and she licked her lips as the tension stretched and stretched between them.

'So that...?' Javier prompted softly.

'So that *you* could ogle me...'

CHAPTER SEVEN

THIS WAS WHAT he had been waiting for, the slow burn until the conflagration, because he knew that it would be a conflagration. She oozed sex appeal without even realising it. And she had come to him. He hadn't been mistaken about those invisible signals his antennae had been picking up and he marvelled that he had ever doubted himself.

Of course, he would have to make it clear to her that this wasn't some kind of romance, that whatever they did would be a purely physical animal act. They'd had their window for romance once and she'd put paid to that. Romance was definitely off the cards now.

He smiled slowly, his beautiful, sensuous mouth curving as he lazily ran his eyes over her flushed face, taking in everything from the slight tremor of her hands to the nervous tic in her neck, a beating pulse that was advertising what she wanted as loud and as clear as if it had been written in neon lettering over her head.

Him.

She wanted him.

The wheel had turned full circle, and having walked away from him, she was now walking back.

That tasted good and it would taste even better when he laid down his conditions.

'Is that so?' he breathed huskily, his erection threatening to hamper movement.

Sophie didn't say anything in response to that. She read the satisfaction in his gleaming eyes and a primal lust that was so powerful that it easily swept aside any nagging doubt that she might be embarking on the wrong course of action.

He caught the lapels of his jacket and drew her a few inches towards him. 'There were less complicated ways of getting my attention, Soph...' he murmured. 'A simple *I want you* would have done the trick.'

The fact that he made no attempt to kiss her or touch her acted as an unbearably powerful aphrodisiac. Her heart was beating so fast that it felt as though it was going to explode and she was melting everywhere. She licked her lips and Javier followed that tiny movement with such intense concentration that it made her blood heat up even further.

'That would have been...too much,' she breathed. 'It was tough enough...' She gestured down to her lack of outfit and Javier half-smiled, remembering how shy she had once been, despite the fact that she had the face and figure that could turn heads from a mile away.

'Getting into your skimpy little get-up? Let's go inside. It's getting breezier out here.' He kept his distance but the electricity crackled between them. He wasn't touching her and he hardly dared because one touch and he would have to have her at once, fast and hard, up against a wall.

He didn't want that. He wanted slow and leisurely. He wanted to explore every inch of the woman who had escaped him. Only then would he be able to walk away satisfied.

Walking towards the house, he really noticed the signs of disrepair which he had failed to see when he had arrived earlier. He paused and looked critically at the façade and Sophie followed the leisurely and critical inspection, marvelling at the damage that had been done over a handful of years.

She longed to reach out and touch him. She longed to link her fingers through his in the same careless gesture of ownership to which she had once been privy. She reminded herself that times had changed since then. This was something quite, quite different.

'You're right,' Javier said drily, stepping back as she pushed open the front door. 'The place is falling down.'

'I know.' Sophie looked around her, seeing it through his eyes. He was now used to the best that money could buy. The apartment loaned to her was pristine, like something from the centre pages of a house magazine. This house, on the other hand...

They were in a cavernous hall. Javier could see that this would have been an enormous and elegant country estate once upon a time but the paint was peeling, the once ornate ceiling was cracked and he was sure that further exploration would reveal a lot more problems.

'I'm sorry,' he said gravely and Sophie looked at him, startled.

'What for?'

'You told me that penury was harder for you than it ever had been for me and you were probably right. I knew no better and things could only go up. You knew better and the journey down must have been swift and painful. But...' he tilted his head to one side and looked at her '...you coped.'

'I didn't have a choice, did I?' She suddenly felt shy. Should they be heading up to the bedroom? What was the etiquette for two people who had decided that they are going to sleep together? Not in the 'clutching one another while stumbling up the stairs' kind of way, but in the manner of a business transaction. At least that was what it felt like—two people putting an end to their unfinished business.

They wanted each other but neither of them liked it.

'Show me the rest of the place.'

'Why?' She was genuinely puzzled.

'I used to wonder what it was like. You talked about your home a lot when we were…going out. At the time, it had sounded like a slice of paradise, especially compared to where I had grown up.'

'And I bet you're thinking, *how the mighty have fallen…*' She laughed self-consciously because all of a sudden she was walking on quicksand. This was the man she had fallen in love with—a man who was interested, warm, curious, empathetic… For a minute, the cynical, mocking stranger was gone and she was floundering.

'No. I'm not,' he said quietly. 'I'm thinking that it must have taken a lot of courage not to have cracked under the strain.'

Sophie blushed and began showing him through the various rooms on the ground floor of the house. There were a lot of them and most of them were now closed with the heating off so that money could be saved. When she and Oliver had realised the necessity of putting the house on the market, they had made an effort to do a patch-up job here and there, but not even those dabs of paint in some of the rooms could conceal the disintegrating façade.

The more she talked, the more aware she was of him there by her side, taking it all in. If this was his idea of foreplay, it couldn't have been more effective, because she was on fire.

Talking…who would have thought that it could have changed the atmosphere between them so thoroughly?

Her nipples were tight and tingling and the ache between her thighs made her want to moan out loud. She could *feel* him, could feel herself warming to him, and she had to fight the seductive urge to start mingling the past with the present, confusing the powerful, ruthless man he had become with the man she had once known.

When they were through with the ground floor, she gazed up the sweeping staircase before turning to him and clearing her throat.

'The bedrooms are upstairs.' She wanted to sound controlled and adult, a woman in charge of a situation she had engendered. Instead, she heard the nervous falsetto of her voice and inwardly cringed.

Javier lounged against the door frame, hoping that it wouldn't collapse under his weight from dry rot or termites. He folded his arms and looked at her as she fidgeted for a few seconds before meeting his gaze.

'Why are you so nervous?' he enquired, reaching out to adjust the collar of the jacket which she was still clutching around her, and then allowing his hands to remain there, resting lightly on her. 'It's not as though you haven't felt the touch of my lips on yours before...'

Sophie inhaled sharply.

She had got this far and now realised that she hadn't actually worked out what happened next. Yes, on the physical level, terrifying and exciting though that was, her body would simply just take over. She knew it would. She remembered what it had felt like to be touched by him, the way he had made her whole body ignite in a burst of red-hot flame.

How much more glorious would it feel to actually *make love* with him...?

She was nervous, yes, thrillingly so at the prospect of making love with him. But there were other things... things that needed to be discussed...and now that the time had come she wondered whether she would be able to open up to him.

'I'm... I'm not nervous about...about...'

'Going to bed with me? Being touched all over by me? Your breasts and nipples with my tongue? Your belly...?' He loved the fluttering of her eyes as she listened, the way

her tongue darted out to moisten her lips and the way she
was breathing just a little faster; tiny, jerky breaths that
were an unbelievable turn-on because they showed him
what she was feeling. He doubted that she could even put
into words what she was feeling because…

Because of her inherent shyness. It almost made him
burst out laughing because she was far from shy. She was
a widow who had been through the mill.

'I'm not nervous about any of that!' Sophie glared at
him. 'Not really.'

'You're as jumpy as a cat on a hot tin roof, Sophie. If
that's not nerves, then I don't know what is.'

'I need to talk to you,' she said jerkily and watched as
the shutters instantly came down over his beautiful eyes.

'Is this the part where you start backtracking?' he
asked softly. 'Because I don't like those sorts of games.
You did a runner on me once before and I wouldn't like
to think that I'm in line for a repeat performance…'

Sophie chewed her lip nervously. To open up would
expose so much and yet how could she not?

How else would she be able to explain away the fact
that she was still a virgin?

A virgin widow. It wasn't the first time that she'd
wanted to laugh at the irony of that. Laugh or cry. Maybe
both.

Would he even notice that she was a virgin? He would
know that she lacked experience but would he really notice just how inexperienced she truly was?

Could she pretend?

'I'm not backtracking.' She glanced up the stairs and
then began heading up, glancing over her shoulder just
once. At the top of the staircase, she eased the jacket off
and slung it over the banister. 'If I didn't want to do this…'
she half-smiled '…would I be doing *this*?'

Javier looked at her long and hard and then returned that half-smile with one of his own.

'No, I don't suppose you would be,' he murmured, taking the steps two at a time until he was right by her, crowding her in a way that was very, very sexy.

He curved his big hand behind the nape of her neck and kissed her.

With a helpless whimper, Sophie leant into him. She undid a couple of his shirt buttons and slipped her hands underneath the silky cotton and the helpless whimper turned into a giddy groan as she felt the hard muscle of his chest.

This was what she had dreamed of and it was only now, when she was touching him, that she realised just how long those dreams had been in her head, never-ending versions of the same thing...*touching him.*

Javier eventually pulled back and gazed down at her flushed face.

'We need to get to a bed.' He barely recognised his own voice, which was thick with desire, the voice of someone drunk with *want.* 'If we don't, I'm going to turn into a caveman, rip off your clothes right here on the staircase and take you before we can make it to a bedroom...'

Sophie discovered that she was wantonly turned on by the image of him doing that.

'My bedroom's just along the corridor,' she whispered huskily, galvanising her jelly-like legs forward.

There were numerous bedrooms on the landing and most of the doors were shut, which led Javier to assume that they were never used. Probably in as much of a state of disrepair as some of the rooms downstairs which had been sealed off.

Her bedroom was at the very end of the long, wide corridor and it was huge.

'I keep meaning to brighten it up a bit,' she apologised,

nervous all over again because, now that they were in the bedroom, all her fears and worries had returned with a vengeance. 'I've had some of the pictures on the walls since I was a kid and now, in a weird way, I would feel quite sad to take them down and chuck them in the bin...'

He was strolling through the bedroom, taking in absolutely everything, from the books on the bookshelf by the window to the little framed family shots in silver frames which were lined up on her dressing table.

Eventually he turned to face her and began unbuttoning his shirt.

Sophie tensed and gulped. She watched in fascination as his shirt fell open, revealing the hard chest she had earlier felt under her fingers.

He shrugged it off and tossed it on the ground and her mouth went dry as he walked slowly towards her.

'There's...there's something I should tell you...' she stammered, frozen to the spot and very much aware of the great big bed just behind her.

Javier didn't break stride.

Talk? He didn't think so. The marriage she had hoped for and the guy she had ditched him to be with hadn't gone according to plan. That changed nothing. She still remained the same woman who had strung him along and then walked away because, when you got right down to it, he had not been good enough for her.

'No conversation,' he murmured, trailing his finger along her collarbone until she sighed and squirmed and her eyelids fluttered.

'What do you mean?'

'No confidences, no long explanations about why you're doing what you're doing. We both know the reason that we're here.' He hooked his fingers under the checked shirt and circled her waist, then gently began to undo the buttons on the shirt. 'We still want one another,' he murmured, nibbling her ear.

'Yes...' Sophie could barely get the word out. Her body tingled everywhere and his delicate touch sent vibrations racing through her. She rubbed her thighs together and heard him laugh softly, as if he knew that she was trying to ease the pain between them.

'This is all there is, Soph.' There was a finality to stating the obvious which, for some reason, set his teeth on edge, although he didn't quite understand why when it was pretty straightforward a situation. He was propelling her very gently towards the bed; she realised that only when she tumbled back, and then he leant forward, propping himself up on either side of her, staring down at her gravely.

Sophie couldn't have uttered a word if she'd tried. She was mesmerised by the compelling intensity of his expression, the soft, sexy drawl of his voice, the penetrating, opaque blackness of his eyes.

Somehow he had managed to undo every last button of her shirt and the cool air was a sweet antidote to the heat that was consuming her.

He stood up and paused for a few seconds with his fingers resting loosely on the zipper of his trousers.

She could see the bulge of his erection and half closed her eyes when she thought about the mechanics of something so impressively large entering her.

But no talking, he'd said...

No talking because he wasn't interested in what she had to say.

As though reading the anxious direction of her thoughts, he dropped his hand and joined her on the bed, manoeuvring her onto her side so that they were lying stomach to stomach, then she flopped over onto her back and stared up at the ceiling.

'Look at me, Soph.' He framed her face with his hand so that she was forced to look at him. His breath was warm on her cheek and she wanted to evade the deadly seriousness of his gaze. 'Whatever it is you want to tell me, resist, because I'm not interested.' He felt a sharp jab of pain deep inside him but pressed on, because this had to be said, and wasn't this all part of that wheel turning full circle? That she'd come to him and now, with her in the palm of his hand, he could reduce her to humility? That he could let her know, without even having to vocalise the obvious, that the shoe was firmly on the other foot?

That he was the one calling the shots?

He had the uncomfortable feeling that it should have felt more satisfying than it did.

'This is something we both have to do, wouldn't you agree? If you hadn't ended up back in my life in a way neither of us could ever have predicted, well, we wouldn't be here now. But we're here and...' He smoothed his hand over her thigh and felt her shudder, wishing she wasn't wearing clothes because he was itching to feel all of her, naked, supple and compliant. 'We have to finish this. But finishing it doesn't involve tender sharing of our life histories. This isn't a courtship and it's important for you to recognise that.'

Sophie felt the hot crawl of colour seep into her cheeks. Of course, he was just being honest. Of course, this was just about the sex they should have had all those years ago. Nothing more. If she could, she would have slid off the bed, looked at him with haughty disdain and told him to clear off, but what her body wanted and *needed* was calling the shots now.

'I know that,' she assured him in a calm voice which was not at all how she was feeling inside. 'I'm not on the lookout for a courtship! Do you really think that I'm the same idiotic young girl you knew all those years ago,

Javier? I've grown up! Life has…flattened me in ways you couldn't begin to understand.' Right now, she didn't feel very grown up. Indeed, she felt as unsure and uncertain as a teenager.

But she really wasn't the same girl she had once been. That much, at least, was true.

Javier frowned. Her words were the words of a cynic altered by circumstance, but the tenor of her voice…the soft tremble of her mouth…seemed to be saying something different, which was, of course, ridiculous.

'Good,' he purred. 'So we understand one another.'

'A one-night stand,' she murmured, flattening her hand against his chest as a tingle of unbridled excitement rippled through her. She'd never been a one-night stand kind of girl but a one-night stand with this man would be worth the final demolishing of all her girlhood, or whatever remnants remained in some dark closet at the very back of her mind.

Javier was a little piqued at the speed with which she had accepted the brevity of what they were about to embark on but he was done with thinking.

His erection was so rock-hard it was painful and he took her hand and guided it to his trousers.

'If you don't hold me hard,' he muttered, 'I'm not going to be able to finish what's been started the way it should be finished.'

'What do you mean?'

'I mean it's time to stop talking.'

He stood up in one fluid movement and began undressing. She marvelled at his utter lack of self-consciousness. He looked at her and held her fascinated gaze as he removed his trousers, tossing it on the ground, where it joined his shirt, leaving him in his low-slung silk boxers, which did nothing to conceal the evidence of his arousal.

She did this to him!

Hard on the heels of that thought came another, less welcome one.

How many other women had done this to him? How many women had lain on a bed and watched him with the same open-mouthed fascination with which *she* was now watching him?

He wouldn't have slept with any of *them* because they had started something years ago that needed *to be finished*. He wouldn't have slept with any of them because he'd been *driven to*. He would have slept with them *because he'd wanted to*. The difference felt huge but it was good that she was aware of that, because it would make it easy to walk away when they were finished making love.

It would make it easy to detach.

'I'm really surprised you never got married,' she blurted out and he grinned and slipped onto the bed alongside her.

His erection butted against her thigh and then against her stomach as he angled her to face him.

Javier was accustomed to women who couldn't wait to strip off so that they could show him what was on offer and it was weirdly erotic to be naked and in bed with a woman who was still fully clothed. He couldn't wait to get those clothes off, yet he was reluctant to undress her, wanting to savour the thrill of anticipation.

Once they'd made love, once he'd had her, it would signal the end and where was the harm in delaying that inevitable moment? They had the night to make love and in the morning, with that itch put to rest for ever, he would leave and contrive never to see her again. His relationship with her company would revert to being just another business deal, which would, he knew, be as successful as all the other business deals he had made over the years.

This didn't taste of revenge, not the revenge that he had

seen as his when her brother had first entered his office on a begging mission.

This was a conclusion and it was one over which he had complete control.

He was exactly where he was meant to be and it felt good.

'I don't think marriage and I would make happy bed partners.' He propped himself up on one elbow and began undressing her. 'A successful marriage...' the shirt was off '...requires just the sort of commitment...'

Now she was wriggling out of the shorts, leaving just a pair of lacy briefs that matched her bra. Her breasts were full and firm and he could see the dark circle of her nipples through the lace.

'That I don't have...' He breathed unsteadily. 'Your breasts are driving me crazy, Sophie...' He bent to circle one nipple through the lacy bra with his mouth and she gasped and arched into his questing mouth.

They hadn't even got this far first time round. She had been as prim and as chaste as a Victorian maiden and he had held off, curbing his natural instinct to swoop and conquer. He closed his mind off to the reasons why she had been so damned prim and chaste because the only thing that mattered now was the taste of her.

He didn't unhook the bra. Instead, he pushed it over her breasts and, for a few unbelievably erotic seconds, he just stared. The big, circular discs of her nipples pouted at him. Her breasts were smooth, creamy and soft. He was a teenager again, with a teenager's crazy, wildly out-of-control hormones, trying hard not to come prematurely.

He almost wanted to laugh in disbelief at the extraordinary reaction of his normally well-behaved body.

He licked the stiffened bud of one nipple and then lost himself in something he had dreamed of, suckling and drawing her nipple into his mouth, flicking his tongue over the tip and just loving her responsive body underneath him.

Without breaking the devastating caress, he slid his hand under the small of her back so that she was arched up, writhing and squirming as he moved from nipple to the soft underside of her breast, nuzzling and tasting.

Driving himself mad.

He had to hold off for a few seconds to catch his breath; he had to grit his teeth and summon up all his willpower to withstand the urge of her hand as she reached up, blindly curving the contour of his cheek, desperate for him to resume what he had been doing.

Without his usual finesse, he clumsily ripped the remainder of her clothes off.

How long had he been waiting for this moment? It felt like for ever as he gazed down at her rosy, flushed body, his breathing laboured as if he had just completed a marathon.

She was perfect.

Her skin was silky smooth, her breasts pert, inviting all sorts of wicked thoughts, and as his eyes drifted lower…

The soft, downy hair between her legs elicited a groan that sounded decidedly helpless.

So this was what it felt like…

This heady sense of power as she watched him watching her and losing control.

By the time she had married Roger, she had known the full scale of the mistake she had made, but she had still been young and naïve enough fundamentally to trust that the lectures from her parents about the follies of youth and the transitory nature of her attraction to the wrong man were somehow rooted in truth. She hadn't, back then, been sure enough of herself to resist the wisdom of the two people she trusted and loved.

Surely time would make her see sense and make her

forget Javier and the new, wonderful feelings he had roused in her?

It wasn't as though she didn't *like* Roger, after all…

But it hadn't turned out that way. Neither of them had been able to find a way through all the muddy water under the bridge and she had discovered fast enough how easy it was for loathing to set in, forging a destructive path through affection and friendship.

She hadn't turned him on and he, certainly, had never, ever had the sort of effect on her that Javier was now having.

It was suddenly very, very important that they do this. Would he walk away if he knew that she was a virgin? Was he hoping for someone experienced, as he doubtless assumed she was, who could perform all sorts of exciting gymnastics in bed?

In her head, she balanced the scales.

Alarm and disappointment with her if he found out that he was dealing with someone who might not live up to expectation…versus her embarrassment at having to come clean and tell him the truth about the marriage into which she should never have entered…

Which in turn would lead her down all sorts of uncertain routes. Because how else could she explain away her mistake without letting him know just how much she had felt for him all those years ago, how deeply she had fallen in love with him?

And, in turn, would that lead him to start thinking that she might just go and do the same again, after he had issued his warnings and told her that this was just sex and nothing more—no romance, no courtship and certainly no repeat performance of what they had once had?

'I've never done this before.' She couldn't face the embarrassment of him pulling away, appalled that he had mistaken her for someone else, someone who might prove to be fun in bed instead of a novice waiting to be taught, guided only by instinct.

It took a few seconds for Javier to register what she had just said and he paid attention to her words only because of the tone in which they had been spoken.

He was still confused, though, as he pulled back to stare down at her.

'You mean you've never had a one-night stand with an ex-flame?'

'No.' Face flaming with embarrassment, she wriggled into a sitting position and drew the duvet cover protectively over her, suddenly shy in the face of his probing dark eyes.

'What, then?' He had never talked so much in bed with any woman. Frustrated, he raked his fingers through his hair and sighed. 'Do I need to get dressed to sit this one out?'

'What are you talking about?'

'What I'm asking is…is this going to be a long conversation involving more confidence sharing? Should I make myself a pot of tea and settle down for the long haul?'

'Why do you have to be so sarcastic?' Sophie asked, stung.

'Because,' Javier pointed out coolly, 'this should be a simple situation, Sophie. Once upon a time, there was something between us. Now there isn't—aside, that is, from the small technicality that we never actually made it past the bedroom door. Indeed, we never made it even near the bedroom door. So here we are, rectifying that oversight before going our separate ways. I'm not sure that there's anything much to talk about because it's not one of those *getting to know you* exercises.'

'I know! You've already told me that. Not that you needed to! I don't have any illusions as to why we're here…and *I know* it's not because we're *getting to know one another*!' Which didn't mean that it didn't hurt to have it laid out so flatly. 'I don't *want to get to know you*, Javier!'

Javier frowned. 'What is that supposed to mean?'

'It means that you're not the sort of guy I could ever be interested in now.'

Did that bother him? No. Why should it? 'Explain!' And if he wanted an explanation, it was simply to indulge his curiosity. Perfectly understandable.

'You're arrogant.' She ticked off on one finger. 'You're condescending. You think that, because you have stacks of money, you can say whatever you want and do whatever you please. You can't even be bothered to make a show of being polite because you don't think you ever have to be...'

Javier was outraged. 'I can't believe I'm hearing this!' He leapt out of the bed to pace the floor, glaring at the shabby wallpaper and the crumbling cornices.

Sophie watched him, shocked at what she had just said but in no way having the slightest intention of taking any of it back. She had to keep her eyes glued to his face because that glorious body of his was still doing things to her, even in the middle of the sudden squall that had blown up between them.

'That's because I bet no one has the courage to ever criticise you.'

'That's ridiculous! I *invite* openness from my staff! In fact, I welcome positive criticism from everyone!'

'Maybe you forgot to tell them.' Sophie glared. 'Because you behave just like someone who has the rack on standby for anyone who dares speak their mind!'

'Maybe...' He strolled towards the bed and then leant over, caging her in, hands on either side of her. 'You're the only one who thinks there's room for improvement in me...'

'Arrogant! Do you honestly think you're *that perfect*?'

'I haven't had complaints,' he purred, suddenly turned on and invigorated by the heat between them. 'Especially from the opposite sex. Stop arguing, Soph. And stop talking…'

There was no way he was going to allow her to dance around this any longer.

And she didn't want to.

She met his eyes steadily and took a deep breath. 'You're not going to believe this…'

'I loathe when people open a sentence with that statement.'

'I've never slept with anyone before, Javier. I'm…I'm still a virgin…'

CHAPTER EIGHT

'DON'T BE RIDICULOUS.' He shot her a look of amused disbelief. 'You can't be.'

Sophie continued to stare at him until he frowned as he continued to grapple with her bolt-from-the-blue remark.

'And there's no need to try to pique my interest by pretending,' he crooned softly. 'My interest is already piqued. In fact, my interest was piqued the second your brother walked through the door with his begging bowl and sob story...'

'What are you saying? Are you telling me that...that...?'

'I suddenly realised what had been missing for the past seven years—completion.'

'You wanted us to end up in bed?'

'I knew we would.'

'Is that why you offered to help us?' Sophie edged away from him, shaking with anger. 'Because you wanted... *completion*?'

'Why are you finding that so hard to believe?' Javier couldn't believe that the tide had turned so swiftly. One minute, he had been touching her, and now here she was, spinning him some tall story about being a virgin and staring at him as though he had suddenly transformed into the world's most wanted.

'I'm surprised...' she said bitterly, grabbing clothes

from the floor and hopping into them, beyond caring that he was watching her dress and wishing that he would follow suit and do the same '…that you didn't try to blackmail me into bed by offering me a deal in return!' Silence greeted this remark and she paused and stared up at him through narrowed eyes that were spitting fire.

'You thought about it, though, didn't you…?' she said slowly.

'This is a ridiculous conversation.' Javier slipped on his boxers and moved to stand by the window, arms folded, his expression thunderous.

'Did you pick all that stuff for the flat? I wondered about that, wondered how come everything seemed to have a personal touch when you didn't actually live there. When your taste, judging from your office, didn't run to old-fashioned… Did you think that shoving me into free accommodation where I'd be surrounded by stuff that made me feel at home was a good way to butter me up into sleeping with you, so that you could have your *completion*?'

Javier flushed darkly and glowered. 'Since when is it a criminal offence to choose what to put in your own property?'

'I'm going to add *manipulative and underhand* to *arrogant and full of yourself*!' He was all those things *and more*, yet she still couldn't tear her eyes away from his masculine perfection as he remained standing with his back to the window, which just went to show how downright *unfair* fate could be.

She should throw him out of the house, tell him what he could do with his deal and order him never to darken her doors again.

Instead, the awful truth was sinking in…

She still wanted him, still wanted to sleep with him, and for her it wasn't all about completion, even though that was what she had told herself, because that was the acceptable explanation for what she felt.

For her...

A jumble of confused, mixed-up emotions poured through her, weakening her, and she feebly pushed them aside because she didn't want to dwell on them.

Javier walked slowly towards her, half-naked, bronzed, a thing of such intense beauty that it took her breath away.

'So I weighted the scales in my favour,' he murmured. 'Where's the crime in that?' He was standing right in front of her now and he could almost *feel* the war raging inside her. Flee or stay put?

She wasn't running.

Because, like it or not, she wanted him as much as he wanted her and getting all worked up about the whys and hows didn't make a scrap of difference. The power of lust.

'I'm accustomed to getting what I want and I want you. And, yes, I did consider holding the offer of financial help over your head in exchange for that glorious body that has disturbed far too many of my nights, but I didn't.'

'Arrogant...' Sophie muttered. But she reluctantly had to concede that at least he wasn't trying to economise with the truth and the fact that he had used whatever ploys he had at hand to get what he wanted was all just part and parcel of his personality. There wasn't a scrap of shame or sheepishness in his voice.

He shrugged and smiled. 'Tell me you don't like it.'

'No one likes arrogance.' Her heart was beating madly. In the space of a heartbeat, the atmosphere had shifted right back to the sexy intimacy they had been sharing only moments earlier, before everything had gone downhill.

Before she had told him that she was a virgin.

'I've always been arrogant and you weren't complaining seven years ago. Why did you tell me that you were a virgin?'

'Because it's the truth,' she whispered stiltedly. 'I know you probably find that hard to believe.'

'Try impossible.'

'Roger...he...'

She wasn't lying or making up something to try to pique his interest. She was telling the truth. He could see it in her face and hear it in the clumsy awkwardness of her voice.

'Sit down.'

'Sorry?'

'You look as though you're about to collapse.' He guided her away from the bed with all its heated connotations of sex towards a chair that was by the window, facing into the room. Perhaps she sat there in the light evenings and read a book. It was the sort of thing he could picture her doing.

What he *couldn't* picture her doing was marrying some man only to spend her married life in a state of frustrated virginity.

Who the hell did something like that?

'You hadn't slept with the man before you...agreed to walk up the aisle with him?' This when she was sitting on the chair like a fragile wooden doll and he had dragged over the only other chair in the room, which had been in front of the oversized, dark mahogany dressing table.

'He...I...' The weight of all those nagging thoughts that she had temporarily pushed aside surged forward in a rush that made her breath hitch in her throat. She couldn't even remember what she had expected from her doomed marriage to Roger. She had half believed her parents when they had told her that her feelings for Javier were just an adolescent crush, the result of being away from home, being free for the first time in her young life. It happened to everyone, they had insisted, and it would blow over in due course. She would gravitate back towards someone on her own level, from her own social class, and the thrill of the unknown would fade away in time.

They had been very convincing, and as all those other reasons for marrying Roger had piled up, so had the tug of war going on inside her intensified.

But had she ever foreseen a satisfying sex life with the man she should never have wed?

Had she properly considered what married life was going to be like for her? Had she simply assumed that forgetting Javier would be as easy as her parents had said it would be and so all those feelings would, likewise, be easily replaced, transferred to Roger? What a complete idiot she had been! Foolish and naïve.

She now knew that what she had felt for Javier hadn't been a passing crush. She had fallen in love with him and he had been spot on when he had told her, just then, that his arrogance had never bothered her when they had been going out.

It was just something else she had adored about him. That and his utter integrity, his dry wit, his sharp intelligence and his sense of fair play.

She was still in love with him and all those traits that should have turned her off him but didn't. He had become the billionaire he had quietly always known he would end up being, and of course he had changed in the process. How could he not? But underneath the changes was the same man and she was still in love with him.

And just acknowledging that appalled and frightened her.

Because things might have stayed the same for her but they hadn't stayed the same for him.

He really did want completion. He hadn't stayed celibate over the years. He was a powerful, wealthy man now who could have any woman on the planet with a snap of his fingers. She was the one who'd got away, and he was determined to put that right, so he was having a little time out with her.

He didn't love her and whatever feelings he had had for her in the past had disappeared over the years. He'd made that perfectly clear. But she still loved him and that was a dreadful state of affairs.

Whilst one part of her realised that she must look very strange, just sitting with a blank expression on her face, another part recognised that there was nothing she could do about that because she couldn't control the racing whirlpool of her thoughts.

One thing was emerging very fast, though. She couldn't let him know how she felt. If he could be cool and controlled, then she must be as well. There was no way that she would allow him to see just how weak and vulnerable she was inside.

'There's no need to explain,' Javier said gently. He was beginning to feel all sorts of things and top of the list was intense satisfaction that he was going to be her first. He'd never thought that he was the sort of primal guy who would actually be thrilled to the core by something like that but he had clearly underestimated his own primitive side. Under the civilised veneer, he was as untamed as they came.

'What…what do you mean?' Sophie stammered. Of course, he had no insight into her murky past, but she still had a moment of wondering whether he had somehow worked everything out, including her feelings for him.

'I don't suppose you ever anticipated entering into a sexless marriage.'

Sophie went beetroot-red and didn't snatch back her hand when he reached out and idly played with her fingers.

'I…er…I…'

'No.' He stopped her mid awkward sentence. 'Like I said, there's no need to explain because I understand.'

'You do?'

'You were young. You weren't to know that it takes all sorts to make the world go round and some men find it harder than others to face their sexuality.'

'Sorry?'

For the first time in living memory, Javier wasn't seeing red when he thought about the loser she had tossed him over for. In many ways, he felt sorry for her. With financial problems surfacing on the home front, and a man with control over purse strings her family needed, she had failed to see that he had his own agenda and had tied the knot in the expectation that life would be normal.

She'd been sorely mistaken.

Javier shunted aside thorny questions about whether she had loved the guy or not. That was then and this was now and, in the interim, she sure as hell had had her wake-up call on that front.

A virgin widow and now here she was. Here they both were...

Sophie was reeling from the series of misunderstandings and misinterpretations. Red-blooded alpha male that Javier was, he had jumped to the simplest conclusion. She was good-looking, she and Roger had married... The only possible reason they might not have consummated their marriage would be because he physically hadn't been able to, and the only reason that might have been the case would be because he just wasn't attracted to women.

End of story.

Was she going to set him straight on that count? Was she going to tell him the series of events that had led to her sexless union? The depth of feeling she had carried for him, Javier? Was she going to risk him knowing how madly in love with him she had been and then finding

the link and working out just how madly in love she still
was with him?

'Roger, gay...' He might as well have been for the
amount of notice he had paid her.

'Key thing here is this, Soph—it was nothing you did.'

'Really?' She very much doubted that but Javier nodded briskly.

'I went out with a functioning alcoholic a couple of
years ago,' he confided, drawing her closer to him and liking her lack of resistance. 'You would never have guessed
that she drank her daily intake of calories. She was a
model with an erratic, hectic lifestyle and she was very
careful.'

'Didn't you suspect anything?' Sophie stared at him,
round-eyed. It was a relief to have the conversation off
her for a moment.

'We were both busy, meeting in various foreign locations either where she was modelling or where I happened
to be. I only twigged when she started having more ambitious plans for our...relationship.'

'What does that mean?'

'It means she decided that meeting in various foreign
locations wasn't enough. She wanted something of a more
permanent arrangement.'

'Poor woman,' Sophie said with heartfelt sympathy.

'Misplaced sympathies,' Javier said wryly. 'She knew
the game before it started. Not my fault if somewhere
along the line she forgot the rules.'

She knew the game the way I know the game, Sophie
thought, *and I'd better make sure I don't forget the rules
or else...*

And with a finger in the family company—frankly
more than just a finger—parting company might be a
little more difficult than he would want. Not just a simple case of ignoring calls and text messages after signing

off with a bunch of flowers and a thanks-but-no-thanks farewell note...

'So how did you, er, find out that there was a problem?'

'She surprised me by inviting me over to her place in London for dinner.'

'And it was the first time you'd been there?'

'Like I said, the rules of the game...they don't include cosy domestic scenes.'

'You eat out all the time?'

Javier shrugged. 'It works. I'm only interested in the bedroom when it comes to any woman's house.'

Sophie thought that he'd seen more than just the bedroom of this particular house, but then, she knew, circumstances weren't exactly typical even though the ground rules would be exactly the same.

'But I went along and it didn't take me long to see just how many bottles of alcohol there were in places where food should have been stored. And it took even less time to unearth the mother lode because there had been no reason for her to hide any of it as she didn't share the flat with anyone. When I confronted her, she tried to make me believe that it was somehow my fault that she drank as much as she did, because I wouldn't commit to her. She clung and cried and said that her drinking had gone through the roof because she was depressed that our relationship wasn't going anywhere. Of course, I left her immediately and then got in touch with a private counsellor specialising in people with alcohol-related addictions. But the point I'm making is that there are just some people who won't face up to their own shortcomings and will take every opportunity to shift the blame onto other people.'

'And you think that, er, that Roger...'

'I think nothing.' Javier gestured in a way that was exotically foreign and then leant in closer to her. 'It would be a tough call for a man to find the courage to face up to his own sexual inclinations when those sexual inclinations risk putting him outside his comfort zone and alienating him from the people he has grown up with.'

'Roger was certainly a coward,' Sophie said bitterly.

'But all that is in the past.' He waved his hand elegantly. 'We find ourselves here and I'm glad you felt comfortable enough to bare all to me.'

'You would have found out anyway,' she said vaguely.

'You shouldn't have put your clothes back on. Now I'm going to have to strip them off you all over again. No, scrap that—what I'd really like is for you to take them off for me, bit by slow bit, a piece at a time, so that I can appreciate every delectable bit of your glorious body...'

'I...I can't do that.'

'You're shy...' Had she ever undressed in front of her husband? he wondered. Was all of this completely new to her? He confessed to himself that he was tickled pink and turned on like hell by the thought of that, the thought of him being the absolute first on so many counts.

Shy but unbelievably turned on...

She liked the way his dark, appreciative eyes roved over her like a physical caress. She liked the way he made her feel. She had never done any kind of striptease for a man before but now she began undressing as he had asked, very slowly, eyes never leaving his as she removed her clothing.

He made her feel safe and she knew why. It was because she loved him. She knew that he could hurt her beyond repair—knew that her love would never be returned and, after tonight, she would be left with only the memory of making love and the knowledge that what she wanted would never happen—but none of that seemed to matter. She'd thought that her heart could never again be made

to beat but she'd been wrong. Her love overrode common
sense and she couldn't fight it.

And what was the point of fighting anyway? She lived
with enough regret on her shoulders without adding to
the tally. If she had this one opportunity to grasp a bit of
happiness, then why shouldn't she take it? She would deal
with the aftermath later.

She unhooked her bra, stepped out of her undies and
then walked slowly towards him, sashaying provocatively
and seeing for herself the effect she was having on him.

Javier held his erection through his boxers, controlling
the wayward effects of his surging libido. He breathed
deeply and tried to think pleasant, pedestrian thoughts
so that he could gather himself sufficiently to do justice
to the situation.

No rushing.

'You look tense,' Sophie murmured. She was amazed at
how at ease she was with her nakedness. Indeed, she was
positively basking in it. She delicately stroked the side of
his face with one finger and Javier grabbed it and sucked
it, watching her with smouldering passion so that every
bone in her body seemed to go into meltdown.

'*Tense* isn't quite the word I would use...' He drew her
close to him so that their bodies were lightly pressed together and, eyes still locked to hers, he eased his hand over
her hip, along her thigh and then between them.

Her wetness on his finger elicited a moan of pure satisfaction from him.

Sophie couldn't breathe. Her eyelids fluttered. There
was something so erotic about them both standing, looking at one another while he rubbed his finger against the
small, tight bud of her clitoris, rousing sensations like little explosions and fireworks inside her. She shifted and
moaned softly.

'This is just the appetiser,' Javier murmured, kissing

her on her mouth, small, darting kisses that left her breathless. 'And there will be lots of those to enjoy before the main course.'

'I want to pleasure you too...'

'You already are. Trust me—just touching you is giving me more pleasure than you could even begin to understand.'

In one fluid movement, he swept her off her feet and carried her to the bed as easily as if she weighed nothing. He deposited her as gently as if she were a piece of priceless porcelain and then he stood back and looked at her, and Sophie looked back at him, eyes half-closed, her breathing shallow and jerky. The outline of his impressive erection made her heart skip a beat.

She realised that she had never actually considered the dynamics of sexual intercourse; how something so big would fit into her...

'Your face is as transparent as a sheet of glass,' Javier told her drily. 'There's no need to be nervous. I am going to be very gentle.'

'I know you will.' And she did. He might be ruthless on the battlefield of high finance, but here in the bedroom he was a giver and utterly unselfish. That was something she sensed.

Javier decided that he would leave the boxers on. He didn't want to scare her. He was a big boy and he had seen that flash of apprehension on her face and interpreted it without any difficulty at all. He'd said he was going to be gentle and he would be; he would ease himself into her and she would accept his largeness without anything but sheer, unadulterated pleasure.

He had forgotten that this single act was supposed to be about revenge.

He positioned her arms above her head and she shifted into the position so that her breasts were pointing at him.

Hunkering over her, he delicately circled one rosy nipple with his tongue until she was writhing in response.

'No moving,' he chastised sternly. 'Or else I might have to tie those hands of yours together above your head...'

'You wouldn't.' But now that he had put that thought in her head, she found that she rather enjoyed playing around with it in her mind.

Maybe another time, she thought with heated contentment only to realise that there wouldn't *be* another time. This was it. This was all he wanted. A night of fun so that he could get the *completion* he felt he deserved.

She felt a sharp, searing pain as she pictured him walking away from her, taking his sense of completion with him, returning to the queue of beautiful, experienced women patiently waiting for him.

She squeezed her eyes tightly shut, blocking out the intrusive, unwelcome image and succumbing to the riot of physical sensations sparked as he trailed kisses along her collarbone, down to her pouting, pink nipple.

He took his time. He drew her aching nipple into his mouth so that he could caress the tip with his tongue in firm, circular movements that had her gasping for breath. Every time she lowered her arm to clutch his hair, he pushed it back up without pausing in his devastating caress.

'Now let's try this another way,' he murmured, rising up and staring down at her flushed, drowsy face.

'I'm not pleasing you...' Sophie's voice was suddenly anxious and her eyes expressed concern that she was taking without giving anything in return.

'Shh...' Javier admonished. 'Like I said, you're doing more for me than you can ever imagine possible.' *Doing more than any woman had ever done before.*

She made him feel young again. He was no longer the boy who had grown into a man whose only focus was forging the financial stability he had grown up wanting. He was no longer the tycoon who had made it to the top, who could have anything and anyone he wanted. He was young again, without the cynicism invested in him by his upwards journey.

'Straddle me,' he commanded, flipping her so that their positions were reversed, and she was now the one over him, her full breasts dangling like ripe fruit, swinging tantalisingly close to his face. 'And move on me...move on my thigh...let me feel your wetness...'

Sophie obeyed. It was wickedly decadent. She moved against his thigh, slowly and firmly, legs parted so that she could feel the nudge of an orgasm slowly building.

She didn't care that he could see the naked, open-mouthed lust on her face or hear the heavy, laboured breathing which she could no longer get under control.

She didn't care if he watched her, in her most private moment, come against his leg.

She was so turned on, she could scarcely breathe. She gasped when he held her breasts, massaging their fullness, drawing her down towards him so that he could suckle on first one, then the other, while she continued to pleasure herself against him, hands pinned on either side of him.

As limp as a rag doll, she lay for a while on him, taking time out to quell the rise of an impending orgasm because she wanted to have it all. She didn't want to come like this. She wanted to feel him moving hard in her.

The apprehension she had earlier felt when she had seen his impressive size had faded completely.

He was in no rush. He stroked her spine and then, when she propped herself up once again, he kissed her slowly, tasting every morsel of her mouth. Her hair fell around her and he pushed his hand through its tangle and gazed at her in perfect, still silence.

'You're beautiful, Sophie.'

Sophie blushed, unused to compliments. She felt as though she had given away her carefree youth somewhere along the line and that single compliment had returned it to her for a little while.

'I bet you say that to all the women you get into bed with.' Her voice was soft and breathless and he quirked an eyebrow in amusement.

'Is that the sound of someone fishing for compliments?'

Sophie thought that actually it was the sound of someone trying to be casual when in fact she was eaten up with jealousy over lovers she had never met or seen.

'It's been a very long time since anyone paid me a compliment,' she told him truthfully and for a few moments Javier stared at her seriously.

'Weren't you tempted to get some sort of life of your own after your husband died? Or even when he was alive, given the extraordinary circumstances?'

Sophie felt a distinct twinge of guilt that she had allowed him to believe something that couldn't have been further from the truth. But then she reminded herself that she was simply avoiding opening a can of worms and where was the harm in a very small white lie? It hardly altered the fact that she was a virgin, did it?

She decided to completely skirt around the whole thorny business of life as she had known it when she had been married to Roger.

'By the time my husband died,' she said instead, snuggling against him, 'I was so snowed under with financial problems, I barely had time to eat a meal and brush my teeth, never mind launch myself into the singles scene and start trying to find a man.'

'And you must have been pretty jaded with the male sex by then,' Javier offered encouragingly.

'Um...with life in general,' she returned vaguely.

'And with your husband specifically,' Javier pressed.

'Understand one hundred percent—he lied and used you and on top of that managed to ruin what was left of your family company.'

Sophie sighed. Put like that, she marvelled that she had had the strength to go on after her mother had moved down to Cornwall. She marvelled that she just hadn't thrown in the towel and fled to the furthest corners of the earth to live on a beach somewhere.

She had been raised to be dutiful and responsible, however, and she could see now, looking back on her life, that those two traits, whilst positive, had in fact been the very things that had taken her down the wrong road. At the age of just nineteen, she had been dutiful and responsible enough to put herself last so that she could fall in line with what everyone else seemed to want from her.

'Let's not talk about all that,' she said gruffly, sensing the tears of self-pity not too far away. What a fantastic start to her one big night that would be—snotty nosed, puffy eyed and blubbing like a baby in front of him!

It enraged Javier that she still couldn't seem to find it in herself to give the man the lack of due credit and respect he so richly deserved, even with a string of unpalatable facts laid out in front of her. But, he thought with harsh satisfaction, who was she here with now? Him! And he was going to take her to such heights that by the time he walked away from her he would be the only man in her head. No one forgot their first lover.

'You're right,' he breathed huskily, expertly reversing positions so that he was the dominant one now, on top of her. 'I've always found talking superfluous between the sheets...'

Sophie sadly thanked her lucky stars that she had ended her rambling conversation before she could really begin to bore him witless. If he didn't care for women talking when they were in bed with him, then she shuddered to think what he might feel if she began weeping like a baby and clutching him like a life jacket flung into stormy seas to a drowning man.

Javier lowered himself and began to kiss her. He started with her mouth and he took his time there, until she was whimpering and squirming, then he moved to her succulent breasts, nibbling and nipping and suckling. Her skin was like satin, velvety smooth and warm. When he began to lick her stomach, her sides, the path down to her belly button, she moaned with fevered impatience.

She reached down compulsively and tangled her fingers in his hair.

'Javier!'

Sophie met his darkened gaze and blushed furiously. 'What…are you doing?'

'Trust me,' he murmured roughly. 'I'm taking you to heaven…' He gently pushed her thighs open and she fell back, then sucked in a shocked breath. The delicate darting of his tongue as he explored her was agonisingly, explosively erotic.

She moved against his mouth, rocking and undulating her hips, and groaning so loudly that it was a blessing the house was empty. She arched up, pushing herself into that slickly exploring tongue, and cried out when two fingers, gently inserted into her wetness, ratcheted up the wildly soaring sensations racing through her as fast as quicksilver.

'I'm going to…' She could scarcely get the words out before a shattering orgasm ripped through her and she clutched the sheets, driving herself upwards as his big hands supported her tightened buttocks.

It was an orgasm that went on and on, taking her to heights she had never dreamed possible, before subsiding, returning her gently back to planet Earth.

She scrambled onto her elbows, intent on apologising

for being so selfish, but Javier was already out of the bed and rooting through his trousers.

It was only when he began putting on protection that it dawned on her what he was doing.

The last thing he would want was a pregnancy.

She barely had time to register the treacherous stab of curiosity that filled her head... *What would a baby created by them look like?*

'Lie back,' he urged with a wolfish grin. 'The fun is only beginning...'

CHAPTER NINE

SOPHIE QUIVERED WITH anticipation but this time it was her decision to take things slowly. He had pleasured her in the most intimate and wonderful way possible and now it was her turn to give.

She wriggled so that she was kneeling and gently pushed him so that he was lying down. His initial expression of surprise quickly gave way to one of wicked understanding that she wanted the opportunity to take the reins instead of leaving it all to him.

'No touching,' she whispered huskily.

'That's going to be impossible.'

'You're going to have to fold your hands behind your head.' She grinned and then looked at him with haughty reprimand. 'It's only what *you* asked *me* to do.'

'Well, then,' he drawled, 'I'd better obey, hadn't I?' He lay back, arms folded behind his head. He could have watched that glorious body for ever, the shapely indent of her waist, the full heaviness of her breasts, the perfect outline of her nipples, the scattering of freckles along her collarbone, that tiny mole on the side of her left breast…

Her eyes were modestly diverted but he knew that she was aware of him with every ounce of her being and that was a real turn on for him.

He'd never felt so *alive* to the business of making love.

Somehow, he was functioning on another level, where every sensation was heightened to almost unbearable limits.

Was it because he was finally making love to the one woman who had escaped him? Was this what it felt like finally to settle old scores?

Would he be feeling this had he had her the first time round? No. That was a given. However crazy he'd been about her, he knew far more about himself now than he had back then. He knew that he wasn't cut out for permanence. If they had slept together, carried on seeing one another, if circumstances hadn't interrupted their relationship, it still wouldn't have lasted. Because, whether he liked it or not, he'd been focused on one thing and one thing only—the acquisition of the sort of wealth that would empower him, afford him the financial security he had never had growing up.

He no longer questioned his motivation, if indeed he ever had. Some things were ingrained, like scores from a branding iron, and that was one of them.

He had no burning desire for children and not once, over the years, had any of the women he had dated given him pause for thought. He expected that if he ever married—and it was a big *if*—it would be a marriage of convenience, a union years down the road with a suitable woman who would make him an acceptable companion with whom to see in his retirement. A woman of independent means, because the world was full of gold-diggers, who enjoyed the same things he enjoyed and would make no demands on him. He would look for a harmonious relationship.

Harmony in his fading years would be acceptable. Until then, he would make do with his string of women, all beautiful, all amenable, all willing to please and all so easily placated with jewellery and gifts if he ended up being unreliable.

They were all a known quantity and, in a life driven by ambition, it was soothing to have a private life where there were no surprises.

Except, right now, Sophie was the exception to the rule, and a necessary exception.

And he was enjoying every minute of her.

She straddled him and he looked down, to the slickness between her legs, and then up as she leant over him so that she could tease his hungry mouth with her dangling breasts.

He was allowed to lick, but only for a while, and allowed to suckle, but only for a while.

And he wasn't allowed to touch, which meant he had to fight off the agonising urge to pull her down so that she was on top of him and take her.

She did to him what he had done to her. She explored his torso with her mouth. She kissed the bunched muscles of his shoulders and then circled his flat, brown nipples with her mouth so that she could drizzle her tongue over them with licks as dainty as a cat's.

She could feel the demanding throb of his erection against her but it was only when she moved lower down his body that she circled its massive girth with her hand, pressing down firmly and somehow knowing what to do, how to elicit those groans from him, how to sharpen his breathing until each breath was accompanied by a shudder.

Instinct.

Or something else. Love. Love that had been born all those years ago and had forgotten that it was supposed to die. Like a weed, it had clung and survived the worst possible conditions so that now it could resume its steady growth. Against all odds and against all better judgement.

Well, worse conditions loomed round the corner, but before she encountered those she would enjoy this night to the absolute fullest.

She straightened, eyes dark with desire, and half-smiled with a sense of heady power as she registered his utter lack of control. She might be the inexperienced one here, but when it came to the power of *lust* she wasn't the only one to be in its grip. She wasn't the only one who was out of control.

And that balanced the scales a bit.

Hot and consumed with a sense of recklessness she would never have thought possible, she sat astride him so that he could breathe in the musky scent of her, positioning herself over him so that he could explore between her legs with his flicking tongue.

She breathed in sharply as he found her sensitive clitoris and probed it with the tip of his tongue.

He still wasn't touching her, still had his hands behind his head, as she had her fists clenched at her sides.

But the heat between them was indescribable all the more so because of the tantalising promise of fulfilment that lay ahead.

She let him taste her until she could stand it no longer, until her breathing was so fractured that she wanted to scream. She could move against his mouth but there was no way she was going to come again, not like this…

She worked her way down him until she was the one tasting him. The solid steel of his erection fascinated her. She took it into her mouth, sucked on the tip, played with it with her hands, tasted it and loved the way it tasted.

She explored his hard six-pack with the flat of her hand as she sucked, enjoying the hard, abrasive rub of muscle and sinew under her palm.

'Okay.' Javier rose onto his elbows to tangle his hand

in her tumbling hair. 'Enough. My blood pressure can't
take any more.'

Sophie glanced at him from under her lashes.

'You're a witch,' he breathed huskily. 'Come here and
kiss me.'

Their kiss was a mingling of scents and Sophie lost
herself in it. She wanted to wrap her arms around him
and never let him go. She wanted to be needy, clingy and
demanding, and all those awful things that would have
him running for the hills without a backwards glance.

She wanted to be open and honest, tell him how she
felt and declare her love for him, and the fact that there
was no way that she could do that felt like an impossible
weight on her shoulders.

She sighed, rolling as he propelled her gently onto her
back. Balancing over her, he looked at her seriously.

'Still nervous?'

'A little,' she admitted. She could have admitted a lot
more. She could have admitted that what really made her
nervous was the prospect of what happened when this glorious night was over and they both returned to their own
little worlds. There was no way she would duck away from
this but the aftermath still made her nervous.

She didn't think he would like to hear about that.

'Don't be,' he murmured. 'Trust me.'

He nudged her with the tip of his erection, felt her wetness and gently, slowly eased himself in.

She was beautifully tight. Would he have guessed that
she had never made love before? Probably. She would
have winced, given her inexperience away. That said, he
was pleased that she had thought to confide in him and
more than pleased that he was going to be her first lover.

Whatever feelings still lingered for the creep who had
married her for all the wrong reasons, *he* would be the
man who would be imprinted in her head for the rest of her

life. Not her ex-husband. When she lay in bed, the loser she still refused to hold in contempt would no longer dominate her thoughts. No. Instead, *he* would be in her head now, and the memory of this first night spent together.

Sophie inhaled and tensed but she was already so turned on that the tension quickly evaporated. Nor did she want him treating her like a piece of china that could shatter into a thousand pieces if he happened to be just a little too rough.

She wanted him to thrust long and deep into her. She wanted his *urgency*.

'Move faster...' she moaned.

It was all the invitation Javier needed. He was unbelievably aroused. Holding on had required a superhuman feat of willpower because having her touch him had driven him wild.

He began moving with expert assurance, felt her wince as he drove deeper, then gradually relax as he picked up pace until their bodies were moving in harmony, as sweet as the coming together of the chords of a song.

Still, he refused to satisfy himself at her expense, waiting until her rhythm was inexorably building and he could feel her fingers dig into the small of his back and knew that she had raised her legs, wrapped them around his waist, all the better to receive him...

Sophie came, spinning off to a different world where nothing existed but her body and its powerful, shattering responses. She was distantly aware of Javier arching up, his whole body tensing as he reached orgasm.

Apart yet inextricably joined. She had never felt closer to anyone in her entire life. And it wasn't just because of the sex. Somewhere in the core of her she knew that it was what it was because of what she felt. She couldn't disentangle her emotions from her responses. The two were inextricably linked.

Not good. Yet so right. She couldn't imagine feeling anything like this for anyone else, ever, and that scared her because when this was over she would have no choice but to pick up the pieces and move on. She would have to put him behind her and one day find herself a partner because she couldn't envisage spending the rest of her life on her own.

She was lying in the crook of his arm, both of them staring upwards. His breathing was thick and uneven and with a little chuckle he swung her onto her side so that they were now facing one another, their bodies pressed together.

Somewhere along the line he had disposed of the condom. He was a very generously built man, however, and even with his erection temporarily subsided she was still aware of his thick length against her, stirring her, although she was aching a little and as tired as if she had run a marathon at full tilt.

She wondered what the protocol was for a one-night stand. She couldn't leap out of bed, stroll to get her clothes and head for the door, having thanked him for a good time, because it was her house. Which meant that she would have to rely on him to make the first move, and that made her feel a little awkward, because she didn't want him to imagine that she was hanging around, waiting for an encore.

She was afraid to carry on being intimate, in these most intimate of circumstances, because she didn't want him to guess the depth of her feelings for him.

She wanted to maintain her dignity. It wasn't just a case of self-preservation, but on a more realistic level: he now had a slice of the family company. He might decide to take a back seat now that they had made love and *completion* had been established, might disappear never to be seen again, but on the small chance that she bumped into him at some point in the future the last thing she needed was for him to know her feelings. If she bumped into him, she wanted him to think that she had been as detached from the whole experience, on an emotional level, as he had been. She wanted to be able to have a conversation with him, with her head held high, and preferably with a man on her arm.

'So,' Javier drawled, breaking the silence and stroking her hair away from her face.

'So...' Sophie cleared her throat and offered him a bright smile. 'That was very nice.'

Javier burst out laughing. 'That's a first,' he informed her wryly. 'I've never had a woman tell me afterwards that the sex was "very nice".'

Sophie didn't want to think about the women he had bedded or what sexy little conversations they had had post–making love.

'You don't have to tell me that.' She was going to keep it light, brace herself for when he levered himself out of bed and began getting dressed. She didn't think he'd be spending the night.

'No?'

'I already have a picture in my head of the sort of women you, er, entertain and I guess they'd be busy telling you how great you were and offering to do whatever you wanted...'

'Did you think I was great?'

Sophie blushed a vibrant red.

'Is that a *yes*...?' He nuzzled her neck and then absently rested his hand between her legs.

'What happens about the shoot?'

'I don't want to talk about the shoot. I want to talk about how great you found me between the sheets.'

Sophie didn't want to laugh but her lips twitched because there was just something so incredibly endearing and boyish about his arrogance.

'I'm glad we made love,' she told him truthfully. 'I...'

'Don't go there, Soph.' He fell onto his back and gazed upwards because this was what he didn't want. Any sort of half-hearted, limp excuses and explanations for the choices she had made seven years ago. She'd already told him enough. He knew enough. He wasn't interested in hearing any more.

'Don't go where?'

'This isn't the point where we pick up sharing our life histories.' He gathered her into him, his arm draped loosely around her. He could touch her nipple with his fingers and he liked that. He liked the way the little bud stiffened in response to the gentle pressure of his fingers rolling it. And he liked what that did to his body, the way it made him feel as though he could keep going indefinitely, his body resting between bouts of lovemaking only long enough to build back up the vigour to carry on.

After sex, no matter how good the sex had been, his instinct had always been to get out of bed as fast as he could and have a shower, his mind already racing ahead to work and business, deals that had to be done.

He'd never been one for hanging around between the sheets, chewing the fat and talking about a future that wasn't going to happen.

But he wanted to hang around between the sheets now.

Minus the chat.

He'd managed, just, to relegate her loser ex-husband to a box somewhere in his head that he could safely ignore. The last thing he wanted was for her to begin recapping her past, forcing him to confront the unpalatable truth that, whether she had come to him a virgin or not, she had still ditched him for someone else and probably still loved that someone else, even though the man in question had failed to deliver.

'No,' she agreed quickly. 'I was simply going to say

that it's probably a good idea if you head back now. Unfortunately...' she gave a derisive laugh '...the guest bedrooms aren't exactly made up for visiting crowds. No crisp white sheets and fluffy towels, I'm afraid.'

She began to slip her legs over the side of the bed and he tugged her back against him.

He wasn't ready for her to leave just yet. He hadn't quite got his fill of her. Surprising, all things considered, but nevertheless true. And he didn't want to give her time to think things over. He wanted her warm, ripe and soft like she was now; yielding.

'I'm not sure I can face the horror story of a long drive back to London,' he murmured, curving his big body against hers and pushing his thigh between her legs.

'There are hotels,' Sophie told him as her heart gave a silly little leap in her chest.

She didn't want him to go. It was exhausting pretending that she didn't care one way or another.

'This may be the back of beyond for you,' she carried on, 'compared to London, but we still have our fair share of excellent hotels. All come complete with mod cons like clean sheets, windows that open and no lingering smell of mustiness from being shut up for too long.'

Javier burst out laughing. He'd forgotten how funny she could be and that was something that hadn't been apparent over the past few weeks.

Probably over the past few years, he thought, sobering up.

'Bit of a trek going to a hotel,' he murmured. 'That would entail me getting up, getting dressed...and who's to say that they aren't all full?'

'What are you saying?'

'I could always save myself the hassle and spend the night here,' he told her.

'Some of the bedrooms... Well, I guess I could make

up the one at the end of the corridor. It's shocking to think how fast things have gone downhill here...' She sighed. 'It's as if the whole place was glued together with sticking plaster and then, one day, someone tugged some of the plaster off and everything else just came down with it. Like a house of cards being toppled. I can't imagine the stress my dad had been living under for ages. It's as well he's not alive to see the way the house has gone downhill. And it's a blessing that Mum is down in Cornwall. She honestly doesn't know the half of what's been going on here.' She pulled back and looked at him gravely. 'Sorry. I forgot you don't like conversing between the sheets.'

'That's not what I said,' Javier felt constrained to mutter. But she had hit the nail on the head. It was all tied in with his driving need to focus on the essentials—work and financial security. For the first time, he found himself projecting to places beyond those confines, the sort of places most people seemed ridiculously keen to occupy, places which he had shunned as irrelevant. 'How can your mother not know what's been happening here?' he found himself asking. 'How often do you go down to Cornwall to visit her? She surely must return here on occasion?'

'Are you really interested? Because you don't have to ask a load of questions just because you happen to be staying on here for a few more hours.'

'So you're going to put me up?'

Sophie shrugged. 'It's no bother for me.'

'Good, because I'd quite like to have a look around the house in the morning—see how bad it is in the unforgiving light of day.'

'Why?' She propped herself up on one elbow and stared down at him.

'Curiosity. You were explaining the mystery of how it is that your mother doesn't know the situation here.'

'Would you like something to eat? To drink?'

'I'm fine here.'

But, even to her, chatting like this in bed felt weirdly intimate and she could understand why he avoided doing it. It would be easy to find herself being seduced into all sorts of cosy, inappropriate feelings, into thinking this was more than it actually was.

'Well, I'm starved,' she declared briskly, disentangling herself from him and scrambling for the door so that she could head to the bathroom for a shower.

Caught on the back foot, Javier frowned as he watched her hastily departing figure.

Since when did women turn down invitations from him to stay in bed—*talking*?

Actually, since when had he made a habit of issuing invitations to women to stay in bed, talking?

He levered himself out and strolled to the bathroom which was a couple of doors along. He was surprised that the bedrooms weren't all en suite and then surmised that the house predated such luxuries and, somewhere along the line, it had become too costly to have them installed.

He pushed open the door to the succulent sight of her bending over the bath to test the water.

Her hair was swept over one shoulder, the tips almost touching the water in the bath. She had one hand on the mixer tap, the other gripping the side of the cast-iron clawfoot bath. He could see the low hang of one breast swinging as she adjusted the temperature of the water, and he moved to stand behind her, grinning as she gave a little squeak when he straddled her from behind, cupping both breasts with his hands.

'Couldn't resist,' he murmured into her hair as she straightened and leant into him so that her back was pressed against his torso.

He massaged her breasts and bent to nibble and kiss the

slender column of her neck. With a sigh of contentment, Sophie closed her eyes and covered his hands with hers.

'What are you doing?' she asked thickly.

'Is there any doubt?'

'I was just going to have a bath...then maybe get something for us to eat.'

'I have all I want to eat right here, right now...'

Sophie moaned softly at the provocative image that hoarsely spoken statement planted in her head.

They hadn't talked at all. Not really. Not about the one thing they needed to talk about. Which was *what happened next*. She knew that she shouldn't be sinking into his arms like this, should be maintaining some distance, but her body was turning to liquid as he continued to assault her senses.

She could have locked the door, of course, but somehow that would have felt silly and childish after they had just finished making love.

And maybe, she thought weakly, there was a part of her that wouldn't have wanted to stop him from coming into the bathroom anyway.

She breathed in sharply as his wicked hand drifted lower. Now he was just caressing one breast, playing with the pulsing, pink nipple while his other hand roamed over her ribcage, exploring downwards at a leisurely pace.

'Spread your legs,' he instructed softly and Sophie obeyed, as weak as a kitten.

She knew what he was going to do, yet she still gasped as he immediately found the swollen bud of her clitoris with the flat of his finger.

He knew just how to rub her there, applying just the right amount of pressure. His fingers were devastating. She could feel her wetness on his hand, and she reached behind her to hold his erection, although the angle was awkward and she couldn't begin to do half as much as she would have liked to.

And she didn't have time.

Because the rhythm of his touching grew faster, his fingers sending a million darting sensations flowing through her body until she was rocking under the impact of an orgasm, bucking against his hand, unable to contain her low groaning cries as she reached the point of utter physical fulfilment.

She spun round, blindly kissed his neck, just as he had done to her only minutes previously, and then she knelt in front of him, tossing her hair behind her, and took his rock-hard bigness into her mouth.

He tasted…like heaven.

She sucked him and he curled his fingers into her hair. She could feel his loss of self-control as she continued, sucking and licking him at the same time, her slender fingers gripping his erection, moving and massaging, working her own rhythm.

Javier had never felt so wildly out of control before. She was exciting him in ways no other woman ever had and he could no more control his own orgasm than he could have stopped the sun from rising or setting.

Spent, he pulled her back to her feet and for a few seconds their bodies were entwined into beautiful, sated pleasure, the aftermath of their physical satisfaction.

'I might have to share that oversized bath with you,' he murmured, tilting her face so that he could gently kiss her on her mouth.

Sophie smiled, as content as a cat in possession of a full tub of cream.

This was just the sort of thing he might take for granted, think nothing of, but she was so scared of taking yet another step into *him*…into losing herself in a non-relationship that wasn't going anywhere and never would.

But what was the harm in having a bath with him? What was the harm in another first experience?

'Okay.'

'And then you can cook something for me to eat.' He had never uttered those words to any woman before.

'Don't expect cordon bleu food,' Sophie warned him in alarm and he laughed.

'Beans on toast would be fine.'

Sophie lowered herself into the water a little self-consciously, drawing her knees up as he took the other end. It was an enormous bath, easily accommodating the both of them, and he made a few approving noises as he settled into the water, pulling her legs out to tangle with his, looking for the inevitable signs of deterioration in the fabric of the building as he was now accustomed to doing after only a short space of time.

'Really?' she couldn't help but ask drily. Once upon a time, perhaps, but he was no longer a 'beans on toast' kind of guy.

'And then you can tell me about your mother and how you've managed to keep this situation from her.'

He stroked her calf, which sent a frisson rippling through her body. She literally couldn't seem to get enough of him and she marvelled at her body's capacity to rouse itself at the speed of light, from satiated, pleasant torpor to wakening hunger to be touched again.

'And then we can talk about this house, which appears to be on the point of collapse. But before all that you can wriggle up and turn round so that I can begin soaping you...'

Sophie looked at the newspaper spread out on the kitchen table in front of her.

It had been *that* easy to become accustomed to having him around. It had felt so natural. Working in London, having him in and out of the office, going through paperwork with him, sitting in on interviews, being consulted on absolutely everything to do with the company…

And then, when they were on their own, those precious times when they would talk, laugh, make love…

The company had picked up in the space of just a few short months. Swept along on the coat-tails of Javier and his remarkable reputation, business that had been lost to competitors was gradually returning and returning customers were treated to reward schemes that secured their loyalty.

Little changes had been incremental and she marvelled at how simple some of the solutions were to turn the company around.

With profit came money to start working on the house. And the profits had also secured Oliver's release from the work he had never enjoyed doing.

He had returned to America to become a sports teacher at one of the prestigious private schools.

Everything had slotted into place and, of course, she had grown complacent.

Who wouldn't have?

She had actually begun secretly to see a future for them, even though he never, ever made plans; never, ever mentioned doing anything with her at some point in the future.

The one-night stand had grown into a relationship that was now almost four months old.

They hadn't talked about Christmas but she could envisage them spending at least a part of it together.

All told, hope, that dangerous emotion, had begun to take root. Loving him had taken away her objectivity, made her vulnerable to all kinds of foolish thoughts about them having a proper relationship, a relationship in which he might actually be persuaded to try to make a go of it, persuaded to think about commitment.

It was her own fault for not listening to the dictates of common sense...

No sooner had she told herself that she had to maintain some sort of emotional distance than she had hurled herself headlong into a relationship that was the equivalent of a minefield.

And this was where it had got her.

She was driven to stare at the picture occupying a large portion of the tabloid newspaper she had bought on the spur of the moment from the local newsagent. Lord knew, she wasn't much of a newspaper reader. She had an app on her mobile that kept her fully updated with what was happening in the world.

The picture had been taken at a London gallery opening. She hadn't even known that Javier had been invited. Ensconced in Yorkshire, where she had been for the past couple of weeks, getting the local offices in order and supervising decorating and refurbishment, she had seen him in fits and starts.

She looked forward to his arrivals with eager, edge-of-seat anticipation. She dressed in clothes she imagined him ripping off. She no longer felt constrained to hide how much he turned her on. Lust and the physical side of things were the only things that were out in the open between them.

She knew how much he wanted her and he knew how much she wanted him.

And he was going to be arriving any minute now. She had cooked and could smell it wafting aromatically from the kitchen, which had seen recent updates and now functioned the way it once had, with everything working and in spanking new condition.

She neatly folded the paper and then hovered until, at

seven promptly, she heard the insistent buzz of the doorbell. She closed her eyes and breathed in deeply to calm her shaky nerves.

She found that she'd even memorised the way he rang the doorbell, as if he couldn't wait to stride into the house, shedding his coat even as he reached to scoop her towards him.

She still hadn't become accustomed to that first sight of him. Even if she'd seen him the evening before, even if she'd seen him five minutes before, he still always blew her mind and took her breath away.

As always when he drove up north—quitting work earlier than he normally would because, he had confessed, those few hours behind the wheel of his car afforded him a certain amount of freedom which he deeply valued—he arrived still in his suit.

Minus jacket, which, she knew, he would have flung into the back seat of the car, oblivious to the fact that what he treated with such casual indifference had cost more than most people earned in a month.

'Have I told you that I missed you...?' Javier growled, closing the space between them in one fluid stride.

He had. It had been three days and he'd gone to sleep every evening with an erection and woken up with one. Not even those sexy phone calls late at night to her had been able to do the trick. There was only so much pleasure to be had satisfying himself.

He kissed her thoroughly, so thoroughly that Sophie forgot that this wasn't going to be the sort of evening they had both been anticipating: an evening of chat, food and lots of very satisfying sex. No, things were going to be different this evening because of that picture.

She pushed ever so slightly against him but immediately weakened as he plundered her mouth, driving her back until she was pressed against the wall.

She'd stopped wearing a bra in the house, liking the fact that he could touch her whenever he wanted without the bother of removing it, and she hadn't thought to put one on this evening. Her head fell back as he pushed up her long-sleeved tee shirt to feel her.

He'd thought of nothing but her on the drive up and now to touch her breast, feel the tautness of her nipple between his fingers, was almost indescribable.

'I want to take you right here,' he confessed unsteadily. 'I don't even think I can make it to the bedroom. Or *any* room...'

'Don't be silly,' Sophie returned breathlessly. She *needed* to talk to him. She knew that it wasn't going to be a comfortable conversation, but talking couldn't have been further from her mind as he dragged at the waistband of her jeans, fumbling to undo the button and pull down the zipper.

She rested her hands on his broad shoulders and her mind went completely blank, swamped by the powerful churn of sensation. Her tee shirt was still over her breasts and she could feel the air cooling her heated nipples. She wanted him to lick them, suckle at them, but, like him, she was frantic for them to unite, to feel him moving in her, free and unencumbered, because she was now on the pill, so there was no need for him to reach for protection.

She helped with the jeans, tugging them down and then somehow wriggling out of them, while he, likewise, dealt with his trousers and boxers.

When she opened drugged eyes, she saw that his white shirt was unbuttoned all the way down, revealing a broad slither of bronzed chest, and he had dispensed with his shoes and socks. When had that happened? Her socks were tangled up with her trousers.

They'd barely closed the front door and here they were,

practically naked in the hall, unable to keep their hands off one another.

Hands balled tightly behind her back, she literally couldn't keep still as he crouched in front of her and began tasting her, savouring her. She planted her legs apart to accommodate his questing mouth, barely able to breathe. When she glanced down to see his dark head moving between her legs, she felt unspeakably turned on.

'You need to come in me *now*!'

She heard his low laugh and then he was lifting her up and she was wrapping her legs around him, clinging to him as he began thrusting hard inside her, his hands supporting her bottom, her breasts bouncing as they moved together.

It was fast, furious, *raw* and earth-shattering. And utterly draining. For a short while, Sophie was transported to another place, another dimension, one in which difficult, awkward conversations with unpredictable outcomes didn't have to take place.

But as soon as she was back on her feet, hurriedly snatching clothes to put them on, her mind returned to what it had been chewing over before and she edged away from him, horrified at how easily she had dumped all her worries the second he had touched her.

And that was the essence of the problem, wasn't it? He did things to her, turned her to putty in his hands. He put her in a position where she couldn't seem to say *no* to him, which meant that this could go on until he got bored, and then he would chuck her aside and move on and where would her precious dignity be when that happened?

She was so cautious about never revealing the depth of her feelings for him, so fearful that he might gaze back into the past, understand how much she had meant to him then and work out how much he meant to her now. She was just so damned careful to play the adult game of keeping it cool, matching his control with control of her own.

She'd still be a mess when he decided that it was time to move on and he'd spot that in an instant.

The mere fact that she was about to tell him about that picture said it all but she didn't care because she had to find out.

'There's something I want to show you,' she told him in a rush, having put some vital distance between them. 'Well, something I want to ask you.' She sighed on a deep breath. 'Javier, we need to talk…'

CHAPTER TEN

'WHAT ABOUT?' HE TOOK his time getting dressed while she watched him from the door, arms folded, her expression revealing nothing. 'There's nothing more guaranteed to kill a good mood than *a talk*.'

'Are you speaking from personal experience?' Sophie asked coolly. She held up one interrupting hand even though he hadn't said anything. 'Of course you are. I suppose some of those women you went out with might have wanted a bit more from you than sex on tap.'

'Is that what this talk of yours is going to be about?' Javier's voice was as cool as hers, his expression suddenly wary and guarded.

Sophie spun round and began walking towards the kitchen. She could feel stinging colour washing over her because, in a way, this *was* about that. This *was* about more than just sex on tap.

'Well?' He caught up with her and held her arm, staying her, forcing her to turn to look at him. 'Is that what this *talk* of yours is going to be about? Wanting more?' He hadn't worked out the exact time scale, but it hit him that he had been seeing her now for several months, virtually on a daily basis, and he wasn't tiring of her. Immediately he felt his defences snap into position.

'I'm not an idiot,' Sophie lied valiantly. 'You'd have to be completely stupid to want *more* from a man like you!'

She yanked her arm free and glared at him. Her heart was thumping so hard and so fast in her chest that it felt as though it might explode.

She wanted to snatch the conversation back, stuff it away, take back wanting to *talk*. She wanted to pretend that she hadn't seen a picture of him at a gallery opening with some beautiful model clinging like a limpet to his arm, their body language saying all sorts of things she didn't want to hear.

'You're not capable of giving anyone anything more than sex,' she fumed, storming off towards the kitchen and the offending picture that she intended to fling in his face as proof of what she was saying.

'You weren't complaining five minutes ago,' he pointed out smoothly.

Below the belt, Sophie thought, but her face burnt when she thought about how her talk had taken a back seat the second he had touched her. He was right. She hadn't been complaining. In fact, at one point she remembered asking for more.

'I don't want more from you, Javier,' she gritted, reaching for the paper with shaking hands and flicking it open to the piece in the centre section. She tossed it to him and then stood at the opposite end of the table with her arms folded, nails biting into the soft flesh of her forearms. 'But what I *do* want is to know that you're not running around behind my back while we're an item!'

Javier stared down at the picture in front of him. He remembered the occasion distinctly. Another boring opening, this one at an art gallery. It had been full of just the sort of types he loathed—pretentious, champagne-drinking, caviar-scoffing crowds who had never given a penny to charity in their lives and had all attended top private schools courtesy of their wealthy parents. He could have given them a short lecture on the reality of being poor, but instead he had kept glancing at his watch and wondering what Sophie was doing.

As always, mixing in the jabbering, wealthy intellectual crowd was the usual assortment of beautiful hangers-on dressed in not very much and on the lookout for men with money. He had been a target from the very second he had walked through the door. He had shaken them off like flies, but by the end of the evening he had more or less given up and that was when the photographer had obviously seen fit to take a compromising snap.

In under a second, Javier could understand why Sophie had questions. He couldn't even remember the woman's name but he knew that she was a famous model and the way she was looking at him…the way she was holding on to his arm…

She didn't look like a woman on the verge of being cast aside by an indifferent stranger. Which she had been.

And snapped when, for five seconds, his attention had been caught by something the guy standing next to her had said to him and he was leaning into her, the very image of keen, while the guy to whom he had been speaking had been artfully cropped from the photo.

Not for a second was Javier tempted to launch into any kind of self-justifying speech. Why should he? He looked at her angry, hurt face and he ignored the thing inside him that twisted.

'Are you asking me to account for my actions when I'm not with you?'

'I don't think that's out of order on my part!'

'I have never felt the need to justify my behaviour to anyone. Ever.'

'Maybe you should have! Because when you're sleeping with someone, you are, actually, travelling down a two-way street whether you like it or not!'

'Meaning what?'

'Meaning it's not all about your world and what you want.'

'And maybe that will be the case one day, when I decide that I want more than a passing...situation with a woman.'

Sophie recoiled as though she had been physically struck. Suddenly all her anger seeped out of her and she was left feeling empty, hollow and utterly miserable.

Of course he would account for his behaviour one day. When he had met the right woman. In the meantime, he was having fun, and that was all that mattered. He wasn't tied to her any more than he had been tied to any of the women he had dated in the past, so if someone else came along and he was feeling energetic, then he probably thought, *why not?*

Facing up to that was like being kicked in the stomach. She literally reeled from the truth but she faced it anyway, just as she had faced the fact that she was still in love with him.

What was the point hiding from the truth? It didn't change anything. Having to deal with the mess her father had made of the company and the horror of her doomed marriage had taught her that, if nothing else.

'Did you sleep with that woman?'

'I'm not going to answer that question, Sophie.' Javier was incensed that, picture or no picture, she dared question his integrity. Did she think that he was the sort of man who couldn't control his libido and took sex wherever he found it?

He was also annoyed with himself for the way he had drifted along with this to the point where she felt okay about calling him to account. He'd been lazy. This had never been supposed to end up as anything more than an inconvenient itch that needed scratching. This had only ever been about finishing unfinished business.

'And maybe,' he said carefully, 'it's time for us to re-assess what's going on here.'

Sophie nodded curtly. The ground had just fallen away from under her feet, but she wasn't going to plead or beg or hurl herself at him, because they really *did* need to 're-assess', as he put it.

'Your company is pretty much back on its feet.' He gave an expansive gesture while she waited in hopeless resignation for the Dear John speech he would soon be delivering.

She was too miserable to think about getting in there first, being the first to initiate the break-up. It didn't mat-ter anyway. The result was going to be the same.

'Your brother's disappeared back across the Atlantic and there's no need for you to continue taking an active part in the running of the company. The right people are all now in the right places to guide the ship. You can do whatever you want to do now, Sophie. Go back to uni-versity…get another job…disappear across the Atlantic to join your brother…'

Sophie's heart constricted because that was as good as telling her what he thought of her and she could have kicked herself for having been lulled into imagining that there was ever anything more to what they had.

'Or France.'

'Come again?'

'I've been thinking about it for a couple of weeks.'

Javier was at a loss as to what she was talking about. 'Thinking about…what, exactly?'

'Ollie's job is still up for grabs,' she said, thinking on her feet. 'And it's dealing with marketing, which is some-thing I've found I rather like and I'm pretty good at.'

'You've been thinking about going to France?'

Sophie straightened. Did he think that she wasn't good enough for the job? Or did he think that she was always going to hang around until he got fed up with her, without giving any thought at all to life beyond Javier?

'Pretty much decided in favour of it,' she declared firmly. 'The house has found a buyer, as you know, who's happy to take it on and complete the renovations I've started, so there's literally nothing keeping me here. Aside, that is, from Mum. And I think she'd be overjoyed to come and visit Paris once a month. And, of course, I can easily get to Cornwall to see her.'

'So you're telling me that you've been concocting this scheme behind my back for weeks?'

'It's not *a scheme*, Javier.' The more she thought about it, the better it sounded. How else would she get over him if she didn't put as much distance as she possibly could between them? Affairs were in order here. Why not? Too much of her life had been taken up having other people make decisions on her behalf. 'I wasn't sure exactly when, but seeing that picture of you in the newspaper...'

'For God's sake!' He tried hard to temper his voice. 'What the hell does some half-baked picture in a sleazy tabloid have to do with anything?'

'It's made me realise that it's time for me to take the next step.'

'Next step? What next step?' Javier raked his fingers through his hair and wished she would settle on one topic and stick there. He felt as though the carpet had been yanked from under his feet and he didn't like the feeling. 'Of course you can't go to bloody France! It's a ludicrous idea!'

'You can do what you like with whoever you want to... er...do it with, Javier, but it's time for me to get back into the dating scene, meet someone I can share my life with.' She tried to visualise this mystery man and drew a blank. 'I feel like my youth has been on hold and now I have a great opportunity to reclaim it.'

'In France?' He laughed scornfully.

'That's right.'

'And what if you'd never seen that picture?' He stopped just short of doing the unthinkable and telling her that he'd never met that woman in his life before and had no intention of ever meeting her again. Because his head was too wrapped up with *her*.

Unthinkable!

'It was just a question of time,' Sophie said truthfully. 'And that time's come.'

'You're telling me, after the sex we've just had, that you want out…' He laughed in disbelief and Sophie wanted to smack him because it was just the sort of arrogant reaction she might have expected.

'I'm telling you that the time has come when it has to be more than just the sex. So I'm going to find my soulmate,' she added quickly.

'You're going to find your *soulmate*?' Javier hated himself for prolonging this conversation. As soon as she had started kicking up a fuss about that picture, he should have told her that it was over. He didn't need anyone thinking that they had claim to him. Never had, never would, whatever he had told her about a woman coming along who could tame him. Wasn't going to happen.

Except… *She hadn't been trying to claim him, had she?*

She'd just reasonably asked him if there was anything going on with the airhead who had been dripping off his arm at a forgettable gallery opening and, instead of laughing and dismissing the idea, he had returned to his comfort zone, dug his heels in and stubbornly refused to answer.

And it was too late now to do anything about that.

Not that it would have made any difference, considering she had been making all sorts of plans behind his back.

For the best, he decided. So he'd become lazy but in truth the itch had been scratched a long time ago.

'Fine.' He held up both hands and laughed indulgently. 'Good luck with that one, Sophie. Experience has taught me that there's no such thing. I'm surprised given your past that you haven't had the same learning curve.'

'Just the opposite.' She felt nauseous as she watched him start heading for the door. 'Life's taught me that there are rainbows around every corner.'

'How…kitsch.' He saluted her and she remained where she was as he strode out of the kitchen.

And out of her life for good.

From Spain to France.

When you thought about it, it was a hop and a skip and it made perfect sense. He had had no input in Sophie's company for over three months. He had delegated responsibility to his trusted CEO and withdrawn from the scene.

He'd done his bit. He'd taken over, done what taking apart had needed doing and had put back together what had needed putting back together. The company was actually beginning to pull itself out of the quagmire of debt it had been languishing in for the past decade, and it was doing so in record time.

It was a success story.

He'd moved on and was focused on another takeover, this time a chain of failing hotels in Asia.

He was adding to his portfolio and, furthermore, branching out into new terrain, which was invigorating. By definition, branching out into anything new on the business front was going to be invigorating!

He had also just had a good holiday with his parents and had persuaded them to let him buy them a little place on the beach in the south of France, where they could go whenever they wanted to relax. He had pulled the trump card of promising that he would join them at least three times a year there and he had meant it.

Somehow, he had learnt the value of relaxation.

So what if he hadn't been able to relax in the company of any woman since he had walked out of Sophie's life?

He'd been bloody busy, what with his latest takeover and various company expansions across Europe.

But he was in Spain.

France seemed ridiculously close...

And he really ought to check, first hand, on the progress being made in the Parisian arm of a company which, all told, he part-owned...

And, if he *was* going to go to Paris, it made sense to drop in and see what Sophie was up to.

He knew that she had been working there for the past six weeks. It was his duty, after all, to keep tabs on the company. Everything was easily accessible on the computer, from the salary she was pulling in to where she lived and the apartment she was renting near Montmartre.

He was surprised that she hadn't headed off to more fulfilling horizons, leaving the running of the company to the experts, as her brother had.

His decision was made in moments. Already heading away from the first-class desk, he walked briskly back, ignoring the simpering blushes of the young girl who had just seen him.

A ticket to Paris. Next flight. First class.

Sophie let herself into her apartment, slamming the door against the fierce cold outside.

She was dressed in several layers but, even so, the biting wind still managed to find all sorts of gaps in those layers, working their way past them and finding the soft warmth of her skin.

Her face tingled as she yanked off the woolly hat, the scarf and the gloves, walking through her studio apartment and luxuriating in the warmth.

She had been incredibly lucky to have found the apartment that she had. It was small but cosy, comfortable and conveniently located.

And Paris was, as she had expected, as beautiful as she remembered it from the last time she had been there nearly ten years ago.

She had wanted to leave her comfort zone behind and she had! She had climbed out of her box and was now living in one of the most strikingly beautiful cities on the planet. Her mother had already been to visit her once and was determined to come again just as soon as the weather improved.

All in all, there were loads of girls her age who would have given their right arm to be where she was now!

And if she happened to be spending a Friday night in, with plans to curl up with her tablet in her flannel pyjamas and bedroom socks, then it was simply because it was just so cold!

When spring came, she would be out there, jumping right into that dating scene, as she had promised herself she would do before she had left England.

For the moment, she was perfectly happy just chilling.

And expecting no one to come calling because, although she had been out a few times with some of the other employees in the small arm of the company in Paris, she had not thus far met anyone who might just drop by on a Friday evening to see what she was up to.

That would come in time.

Probably in spring.

So when the doorbell went, she didn't budge. She just assumed it was someone selling something and she wasn't interested.

She gritted her teeth as the buzzer kept sounding and eventually abandoned all pretence of Zen calm as she stormed to the door and pulled it open, ready to give her uninvited caller a piece of her mind.

Javier had kept his finger on the buzzer. She was in. She had a basement apartment and he could see lights on behind the drawn curtains. He wondered whether she knew that basement apartments were at the highest risk of being burgled.

Since leaving Spain, he hadn't once questioned his decision to spring this visit on her, but now that he was here, now that he could hear the soft pad of footsteps, he felt his stomach clench with an uncustomary attack of nerves.

He straightened as she opened the door and for a few seconds something bewildering seemed to happen to him: he lost the ability to think.

'You're here...' he said inanely. Her long hair was swept over one narrow shoulder and she was wearing thick flannel bottoms and a long-sleeved thermal vest. And no bra. 'Do you always just open your door to strangers?' he continued gruffly, barely knowing where this unimaginative line of conversation was coming from.

'Javier!' Temporarily deprived of speech, Sophie could just blink at him, owl-like.

She'd pretended that she'd moved on. She was in Paris, she was enjoying her job, meeting new people...

How could she *not* have moved on? Hadn't that been the whole point of Paris?

But seeing him here, lounging against the door frame in a pair of faded black jeans and a black jumper, with his coat slung over his shoulder...

She was still in the same place she'd been when she'd watched him stroll out of her flat without a backwards glance.

How dared he just show up like this and scupper all her chances of moving on?

'What are you doing here? And how the heck did you find out where I live!'

'Computers are wonderful things. You'd be shocked at the amount of information they can divulge. Especially considering you work for a company I part-own...' Javier planted himself solidly in front of her. He hadn't given much thought to what sort of welcome he was likely to receive but a hostile one hadn't really crossed his mind.

Since when were women hostile towards him?

But since when was she just *any woman*?

She never had been and she never would be and, just like that, he suddenly felt sick. Sick and vulnerable in a way he had never felt before. Every signpost that had ever guided him, every tenet he had ever held dear, disappeared and he was left groping in the dark, feeling his way towards a realisation that had always been there at the back of his mind.

'Go away. I don't want to see you.'

Javier placed his hand on the door, preventing her from shutting it in his face. 'I've come...'

'For what?' Sophie mocked.

'I...'

Sophie opened her mouth and shut it because she didn't know what was going on. He looked unsettled. Confused. *Unsure.* Since when had Javier *ever* looked unsure?

'Are you all right?' she asked waspishly, relenting just enough to let him slip inside the apartment, but then shutting the door and leaning against it with her hands behind her back.

'No,' Javier said abruptly, looking away and then staring at her.

'What are you saying?' Sophie blanched. 'Are you...?

Are you ill...?' Fear and panic gripped her in equal measure.

'Can we go sit somewhere?'

'Tell me what's wrong!' She was at his side in seconds, her small hand on his forearm, her eyes pleading for reassurance that he was okay because, whatever he was, he wasn't himself and that was scaring her half to death.

And if he saw that, she didn't care.

'I've missed you.' The words slipped out before Javier could stop them in their tracks. He had put everything on the line and he felt sick. He wondered why he hadn't thought to down a bottle of whisky before embarking on this trip.

'You've missed me?' Sophie squeaked.

'You asked what was wrong with me,' Javier threw at her accusingly.

'Is missing me wrong?' Something inside her burst and she wanted to laugh and cry at the same time. She had to tell herself that no mention had been made of love, and if he was missing her, then chances were that he was missing her body. Which was something else entirely.

She walked on wooden legs into the sitting room, where she had been watching telly on her tablet, and watched as he sat down, briefly glancing around him before settling those dark, dark eyes on her.

'Missing...' he sat down, arms loosely resting on his thighs, his body leaning towards hers '...isn't something I've ever done.'

'Then it's a good thing,'

'I couldn't focus,' he admitted heavily. Now that he had started down this road, he had no alternative but to continue, although she hadn't chucked him out and that was a good thing. 'I couldn't sleep. You got into my head and I couldn't get you out of it.'

Sophie's heart was singing. She didn't want to speak. What if she broke the spell?

'I wanted you, you know...' He looked at her gravely. 'I don't think I ever really stopped wanting you, and when your brother showed up at my office, I figured I'd been handed the perfect way of putting that want to bed for good. Literally. I was going to just...go down the simple "exchange for favours" road. Cash for a little fun between the sheets, but then I decided that I wanted more than that...I didn't want a reluctant lover motivated for the wrong reasons.'

'You're assuming I would have given you your fun between the sheets because I needed money!' But she couldn't fire herself up to anger because her heart was still singing. She itched to touch him but first she wanted to talk.

'I'm arrogant.' He shot her a crooked smile. 'As you've told me a million times. I thought that it would be a one-night stand, simple as that, and then when you told me that you were a virgin...that the ex was gay...'

'Um, about that...'

'Sleeping with you that first time was...mind-blowing.'

'Er...'

'And it wasn't just because I'd never slept with a virgin before. It was because that person was *you*...'

'I should tell you something.' Sophie took a deep breath and looked him squarely in the eyes. So what if he hadn't said anything about love? He had opened up and she could tell from the way he was groping with his words that this was a first for him. A big deal. Her turn. It would be a bigger deal, but so be it.

'He wasn't gay. Roger wasn't gay. The opposite. He was one hundred percent straight as an arrow.'

Javier stared at her, for once in his life lost for words. 'You said...'

'No, Javier, *you* said.' She sighed wearily and sifted her fingers through her hair. 'It's such a long story and I'm sorry if I just let you think that Roger...'

Javier just continued staring, his agile brain trying and failing to make connections. 'Tell me from the beginning,' he said slowly.

'And you won't interrupt?'

'I promise nothing.'

Sophie half-smiled because why would this proud, stubborn, utterly adorable man ever take orders from anyone, even if it happened to be a very simple order?

'Okay...' Javier half-smiled back and a warm feeling spread through her 'I as good as half promise.'

'I'd been sort of going out with Roger by the time I went to university,' Sophie began, staring back into the past and not flinching away from it as she always did. 'I honestly don't know why except he'd been around for ever and it was something I just drifted into. It was cosy. We mixed in the same circles, had the same friends. His mother died when he was little and he and his father spent a good deal of time at our place. When his father died, he became more or less a fixture. He was crazy about me...' she said that without a trace of vanity '...and I think both my parents just assumed that we would end up getting married. Then I left home to go to university and everything just imploded.'

'Tell me,' Javier urged, leaning forward.

'Roger didn't want me to go to university. He was three years older and hadn't gone. He'd done an apprenticeship and gone straight into work at a local company. His parents had been very well off and he'd inherited everything as an only child, so there was no need for him to do anything high-powered and, in truth, he wasn't all that bright.'

She sighed. 'He wanted to have fun and have a wife

to cater to him. But as soon as I went to university it hit me that I didn't love him. I liked him well enough but not enough to ever, ever consider marrying. I told him that but he wasn't happy and then I met you and…I stopped caring whether he was happy or not. I stopped caring about anyone or anything but you.'

'And yet you ended up marrying him. Doesn't make sense.'

'You promised you wouldn't interrupt.'

Javier raised both his hands in agreement. In truth, he was too intrigued by this tale to ask too many questions.

'My father summoned me back home,' she said. 'I went immediately. I knew it had to be important and I was worried that it was Mum. Her health hadn't been good and we were all worried for her. I never expected to be told that the family was facing bankruptcy.' She took a deep breath, eyes clouded. 'Suddenly it was like every bad thing that could happen at once had happened. Not only was the company on the verge of collapse but my father admitted that he had been ill—cancer—and it was terminal. Roger was presented to me as the only solution, given the circumstances.'

'Why didn't you come to me?'

'I wanted to but it was hard enough just fighting your corner without presenting you to my parents. They wanted nothing to do with you. They said that Roger would bring much-needed money to the table, money that would revitalise the company and drag it out of the red. Dad was worried sick that he wouldn't be around long enough to do anything about saving the company. He was broken with guilt that he had allowed things to go down the pan but I think his own personal worries, which he had kept to himself, must have been enormous.

'They told me that what I felt for you was…infatuation. That I was young and bowled over by someone who would be no good for me in the long run. You weren't in my social class and you were a foreigner. Those two things would have been enough to condemn you but, had it not been for what was happening in the company, I don't think they would have dreamt of forcing my hand.'

'But they persuaded you that marrying Roger was vital to keep the family business afloat,' Javier recapped slowly. 'And, with your father facing death, there wasn't time for long debates...'

'I still wouldn't have,' Sophie whispered. 'I was so head over heels in love with you, and I told Roger that. Pleaded with him to see it from my point of view. I knew that if he backed me up, Mum and Dad might lay off the whole convenient marriage thing, but of course he didn't back me up. He was red with anger and jealousy. He stormed off. At the time, he had a little red sports car...'

'He crashed, didn't he?'

Sophie nodded and Javier picked up the story.

'And you felt...guilty.'

'Yes. I did. Especially because it was a very bad accident. Roger was in hospital for nearly two months and, by the time he was ready to come out, I had resigned myself to doing what had to be done. I'd even come to half believe that perhaps Mum and Dad were right—perhaps what I felt for you was a flash in the pan, whereas my relationship with Roger had the weight of shared history, which would prove a lot more powerful in the long run.'

Javier was seeing what life must have been like for her. In a matter of a few disastrous weeks, her entire future and a lot of her past had been changed for ever. She hadn't used him. He had simply been a casualty of events that had been far too powerful for her to do anything about but bow her head and follow the path she had been instructed to follow.

Not old enough to know her own mind, and too attached to her parents to rebel, she had simply obeyed them.

'But it didn't go according to plan...' he encouraged.

'How did you guess? It was a disaster from the very start. We married but the accident had changed Roger. Maybe, like me, he went into it thinking that we could give it a shot, but there was too much water under the bridge. And there had been after-effects from the accident. He very quickly became addicted to painkillers. He used to play a lot of football but he no longer could. Our marriage became a battleground. He blamed me, and the more he blamed me, the guiltier I felt. He had affairs, which he proudly told me about. He wreaked havoc with the company. He gambled. There was nothing I could do because he could quickly turn violent. By the time he died, I'd... I'd grown up for ever.'

Javier looked at her long and hard. 'Why did you let me believe that he was gay?'

'Because...' She took a deep breath. 'I thought that if you knew the whole story, you would know how much you meant to me then and you would quickly work out how much you mean to me now.' She laughed sadly. 'And, besides that, I've always felt ashamed—ashamed that I let myself be persuaded into doing something I really didn't want to do.'

'When you say that I *mean something to you now*...'

'I know what this is for you, Javier. You believed that I ran out on you, and when you had the chance, you figured you would take what should have been yours all those years ago.'

Javier had the grace to flush. What else could he do?

'And, for a while, I kidded myself that that was what it was for me too. I'd dreamt about you for seven years and

I'd been given the chance to turn those dreams into reality, except for me it was much more than that. You won't want to hear this but I'll tell you anyway. I never stopped loving you. You were the real thing, Javier. You'll always be the main event in my life.'

'Sophie…' He closed the distance between them but only so that he could sit closer to her, close enough to thread his fingers through hers. His throat ached. 'I've missed you so much. I thought I could walk away, just like I thought that sleeping with you would be a simple solution to sorting out the problem of you being on my mind all the time through the years. There, at the back of my mind like a ghost that refused to go away. You'd dumped me and married someone else. It didn't matter how many times I told myself that I was well rid of someone who used me for a bit of fun until she got her head together and realised that the person she really wanted to be with wasn't me…I still couldn't forget you.'

Sophie thought that this was one of those conversations she never wanted to end. She just wanted to keep repeating it on a loop, over and over and over.

'We slept together, Sophie, and just like that my life changed. Not having you in it was unthinkable. I didn't even register that consciously until you presented me with that picture and I suddenly realised that I had succumbed to all the things I'd thought I'd ruled out of my life. You'd domesticated me to the point where I didn't want to be anywhere unless you were there, and I hadn't even realised it. I took fright, Soph. I suddenly felt the walls closing in and I reacted on instinct and scarpered.'

'And now that you're back…' She had to say this. 'I can't have a relationship with you, Javier. I can't go back to living from one day to the next, not knowing whether you'll decide that you're bored and that you have to take off.'

'How could I ever get bored with you, Sophie?' He lightly touched her cheek with his fingers and realised that he was trembling. 'And how can you not see what I need to tell you? I don't just want you, but I need you. I can't live without you, Sophie. I fell in love with you all those years ago and, yes, you're the main event in my life as well and always will be. Why do you think I came here? I came because *I had to*. I just couldn't stand not being with you any longer.'

Sophie flung herself at him and he caught her in his arms, laughing because the chair very nearly toppled over.

'So, will you marry me?' he whispered into her hair and she pulled back, smiling, wanting to laugh and shout all at the same time.

'You mean it?'

'With every drop of blood that flows through my veins. Let me show you how great marriage can be.' He laughed. 'I never thought I'd hear myself say that.'

'Nor did I.' She kissed him softly and drew back. 'And now that you have, I won't allow you to take it back, so, yes, my darling. I'll marry you...'

* * * * *

*If you enjoyed this story, check out these
other great reads from Cathy Williams*
SEDUCED INTO HER BOSS'S SERVICE
THE SURPRISE DE ANGELIS BABY
WEARING THE DE ANGELIS RING
THE WEDDING NIGHT DEBT
Available now!

*Uncover the wealthy Di Sione family's sensational se-
crets in the brand-new eight-book series*
THE BILLIONAIRE'S LEGACY,
beginning with
DI SIONE'S INNOCENT CONQUEST
by Carol Marinelli
Also available this month